# VERTICAL
# BURN

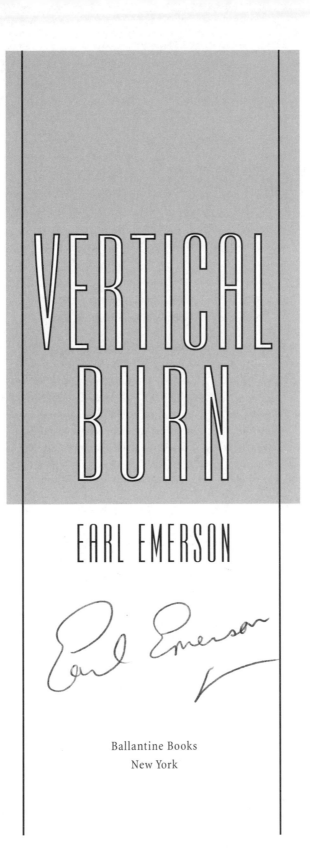

# VERTICAL BURN

## EARL EMERSON

Ballantine Books
New York

LIBRARY OF CONGRESS CATALOGING-IN-PUBLICATION DATA
Emerson, Earl W.
Vertical burn / by Earl Emerson.
p.   cm.
ISBN 0-345-44589-9
1. Fire fighters—Fiction.   I. Title.
PS3555.M39 V4 2002
813'54—dc21        2001035969

Text design by Holly Johnson

Manufactured in the United States of America

First Edition: June 2002

10   9   8   7   6   5   4   3   2   1

This book is dedicated to the brave men who've been assigned with me on Ladder 3-C over the years: George Ramos, Jerry Travis, Craig Davillier, Greg Mejlaender, Mark Buck, Dan Bachmeier, Dave Iranon, Jay Mahnke, Matt Hougan, Ron MacDougall, Erik Lawyer, Chris O'Reilly.

# AUTHOR'S NOTE

Because this novel was written over a period of three years, various sections of the narrative were created while the Seattle Fire Department was undergoing fundamental changes in equipment carried, staff, and operating procedures. The author has taken the liberty of leaving several anachronisms in the story. For instance, the novel has a Battalion 1 and a Battalion 1 aide, while the department has eliminated these positions. The novel operates with three-person engine companies while most engine companies in Seattle now operate with four firefighters via the NEPA two-in/two-out rule. This is a work of fiction. Any resemblance the characters have to real people is purely coincidental.

He had never been more alone. Smoke and flames engulfed him in dizzying waves. The truest form of death, the knowledge that death is imminent and unavoidable, pressed on him from every side. Such fear sends a torrent of chemicals raging through the body, numbing every thought except concern for self.

—John N. Maclean, *Fire on the Mountain*


We are all dead men on leave.

—Eugene Levine

# PART ONE

# LEARY WAY

# 1. I WAKE UP SCREAMING

When the lights came on, John Finney found himself admiring the arch of Diana's lower back through her ribbed undershirt, admiring her supple thigh muscles as she swung her legs over the edge of the bunk and the way two hours of sleep had frizzed her chestnut hair. Her back was to him as she stepped into her boots and pulled her pants up over blue silk running shorts.

It was 0304 hours, June 9.

On their way out of the bunk room they passed evidence of Engine 10's earlier departure: twisted blankets, pillows darkened with swirlies of drool, a set of reading glasses askew on a *Fire Engineering* magazine. Finney always turned his pillow over when they got a run in the middle of the night. He reached the hole just as Moore grabbed for the thick brass pole. In a voice husky with sleep and as rough-edged as Rod Stewart's, she said, "I guess this is the most dangerous thing we'll do all night, huh?"

"It's a long drop," he joked.

She wrapped herself expertly around the pole and vanished. They'd been bantering back and forth all evening, flirting really, and she was teasing him for warning her about the long drop at Station 10. Finney cautioned everyone. Two years earlier a sleep-addled firefighter let go of the pole ten feet too soon and woke up screaming.

By the time the bearlike captain lumbered around the front of the rig and climbed into the high cab, Finney had fired up Ladder 1's diesel engine and turned on the department radio. Reidel, the tillerman, checked in through Finney's headset. "Ready to rock 'n' roll, boss." Reidel kept at his fingertips an ample supply of the worst action movie lines. Finney grinned.

"How the hell could we possibly be the first-in truck all the way out on Leary Way?" asked Captain Cordifis.

"I don't know," Finney said. But it had surprised him, too. There were thirty-three engine companies and eleven aerial truck companies in Seattle, and at least five of those truck companies should have been dispatched ahead of them.

As they traveled north through downtown on Third Avenue, the electronic whoop of the siren reverberated off the tall buildings. Finney heard the familiar clinking of the alarm bells on the MSA air masks Moore and Baxter were donning in the crew cab behind him. Then, from the east shore of Lake Union on Westlake, he saw smoke in the northern sky. Lots of smoke. They had a good one. This was what Finney was bred for, fighting fires.

He glanced at Cordifis, who was putting a piece of chewing gum into his mouth. Bill Cordifis had been to the Ozark Hotel fire, where they lost twenty-one civilians. He'd been at the Villa Plaza apartments, where eight hours of fire burned more than two hundred people out of their homes. He'd seen a woman jump six hundred feet off the Space Needle. Smoke in the sky didn't bother Cordifis any more than it bothered Finney.

Engine 22's radio report came over the air. "Engine Twenty-two at Leary Way Northwest and Eight Avenue Northwest. We have a three-story warehouse approximately seventy by fifty. Constructed of tilt-up concrete. Heavy black smoke coming from the rear of the building. Engine Twenty-two laying a preconnect and establishing Leary Command."

Captain Vaughn was riding Engine 22 tonight, and if Cordifis didn't take command from him, he would be the Incident Commander until a chief showed up.

The building was set back from the north side of Leary Way, a couple of blocks north of the Lake Washington Ship Canal in a neighborhood that was evenly divided between residential and commercial properties. When they got close, the smoke in the street forced Finney to slow to a crawl. He didn't want to run over anybody.

Then the wind shifted, and it became clear that Vaughn had under-estimated the size of the building by at least half. In front were several moving vans parked close enough to the loading dock that radiant heat would ignite them should the fire grow worse. But it wasn't going to grow worse. They would go inside and put it out just like they always did.

# 2. THE GIRL WITH THE FAN

Although no flame was showing, heavy black smoke floated off the roof area, curled down the walls, and blotted out large portions of the street. As far as Finney could tell, nobody had approached the building yet. Engine 22's crew was off somewhere in the smoke, probably looking for a hydrant. Standing in his thick yellow bunking pants and coat, the captain from Engine 22 was surveying the building and evaluating their resources. One engine company. One truck company. By now the street should have been swarming with units.

On the rig radio, Cordifis said, "Ladder One at."

"Okay, Ladder One," answered the dispatcher.

"Moore, Baxter," Cordifis said, "get a door open. Reidel, follow me."

After parking the ladder truck, Finney strapped on an MSA backpack and regulator with thirty minutes of compressed air in the cylinder. Then he grabbed a chain saw and a pike pole out of their respective compartments and approached the building, crossing paths with Diana Moore as she headed back to the apparatus. As the driver, Finney was almost always the last one ready. "What's going on?" he asked.

"A fan. I got it."

Baxter broke a large window in front of the building with the Halligan tool, the falling glass sounding like an armload of dropped plates. Captain Cordifis, who had been speaking with Captain Vaughn near Engine 22, turned and walked toward the broken window. "Supposed to be somebody trapped inside," he said. "I guess a band practices in there all night."

"Hell," said Baxter. "We'll never find them in that smoke."

Near the front of the building the four of them, Finney, Cordifis, Baxter, and Reidel, were suddenly enveloped in a pall of smoke that made their eyes water. Cordifis began masking up as Baxter and Reidel, already covered, disappeared through the opening. Speaking to their backs, Cordifis said, "Tommy and Art, you guys go left. Find an exit for that smoke. John, you and I'll go right. The girl's going to stay with the fan."

Cordifis was an old-timer who meant no disrespect by calling Moore a "girl," or by leaving her outside to tend the fan. Finney hoped she realized that, but thought she probably didn't.

5

Finney put down the chain saw and pike pole. He wouldn't be needing them to search. Now his tools consisted of the small department-issued flashlight on a clip on his chest and the four-pound service axe in a scabbard on his belt, the axe no truckman was ever without.

Inside, Finney could see Cordifis's lantern for about four feet, after which it vanished. He kept track of the captain through the Darth Vader sound of his breathing in the facepiece and the casual conversation they always maintained when they worked together. He liked to keep a leash on the captain so he didn't get into trouble. Cordifis had seen better days and sometimes couldn't keep up with the rest of the crew.

It wasn't too many minutes before Finney heard the wooden-bladed, gasoline-powered fan firing up behind them, sounding like a small airplane. The racket would serve as a marker for their entrance point. They were searching a forty-five-thousand-square-foot building, but Finney couldn't see past the end of his arm.

Department protocol decreed that fans wouldn't be set up without hose lines in position, lest the additional fresh air being pushed into the building feed the fire, but Finney knew Cordifis wasn't afraid to bend the rules whenever the rules didn't suit the situation. Finney had worked under by-the-book officers before, and he would take Cordifis's commonsense approach any day. At least Cordifis knew how to think for himself—a quality Finney valued in emergency situations. Once the fan was running, the air would clear and they could finish their search before their rescue operation turned into a body recovery. If it turned out they were fanning the fire, they would turn it off after their search was complete.

The building would begin clearing as soon as Baxter and Reidel opened an outlet for the fumes, preferably smaller than the entrance and near the seat of the fire. The structure would become like a balloon with a pinhole in it, smoke rushing out that pinhole. The technique was amazingly effective. Finney heard a second fan rev up and knew Moore had set it up in tandem with the first to generate additional pressure inside the building. Still, the smoke wasn't clearing. What the hell were Baxter and Reidel doing? They should have had an outlet hole by now.

Finney and Cordifis searched a series of small interconnecting rooms along the front side of the building, and as they exited each room, Finney placed a piece of white tape diagonally down the outside of the door to signal that the room had been searched.

Even though they weren't doing much more than walking, Cordifis was breathing with effort. Their PPE—personal protective equipment—weighed more than fifty pounds; when fastened, their heavy coats were as warm as Arctic expedition parkas. Just walking was a chore. Much as he wanted to move more quickly, Finney forced himself to adapt to the captain's pace. There was no point in wearing him out.

They moved about in the smoke for five minutes before they both bumped into a high counter and found themselves treading on material that felt like gravel. Moments later, the smoke abated somewhat and Finney suddenly realized he was outside the building, walking on nuggets of broken glass from the window Baxter had broken. They'd circled back through the interconnecting rooms without realizing it. It was easy to do and embarrassing as hell.

"Where's that damned fan?" Cordifis asked irritably, when he realized they'd screwed up. "This place should be clear by now." Both fans were gone, as was Diana Moore. It surprised Finney. Usually you could count on her.

"You want to go back in and search, or do you want me to get the fans back?"

Cordifis's reply was to head back inside. Bypassing the rooms they'd already searched, they moved along the front wall of the building. Minutes later, they found a door at the right corner of the building on the far side of a loading area. When Finney opened it, he was greeted by a long flight of descending concrete steps.

In the basement they found a huge subterranean space with a high ceiling and a floor of rough concrete. There was no smoke. By the time they'd searched the area, Cordifis's five-minute warning bell was ringing, though Finney had two thousand pounds left in his bottle, a little less than half what he'd started with. Cordifis generally ran out of air before he did, but Finney was thinking this was too soon even for him. They would get fresh bottles together.

When they'd made their way outside, a ragged group of spectators in robes, T-shirts, and slippers were congesting the smoky area where Captain Vaughn had set up his command post. Finney grabbed a battle lantern for more light and two spare bottles off Ladder 1. He looked up the street for additional units but saw none. By now they should have had two chiefs—three, counting the safety chief. There weren't even any additional engines on scene. What the hell was going on? Finney carried the spare bottles over to Cordifis and changed the bottle on his back while Cordifis spoke to Vaughn.

"But she was right there," Cordifis said angrily. "She could have shut it off in two seconds."

"You know that's not the way we fight fire," answered Vaughn.

"With the fan up, we'd be able to see something. What we're doing now, this is like playing Pic-Up Sticks with our butt cheeks."

"I've got Ladder Five going to the roof from the other side of the building. If you want them inside searching with you, I can do that."

"More butt cheeks isn't going to help. I want ventilation is what I want. I want those fans."

Vaughn walked away. A chain saw started up somewhere, the two-stroke engine screaming as the crew of Ladder 5 cut holes in the roof. Cordifis gave Finney a disgusted look, while Finney shrugged out of his own backpack and laid it on the ground to change the bottle. Bill was right, as usual. This would be a whole lot easier with the fans.

Cordifis stepped around Ladder 1 and addressed someone Finney couldn't see. "Hey, you bastard . . ." Finney missed whatever insults came next as Engine 22's engine and built-in pump roared.

As Finney slung his backpack and tightened the shoulder straps, Robert Kub stepped into view from around the front of Ladder 1. He wasn't the one Cordifis was giving a hard time to, for Finney could still hear Cordifis's loud, angry voice.

Finney had come into the department with Kub, the only African American in his recruit class, and as with most of those he came in with, he felt a special bond toward the man. For the past twelve years Kub had been working for the fire investigation unit, Marshal 5, so he often didn't arrive at a fire scene until the firefighting units were packing up to leave. Finney thought it was unusual to see him this early in a fire. "What are you doing here?" Finney asked, screwing his low-pressure hose onto the regulator at his waist.

"Dispatcher called me at home. There's another good fire down on Othello, but I came here." He wagged his eyebrows. "More potential."

"Oh, we got potential all right." Finney grinned, as he left Kub and walked around the nose of Ladder 1 in time to see Cordifis heading toward the building and away from another off-duty firefighter, Oscar Stillman. Finney knew Cordifis and Stillman were good enough friends that a greeting of "Hey, you bastard!" often served as an endearment between them. Just like every other big fire, this was turning into a reunion.

Stillman, who had nothing to do here but watch, turned around and flashed his gapped teeth at Finney. "God, how the hell are you, young man?"

"A little early to be up, isn't it?" Finney followed Cordifis while Stillman tagged along behind him.

"I was coming back from my biannual Tuesday-night card game when I saw the smoke from Aurora. I was the first motherfucker on the scene."

"You see any band members come out of there?"

"I ain't seen nothing but this goddamn smoke. Thought maybe my first wife was in there cooking dinner."

When Finney caught Cordifis, they donned their face masks and stepped into the building just as Baxter, Reidel, and Moore emerged, accompanied by ringing alarm bells. The trio told them they had searched along the left wall of the building and found only storage racks and empty rooms.

Diana Moore stepped up to Cordifis as he was pulling the straps tight on his blue rubber facepiece and said, "Sorry about the fans. The IC told me to put them back. I didn't know what to do, so when I saw these guys through the smoke, I joined up."

"Don't worry about it, darlin'. You did right." Finney thought he detected an amused twinkle in Diana's eye at the word *darlin'*. He had to hand it to her. She had enough self-confidence to let things pass.

Finney was beginning to get a bad feeling about this building. Even though he could hear more units rolling up the street behind them now, he knew you didn't find this much smoke in a building and then squander fifteen minutes without putting water on it. You found the seat of the fire as expeditiously as possible. You stormed in and you tapped it. Ninety seconds could make the difference between a tapped fire and a grounder. They'd already been here ten minutes. Engine 22's pump was running, but the lines on the ground were not yet flowing water. So far, nobody had found the seat of the fire. Or any fire at all.

In a building this large there was too much space for superheated gases to accumulate. Finney knew that if those gases got hot enough and blended with oxygen in the proper ratio, they would ignite, and anyone luckless enough to be inside would be trapped in a flashover. In a house fire the rooms would go from two or three hundred degrees to twelve hundred in the time it takes to snap your fingers. In a place this big the higher temperatures would chop a man down where he stood. The body recovery team would find the soles of his rubber boots melted to the concrete floor.

# 3. REARRANGING DECK CHAIRS ON THE *TITANIC*

Back inside, Finney and Captain Cordifis found the door to the basement they'd already searched and, using the east wall as a benchmark, they moved north from there. The building was filled with home furnishings shrink-wrapped in thick plastic and loaded onto wooden pallets, the pallets stacked on huge metal racks, the racks extending higher than they could see in the smoke.

They were moving faster now and they both knew they needed to cover as much ground as possible. The wall they were using as a reference point was mostly bare, as was the space nearby, and they moved almost without impediment.

Sooner than Finney thought possible, they arrived at the far right corner of the rear wall and worked their way along it, Cordifis an arm's length from the wall, Finney an arm's length from Cordifis. They were heading west, paralleling their original traverse across the front wall.

Finney was beginning to feel warm from the movement, so he knew Cordifis had probably been sweating profusely in his bunkers for some time. Although the manufacturers boasted of breathable fabrics in the liners, anyone who actually bothered to put on a set of bunking clothes and do any work knew that firefighters were sealed up like fresh-cooked muffins in a plastic bag. It could be like running a marathon in the desert, and some tolerated it better than others. Finney loved it. Cordifis sweated nearly to death each time they had a working fire.

"This way," Cordifis said. "I got a door here."

Finney stepped through the half-open door and for the first time in more than five minutes he could actually see his partner. Wrapped in a cocoon of smoke, the two men had been communicating by touch and sound alone. Now Finney followed Cordifis's gaze and was startled to realize he was looking at stars. They were standing in a closed, rectangular well, the high, windowless walls of the warehouse behind them, a lower wall of red brick in front, the structures cobbled together by walls at either end.

From time to time pockets of filthy brown smoke from the roof dipped down into their canyon. An orange glow reflected off smoke in the sky, though it was hard for Finney to tell whether the glow came from behind or in front. Wherever it was, the fire was growing larger.

"This is where the goddamned band is," said Cordifis, looking at the smaller building across from them. "Nobody's going to let a bunch of punk-ass kids mess around with all that furniture back there. Hell, they'd be banging their girlfriends on the sofas. They're in here."

He was right, Finney thought. There were three doors; two of them looked impenetrable. Finney took his axe out of its scabbard and approached the third, knocking off the paint-splattered two-by-fours nailed across the edges. He ended up demolishing the entire door when he found it had been screwed to the frame.

Devoid of smoke, the space appeared to be an abandoned machine room with steel counters built into the walls, a dilapidated drill press on its side on the floor. Maybe the fire hadn't touched this side. It was possible the band members were unaware even that the building was on fire.

The room had two interior doors, both closed and locked, one of which looked as if it led farther into the building. Finney used his axe again.

The door opened onto a long passageway, a small ghost of smoke hovering near the ceiling at the far end. They worked their way down a row of doors, searching the rooms one by one. The rooms to the left were clear, the rooms to the right increasingly smoky. It was disconcerting to be this deep into a building without a hose line, even worse to realize the smoke was compartmentalized in a manner they didn't often see. Finney could tell it bothered Cordifis, too.

When Cordifis opened an unlocked door near the far end of the corridor, torrents of smoke poured out over their heads, the first really hot smoke they'd encountered. Visibility in the room was near zero and the smoke swirled in angry circles. Finney stepped inside and stumbled into a set of drums.

A pair of cymbals crashed to the floor. "You go right," Cordifis said from behind. "I'll go left."

"I don't like this," Finney said.

"Me neither, but we got to do it."

There were other ways to search a room, but this would do. Split up. Right. Left.

Finney could see maybe twelve to eighteen inches in front of his light, and expecting to touch a body at any moment, he kicked some bedding on the floor—and then, as he advanced, a sleeping bag, a pile of clothing, a guitar case, some loose beer bottles. It was slow going, because even though they'd left the door open, the smoke wasn't clearing.

Finney found a low sofa, a table, a lamp. He couldn't tell until he had his facepiece up against it that the lamp was on, the bulb staring at him like an eyeball. The walls were made of rough brick, and pieces of mortar fell out when he brushed them with his gloves.

"Hey, take a look here," Cordifis said. "Down here at the end."

Finney quickly located Cordifis, who was studying the wall with his battle lantern. Finney took off a glove and held his bare palm close to the hot bricks.

"You know what I think?" Cordifis said.

"God, that's like a stove." Finney pulled his glove back on and heard a loud crunching sound. He began moving. "Let's get out of here."

As he turned, Finney heard a crack that sounded like a gunshot. He managed two running steps before something knocked his legs out from under him. It was as if he'd been tackled from behind on a football field.

The urgency of the situation became instantly clear to him. He sprawled on his stomach and scrambled forward while debris continued to rain down on him. A particularly heavy projectile slammed into his helmet and knocked him flat. Before he could start crawling again, more debris fell, and he was half-buried under the weight. The noise and confusion persisted for another twenty seconds and then died out like a spent avalanche.

When he heard the brittle clicking sound of a single brick falling against another single brick, he shook off some of the debris. The left shoulder strap of his breathing apparatus felt like it had claws. He was pretty sure something in his shoulder was broken.

Using his good arm, he pushed himself to his knees and then his feet. "Captain? You all right?"

Finney looped the thumb of his left hand under his right chest strap in a makeshift sling, then began making his way to where he'd last seen Cordifis. The pain in his shoulder throbbed with his heartbeat. The temperature in the room had soared, and even with the battle lantern in his right hand he could see nothing but blackness.

"Bill! Bill? Are you all right?"

He took two steps and stumbled into a pile of debris, the jolt from the fall hitting his shoulder like a .38 slug. He moved the battle lantern across a large mound of bricks and mortar. Around the central pile dozens of individual bricks littered the floor helter-skelter.

Cordifis was gone.

Circling the mound, he discovered that the place where the brick wall had stood earlier was nothing but a wooden core now, a few bricks still embedded in the wall at knee level. As he moved backward, he nearly knocked himself out on a heavy beam, one end of which was jammed into the corner at the ceiling, the other anchored in the rubble behind him. "Bill? Bill?"

He searched the area around the rubble, and just as he was about to call out again, he found the toe of a rubber boot protruding from the pile.

# 4. TWENTY-EIGHT PACES

Working frantically with one arm, Finney began pulling bricks from the mound. He worked in darkness because he couldn't hold his light and work at the same time. He cleared a layer almost a foot deep before he uncovered the top of a helmet, then part of a head. He clawed the material away from Cordifis's face mask, picked up his light, and shone it into the hole. Peering into his partner's facepiece, he realized his lens was fogged over, which meant Bill wasn't moving air.

More frantic than ever, Finney worked until he'd removed enough debris so that Cordifis's entire head and neck were free and he could hear the mask leaking air out the sides. Cordifis stirred. Finney reached down and adjusted the facepiece until the seal was tight; the lens cleared. Miraculously, Cordifis blinked.

"You all right?" Finney asked.

Cordifis mumbled, "Where am I?"

"Leary Way. We're looking for musicians."

"Christ on a crutch. I guess I was dreaming. What happened?"

"The wall collapsed on us."

"What wall?"

"The one that's still on top of you."

For the first time the captain grasped his situation.

Now his partner's chest and arms were free, but Finney couldn't pull the rest of the mound apart without moving the heavy beam that had Cordifis's lower body pinned. It was clear that Bill had made a run for it, though he hadn't gotten far. If Finney hadn't continued to scramble after he'd been knocked off his feet, he would have ended up directly under the end of the beam himself. It would have killed him. Both of them would have died here. Finney put his back against the beam and tried to dislodge it, but it was like trying to move a house, and the pain in his shoulder increased exponentially as he exerted himself. He stopped only when he heard Cordifis yelling, "God, don't move that. You're killing me."

"What's wrong?"

"I don't know. It feels like I'm all twisted around down here. Don't move it."

"Doesn't matter. It's a two-man job."

"Let me have your portable. I'll tell them where we are while you scout around."

While Cordifis made radio contact, Finney discovered a second massive wooden beam angled across the doorway flush with the door. Six by ten inches, the beam appeared to be supported at the far end by what was left of the collapsed wall. He tried to trace the beam with his lantern but detected nothing but smoke and dust. It crossed directly in front of the door, and it rocked precariously when he touched it. Should it fall, it would likely land on Bill, or at least on the pile under which Bill was trapped. And it *would* fall if anyone tried to open the door, which had become the trip-hammer in a deadly booby trap.

Quickly, Finney traced the perimeter walls a second time, searching for another exit. He didn't have the strength or the means to get the beam away from the door without compromising Cordifis, nor did he have the tools to lever Cordifis out from under the pile. It didn't much matter. Even if he freed him, Cordifis weighed 265 pounds buck naked, and his protective equipment and clothing weighed an additional fifty. Finney was six feet, muscular, and in the best condition of his life. If he were uninjured, he just might *drag* Cordifis out of the building. But there was no way he could carry him. Not tonight. Not without help.

Breathing heavily, Cordifis said, "I talked to Smith."

"He say who he was sending?"

"Everybody he's got."

"Tell them not to come through this door."

Finney was in a locked room, had one good arm, limited air, a light, a Buck knife on his belt, and a service axe in a scabbard. For a few seconds he found himself incapable of productive thought. Death wasn't the enemy. He knew that. Panic was the enemy.

They were both running out of compressed air. Any minute one or both of their five-minute warning bells would begin ringing.

Crossing to the wall opposite the doorway and placing his back against it, Finney swung the service axe one-handed down between his legs, using the pick-head side of the axe. He swung again, again. The concussion of each blow spewed pain through his shoulder. He broke one brick into pieces, chipping out the mortar around it. Then a second brick, a third.

Fortunately, this wall did not have the same solid planking at its core as the wall that had collapsed.

Even so, his five-minute alarm bell began ringing as he pulled out the broken bricks. On the other side of the bricks he encountered a layer of plaster and lathe and then an empty space about four inches deep, the back side of newer wallboard beyond that. When he punched that with his fist, he broke through to another room.

Using his axe, he chewed away at the edges of his escape hole until the opening was large enough for a man with a bottle on his back. Then he went back to Cordifis, reaching behind his back to muffle his own ringing bell so they could hear each other.

"I'm going for help. If they get here before I come back, don't let them through that door." As he spoke, the ringing bell behind his waist stopped and Finney found himself sucking on the rubber facepiece. It felt as if somebody were clamping his nostrils and mouth at the same time. His bottle was dry, and he might as well have had a plastic bag over his head. He loosened the chin strap, tipped his helmet back, and lifted the facepiece off his chin.

He'd forgotten how abrasive and gritty and putrid a lung full of hot smoke tasted. He knelt instinctively to get some of the better air near the floor.

"You okay, John?"

"Are you kidding?" Finney gasped. "I love this stuff."

"Plug into my bottle. I don't need all this air."

"There's no time. Listen, Bill. I've got a hole. I'm going out to find help. I'll leave my PASS device outside that wall so when help comes, they'll hear it and know you're in here."

"Here. You take the radio."

"Quit offering me stuff. I'll be back with help in a few minutes. Breathe slow, old man." Finney stooped down, their faces glowing in the gray-yellow soup formed by the light of Finney's battle lantern. It was important that he make eye contact before leaving.

Cordifis chuckled. "Have fun, kiddo." Bill hadn't called him kiddo in years. "And don't go have a brain fart and forget where I am."

"I won't."

After Finney had squirmed through the small opening on the floor, he found the next room was as smoky as the one he'd left. He reached back and pulled his MSA backpack into the room, along with the PASS device, which was designed to let out a high-decibel screech when it ceased moving. Jiggling the device shut off the noise, but it would resume after twenty-four seconds of no movement.

Which way? He tried to recall all the changes of direction they'd put themselves through. Keeping low, he ran his gloved hand along the wall and moved left through a doorway, where he found a room that was hotter than anything they'd encountered so far. He crouched on hands and knees until he found a layer of semi-breathable air, his mouth inches off the floor. He made his way around the wall, around tables, around counters and machines.

Minutes later he felt a gush of air waft into the building. Before he could think about it, an orange-yellow glow lit up the room.

The incoming air brought oxygen with it. The oxygen mixed with the hot gases at the ceiling, and the room flashed over, fire roaring above his head. Now, even if he knew which direction to take, he wasn't sure he could get out. At head height, the temperature would be somewhere around twelve hundred degrees.

Because he'd been low, the initial ignition hadn't scorched him, but now the heat was so intense that all he could do was curl up and shield his head, the movement exposing a small sliver of skin between his gloves and his sleeves; he could feel the skin beginning to bubble. He was being burned, but the fact that his wrists didn't hurt scared him. He felt only a strange dullness and an incredible need to close his eyes and sleep. He'd never felt this much heat in his life.

He realized at some point that he had assumed the classic fetal position. He was dying. Or as good as dead. It had all been so quick. So this was how it was going to end, he thought. Here on the floor in this dirty building where it was too hot to move.

As he began to drift off, he remembered that Bill was depending on him. Bill was going to die because he was taking a nap. The thought woke him up.

Using both arms, he rolled himself over and began crawling on his stomach, feeling the painful heat once again as it singed his wrists and neck. He tried to remember if he'd repositioned the Nomex hood after removing his mask. He couldn't recall; he wondered if they'd be able to save his ears.

He crawled until he found a wall, followed it to the right, praying he would find a door, any door. If he was going to die, at least he was going to die moving. Nobody was going to say he'd given up, that he'd stopped trying.

He continued to crawl, taking shallow, painful gasps, barely able to suck any breathable air off the floor. The wall stretched on, seemingly without end.

He wasn't sure how much time had elapsed. All he knew was that somehow he was standing now, walking. It wasn't as hot as it had been. Or maybe he was simply too numb now to feel the pain. Dizzy and disoriented, he had somehow groped his way out of the back room. He remembered stepping over his own screeching PASS device once again and knew that with great effort he had been counting his footsteps as he worked his way toward what he hoped was an exit.

At twenty-eight paces from the PASS device, two firefighters in full gear hove into view, flashlights wagging in front of them.

He couldn't tell if the firefighters were real or a figment of his delirium. And then as he moved forward, seemingly in slow motion, something heavy and metallic fell in the corridor just behind him. The earth seemed to shake.

Before he could turn around to see what it was, the shorter firefighter spoke. They were real. "Christ, what was that? You see Ladder One anywhere in here?"

The taller man stepped close and shone his light on Finney's naked face. "This is Ladder One right here," he said. "Look at his helmet. Where's your mask, buddy?"

"Bill's back there behind me," Finney heard himself saying. "He needs help."

"Bill who?"

Finney tried to recall the captain's last name, but he couldn't dredge it up through the fog in his brain. It scared him. In five minutes he'd turned into a moron. He knelt to get out of the hottest smoke, straining to align his thoughts so he could describe Bill's predicament. When his voice came, it sounded thick and slurred, even to him, his words tumbling out as if they had spurs on. As he explained how to locate Bill and said he would take them back to Bill himself, he felt as though he were talking in his sleep, uncertain whether he was actually speaking the words or merely thinking them.

"We'll get him. You just go that way. You'll find a doorway down there."

The shorter firefighter spoke into his remote microphone. "Leary Command from Division D. We've found Ladder One. We're sending the first member out. We'll be bringing out the other member in a few minutes."

"Leary Command, okay. Do you need help?"

Finney didn't hear the rest of the transmission. He was walking upright in the smoke now, sensing clean air just footsteps away. He could almost taste the paper cup of cool Gatorade he knew was waiting for him. What a nightmare this whole thing had turned into. For some minutes there he'd actually thought he and Bill weren't going to make it.

# 5. HOSPITAL LINEN LIKE BOARDS

The lights pierced his eyes like lasers, and his eyeballs felt as if they'd been sandpapered with #80 grit. The bedsheets might as well have been made out of boards. He knew his ears and neck and wrists had been daubed with something, and he could tell he'd been given medication, though he hadn't asked what. In fact, he hadn't spoken. Not for some time now. He didn't know why. It wasn't until his brother, Tony, a captain at Station 17, showed up that he felt any inclination to use his voice.

"You're going to be okay," Tony whispered, the way some people did in sickrooms. "Just take it easy. Right now your only job is to rest up and heal."

Finney's throat was dry and raw. "How's Bill?"

"They're going to put you into a decompression chamber to help get the carbon monoxide out of your blood. Fact is, they're still a little worried over whether you're going to make it. But you'll bounce back. Just do what the doctors say and stay relaxed."

"Bill. Where is he?"

"I'm not sure."

"He okay?"

"You don't need to worry about him."

"Was his leg broken?"

"I don't know. You just lie back and don't think about anything but getting some rest."

"Was I burned?"

"Oh, yeah."

"Bad?"

"Not too bad."

"My ears?"

"Your ears'll be okay."

"I don't feel any pain."

"Don't worry. You will."

# 6. DODGING THE BULLET

In the rest area 150 feet from the fire buildings, the radiant heat on Diana Moore's face felt like a fresh sunburn. Crews manning hose lines in the parking lot were directing water, tons of it, into the buildings. Some of the more alert firefighters on the hose lines tried to knock down embers so they wouldn't drift out of the neighborhood and ignite secondary fires, but Diana could see it was a losing battle. Propelled by the tremendous heat rising off the buildings, sparks raced unhindered up into the night sky like antiaircraft rounds.

The structures to the north had taken off first, but now spirals of flame were shooting out the high windows on the warehouse. Electrical wires on nearby utility poles had burned off and were dancing in the street. Pools of water spread under hose connections in the parking lot and drained downslope toward the fire, where the water evaporated. When the moving vans outside the building burst into flame, one ill-fated firefighter was sprayed with hot rubber from an exploding tire.

Across the street the damp from the high hose streams drizzled onto a crowd of spectators. Water beaded up on parked cars and fire engines. Two women in bathrobes huddled under an umbrella watching the fire.

So many spaghetti lines crisscrossed in the street that in places the hoses were layered several feet deep. On the warehouse roof flames leaped fifty feet into the air. Engine companies manning deck guns shot eight hundred gallons a minute into the conflagration.

Diana wished she knew how a pair of experienced firefighters like Captain Cordifis and John Finney had gotten into so much trouble. She had been on the crew all day, had worked with these men, joked with them, and through some serendipitous order of events had escaped tonight's catastrophe unscathed.

Eleven minutes after Finney came out, Battalion Chief Reese and Robert Kub were ejected from the building like corks popping out of a bottle. She'd never seen anything quite like it, and apparently neither had the newspaper photographers who captured it on film: two men running, ducking low, only a couple of feet in front of a fireball that obliterated everything else in the frame.

Moments after Reese and Kub emerged, Reidel approached the fiery doorway from the side, stooped low, and peered inside for signs of Cordifis.

Until she saw the stricken look on Robert Kub's face as he plowed through the gang of reporters, Diana assumed Cordifis had been taken out another exit by a second team. But Kub didn't resemble a man returning from a successful mission; he seemed like a man in need of a quiet place to cry.

As soon as he whipped off his mask, film and radio crews swarmed Chief Reese like flies on bad meat, pushing their microphones under his nose as they lobbed questions. Over the years Diana had heard contradictory stories about Reese, but it was amazing that he had so much command of both emotion and intellect at a time like this. He'd risked his life but had lost neither his equilibrium nor his composure. Diana watched as the battalion chief looked stolidly at the cameras.

"We went in and within a minute we found one firefighter wandering around alone," Reese began. "He was in a panic and wasn't any help at indicating where his partner was. We guided him outside and then went back down the direction he came from, but there wasn't anything there. We searched as long as we could, but were finally forced out by the heat."

"So who's bringing him out?" one of the reporters asked. "There were two men lost, right? Who's bringing out the other one?"

"To the best of our knowledge, he's still in there."

At that moment a section of the roof collapsed. Diana watched a thin tongue of orange shooting out the top of the doorway Cordifis and Finney had gone in, the doorway she herself had used earlier. It was inconceivable that anybody else was emerging alive from that tinderbox.

For a while Baxter stood next to her. Thomas Baxter was one of those people who talked out his problems, the nexus between his mouth and brain unencumbered by the normal barriers associated with self-censorship or second thoughts.

"How?" Baxter asked in his faded southern accent. "How in hell could he work thirty-six years and then have this happen? With all his experience. Christ! John must have killed himself getting out. You see his neck?"

"I saw it," Diana said, shuddering to herself. Most firefighters didn't think about getting burned because it didn't happen all that often. But when it did, it was ugly.

"Bill almost went off a roof over on King Street last winter. House fire. His knees buckled. If John hadn't been there . . . Last couple of years John's been following Bill around like a mother hen. Cordifis should have retired a long time ago. Boy, we sure dodged the bullet tonight, didn't we?"

Diana turned her back to the fiery spectacle. "I guess you could say that."

# PART TWO

# OCTOBER:

## FIVE MONTHS LATER

# 7. TOUGH TITTY

John Finney's story was one of the first things the current batch of SFD drill instructors told probationary firefighters when they tried to spook them into quitting.

Finney didn't know how specific the storytelling was, or whether the drill instructors mentioned that Finney was obsessed with Leary Way—that he'd grilled every member of every crew on the alarm, that he'd even constructed a miniature model of the complex as it was before the fire. Finney was well aware that some people thought he was losing his mind. But if people thought he was waging a futile crusade, tough titty.

Leary Way had ripped his life in half. Since that night in June he had not once gotten more than five hours of sleep in a twenty-four-hour period. Leary Way was all he thought about, and he knew it was all others thought about when they saw him. He wasn't the same as before the fire, and he wouldn't be until he'd tamed the fundamental conundrum. Would Bill Cordifis be alive if Finney had done anything differently? And had he panicked after leaving Cordifis?

Most people said nothing to his face, but his brother, Tony, relayed the rumors, the worst of which was that at Leary Way he'd been running around like a chicken with its head cut off. Chief Reese had publicly announced that Finney had panicked, and nobody could forget that. Nobody wanted to fight fire with a fireman who'd panicked.

But he hadn't panicked and he knew it.

Still, not an hour passed without Finney wrestling to understand what went wrong. Heat stress and carbon monoxide poisoning from that night had blanked out much of his memory, and what he did remember he didn't trust to be true. He knew he'd been hallucinating in the hospital but couldn't be certain whether he'd been hallucinating during the fire itself. It was impossible to know in the confusion caused by heat exhaustion and smoke inhalation whether he had imagined telling Reese and Kub that they had to go twenty-eight paces to find the hole in the wall, or whether he'd actually told them.

Reese said Finney hadn't told them anything. In dozens of interviews he'd implied that Finney's primary concern was getting out of the building, not helping them find his partner. What Finney didn't understand was how they'd missed Cordifis. Reese and Kub had been inside the building eleven minutes after Finney left them, plenty of time to find Bill, dig him out, and carry him to safety. Still, if they hadn't known where to look . . .

Nobody blamed Bill's death on him, not directly, but even so, the indictment floated about in the ether. If he'd been coherent enough to get himself out of the fire, why hadn't he done as much for his partner?

Finney was beginning to believe it was not possible for a man to endure as many sleepless nights as he had without stepping over the precipice into madness. He had moods that nobody knew about, fugues that he hadn't mentioned even to the tight-lipped psychologist the department sent him to, a woman who gawked at him over the top of her tortoiseshell reading glasses and urged him to tell her what he was feeling. What did she think he was feeling? He and Bill Cordifis had gone into a burning building together. He'd come out alone. It didn't get any simpler than that. He felt guilt. Grief. He felt incompetent. Dim-witted. Alienated. Evil, even.

It was bad enough to lose a partner. It was untenable to be the cause of that loss, unconscionable, and, ultimately, unendurable.

Leary Way was the sort of catastrophe that might happen to a firefighter at his first fire, yet Finney had been wading through smoke for eighteen years. Firefighting ran in the family blood. Finney's brother had been in the department twenty-one years. And just a few months ago, after nearly forty-two years of service, their father had retired with the rank of battalion chief. Their grandfather had been a volunteer in his youth during the Depression in Michigan. Accounts of unexpected endings, ill-fated victims, and unimaginably bad luck had been ricocheting around the supper table since John Finney's childhood, yet as far as he could tell, until now no one in the family had ever been the cause of one of those cataclysms.

He knew there was usually some permanent damage that went along with something like this. So far, aside from the skin grafts on his neck and wrists, he'd been left with an ineluctable and sometimes incapacitating depression. The possibility that he could no longer trust his own skills on the fire ground—or anywhere else—plagued and horrified him. First and foremost he was a firefighter. Losing that, even in spirit, was more painful than anything he could imagine.

Finney was, as always, obsessing on these thoughts in the officer's room of Station 26 on a Tuesday morning in late October. He stared at his own reflection in the computer screen, trying to figure out who he'd become. The image he saw didn't tell him anything new: dark brown hair, a relatively square face with only a few telltale lines to suggest his thirty-nine years, a blocky jaw. He saw a strong face, not quite handsome, with blue eyes his ex-wife had once called dreamy. Later, during the divorce, she'd decided they were vacant. Now they were underscored with dark circles.

Situated near the southern city limits of Seattle, Station 26 was the kind of sleepy little firehouse that Finney had discovered attracted misfits, misanthropes, bathroom philosophers, backyard mechanics, geezers on their way to retirement, or people who habitually reduced their life philosophy to a few words on a bumper sticker. Finney had been transferred here to be the acting officer while Lieutenant Sadler was on disability, but Sadler had returned unexpectedly, and now Finney was stuck riding the tailboard. He wasn't particularly happy about it, but then he wasn't particularly happy about anything these days.

In the officer's room with him was Jerry Monahan, one of only a handful of firefighters whose attitude toward Finney wasn't influenced in some manner by Leary Way. "Whatcha doin'?" Monahan asked.

"Trying to track down the last band member from the fire. I've talked to the others. This guy's supposedly moved to Montana."

"Don't you think you'd be better off putting all this behind you, John?"

"No."

"It was me, I'd move on and try to forget it."

"No, you wouldn't."

In his late fifties, Jerry Monahan was a roly-poly man with an ingratiating smile and rumpled clothing. His skin was so gray it looked like ash. There was always something a little off about Monahan; Finney regarded him as a real-life "what is wrong with this picture?" puzzle. This morning it was a brown shoelace in one of his black boots. Monahan overflowed with elaborate government conspiracy theories and was a frequent caller to extreme-right-wing radio shows. Finney had reason to believe he often went several days without bathing. He suspected Monahan was allergic to soap and the federal government in equal proportions.

While Finney stared at the computer screen, Jerry Monahan sat on Lieutenant Sadler's bunk next to the desk and fiddled with a Teflon-coated cable on an aluminum spool, explaining how the spool fit into a contraption he'd designed to evacuate civilians from high-rise fires and how the whole thing was going to make him a billionaire. Finney had heard it all a hundred times before.

"Calling it Elevator-in-a-Can," Monahan said. "What do you think?"

"Catchy."

"All I need is a little luck. Just a little luck and two hundred grand for promotion. The potential with this dealybobber is staggering."

"I'll bet."

Finney knew that plenty of people in the department called Monahan a crackpot to his face, and he found it easy to assume this latest invention would never work, much less make Monahan wealthy. It was an undeniable fact though that Monahan had already collected fortunes from two similar schemes. But then, true to his karma, he had never been wealthy for long and had quickly reinvested each of those fortunes in doomed projects.

"Quiet," Monahan whispered, as an alarm came over the radio in the other room.

Finney followed as Monahan dragged the snarl of cable out into the watch office at the front of the station and stood next to the radio scanner. The dispatchers were adding Engine 38, Engine 17, and Ladder 9 to an ongoing incident in the Northgate area. There had been heavy radio traffic all morning, but this was the first time Finney paid any attention to it.

"All of the Fourth Battalion is tied up at that ship fire, and now they're calling for more units," Monahan said. "Two major alarms at once. There won't be a rig in service north of the ship canal."

The term *in service* referred to an apparatus that was ready to respond. A rig that was out of service was one already on an alarm or one that couldn't be dispatched because of mechanical problems or some other reason.

"The whole town's going to be jammed up," said Monahan excitedly.

"A couple of fires aren't going to overwhelm us."

"You watch. This is going to be nuts."

Even as he spoke, the bell in the corridor clanged.

Lieutenant Sadler came bustling down the hall from the beanery and immediately began tripping in the lengths of loose cable Monahan had left on the floor. He stood at the console waiting for the printout with the alarm information on it. Half a foot taller than Finney, Sadler had a thick black mustache that dominated his long face and a shock of salt-and-pepper hair he combed to one side. He spent much of his free time at the station talking on the phone to girlfriends, former girlfriends, prospective girlfriends, ex-wives, and women whose phone numbers he'd collected but whose names he'd lost or forgotten. Finney felt sorry for all of them.

"Four Avenue South and South Main Street?" Sadler said, scanning the run sheet on his way to the apparatus floor. "This has got to be a mistake. That's nowhere close to our district."

"They've got two working alarms in the north end," said Monahan with an exuberance Finney found out of character. There were firefighters who responded to every fire call as if they'd just been handed a ticket to the World Series, but he knew Monahan typically reacted to each alarm as if he were about to have his ass sewn shut.

A mile from the station, turning off East Marginal Way onto Fourth Avenue South, Finney heard the radio crackle. "Engines Twenty-six, Twenty-two, Thirty-two, and Eleven; Ladders Twelve and Six; Aid Five, Medic Sixteen; Air Twenty-six, Battalion One: Four Avenue South and South Main Street, the Downtowner," said the dispatcher. "Channel two. Engine Twenty-six?"

Lieutenant Sadler keyed the mike in his hand. "Engine Twenty-six, okay."

"Engine Twenty-six. This was a pull station activated on floor seven."

"Engine Twenty-six, okay."

Sadler pressed the mechanical siren button on the floor. After all these years the growling of the old-fashioned siren still gave Finney a bit of a thrill. These days it was about the only thrill left.

# 8. FOOD ON THE STOVE

Racking the microphone on the dash, Lieutenant Sadler wrenched around in his seat and raised his voice so Finney could hear him over the siren and the roar of the diesel motor. "That's your old stomping grounds, isn't it? Ten's district?"

"The Downtowner's a residential hotel," said Finney. "The panel's inside the front door on the left."

Formerly a hotel serving travelers from the King Street train station a block away, the Downtowner was now a low-rent, nine-story apartment building inhabited by elderly pensioners, immigrants who spoke little or no English, alcoholics, the formerly homeless, and the recently paroled. Nine times out of ten a call there was a false alarm. In eighteen years at Station 10, Finney had been there hundreds of times.

It was a long drive up Fourth Avenue through the industrial area, past Sears, the new baseball stadium, the Amtrak depot, and into the lower reaches of Chinatown. This area had been tide flats a hundred years ago. As they passed Station 14, Finney caught a momentary glimpse of recruits practicing behind the tower. His brother had told him they all knew him by name and his story. It pissed him off that most of them probably felt superior to and sorry for him.

Driving faster than department regulations decreed or his own skills dictated, Jerry Monahan gripped the wheel tightly, his body tipped forward. Monahan was one of those people who, no matter how much training he had under his belt, would still panic in an emergency.

Finney knew it was a trademark of the Seattle Fire Department that ineptitude such as Monahan's would be either studiously ignored or steadily rewarded—never punished, rarely corrected, and in most cases barely acknowledged. Common sense having been crippled by an elaborate set of civil service regulations and union rules, chiefs tended to shuffle their problems to other battalions or isolate them in quiet stations where they could do the least amount of damage. In order for Monahan to lose his job or even be demoted from the coveted driver's position, he would have to be convicted of a felony or commit some other egregious act. Finney feared that what would finally do Monahan in would be running over an innocent pedestrian on the way to a false alarm.

When they were a mile away, the dispatcher fed them an update. "Engine Twenty-six, we have a report of smoke on floor seven."

Facing backward in the crew cab, Finney was already in his tall, rubber bunking boots and multilayered bunking trousers. He'd put on his coat and slipped his arms through the straps of the MSA backpack and air cylinder stored behind the seat. As they approached the address, he saw people spilling out the main entrance onto the sidewalk. This should have been routine for him, the Downtowner, but these days, all he could think about when they went to an alarm was not screwing up.

"Jesus Christ, stop here," Sadler yelled at Monahan, who had bypassed the front entrance and was rolling toward the northwest corner of the building. "What the hell's wrong with you? You should have parked at the front door."

Meek as a kitten, Monahan said, "Aren't we going to charge the standpipe? It's a fire call, right? A high-rise . . . I charge the standpipe at a high-rise, right?"

"You stop in front when I tell you to stop in front, goddamn it!"

These two had been going at each other for the past week. It was hard for Finney to keep from laughing. He'd never worked on a crew quite like this.

Sadler gave his radio report and then he and Finney jostled their way through the crowd at the front entrance, Finney carrying a heavy dry chemical extinguisher, Sadler a pressurized pump can. Inside, the alarm bell was deafening.

When a high-rise went into fire mode, elevator cars were supposed to return automatically to the lobby, but the elevator wasn't there. "Where the hell's that car?" Sadler yelled to no one in particular.

A man with several missing teeth approached through the pack of evacuating citizens covering their ears with their hands. Like Sadler and Finney, he was a head taller than everyone else in the lobby and probably one of the few people in the building who spoke English. "The manager took it up to check on the fire."

"To floor seven?" Sadler asked.

"I guess so. The way I—"

Finney and Sadler ran to the narrow stairs leading from the back of the lobby and began climbing. In their cumbersome gear they left little room for nervous civilians, who flattened out against the walls when they saw them coming.

"*Cuidado!*" Sadler shouted at the descending citizens, his voice echoing in the marble staircase. Finney realized Sadler didn't know much Spanish, but he liked to flaunt what he did know. "*Cuidado!*"

Before they'd gone two flights, Finney could hear Sadler's heavy breathing, the tax for a lifetime of smoking. Including the weight of the extinguishers, they were each carrying more than eighty pounds of protective equipment. If nothing else, Finney knew he was still one of the fittest firefighters in the department. He would run Sadler into the ground and pretend it was easy. He could do that.

By floor three Finney was breathing hard, too. By four he felt as if the dry building air was scarring his lungs. Three floors left. Two left. As he approached seven, his legs grew noticeably wobbly. Still, he was far ahead of Sadler.

Finney waited for Sadler on the seventh-floor landing, breathing deeply. When he finally caught up with Finney, Sadler banged his pump can noisily onto the landing, dropped to his knees, and tried to catch his breath.

Finney took a few more deep breaths and said, "You all right?"

"Hell, no, I'm not all right."

"Want me to go back and get the Lifepak?"

"Why don't you go look around if you have so much extra energy?"

"Sure it's not your heart?"

"Get out of here!"

Smiling, Finney left Sadler in the stairwell while he went onto the floor, passing two Hispanic men who were punching the elevator buttons as if playing a video game. Unlike the old days when firefighters left their masks outside on the rigs and braved the smoke on their own, now the only time a Seattle firefighter was permitted into a fire building without an SCBA—a self-contained breathing apparatus—was to effect a rescue, and then only if other members with SCBAs weren't available. Medical treatment for smoke inhalation, once a badge of courage, triggered disciplinary charges these days.

Two doors down he came upon an apartment with light smoke drifting out of it.

"Fire department," he said loudly as he entered.

Standing in a semicircle around the stove were three mop-haired children and an elderly Asian man. They were mesmerized by a sheet of flame flowing out of the back burner on the stove, consuming a pot and lazily working its way up the wall. Finney hit the pot with a blast from his dry chemical extinguisher, snuffing the flames in a cloud of retardant. He plucked up the pot and set it in the sink, then turned off the burner and opened a window to let in the autumn breeze.

"When the alarm goes off, you're supposed to leave the building," Finney said, turning to the old man, who smiled and nodded. In another minute or two it would have eaten into the walls and ceiling. Finney took off a glove and put his hand an inch above each of the burners to make sure they were off. Dropping onto one knee to address the oldest of the children, Finney said, "Tell him that first you turn off the stove, then you leave the room and call the fire department. Close the door but do not lock it."

"Tapped food on the stove?" Sadler asked, walking through the door and sniffing.

"Tapped food on the stove."

While Sadler code-greened the rest of the incoming units and tried to communicate with the elderly man, who continued to smile and bow politely, Finney looked out the double windows. Seattle sat next to Puget Sound in a huge basin a hundred miles across, mountains on either side. Even low-income housing had a panoramic vista. Finney admired the way the morning sun etched the container ships on the slate-blue waters of Elliott Bay. The angled October sunshine, brightening the whitecaps and making them look like sharks' teeth, also highlighted the jagged mountains along the western horizon. Finney had always been awed by the snowcapped Olympic Mountains to the west, the Cascade range to the east, and especially Mount Rainier looming in the distance at the south end of Rainier Avenue, as if the city fathers had planted it there.

Funny. Peering down at the street, he was surprised to see no other units had arrived. Had he and Sadler followed protocol and waited downstairs, a simple food-on-the-stove would have escalated to an apartment fire. It was even possible it would have burned out the whole floor.

As they left, Finney tousled the hair of all three children. The oldest boy cracked a gap-toothed smile. The old man grinned and half bowed once again. Finney bowed back.

Downstairs they reset the alarm system and then Sadler chased down the building manager so he could chew him out for his hijinks with the elevator. In the short time he'd worked with Sadler, Finney had noticed the one aspect to the job Sadler relished: dressing down subordinates and civilians.

# 9. THE DANGEROUS BUILDINGS LIST

As a rule, Octobers in the Northwest are soggy, but several weeks earlier an unseasonable drought had developed, bringing with it clear, cold nights and cool, sunny days. When the rains came, the omnipresent dust in this neighborhood would transform into the kind of mud firefighters on Engine 26 had been grumbling about for as long as anyone could remember, the kind that reappeared as a sloppy film on the side panels after you washed them. At least they didn't have to wipe down the apparatus with a damp chamois, top to bottom, every time it returned to the barn—the procedure during Finney's first few years in the department, a mandate he assumed had originated from grooming sweaty horses after a run.

Finney stepped down out of the driver's seat and began pacing beside the rig, anxious about his scheduled meeting in less than an hour with the chief of the department. He was number one on the lieutenant's list, and everybody knew the first promotion was to be given out this week. He'd avoided taking the test for years, his reluctance stemming from family dynamics. His father had started browbeating him about becoming an officer the minute he entered the department, and falling into a lifelong pattern, Finney automatically resisted. At thirty-nine he finally saw his extended adolescent rebellion for what it was and realized that his refusal to accede to his father was keeping him from doing the very thing he wanted. Once he'd decided, it was a simple matter to follow through with the requisite studying. Coming out first on the list hadn't been difficult. The difficulty had been the initial resolve. After Leary Way he went through a period where he regretted having taken the test, wanting to keep as low a profile as possible. But his attitude was slowly shifting, and he now saw making lieutenant as partial redemption.

While Sadler and Monahan were across the street inspecting buildings, Finney waited alone in the rig parked on Riverside Drive, the Duwamish Waterway a stone's throw to his right. Somewhere nearby a metal grinder shrieked. It was a sad neighborhood, Finney thought. After World War II these lazy streets had been taken over by industry and commerce, children and families chased away by the screech of trucks and the thump of heavy machinery. Before the war it had been a community of Italian truck farmers, some of whom still resided in tiny houses dwarfed by tall warehouse walls. It seemed to Finney that everywhere he looked industry, commerce, and the need for a profit were overtaking humanity.

With nothing else to occupy his time, Finney picked up his portable radio and made a circuit of a two-story vacant house just this side of the waterway. Wind, time, and dust had abraded most of the paint from the outer walls and the boarded-over windows. Long-neglected azaleas and rhododendrons still thrived in the yard. A sepia swoosh marked the front porch, where it looked as if the boards had recently been swept clean of the neighborhood grit. Finney wondered who'd been here.

Stepping past an old wringer washer on the slanted back porch, he found the door had been forced recently. His small yellow department-issue flashlight in one hand, portable radio in the other, he stepped inside.

The house was at least a hundred years old, its wood floors scarred from generations of shoes. Mold and the smell of old apples permeated the rooms. The only piece of furniture on the main floor, a couch in the sitting room, was cancerous with black industrial grime that had infiltrated the structure. To the left of the front door a set of stairs led to the second floor, where Finney found three small bedrooms and a bathroom with a claw-foot tub. One bedroom was almost bare, but the others were cluttered with empty Corn Flakes boxes, Pepto-Bismol bottles, crushed Pepsi-Cola cans, prescription containers, crumpled newspapers, and filthy bedding. A vagrant must have set up camp here years ago and left after the disorder defeated him.

Throughout the house the grimy floors were dappled with fresh boot prints. Somebody had been here recently. Not a lot had been disturbed, but it was all to one purpose, and Finney gleaned that purpose quickly.

Outside in the sunshine Lieutenant Sadler and Monahan showed up at the apparatus just as Finney did.

"Come on," said Sadler. "We gotta get you back so you can see the chief."

"This place needs to be on the dangerous buildings list," Finney said.

Sadler put his clipboard and Notice of Violation pad inside the rig. "You went inside?"

"Somebody's got it all set to burn."

"This old wreck?" said Monahan dubiously. "Who would bother?"

"I don't know, but the wallboard is kicked out around the stairs.

There are combustibles stacked in all the right places. It's balloon construction, too, so the walls don't have any fire stops in them."

"Heck," said Monahan. "Half the places around here are like that. How about that double-wide trailer down the street? We going to put everything on the list?"

"We should put *this* on it. I'll fill out the form when we get back."

"Don't bother," said Monahan. "I've got a building I've been meaning to do myself. I'll do them both at the same time. You just go downtown and get those bars and make us proud."

As they drove back to the station, Finney let the full impact of his promotion wash over him. To be truthful, he had butterflies in his stomach. He'd waited a long time to become a lieutenant. Eighteen years.

He had to laugh when highfliers outside the department presumed that remaining a firefighter was the mark of a loser. Perhaps it wasn't exactly the fast track, but riding tailboard had always suited Finney just fine. Reporting for eight twenty-four-hour shifts a month gave him all the time in the world to keep in shape, to take long, rambling hikes in the Cascades or kayak trips through the San Juans, even to start a second business. For a while now he'd been toying with the idea of building kayaks professionally. He'd already built six of them, sold four, given away two. He liked the work and had every reason to believe that once he set his mind to it, he could make a business out of it.

But first and foremost he loved the straightforward hard work of firefighting. As a lieutenant he would still be fighting fire, and as a captain; but a chief's job was all paperwork, personnel problems, and incident command. And those dreadful meetings. Finney couldn't imagine being old enough or tired enough to want to be a chief.

Until recently Finney had worked his entire career on one of the city's eleven aerial ladder rigs, referred to as trucks or sometimes simply ladders, to distinguish them from the thirty-three engine companies in Seattle.

Engines carried hose, couplings, and nozzles—and usually five hundred gallons of water. The motor served double duty and could run either the rear wheels or a built-in pump. At a fire the driver ran the pump and made the hose connections, while the officer and the nozzleman took a line into the building, where they located the seat of the fire and put water on it.

Trucks carried ladders, including a hundred-foot aerial, power saws,

forcible entry equipment, hydraulic extrication tools, and high-angle rescue ropes and hardware. At fires, truck companies performed forcible
entry, searched for victims, and ventilated the fire building, which was
just as necessary to putting out a structure fire as a chimney is to a fire-
place. Ventilation was accomplished either by laddering the roof and cutting a hole with a chain saw, or by mechanical means, with fans.

Finney treasured the unique challenges of truck work, and to him, a
lieutenant's spot on a truck seemed about as perfect as life could get.

# 10. CHUB O'MALLEY RETIRES

Finney always thought Station 10's red apparatus doors, in contrast to its pale walls, looked like bright lipstick on a sickly streetwalker. The monolithic, four-story structure at Second Avenue South and South Main Street was in a small corner of old town called Pioneer Square and had been Finney's home away from home until last June, when he'd requested a transfer after Leary Way. He still loved the place, but there was no way he could work here again. Every time he showed up, he expected to see Bill coming around a corner.

Except for the occasional Saturday-night rowdiness next door at The Fenix Underground and the traffic tie-ups when one of the nearby stadiums scheduled a ball game or a new-car expo, these were sleepy streets, frequented by lost tourists, homeless schizophrenics, and panhandlers trying to put together enough quarters for another bottle of Night Train. Finney and the others on his crew had spent countless hours people-watching from the windows upstairs.

He couldn't begin to count all the times his father had brought him here as a tot; he still had vivid memories of concealing himself in the cubbyholes around the station. Once, after his father told him how his own dad had thrown him into Lake Missaukee in Michigan to teach him to swim, Finney had leaped into the pool upstairs only to be fished out by kindly Captain Gagliani, who had only three fingers on one hand—a fact that both terrified and fascinated the five-year-old. Like a lot of other old-time firefighters, Gagliani was long dead from lung cancer by the time Finney joined the department.

The third and fourth floors of Station 10 housed the department's administrative offices. Floor two contained the living quarters for the crews of Engine 10, Ladder 1, and Aid 5: bunk rooms, officers' rooms, the beanery, a small inspection room, an enormous TV room, a handball court, a weight room, meeting rooms, and the same indoor swimming pool Finney had jumped into so long ago. There was a mezzanine between floors one and two where the department fire investigators maintained offices. The ground floor contained the apparatus bay.

Firefighters parked their cars beneath the station in an underground garage that was so crowded the outgoing shift had to shuttle its vehicles to a pay lot across the street before the incoming shift could squeeze in. This rite was performed each morning before the 0700 bell-testing that was still called the hitch, one of many terms passed down from the horse culture of ninety years before, when each morning that day's team was fitted in harnesses. Finney loved all the historical ties. The apparatus bay was called the barn and, as if galloping horses were still involved, alarms were called runs.

Finney hadn't visited Station 10 in months, and though he expected to be overwhelmed by nostalgia, oddly, he wasn't struck by anything except the fact that Diana Moore was in the watch office. He was surprised that spotting her sent a shot of low-voltage electricity through him.

Also in the watch office were Lieutenant Balitnikoff and his crew, the two Lazenby brothers. The assigned engine officer on C-shift, Marion Balitnikoff was slightly shorter than Finney but heavier, most of it in his bulky torso. Balitnikoff had made his share of enemies in the department by letting his mouth run too far ahead of his brain, and then laughing loudly as if his crude comments were harmless gags. He'd offended Finney as often as anybody else, but Finney figured that was just the way he was and tried to ignore it. Off shift he was a hunter and drinker; on shift he bragged about empty bottles and whatever animal he'd killed recently, when he wasn't boasting about his sons, three young men attending various state colleges on second-string football scholarships. He was married to a mousy woman who took his excesses in stride. For years he'd tried to kindle a romance between one of his sons and any of Cordifis's three daughters, but Cordifis's daughters were too well-bred to be interested.

"Hey! There he is," Michael Lazenby said, grinning at Finney. "You come down to talk to the big cheese?"

"The cheese himself."

"Don't drop your pants for him," said Paul Lazenby. "That's the wrong way to get a promotion."

"Yeah," said Michael Lazenby. "They'll want to do it to you again when you make captain. Pretty soon you'll start liking it."

Both brothers laughed raucously. The Lazenbys were hard drinkers and amateur bodybuilders. Michael was good-looking in a California surfer style, while Paul was stockier, darker, and less amiable. Paul, who had all his department shirts tailored and rarely buttoned the top four buttons, touched the gold medallion dangling in the hair on his chest. He must not be doing a bodybuilding show anytime soon, Finney thought. He shaved his whole body for shows. Paul Lazenby was the only person Finney knew who managed to look like a lounge lizard in a fire department uniform. Despite their rough personalities, or perhaps because of them, in straight-ahead firefighting the crew of Engine 10 had few peers.

Finney looked around the group, his eyes settling on Diana Moore. "Where was everybody this morning?"

"What's the matter? Couldn't you guys handle a little food-on-the-stove by your lonesome?" Lieutenant Balitnikoff asked derisively, stepping between Finney and Diana. "Shit, man. Helen Keller could put out a food-on-the-stove."

"Now that you mention it, I think it was Helen Keller. She put it out and then she gave the radio report and helped us with our gear. She's coming back to the station tonight to tuck us in."

Unable to goad Finney, Balitnikoff stalked out of the room, humorless and cold as stone, rolling slightly on the outer edges of his feet, his blue officer's shirt stretched over his abdomen like spandex. Five months ago, before Cordifis's death, Finney had enjoyed a raucous camaraderie with these men. Now they seemed like strangers.

As he followed his lieutenant out of the room, Michael Lazenby turned to Finney and said, "Just remember us when you make chief."

"I'll keep a bag of peanuts in my desk drawer for the little people."

"Paul likes corn nuts."

"I'll keep some of those, too."

After the others left, Diana's gray eyes swiveled expectantly to Finney. "Don't pay attention to them. They think the sun rises and sets out of that tailpipe on Engine Ten. I've even seen them out there taking pictures of it like they're going to send them to their grandma or something."

"I think their grandma is a bodybuilder."

Diana laughed. He liked that she laughed at his lame joke. He'd been thinking ill of her for some time. He wasn't quite sure why. Maybe it was survivor's guilt. Maybe it was because he hadn't yet apologized for speaking rudely to her after Leary Way, when she tried to console him. He hadn't thought about that in weeks. He'd been terrible.

Finney knew that, despite strenuous objections from her well-to-do family, Diana had taken the job in the fire department after receiving an education in private schools and following a course of studies in English literature at Pepperdine. Four months ago, after the Leary Way fire, she'd been moved to his empty spot on Ladder 1. Maybe that was why he held a grudge against her.

"How have you been, John?"

"Except for the heart palpitations and the random paranoia, just fine," he said, smiling. He could tell she didn't know whether to believe him or not. The funny thing was, it was half-true.

He could also tell that she'd been trying not to look at the side of his neck where the doctors had grafted fresh skin onto the worst burns. "I probably shouldn't ask," she said, "but did that hurt?"

The burns had been nothing compared to what had been going on inside his head. "I cried like an orphan at the train station."

"I doubt that. Are you all right? I worry about you. They don't talk about it around here, but I don't think anybody's handling Bill's death too well. No one except Reidel, who turned to religion and acts as if it was God's will. I wish I had a nickel for every time he's said 'Bill's with Jesus now.' The engine guys don't talk to the truckies, and Baxter's in retirement mode."

"The chemistry of a crew is a delicate thing. It'll get better." Neither of them spoke for a few uneasy seconds. "All those missing units this morning weren't at a class?"

"There were two fires in the north end. Then a bunch of runs came in all at once and tied everyone up."

"The last time I remember that happening was June seventh. The night of Leary Way."

"I hadn't thought about that, but you're right."

"If Helen Keller hadn't been at the Downtowner, we wouldn't have had any help at all."

She smiled good-naturedly. It had taken a long time for Diana to be accepted in the ranks. Eleven years ago, when she started at Station 2, the old salts spent weeks trying to break her—their primary weapon the rumor mill. They said she was too weak to meet the department's physical standards, that she was a lesbian, or that she had slept with the captain at training to get the job. After her physical strength was tested and found sufficient, a rumor circulated that she was on steroids.

None of the rumors seemed to rattle Diana, who somehow remained even-tempered and pleasant throughout. Two years before entering the department she'd finished in the top ten at the Hawaiian Iron Man competition, so she was stronger than many of the men she worked with and had more endurance than all but a handful. Among eighteen hundred candidates, she'd passed the physical agilities section of the department's entrance exam at eighth. She told this to no one. If the old-timers wished to believe she wasn't strong enough, that was their problem.

It was a slow process, but eventually she was welcomed into the fold. The lone holdout was Chub O'Malley, who'd been the driver on Engine 2 since the late Sixties. One day the other crew members egged Chub into betting two gallons of ice cream that he could bench-press 150 pounds more times than Diana. O'Malley felt confident that even a flabby male was stronger than the fittest female. "One Rocky Road," he said, as they walked into the weight room at Station 2. "And one chocolate chip mint." Ten minutes later O'Malley was on his way to the hospital with a torn ligament in his elbow. While he was being wheeled out, Diana said, not unkindly, "Two vanilla."

Six months later, on his first day back from disability, the crew taunted Chub about still owing ice cream, taunted him until he made a second wager. Double or nothing. At first Diana refused, but if Chub could do nothing else, he could make her angry. She stormed into the weight room and bench-pressed 150 pounds twenty-seven times.

O'Malley performed the exercise four times and tore the ligaments in his other elbow. This time he retired.

Diana was almost as tall as Finney, and moved with the grace of a large cat, certainly without the clumsy, masculine affectation Finney noticed some of the women in the department strove for. Her uniform always looked as if it had been pressed minutes earlier and might still be warm from the iron. She had perfect white teeth, chestnut hair, and wide cheekbones.

Finney was aware that she'd been looking at him for some time now, and her look was about as personal as he'd gotten with a woman in some time. Judging by the question in her eyes, she'd meant it to be personal.

"You don't like me, do you?" she said.

"Pardon?"

"I just get the feeling you don't like me."

"Where did that come from?" She was right, but he was defensive, had thought he was hiding it better than he probably was. She was some kind of mind reader or something. He hoped she couldn't see his chagrin.

"I can understand why. I mean, we went through that fire together, and now you're getting shuffled around the city like a recruit, while here I am working out of your old locker."

"I'm getting shuffled around because I'm on the lieutenant's list. And if I'm acting uneasy, it's because I owe you an apology." He thought about the clumsy things he'd said after Leary Way, to her and others. He'd been particularly horrid to her. She'd been trying to help, and all he'd wanted was to be left alone. Their intentions had collided and he'd said things he wished he hadn't. "I was rude. I should have apologized earlier."

"I know you weren't yourself after Leary Way. I wasn't angling for an apology."

"You got one anyway. I'm sorry."

"Thank you. But apology aside, you don't like me, do you?"

She was on to him. From what little he knew about her, she'd always been an astute judge of character. He might as well have been naked. "I like you fine."

"Is it because Bill had me stay outside that night?"

"I can't get into this now."

"Okay, when?"

"I'm sorry if I gave you the impression I don't like you. I like you just fine." Her eyes remained fixed on his, and it was clear she didn't believe him, as well she shouldn't. He *didn't* like her. Undeniably, he felt electricity in his stomach when he was around her, but he hadn't liked her since Cordifis's funeral, and it bothered him that she had found him out and that he didn't have a good reason for his attitude. Or any reason. Hell, everybody liked Diana. And why wouldn't they? She was sharp as a tack, amiable, straightforward, and she was a first-rate firefighter—that last a quality one wouldn't necessarily expect to find in a beautiful woman. And without an ounce of snoot to her, as Bill had said that last day they worked together. Finney took a step back and looked around the room. "I miss this place. I thought I would, and now I do." He turned to leave.

"Break a leg."

"That's the plan."

# 11. THE GOVERNOR'S LIFESAVING AWARD

When Finney stepped out of the elevator onto the fourth floor, a business-like secretary with green-tinted contacts and a pile of brunette hair told him the chief would be with him in a minute.

She left him to his own devices in a large office with a tall ceiling and a desk sporting photographs of Reese's family. Hanging on the wall behind the desk, where you couldn't miss it if you tried, was a Governor's Lifesaving Award, praising BATTALION CHIEF CHARLES REESE for his actions the night of June 7. Surrounding it were framed photos and newspaper clippings chronicling Reese's meteoric career, including a photo from *Time* magazine of Reese and Robert Kub running out of the Leary Way building in front of a ball of flame. It gave Finney the creeps. Maybe they should all chip in and buy Reese a scrapbook for this stuff so he wouldn't have to plaster his ego all over the walls.

The search for Bill Cordifis had been the pinnacle of Reese's career. Written up as a hero in the regional and national papers, Charlie rode his renown into the chief's office three months later.

It occurred to Finney that Leary Way was the defining moment in the careers of both Reese and himself. Finney went into the burning building with a partner and forty-eight minutes later came out alone, burned, confused, disoriented, barely able to walk. Even though he, too, failed to bring Cordifis out, Reese went into that same burning building and came out as chief of the department. Finney sometimes wondered if his dislike of Reese was nothing more than envy—but no, his opinion had been formed eighteen years before, when they entered the department in the same drill school.

It was twenty minutes before Charlie Reese showed up, which was about ten minutes after Finney figured the chief had succeeded in making his point.

At five foot five, Reese was a short man in a profession of giants. He had unwavering eyes and wavy black hair. He wore loose-fitting trousers and an off-white dress shirt, the collar of which captured a wedge of soft flesh just below his chin. He'd been handsome once, and would still have been handsome, Finney thought, if he hadn't let so much of his personality leach out into his face.

After shaking hands, Reese smiled slowly. "Whoever would have thought, huh? You and me. Here in this room." He laughed.

"From day one you said you were going to be chief of the department."

"And now here I are." Reese laughed again, then walked around the desk and sat heavily in the leather chair. "So tell me, how's your old man?"

# 12. UNTIL THEY PRY MY COLD FINGERS OFF THIS DESK

"Six months ago when they diagnosed it," Finney said, "they told him aggressive treatment might give him a year at the outside, but he opted out of that. He doesn't want to live the twilight of his life driving back and forth from the hospital. Mostly, he's playing golf. When he has the strength."

It was bad enough that his father was dying, worse that he was dying of cancer, an occupational hazard among firefighters, and it prompted Finney to wonder what toxins had banked up in his own system during the nearly two decades he'd been a firefighter. He knew that because of the twenty- to thirty-year gestation period of many cancers, firefighters frequently retired just in time to discover they had six months to live.

"He was a stubborn old fart," said Reese, grinning.

"Still is."

Finney resisted the temptation to toy with the set of lieutenant's bars in his pocket, a gift from his father, who couldn't get enough of the fact that his younger son, with whom he rarely saw eye-to-eye, was finally going to be an officer. If his father didn't live long enough to see him make captain, at least he would see Finney wearing his own battle-tested lieutenant's bars. Finney's older brother, Tony, the apple of his father's eye, made lieutenant twelve years ago and captain shortly thereafter, all according to the old man's schedule. The fact that Tony then went into a long tailspin precipitated by a gambling habit and two volatile divorces from the same woman somehow evaded their father's radar, a situation Finney found amusingly ironic. Finney's father wanted only one thing for his sons. He had climbed through the ranks from firefighter to lieutenant, from captain to battalion chief, and he wanted desperately to see both his sons do the same.

"Did you know your old man was my first batt chief?" Reese asked. "Out at Eighteen's?"

"I guess I'd forgotten." Reese couldn't have looked too impressive just out of drill school. Finney remembered how his strength used to fade toward the end of the day as they were picking up wet hose to hang in the tower at 14's, how he couldn't hide his fear in the smoke room. As a recruit Finney quickly learned which of his fellow trainees he could count on, and Reese had never been one of them. Once in the company, Reese spent thousands of hours studying for promotionals. Despite all the studying, his first test results were mediocre—forty-eighth on a lieutenant's list from which fifty-four firefighters were promoted. Three years later he scored slightly higher on the captain's test, but only enough to get the last captain's spot. If he hadn't been one-sixteenth American Indian, he might not have been promoted at all. Later he was the last battalion chief to be made from that list. Even in drill school Reese had made each cut by a whisker, yet his history of scraping by was transformed in a single stroke by Leary Way, which propelled him directly into the department chief's office.

"Your father. My first day in the company he told us he was going to drill the engine. Most of those guys had been in fifteen, twenty years, and they were worried. I took my cues from them. Your old man was a terror. He finally shows up eating a Wendy's burger. He runs us through five hose evolutions on the back ramp. I thought we were going to suck the main dry. Afterward we're sopping wet and exhausted and shivering, and he comes over to me and says, 'You're pumping into the standpipe to the tenth floor of a high-rise. Upstairs you've got two hundred feet of inch-and-a-half hose line with a Wooster nozzle. Two one-hundred-foot two-and-a-half-inch lines into the standpipe from the engine. What's your pump pressure?' That was his question to me, and that's my question to you now."

"We haven't carried inch-and-a-half hose for years."

"What if I said your promotion depended on the answer?"

What an asshole, Finney thought. Well, he wasn't above jumping through a few hoops if that's what it took to get a promotion. Just so he didn't have to bend over and drop his pants. Although it was starting to look like maybe the Lazenby brothers hadn't been joking about that. "A hundred pounds of pressure for the nozzle, twenty-five for each section of inch-and-a-half, forty-five for the nine stories above grade, and twenty-five for the standpipe. Nothing for the parallel two-and-a-halfs until you're flowing more than two hundred gallons a minute. You're pumping at two-twenty."

"Try doing that out in the rain after you've been drilling for three hours."

"Put me out in the rain and drill me for three hours." Finney smiled.

Reese furrowed his brow. "You think the way your old man treated me was funny?"

"Not at all." Finney had no idea where this was leading. If his father had been hard on Reese, he'd been hard on Finney, too. And on his brother. They'd suffered his wrath for a good many more years than Charlie Reese. Inside and outside the department Gil Finney had been a son of a bitch, and because of that, John had always kept his own counsel regarding his father, as he would now. Gil Finney had come into the fire department under a regime headed by flint-eyed men who'd fought in World War II and Korea, unforgiving men, a gruff bunch who schooled him until he was hard, too, the part of him that wasn't steel to begin with. People either loved him or hated him, and on both sides of the fence they were intimidated by him.

Reese leaned against his desk and clasped his hands together. "Every time I ran into your old man, he made me look like a fool. I swore I was going to get even."

"You're going to outlive him, if that's any consolation." Finney thought it was ironic that Reese groused about Chief Finney, because as feared as his father had been in certain quarters, there were men who would have given their lives for him. On the flip side of the coin, there weren't too many people who would spit the toothpick out of their mouths for Reese. Finney knew it had a lot to do with the indifference he displayed, as if he didn't feel anything for the people working under him and wanted them to know it. In fact, it seemed to Finney that Reese was and always had been proud of how much he was disliked.

Reese gave him a long, withering look. "He used to go home and laugh about me, didn't he?"

"I wouldn't know. I barely spoke to him until after Leary Way."

"Leary Way? Goddamn. I almost forgot about that. You're not still bothering people over that fire, are you?"

Obviously it was poor interview strategy to bring up the night he'd lost his partner, and Finney felt like kicking himself for it. Still, the words were out of his mouth, and there wasn't a damn thing he could do. "I'm looking into it."

"Still?"

"Still."

"Tell you what," said Reese, smugly. "Here's your million-dollar question. Get this right and you've got the job. You're deep inside a fire building. A wall collapses on your partner. You can't dig him out. You have one radio between the two of you, but neither of you knows exactly where you are, so you can't tell anybody how to get there. What do you do?"

"Charlie, is this a joke?"

"I think from now on you'd better call me *chief.*"

Finney felt a rush of heat in his face. Impossible and wrong as it seemed, he knew now that despite having the top score on the list, he wasn't going to get promoted. Thirty-five lieutenants were going to come off that list, but he wouldn't be one of them. Maybe Reese wanted an answer to his question. Maybe he didn't. Finney knew giving him one wouldn't change his mind.

For a few moments, Reese stared morosely at the wall. It wasn't a joke, but he didn't require an answer either. "I'm glad you came up. I needed a breather. You know, this job is like riding a bicycle around the inside of a tornado. Phone calls. Messages. Meetings. The mayor's office. Carla and I are having dinner with Jon Stevenson tonight. The state senator?"

"I know who Stevenson is."

"We're going to see if we can't get a statewide task force on arson fires moving along in the right direction." Clasping his hands behind his back, Reese walked to the window, a world-weary act Finney had seen before, an affectation of thoughtfulness and calm, a commander at the helm of his ship. As a young officer, Reese had been mocked for it, mimics duplicating it within days of each new assignment, the wake of his career strewn with uniformed clowns who could ape him perfectly. Finney had always thought the mockery was a little sophomoric, akin to making fun of the teacher when his back was turned, but now he could picture himself mimicking Reese's self-important pose.

"Am I going to get this job?" Finney asked.

Without turning around, Reese peered at Finney over his shoulder. "You know how long I'm going to be chief?"

"Am I going to get the job?"

"Until they pry my cold fingers off that desk. Meanwhile I'm going to build an officer corps the likes of which this department's never seen. John, I want you to hear this from me. I figure I owe you that much. I'm not going to promote you."

Even though he'd seen it coming, Finney felt as if he'd been hit in the chest. Surely this little pissant who could barely cut the mustard in drill school, who'd been promoted at the tail end of each list, who'd been despised by each of his crews, wasn't going to sink Finney's career over one fire? Or because of his father.

He tried to concentrate, vaguely aware that Reese was talking, though the words came to his ears as if through water.

". . . and it wasn't until I got a few years under my belt and gained some experience that I was able to appreciate what a power-mad, incompetent jackass your old man really was. . . . After what happened I know a lot of people still believe you're a good firefighter, but for the time being I think, rather than giving orders, you should learn how to take them. You study for the next test two years from now. Meanwhile I'm going to keep you at Twenty-six's. That should help settle you down."

"I deserve this promotion and you know it."

Reese walked over to the office door and dropped his hand onto the knob. "I can't promote a man who would abandon his partner and then sabotage the efforts of the rescue team."

"Abandon? What the hell are you talking about? I went for help. And just how did I sabotage the rescue team? I did everything but take your hand and lead you down that corridor. In fact, I offered to do just that."

"You were in a blind panic," Reese said quietly. "I almost lost my life because of you."

Finney stared into Reese's unwavering dark eyes. He'd never seen a man more sure of himself.

"You're making a mistake," Finney said. "I'm a good firefighter and I'd be a good officer."

"There are two of us in this room, John. One of us has a citation on the wall. The other has a dead partner. Think about it."

# 13. SICK CHICKENS WITH MATCHES

The rig was out when Finney got back to Station 26, and for a few crazy minutes he considered emptying his locker and leaving his resignation scrawled on a roll of toilet paper the way one contemptuous old-timer had done years before. There were several actions he could take. He still had a vague hankering to go back to school, get a degree, and teach high school history. He'd worked for a commercial painting outfit and he'd always liked the smell of paint and the routine of good honest labor every day. The fire department wasn't the air in his lungs or the blood in his veins. Then again, nothing would destroy his father quicker than to see him quit. And as he thought about it, he realized maybe the fire department *was* the air in his lungs and the blood in his veins. Maybe it was those things and more.

As he stood there thinking, Finney became aware of a woman rapping on the glass door to the station, her face less than a foot from his. Apparently she'd been in front of him for some time. It was Annie, one of their regulars. From dawn to dusk Annie roamed the streets of South Park, the neighborhood Station 26 protected, pulling a two-wheeled wire shopping cart behind her, obsessed with making right-angle turns, which meant she had surely been in his direct line of vision for the last thirty feet of her jaunt. Annie was a small woman in her early sixties who wore old-fashioned hiking boots, white knee socks, and, as always, a denim skirt and a lightweight raincoat.

As a courtesy, the Seattle Fire Department tested blood pressures for citizens during business hours; every station had their regulars, and Annie was one of 26's. He knelt beside her, wrapped the blood pressure cuff around her arm, and put the stethoscope to his ears. It was, as always, 120 over 60, perfectly normal.

As she put her raincoat back on, she said, "You going to be here for the war?"

"What war?"

She removed a *Wall Street Journal* from her cart and showed him an article on the front page announcing an agreement between two Mideast powers to lower the price of oil. "Don't you see it? They're lowering the crude prices to lull us into complacency. These men have nuclear weapons. They say they don't, but they do. We're all standing in a pool of gasoline, and now these sick chickens have matches. What I need to know is whether you're here at night."

"Somebody's always here, Annie. We work twenty-four-hour shifts."

"You. I'm talking about *you*."

"I won't be here every minute. But somebody will."

"I want you here. I'm scared."

Finney patted Annie's shoulder. He knew the worlds of the mentally ill and the mentally broken weren't far apart, and even though he had survived those hellish weeks after Leary Way, they were as vivid to him now as if they'd happened yesterday. He'd tiptoed along the abyss, and there were a few hours scattered over several of the worst days when he'd come close to losing his mind. He identified with Annie in a way no one else in the station could.

"Don't worry. Everything's going to work out fine no matter who's here. You have a good day, Annie."

"Bet'cher ass, sweetie."

# 14. THE DOOTER IN THE HELMET

After they'd done the dinner dishes, Finney and Jerry Monahan collapsed in the station recliners, Monahan channel-surfing with the remote control, Finney unable to motivate himself for even the simplest task. The whole battalion knew Finney had lost the promotion, the topic picked over by the twin vultures of gossip and Monday-morning quarterbacking; they were bound to connect it to his performance at Leary Way. It ate at him to know that everybody was talking about him again.

"I didn't want to tell you before you went down there," Monahan said, "but I knew you weren't going to get the job."

"What? How did you know that?"

"Somebody who works down there told me. I'd rather not say who."

"Jesus. Why didn't you warn me?"

"Are you kidding? Who wants to tell a guy a thing like that?" Monahan let his belt out a couple of notches. They'd made fajitas, the four of them—Finney, Sadler, Monahan, and Iverson, who was manning the air rig, Air 26—and except for Finney, who'd lost his appetite, they'd eaten too much. Iverson was hiding out on the other side of the station with a calculator and a stack of personal bills. Sadler was in his office on the phone.

Monahan ballooned his belly out, lifted his leg, and farted. He wouldn't swear out loud, but he would fart in a cathedral. "Geez-Louise, why do I eat so much?"

"Same reason you break wind in public," Finney said, still smarting over the fact that Monahan had known in advance about his not getting the promotion. "Lack of character."

Passing off the insult, Monahan chuckled as if it were a joke and turned his head at the sound of knocking at the back door. Finney crossed the room and opened the door. It was his brother, Tony.

"Just thought I'd come by and see how you were."

"You heard?"

"Oh, yeah."

Monahan rose and scratched the back of his head. "I better go see if I got November seventh off. I've been asking about it all day."

"Why do you need the seventh off?" Finney asked.

"My wedding anniversary," Monahan said, nervously. "I forgot last year. You can bet your booties there was heck to pay. Thirty-two years. I get anything wrong this time, the little woman'll really pin my ears back." Monahan stepped around the corner into the corridor and knocked on Lieutenant Sadler's door.

"Some place we can talk?" Tony asked, giving Monahan a sour look as he left the room.

They walked out into the cold apparatus bay behind Engine 26 and stood facing each other on the concrete floor.

Taking after their mother's side of the family, John was blue-eyed, easygoing, and genial. Tony resembled their father, penetrating dark eyes, blond hair. A captain at Station 17, Tony was three years older and four inches shorter than Finney. Tony and their father were the hardnoses in the clan, both calculating and intense, and each with a mean streak, though recently they'd both worked at taming it—Tony, perhaps because of the bad marriages; their father, because of the cancer.

"He's not trying to put this off on Leary Way, is he?" Tony asked.

"Maybe a little."

"You know, when he was a captain at Thirty-one's, somebody dumped a dooter in his helmet. You ever hear that story? You got to really hate somebody to drop a hot turd in his helmet."

"Thanks, Tony. Thanks for coming by."

"You should have called the minute it happened. You got anybody else to talk to? How about Laura?"

Finney had been divorced from Laura almost six years. "Not likely."

"Jesus, you're right. I know how pissed Doris gets at me when we're not married. God, I was at Seventeen's to pick up my check, and they were saying you and Reese almost came to blows. Until now everybody's pretty much been waiting to figure out his style. But this goes against all tradition. You were top dog on the list. By rights you should have snagged that first job. Nobody's ever been head man on the list and not gotten a job. Now everybody's going to ask why the hell they should even take the test."

"I didn't screw up at Leary Way." Finney hadn't meant to say the words; they'd just come out.

"I know that, John. We all know that."

"You might. Plenty of others don't. And I didn't almost come to blows with him." Finney sat next to Tony on the cold steel of Engine 26's diamond-plate tailboard, looking out at the darkness through the windows in the roll-up rear door of the apparatus bay. He and Tony had never been close, and Finney wished it hadn't taken their father's illness to unite them.

For some minutes neither spoke. Then Tony opened his billfold and handed Finney fifty dollars. "Two weeks ago. Remember?"

It was a rare month when Tony didn't put the touch on him. In the past it had been the horses, but these days he spent his free time at the Indian casinos, a predilection that was beginning to rock his third marriage the same way the horses had rocked the two marriages to Doris. So far his new wife, Annette, was more forgiving than Doris, but Finney could see the handwriting on the wall.

"Thanks for dropping by, Tony."

"The gossip about Leary Way is bound to speed up after this. Not too many people like Reese, but he's the man in the catbird seat. Watch your backside, too. Balitnikoff's been telling everyone the reason you and Cordifis were paired up at fires was because Bill was baby-sitting you."

"You kidding?"

"I know; I know. Anybody ever worked with you two knows it was the other way around. But a rumor is like busting a feather pillow in a windstorm. You never get all the feathers back. No point in trying."

"Rumors are the least of my worries."

"I'm glad you're taking it so calmly."

But he wasn't taking it calmly. Balitnikoff. Besides having worked at Station 10 for the past three years, Marion Balitnikoff had been in and out of Finney's life since he'd known Bill Cordifis. Finney had long ago been conscripted into the weekly Cordifis clan get-togethers, and frequently this meant spending time with Bill's department pals, Marion Balitnikoff among them. Finney and Balitnikoff had crossed swords more than once. Uneasy about the way he ogled Heather, Cordifis's youngest daughter, Finney had mentioned it to her father, who, either unwilling or incapable of thinking ill of his friends, dismissed Finney's concerns out of hand. Balitnikoff was a family friend, and that was that. To make matters worse, Cordifis, for some reason, told Balitnikoff what Finney had said. Balitnikoff had never forgiven him.

Tony picked a piece of lint off his younger brother's collar. "God, I was worried for you that night. We pulled in just as the roof on the west side caved in and fired up the sky. I thought you were going to die. They must have been working on you, oh, fifteen minutes, had all your clothes except your jockeys stripped off and were putting ringers into you, when one of the medics decided to get a core temperature. A hundred and six. The doctors told me hallucinations start at a hundred and five. Can you imagine how hot you must have been twenty minutes earlier when you were inside?"

To Finney's way of thinking, the modern fire service had gone overboard in mandating protective equipment. During his first years on the job full bunkers had been optional. He'd worn a heavy bunking coat, a helmet, gloves, cotton—and later Nomex—pants, along with steel-toed work boots. Only at night or at the more hazardous fires would he climb into knee-high rubber bunking boots and the heavy bunking pants that came with them. In the old days their ears, necks, and skin around their facepieces were exposed. People who'd worked with that system liked it because, despite occasional steam burns, it gave them a valuable temperature gauge.

Now, mummified in a variety of heavy, fire-resistant garments, they often went so far into fire buildings they couldn't get out safely. There was no way to tell how hot it was until it was too late.

And though the manufacturers touted the latest materials in heat transference properties, the fact was that even the best-conditioned firefighters sweated heavily while working in the multilayered bunking coats and trousers. The body produced sweat in order to cool, yet in bunkers there was no cooling effect. To Finney, compared to the old days, it seemed as if fires were being fought in slow motion. Teams were sent to rehab to drink and rest after depleting a single half-hour air bottle.

Fire departments across the country were fighting forty percent fewer fires but losing more people than ever. Firefighters were dropping from heart attacks and heatstroke and from getting trapped deep inside burning buildings, while the industry adjusted its blinders and tried to figure out why. Finney and plenty of others knew why. They were going into these buildings carrying the earth and sky on their backs like Atlas.

"John. I'm really sorry about what happened today."

"Thanks, Tony."

"Jesus! How are you going to tell Dad? This'll kill him."

"I'll figure out something."

Finney let Tony out the rear door of the apparatus bay, his brother's final comment ringing in his ears. Despite their recent closeness, it was just like Tony to point out that this was going to hurt their father—kill him, in fact. It was also like him to make sure it was the last thing he said, a dig that appeared accidental yet probably wasn't, the sort of double-edged comment Tony had honed to perfection over the years.

# 15. NOBODY GETS OUT ALIVE

Uffocating, blinded, choking on smoke, Finney crawled down the dark corridor, his right glove skimming the wall. He'd been without bottled air for some time, and his mouth tasted of blood and burnt rubber and something that might easily have been roadkill. Nothing was nastier than smoke from a building fire.

Piloting by the dim sounds of a fire engine pump somewhere outside, he made his way forward, but each time he inched ahead, it seemed as if the floor pulled him back, as if the floor were moving. When he finally looked down, he realized he was staggering through dead men tiered up like logs, each burned beyond recognition.

Then his eyes were open and it took a few seconds to decide whether he was awake or only dreaming he was awake. When he rolled his head on his pillow to check the bedside clock, a mixture of sweat and tears crackled in his ear. It was 0305 hours, almost to the minute they'd been dispatched to Leary Way five months earlier. It was uncanny how some circadian clock in his brain knew what time to bring on the dream.

Always Leary Way. Always a few minutes after three in the morning.

Finney sat up and let the air in the houseboat cool him. He knew from experience he wouldn't sleep again tonight. Sleep would be too great a gift. In an attempt to clear the cobwebs, he climbed out of bed and walked around the boat. He undressed and stepped into the shower, languishing like a drunk trying to sober up. He felt better after he'd toweled off and climbed into sweats and a thick pair of hiking socks. He went outside to the small deck, where he gazed across the black-glass surface of the lake.

Along with seven other floating homes and a mixture of pleasure craft, his houseboat was moored to a dock just north of Crockett Street on Westlake Avenue North, the second slip from the end. To his east he could gaze out over Lake Union to the freeway and the lights of apartment buildings, condos, and vintage homes residing shoulder-to-shoulder on the western slope of Capitol Hill. To his north were the shadowy, surreal comic book shapes of the old burners and smokestacks in Gas Works Park. To the southwest the Space Needle appeared from his vantage point to be keeping watch over an ever-expanding clutch of downtown sky-scrapers, their reflected lights twinkling on the surface of the lake.

The houseboat had originally belonged to his aunt Julie, who twenty-two years earlier had lost her husband, a mechanic at Boeing Field, to a freak accident, when he was sucked into a jet intake. The event had been captured by some clown with an eight-millimeter camera. The footage ended up on the national news, and it did more to destroy his aunt than the death itself. In fact, she never stopped ranting about the news footage and how cruel it had been to both her husband's memory and her sanity. The proceeds from the insurance settlement along with a small pension allowed her to hibernate in her bedroom, drugged by soap operas, smoking three or four packs of unfiltered Camels a day, seeking final solace in the bottom of a wineglass. After twelve years of this, her body betrayed her in the same way the world had, and one morning she found she could no longer walk.

She'd been Finney's favorite aunt, and when she started her long downhill slide, he was the only family member to stand by her. Where others saw a cynical old woman who crabbed about every little thing, Finney saw the Aunt Julie who'd taken him on pony rides when he was four, to Disneyland when he was ten, on college visits when he was seventeen. Twice a week Finney would buy her groceries, put them away in the kitchen, then sit and chat while she sipped wine. After she nodded off, he'd clean the place up and do whatever odd jobs needed doing.

She'd had no children, just a battered houseboat on Lake Union and a tailless cat named Dimitri, both bequeathed to Finney when her heart finally gave out earlier that year.

His initial plan was to neuter the cat and sell the boat, but he soon found himself living on the boat and treasuring the cat, testicles and all. The battle-scarred Manx followed him everywhere just like a dog. He was fearless, and Finney loved him for it.

Since Leary Way, Finney had been stalled out in the middle of re-modeling the houseboat. It would have been embarrassing if he'd ever had any visitors. As things stood, it was possible to launch one of his kayaks from the spare bedroom by stepping out past the blue plastic tarp hanging over the unfinished outer wall. Currently, he owned three kayaks and was building another from a kit. Kayaking was his one interest that continued unabated since Leary Way.

He went back inside and pulled a small tape recorder off the nightstand. His hands were shaking. This was one of the hardest things he could do, but he was helpless to stop himself. In the beginning he'd listened to the tape at all hours of the day, but now it seemed to beckon only when he couldn't sleep. The recording had been copied from the master tape the dispatch center kept of all radio transmissions made during the fire.

On tape Cordifis's tone was surprisingly calm, almost nonchalant: "I want to say a few things while I still have a clear head. Emily, I love you. You are my life. I don't know how I ever got so lucky thirty-four years ago. There has not been a day that I regretted meeting you. Heather, you're the youngest, and I'm afraid we spoiled you. I'd do it again. I hope you have that child you want. Marge, you just go ahead and do whatever you think is right. I've always trusted your judgment. Ever since you were little, you knew what you were about. Linda, I hope you and the kids get through this divorce and come out happier on the other side. You girls and your mother are what make my life worth living. And the crew of Ladder One. You're all great. I love you guys. I don't think I've ever had a crew member I didn't think of as family."

(There was a sound that might have been gasping.)

"I know I'm not getting out of here tonight, so I'm telling you right now, I don't want anyone feeling bad over this. None of us get out alive. It's just a question of when and where and how we do it. I'm at peace with this. I knew when he left, the odds of John getting back with help were zero. God bless him, though. He really thought he was going to make it. I'm sure he's out there busting his gut. I only hope you're not in trouble your own self, and I pray that you make it, John. You and I both know you only strike out once in this game."

(At this point there was a pause and then the tape grew scratchy. The next sound was Cordifis coughing. He hadn't been wearing his mask.)

"The smoke's been down on the floor for a while, but this is *hot*. . . . John, I want you to know something about tonight . . ."

(More coughing.)

The tape ran on for a few moments before it ended with a clicking sound. Most people figured it had simply stopped, but Finney knew from the noises in the background that the fire had been pushing in on him, that Bill had deliberately shut off his transmission to spare the feelings of his friends and loved ones—that he didn't want anybody to hear him die.

Finney had endlessly speculated as to what Cordifis's last words to him would have been had he been able to get them out. Probably not to feel guilty, that he knew it wasn't Finney's fault. Probably not to let this night ruin the rest of his life. Finney often wondered if it would have made a difference to have heard the words. Every time Finney heard that last click he felt as if his heart were trying to beat without any blood in it.

For a month after they extracted Cordifis's body from the rubble, Finney holed up on the houseboat and pickled himself in alcohol, sobering up only long enough for infrequent visits to his doctor and sometimes not even then. It was his brother who, one afternoon, found him in a pile of dirty laundry on the floor and told him he was turning into Aunt Julie. That was what saved him—Tony's admonition and the vision he'd carried of a drunk Aunt Julie over all those years. That was all he needed to hear. He hadn't had a drop of alcohol since.

For months now he'd been obsessed with his own role at Leary Way, grappling with the generally accepted theory that his disorientation and failure to find an exit quickly was the cause of Cordifis's death. He'd talked to everyone who had been at the fire, trying without success to fill in the incomplete pieces from his memory. There was nothing concerning Leary Way that was either too small or too large for him to dissect.

He had an indistinct recollection of telling Reese and Kub that Bill was twenty-eight paces back, directly along the passageway he'd come down. But was that a memory or only a dream? Reese, the self-appointed spokesperson for both himself and Kub, said the two of them had heard nothing out of his mouth but babbling. It was a fact that he'd babbled a few minutes later when Soudenbury found him standing inside a doorway in the smoke. It was a fact that he'd babbled in the medic unit, and he knew he hadn't made much sense in the hospital.

The doctors said his confusion had been caused by a combination of smoke inhalation and heat stress, that he'd been lucky to survive. They assured him nobody would have been coherent in that condition. What they couldn't tell him was when it was likely to have begun.

It was small comfort to Finney. Bill Cordifis remained dead, and he was taking the rap for it.

He had been obsessed for the past four months with his own actions at Leary Way and it was getting him nowhere. Maybe he needed to look in a different direction. Since the last shift he'd worked, when they'd been called to the food-on-the-stove at the Downtowner, he'd been thinking about the larger picture. On the surface the call to the Downtowner couldn't have been more dissimilar to Leary Way—a routine alarm, no loss of life or property, nothing to think twice about. But Finney noticed a disturbing similarity to the night of June 7. Because there were so many other alarms going on in the city, and because there were no other units available, Engine 26 had been first in—far outside its normal response area. Just like the night of Leary Way. Because of citywide tie-ups, Ladder 1 had been called outside its normal district. None of the first arriving units normally responded to Leary Way. None knew the layout of the buildings or what was inside. Finney couldn't remember such involved tie-ups at any other time during his career. He had to wonder how it could have happened twice in five months.

He walked across the bedroom, fired up his computer, and logged onto the website for the Seattle Fire Department. Among other things, the site gave details of every alarm the department had fielded in the past five years, these divided into fire and medical calls for each twenty-four-hour period, all listed in chronological order.

Finney checked the run lists for the last shift he worked and found a striking increase in alarms throughout the city around the time of the Downtowner incident. A lot of them were false alarms, although there had been two fires going on and the Downtowner was genuine enough.

He went back to the night of Leary Way. In Seattle, taverns closed at two A.M., and between two and three on a Friday or Saturday night there would often be a marked increase in car accidents, stabbings, beatings, man-down calls, many of which required EMS responses from the fire department. But June 7 was a Tuesday, and the taverns didn't have anything to do with the report of a natural gas leak at Sand Point at 0225 hours that tied up one chief, two engines, two truck companies, an aid car, and a medic unit for two and a half hours. Firefighters who'd been on that call told Finney they never found a gas leak. Nor did the taverns have anything to do with the report of smoke from a vacant house on Lake City Way that came in at 0237 hours. Nor the second house fire miles away in the 3900 block of South Othello Street, this also a vacant dwelling. The latter put virtually all of the Fifth Battalion out of service. A smoldering pier fire in West Seattle took the Seventh Battalion out of the picture. A brush fire at Fort Lawton tied up three more engine companies.

The calls were all either unsolved arsons or false alarms, yet there was no known arsonist working in Seattle during that period and the department's activity sheets for the weeks before and after June 7 showed no abnormal flurries of activity and few arsons.

It was tempting to conclude that the alarms during both shifts were orchestrated rather than happenstance, that some unknown party or parties had engineered those fire calls so they would occur more or less at once. If so, the supposed object of that orchestration on June 7 would have presumably been to burn down Leary Way.

What discredited the theory was that, according to the department fire investigation team, Leary Way was caused accidentally by an electrical outlet in a storeroom in an area not far from where Finney and Bill Cordifis found themselves trapped. The head of Marshal 5, the department's fire investigation unit, Captain G. A. Montgomery, even put a photo of the offending wall outlet in the department's union newspaper, *The Third Rail*. For months the melted outlet sat atop his desk, a mute testament to his skills as a fire investigator.

Was the series of alarms that had occurred on June 7 and two days ago beyond the pale for their department, or did it happen once every few years? Finney began with January of that year, scanning the response records for other periods of abnormal activity. After several hours he became aware that the sun had come up, and he knew if he had any appointments that morning, he was going to miss them. By the time he'd finished, it was almost two in the afternoon; he'd pored over five years of records.

He found only one additional shift that fit the rough pattern—an extraordinary number of calls in a very short period of time, so many units out of service when new calls came in that units were responding to fires at the other end of the city. All three shifts had occurred in the past six months, the first just three weeks before Leary Way.

But it was the vacant house he'd found by the Duwamish River that troubled Finney more than anything. It fit in perfectly.

# 16. A CONSPIRACY OF VAST PROPORTIONS

It was after five o'clock and dark outside when Finney parked at a meter on Main Street and pushed his way through a light mist to Station 10. Inside, he skirted the watch office, where Bud Masterson was reading a newspaper, and went up the stairs to the mezzanine, where he found Robert Kub alone in the shadowy fire investigation office watching a Sonics game on a six-inch TV. The office was long and irregular, and the interior windows overlooked Station 10's apparatus bay, like a news booth in a stadium.

Marshal 5, the fire department's fire investigation unit, was comprised of eight firefighters cross-trained as law enforcement officers, along with two cops from SPD, the unit overseen by Captain G. A. Montgomery.

"So, what's up?" Kub said. "You look like something's bothering you."

John Finney and Robert Kub had connections that extended as far back as drill school, not the least of which was that Robert Kub had been Charlie Reese's partner at Leary Way. Unlike Charlie Reese, though, Kub didn't look back on Leary Way as a triumph. Finney found it endeared Kub to him in a way nobody would have guessed.

Kub was tall and lean, four inches taller than Finney, with a dark, nearly black complexion and jaws that stood out like chestnuts when he chewed gum, which he did incessantly. His hair was cropped close, and he had a habit of absentmindedly palming the top of his head. He spoke in a mellifluous baritone and was so deliberate in what he said and did that at times he gave the impression of being dim-witted, though he was anything but. In fact, Finney admired the perceptive way Kub's mind worked, and it was because of this and because he wanted some perspective that he'd come to see him. Kub was one of the few friends he hadn't distanced himself from after Leary Way.

Kub leaned forward in his chair, the long fingers of his hands interlocked. "What's up?"

It took only a few minutes to outline it: the fact that there'd been a plethora of alarms the night of Leary Way, alarms that contributed to the loss of the building and to the death of Captain Cordifis because there was too little help; that two days ago there'd been a similar rash of alarms with a corresponding number of units out of service; and that three weeks before Leary Way there'd been a smaller but nearly identical event with no major fires, but an unusually high percentage of alarms all at the same time; the fact that in the past five years nothing even remotely similar had happened. As with the first event in May, two days ago there had been no major fire losses. Finney figured it for a practice run.

"I don't know," Kub said. "I don't know what to think about this."

"It makes sense, doesn't it? Somebody orchestrating this? They burned down Leary Way and made sure we didn't have any help by lighting a bunch of little nuisance fires."

"I wouldn't call the other ones nuisance fires. We lost two houses in the south end."

"Okay. But they were set, right?"

"Right."

"And you haven't found the arsonist, have you?"

"Lots of times we don't find the bad guys."

"This is organized, Bob. It has to be. That house I found. It's going to be another nuisance fire. It's all primed and ready."

"I still think this is a little off the wall."

"It is off the wall. That's why they think they can get away with it. It's too crazy for anybody to catch on to."

"I don't know. How about you and me go up and talk to G. A.? See what he thinks about it. He's upstairs eating dinner with the crew."

"But I wanted to bounce this off of you."

"I told you what I thought. Let's go talk to G. A."

"G. A.'s the one who declared Leary Way an accident, and he's never changed his mind about anything in his life. You know how proud he was about that investigation. He's not going to reverse himself. He's still got the melted electrical socket from Leary Way sitting on his desk like some sort of bobcat he shot and stuffed."

"Maybe he made a good call. Maybe he's proud of it. Look, a lot of people don't like G. A., but he's dedicated to this unit like no officer I've seen. If you're really on to something here, I think he can hear you out objectively. G. A. looks pigheaded to people who don't know him, but believe me, he can admit his mistakes like anyone else. If what you're saying has any validity, who better to take back his call than him? He'll appreciate that you brought it to him first."

Finney stared into Robert Kub's brown eyes. Although one wouldn't guess it from his implacable exterior, Kub was an intensely emotional man, and having been on the fire ground the night Bill Cordifis died had changed him more than he cared to admit. From Kub's point of view, it didn't matter that he and Reese had almost been incinerated. His guilt over not finding Cordifis was overwhelming. Maybe that was why Finney had remained close to him—their shared guilt.

As they left Kub's office, the house bells rang. Less than a minute later the apparatus bay doors slammed shut on a cloud of blue-gray diesel smoke, the building like a tomb, Engine 10, Ladder 1, Aid 5, and Battalion 1 all roaring down Second Avenue in a ragged parade of red lights and sirens. Finney couldn't help wishing he were with them.

Taking the stairs two at a time, they went up one flight and punched in the lock box code on the door to the crews' private quarters.

The TV in the great room was playing a local news show to no audience. In the enormous kitchen area steam was coming off half a dozen abandoned plates of food set out on the long table. Dinner would be cold by the time they got back; they were accustomed to it. They'd line up and one by one put their plates in the microwave and try again. For a split second Finney found himself looking for Cordifis's plate, but of course, Bill's favorite Harley-Davidson commemorative platter had been returned to his widow along with his Mickey Mouse sheets, his Waterpik, his Bible, the pictures of his daughters, and the six hundred pennies they'd found in the bottom of his office drawer.

Alone in the room, G. A. Montgomery hunkered over a bowl of chili with a moon of margarine in it.

Montgomery had been a member of AA for ten years, could give his sobriety time in months and days. He liked to boast, only a little facetiously, that he would be chief of the department by now if he hadn't become enamored with the taste of bourbon. As a drunk he'd been as cocksure as a man could be, and sobriety hadn't changed that. People were intimidated by G. A., not just firefighters but other captains and chiefs. He was fifty-two years old, with a ruddy face and puffy tea bags of flesh under his eyes. His head was so large it scared small children. He had a shock of pale brown hair he clipped himself and combed straight back, though by mid-morning most of it stuck straight up. G. A. Montgomery put on a suit each morning, but by late afternoon the jacket was rumpled, discarded, or misplaced. This evening he wore a sweater vest over a dress shirt, his tie having lost its battle to hold a knot.

G. A. had been at the helm of the fire investigation unit for fourteen months, not long enough to know what he was doing, although that didn't dissuade him from running it with an iron hand or from taking charge of certain pet investigations. He had taken the requisite courses, read the textbooks, gone through the state police training, traveled to Maryland to the National Fire Academy—and returned feeling he knew everything. But then, he'd known everything before he left. G. A. had always known everything. His rigid policies had caused at least one fire investigator to transfer back to an engine company. Since Cordifis's death he had twice cautioned Finney to stop interfering in the investigation.

"Hey," said Captain Montgomery, speaking around a mouthful of corn bread. "That was a rotten deal you were handed the other day. Charlie should have promoted you." He stood and they shook hands. "So, what's going on? You two look like you just caught the Sears deliveryman banging the old lady."

Finney reiterated the theory he'd outlined for Kub downstairs.

G. A. pushed his bowl away and sat back, evaluating the two men in front of him. "I thought you said you were going to give up snooping around in all this Leary Way nonsense."

"That's not what I said. That's what you said."

G. A. stared hard at Finney, as if he could get him to relent by sheer force of will, then swiveled his eyes to Kub. "So where was the big fire last C-shift? What was the target?"

"It was a practice run," said Finney.

"A practice run?"

"Yeah. It was just like the tie-ups three weeks before Leary Way. Somebody was getting ready, practicing. All of which points to another sizable event on the horizon. What clinched it for me was the vacant house next to the river. It's just sitting there, all prepped for arson."

"Seems strange to me that of all the occupancies in the city, you walked into one that was ready to be torched. You're sure it's set to burn?" G. A. asked. "That house you saw?"

"Absolutely."

"Not just some kids playing around?"

"It was a professional setup."

"You've seen professional setups before?"

"Not before they were lit. But this looked professional."

"Convince me. Not of the setup, but the whole thing."

"If you wanted to cause a lot of distraction for the fire department and you had limited manpower, you'd prepare in advance. I'm guessing there are other buildings ready to burn. I'm betting somebody can drive quickly from one to the other and with a Zippo lighter divert most of our manpower from the real target."

"And what would that be? The real target."

"All I know is that on June seventh it was Leary Way."

"So what you're talking about is a conspiracy," said Kub, "a conspiracy of relatively vast proportions."

G. A. scratched under his armpit. "It's just a little far-fetched, isn't it?"

"That's the beauty of it. It's totally outrageous. If I was doing this, I would figure no one was ever going to catch me."

"There's one big problem here, John. In order for your theory to hold up, Leary Way would have had to be arson."

"It *was* arson." Finney could see G. A.'s face begin to turn red. "I think you made a mistake."

G. A.'s face took on more and more color.

"I investigated it myself," G. A. said. "For days I worked that place with a camera and a shovel and a team of firefighters to help me. I took it apart a layer at a time. It was accidental. Everyone knows it was. Much as you want someone else to take the rap for your captain's death, you have to accept the fact that the fire was not set."

"This is going to happen again," Finney said, "and when it does, everyone will know I'm right. This is too much of a pattern to be accidental. I'm not just talking about one arsonist setting a fire and running off into the night. I'm talking about a bunch of people working together to take the punch out of the department at exactly the right point in time, take most everybody out of service, then light up their target. It's like setting a fire in a city that doesn't have a fire department. Hell, they could burn down anything they wanted."

Kub palmed his shorn scalp. Popping a fresh stick of gum into his mouth, he glanced at Finney without moving his head from G. A. and said, "To my way of thinking, John's got a point about those alarms. Where did they come from?"

The room was silent for fifteen seconds. Finally G. A. pushed a pile of computer paper that had been sitting beside him across the table. "Take a look."

Kub riffled through the half-inch stack and said, "These are run sheets from two days ago on C-shift. The stuff John is talking about. You've already been looking into this?"

"Similar situation to June seventh," G. A. said. "A bunch of bad calls at the same time as a couple of full responses. We were shorthanded. It's the damndest coincidence."

Finney said, "No way it's a coincidence."

"I don't know what else to call it."

"Call it murder."

"Let's not go off the deep end here. He was a friend of mine, too. But it was an accidental fire. *Accidental.*"

"Explain those alarms."

"I can't, but I can't explain the aurora borealis either. I can't explain how the butterflies make it back to Monterey every year. That doesn't mean somebody's deliberately doing this. There's no way to connect Leary Way with any of this other, and you know it. And as far as connecting the dots to that vacant house . . . that's a leap even Michael Jordan couldn't make. You guys were shorthanded at Leary Way. You went in too deep with a very nice old man who should have retired years ago. It's the kind of shit that happens when you stay in this job too long. Don't try to make it into something it's not."

"Okay," Kub said. "Let's just say these incidents *were* choreographed. What would be the purpose? Somebody wanted to burn down Leary Way, they could have done it without going to the trouble of starting other fires."

"They were practicing," said Finney. "Leary Way? Sure, they could have burned that down anyway. They're practicing for something they couldn't burn down anyway."

"Let me reiterate," G. A. said, visibly angry. "The fire was accidental. You think somebody knew an electrical short was going to occur at three in the morning? There were no signs of flammable liquid. No witnesses. No threats against the building. No disputes between tenants and landlord. It was a goddamned accident. And if it wasn't, what the hell were they practicing *for?*"

"That's the big question, isn't it?"

"No, the question is: Why don't you leave this alone and try to put your life back together? That's the question."

Kub's pager went off. An engine company in Wedgwood had a juvenile fire-setter in custody and was asking for a fire investigator.

G. A. looked at Kub and said, "Go ahead. I'll take care of this."

"They can wait."

"No, you go ahead."

After Kub left, G. A. leaned on the tabletop, the thick muscles of his forearms swelling as he pressed down. "You checked the alarm records for all the shifts between June and now?"

"I checked the alarm records for the past five years. We've all seen it happen in wildland firefighting. Somebody'll start a fire and then drive down the highway and start another one until they have fire crews running around like cats trying to bury shit on a tin roof."

G. A. fixed his hazel eyes on Finney, his bushy eyebrows lowering. "I don't buy any of this."

"I don't know why not. You were already looking into it yourself."

"Examined the possibility and dismissed it. These days all companies in the city are taking more alarms than when you and I signed on. It was only a matter of time before this started happening. That's why we have mutual aid pacts with the outlying districts. Let me try to put this delicately, John. I know how hard you took Bill's death. Sometimes transferring the blame to someone else tracks with reality. Sometimes it's wishful thinking."

Finney knew there was some truth to what G. A. was saying. He also knew that if he could prove the events of June 7 had been planned, G. A.'s official interpretation would look foolish, and the investigation would be reopened. It would mean G. A. had made a bad call. With a fire that big and a fire death involved, a department death, it would be embarrassing as hell. There was a good possibility it would ruin him.

"Here's the deal, John. The department report, the Labor and Industries report, and the NFPA reports on Leary Way are all coming out any day now. Why don't you sit tight and see what they have to say? This was a tragedy, but don't try to link it up to the Kennedy assassination or Area Fifty-one."

"Is that how I sound?"

"That's exactly how you sound." They were quiet for a moment. "Listen, I feel as bad about Bill as you. But we have to let it go."

Oddly enough, G. A. Montgomery had been appointed chairman of the panel preparing the SFD report on Leary Way. Finney wasn't convinced that putting the man who'd investigated the fire in charge of the panel investigating the department's performance in extinguishing the fire was kosher, but apparently nobody else had any problem with it.

"You're going to keep after this no matter what I say, aren't you, John?"

"Absolutely."

"I can tell you right now, when all is said and done, what you're going to find is a series of coincidences."

"Then you'll be right and I'll be wrong."

As he turned to leave, G. A. said, "You still seeing that counselor the department set you up with?" Finney looked out the beanery windows at the corona the streetlights formed in the drizzle. "I'm just thinking you can use some help. Anybody in your position could."

"I quit her. She was a little too neurotic for my taste."

"One last thing," G. A. said. "Give me the address of that vacant house. I'll look at it. I can do that much."

It was nearly midnight when Finney picked up his ringing phone. "Seven Avenue South and South Holden Street," said a gruff voice. It sounded as though the call was coming from a phone booth alongside a busy highway, and Finney had to struggle to put the blurred syllables into words. He noticed his caller had given the streets in the standard fire department lexicon, the avenue before the street so that the designators were next to each other, the number clean and without a suffix. "You know where that is?"

"Of course I do. What about it?"

"Meet me there tomorrow morning at zero six-thirty. It's about Leary Way."

"Who is this?"

"I can't say anything over the phone. Zero six-thirty. Don't bring anybody else."

# 17. BLOWING UP GRACELAND

It was early when Finney rolled over in bed and peered out his window at a single light reflected off the inky lake. A heavy fog had moved in overnight, obscuring everything except the boat next door. Power lines buzzed. The weather report said the fog would burn off by noon and that the rest of the day would be clear and sunny, but Finney, a Northwest native, knew this kind of October mist could roost on Seattle indefinitely like a large, wet hen.

At twenty minutes past six, when he drove past Station 26, the rigs were in place behind the roll-up doors, everything dark except for a glow from the beanery lights. On A-shift, Peterson generally woke up a couple of hours before everybody else, rustling around in the beanery and whistling and just generally annoying the others who were still trying to sleep.

Finney drove eleven blocks past the firehouse and parked next to the river where Seventh and Holden merged with Riverside. He saw no pedestrians and no parked vehicles. What little traffic there was came and went in the fog with startling suddenness. After fifteen minutes, he began pacing the short chunk of Riverside Drive that paralleled the water.

Oddly enough, the vacant house Monahan had put on the dangerous buildings list for Finney was two blocks away.

Engine 26's first-in district was small but tricky, bordered on the south by the city limits, bisected at odd angles by Highways 509 and 99. The Duwamish Waterway sliced through it, too, running between 26's and the rest of the city, its muddy water spanned by drawbridges. Half a dozen streets and avenues dead-ended at the river and continued on the other side in Engine 27's district, so that the drivers of both stations had to memorize dozens of individual addresses—or risk watching helplessly as a fire burned across the river.

By seven he was back in the cab of his Pathfinder with the heater running. He'd seen only a handful of cars, none with red IAFF union stickers in the window. Finney was assuming from the way the caller used the street designators and military time that he was meeting with a firefighter.

At 7:25 a pedestrian glided forward through the fog and tapped on his window. "They're coming for you," she said, as he rolled the window down. "The first thing they're going to do is make us sterile. It's only a matter of time before they get around to blowing up the Supreme Court, the Empire State Building, Graceland."

"You're out early this morning, Annie." The homeless woman's knit cap and eyebrows were freighted with moisture. He wondered if she'd been roaming these streets all night.

"The defenders of freedom are few and far between, but we don't sleep in."

She gave him a blank look that made him think she hadn't gotten much sleep, then she turned briskly and pulled her cart away into the murk.

Finney was due at the station at 7:30, in less than five minutes, and it was obvious by now that last night's caller wasn't coming. Everyone in the department knew how to push Finney's buttons, and the phone call the previous night was probably a practical joke. They were probably yukking it up in the beanery at this very moment over the thought of Finney out here in the fog waiting for secret information.

When he got to the station, nobody paid any attention to him. He carried his personal protective equipment over to the engine in the apparatus bay, removed Peterson's gear, and put his own equipment on the rig. He Velcroed his name tags onto the passport name card in the cab, inspected his mask to make sure it was in working order, and signed into the daybook in the watch office. He ran the daily checks on the Physio-Control Lifepak, changed batteries in the three portable radios, and looked inside every compartment door on the rig to ascertain each piece of equipment was in place and in working order.

At 8:36, while he was mopping floors, 26's big metal bell began clanging. The tones on the station speaker signified that it was an aid call, the address only a few blocks north of the station. As the doors rolled up, Monahan fired up the Spartan, turning on the emergency lights, and they rolled out onto Cloverdale and into the mid-morning Boeing traffic. Around the corner the residential streets were empty.

After they stopped in front of the address, Finney procured the aid kit, $O_2$ kit, and Lifepak and carried them into the house. Their ninety-two-year-old patient had flu symptoms. They called an ambulance, and ten minutes later, as Finney was wheeling the empty ambulance stretcher through the front entrance of the home, a fire call came in on his portable radio. Engine 26 received only two or three alarms a day, and it was rare to miss one because they were already out of service.

"Engines Twenty-seven, Eleven, and Thirty-six; Ladders Seven and Eleven; Aid Fourteen, Medic Twenty-eight; Battalion Seven: Eight Avenue South and South Elmgrove Street. Smoke from the building." The location was only a few blocks away, but they wouldn't be included until Lieutenant Sadler radioed the dispatchers that Engine 26 was back in service. In all probability, Engine 27 would get there first.

# 18. BLIND MEN TOSSING HORSESHOES

ven though Lieutenant Sadler cautioned Monahan to slow down and
keep an eye out for the other rigs responding in the fog, Monahan
drove too fast and ended up skidding the 34,000-pound apparatus to a
halt just inches shy of Engine 27's tailboard. They were lucky he hadn't
killed anyone.

Finney had been smelling smoke for blocks, and now it mingled with
the odor of hot brakes and the back-of-the-throat tang of a week's worth
of big-city pollution suspended in the fog. Between the smoke and the
fog, they would be like blind men tossing horseshoes.

For a split second Finney glimpsed the roofline and a wind-blown
chimney, dense black smoke pumping from a dormer at one end. Then
the smoke and fog damped out his view.

After conferring quickly with the driver of Engine 27, Lieutenant
Sadler twisted around in his seat and spoke to Finney through the crew-
cab window. "McKittrick says he thinks there's a hydrant about a hundred yards down. I'm going to send Jerry. You and me are going to take a
second line off Engine 27 and back them up."

"Right."

Finney couldn't have been more pleased. They were taking a line inside. They were going to fight fire. He lived for times like this.

The smoke was thick and acrid, and they coughed as they moved
through it. Even Sadler, the hardened nicotine junkie. Even McKittrick,
who operated Engine 27's pump panel, his nostrils yielding a steady
stream of snot after only a few minutes' exposure to the smoke in the
street.

Air cylinder on his back, Finney climbed down off the rig and went
around the back of Engine 27, where he pulled out the first hundred feet
of inch-and-three-quarter hose load with the gated wye. By the time he
got it on his shoulder, McKittrick had shouldered the second hundred
feet. Ian McKittrick had almost twenty-five years in the department, fifteen of those behind the wheel of Engine 27. He was a fast talker and
knew his job better than he knew his kids. Bald-headed and slack-jawed,
McKittrick placed the gated wye and ten feet of line near a hose-port on
the fire side of the rig—he would connect it later—then followed Finney

through the fog, dropping dry hose flakes onto the ground behind them as they proceeded. Finney, unable to see the house, followed the first line on the ground.

It wasn't until Finney was on the front doorstep that he realized this was the vacant house they'd put on the dangerous buildings list.

McKittrick hollered over his shoulder as he ran back to his rig. "Don't waste any water. All I've got right now is that five hundred gallons in the tank."

The front door was half off its hinges, mute testimony to the rough passage of the earlier crew. Inside, Engine 27's hose stream was being directed into a sheet of orange without any seeming effect, and Finney could see the boots of two firefighters on their stomachs in front of him. He could hear the crackle of burning wood. Even in the doorway he was forced to tip his helmet so that the brim shielded his face from the heat.

Behind, over the roar of Engine 27's pump, he could hear Lieutenant Sadler yelling, "You stupid shit!" He assumed the comment was addressed to Monahan; those sorts of expletives usually were. Later, he learned Sadler had anchored a piece of four-inch supply line in the street while Monahan drove away and recklessly overshot the hydrant, disappearing into the fog.

Finney pulled his facepiece on, tightened the straps on the sides, opened the valve at his waist, and inhaled clean air; then he pulled his hood over the top of the facepiece, put his helmet back on, and knelt in the doorway waiting for his partner. A torrent of hot smoke surged out of the building into his face, but with this much cover, he barely felt the dirty heat.

Sadler reached the porch at the same time as the hose at their feet stiffened, the water knocking the kinks out with the sound of a cardboard box being kicked. Finney worked the bale on the Task Force tip to bleed air off the line. A few seconds later Sadler finished masking up and tapped him on the shoulder.

Finney crawled twelve feet inside before his helmet rapped against the green bottle on another man's back. Even with every bit of skin covered by thick protective clothing, the heat had pinned Engine 27's crew to the floor. Finney and Sadler were still on their hands and knees, but they would get lower as their clothing and equipment began to heat up. He heard the mellow, ripping sound of fire scratching at the structure.

Not realizing Finney had run up against the other crew, Sadler bumped him from behind, hard. Like any other high-danger activity, firefighting could get addictive, and doing it better and quicker than others was addictive, too. Sadler said, "Come on! Let's fight some fire! Let's go, man!"

It was always cooler behind. Finney knew of a man on Engine 6's crew who'd been shoved into a burning basement from behind by an overeager officer. Sadler bumped Finney's back again, harder. When Finney turned to complain, he reached out but felt only empty space and scarred hardwood flooring. For a split second he thought Sadler might have fallen into a hole in the floor or rolled down a stairwell.

Retracing his path along the hose line, he groped his way to the doorway. Inexplicably, Sadler was standing on the porch, McKittrick alongside him. Sadler spoke through his facepiece without turning his gaze from McKittrick. "Ian says there's a victim upstairs."

"This is the house I was in last shift. It's vacant."

"He saw a victim."

Sadler, McKittrick, and Finney trotted through the tall, wet weeds in the yard, McKittrick stumbling on a coiled hose line. When they were almost to the road, McKittrick turned and pointed to a second-story window barely visible in the murk. Sadler gave a report on his portable radio. "Dispatch from Engine Twenty-six. We have a victim on the second floor. Repeat. Confirmed victim on the second floor. We're going to initiate a rescue."

Finney glimpsed coils of black smoke belching out the broken windows, a tongue of flame. Then something upright darted past a window on the second story, something that resembled a human form.

# 19. ABANDON YOUR PARTNER AND DO-SI-DO

As the fog and smoke closed down visibility once more, Finney stepped to the middle of the street looking for another unit, perhaps a truck company, but there were no other companies, only Engine 27 and their own dry supply hose trailing along the center of the street into Jerry Monahan's netherworld.

Sadler had vanished.

It was always a long wait for help down here in South Park, but other units should have been on the scene by now. Engine 11 from West Seattle. Ladder 7 from the industrial area south of downtown. He had no idea how much time had elapsed, but he didn't hear sirens. He approached McKittrick at the pump panel. "Where is everybody?"

"There's an accident on the First South Bridge, and the Sixteenth South Bridge is stuck in the up position."

Finney went back to the front door and, under a scrim of boiling smoke, spotted Sadler's size-thirteen boots just inside the entrance, Sadler on his stomach, trying to crawl through the worsening heat. As Finney crawled in behind him, he noticed the officer and tailboard man from Engine 27 hadn't progressed an inch. Rarely had he seen a house fire this hot or this impervious to water.

"Come on," Sadler yelled. "They're going to protect the stairs while we go up."

"There aren't any stairs," Finney said. "They're burned out. And that fire doesn't even know we've got a line on it."

"You and me are going up. Come on."

"If we go outside, we can get through a window."

"The stairs should be towards the back. Besides, you know the rule. Always a hose line between the fire and the victim." When Sadler began edging around the crew of Engine 27, a pillow of steam from one of their nozzle bursts came down and forced them flat. From his face-down position on the floor, Sadler opened his line, but it went slack. It took a few moments to figure out Engine 27's line had gone slack, too. The five-hundred-gallon tank on the pumper outside had run dry. Now everything would depend upon Monahan or McKittrick finding and opening a hydrant.

It was hard to believe five hundred gallons less what was in the hose lines hadn't made a dent in this fire, but it hadn't.

The rubber facepiece against Finney's cheeks was slick with sweat. A pulse pounded in his temple.

"Okay. Let's go." Sadler began pulling the dead hose line toward where he thought the stairs were. Finney watched Sadler wriggle along the floor until, a full body-length in front of the other crew, he was forced to stop, as Finney had known he would be. It was incredible how much heat Sadler could take. He was crawling into a virtual oven.

"The stairs are gone," Finney yelled. "And we don't have any water, so how are we going to get a line between the fire and the victim?"

It was pointless to argue. They could barely raise their heads, much less stand up to climb a staircase that didn't exist. Again, Sadler inched forward.

"We'll never get there this way," Finney yelled. "I'm going outside."

If Sadler heard him, he didn't acknowledge it.

All professions have cardinal rules, and in modern firefighting there are few crimes as egregious as abandoning a partner. It was a fiat Finney knew better than anybody, yet he backed out on his hands and knees, backed out until he was on the porch by himself.

As he ran through the yard and passed the pump panel on Engine 27, he pushed the throttle in and muffled the screaming of the now-dry pump. McKittrick was off somewhere finding a hydrant. Fed by reservoirs high on the hill, most of these hydrants in South Park carried 135 pounds of head pressure. When McKittrick opened the hydrant, the pressure, even without a boost from the pump's impeller, would cycle through the pump housing and pressurize the hoses.

Without taking his mask off, Finney unhooked the chrome latch mechanism on the heavy twenty-six-foot aluminum ladder on the officer's side of Engine 27, lifted the ladder out of the holder, balanced it on his right shoulder, and ran with it. It was a lot heavier than he remembered. More than a minute had passed since he'd seen the figure in the window.

When he reached the house, he tipped the spurs of the ladder into the soggy grass and muscled it up. Once he had the ladder vertical, he steadied it with his knee along one beam, tugged the halyard hand-over-hand until the sections were fully extended, and dropped it clanking against the house. He couldn't see the tip, only fog and smoke.

He raced up into the chaos.

# 20. FIGHTING FOR AIR

Finney scrambled up the rungs past a sagging gutter and, keeping a grip on the ladder's beam, placed one boot on the steeply pitched roof. For a split second he inspected the roofline, and then a hood of black smoke enveloped him. All he could see was the heavy aluminum ladder in his hands—and a millisecond later not even that.

Bouncing slightly, he tested the integrity of the roof and rafters as he made his way up the incline, crossing thick layers of moss-encrusted three-tab roofing. He was more than two stories above the ground and a fall could prove fatal.

The figure he'd seen from below had been in the gable twenty feet to his right. When the smoke didn't clear after a few moments, he moved higher, slipping on a patch of moss that felt like a balled-up sock, the misstep nudging a shot of adrenaline into his system. The roof was spongier here, and he could feel the fire brushing the rafters under his feet. Sheaves of smoke crept out through overlaps in the roofing material.

He knew the roof was growing weaker, that it wouldn't be long before he would drop into the house like a big yellow squalling Santa Claus.

When he reached the edge of the first dormer, he grabbed the gutter and placed himself directly in front of the window. The glass was intact, though when he put his flashlight to it, he found the windowpane had a mottled, tarlike coating on the inside. Moving close, he squinted through the black film.

It took a moment to realize he was staring at a face, a pair of wild gaping eyes only inches away.

For a moment the eyes inside the window searched his. Then they vanished.

When he broke the window with his gloved fist, heat traveled up his sleeve through the Nomex gauntlets sewn in to protect his wrists.

"Fire department!" he yelled, leaning into the funnel of rapidly escaping heat and smoke. The only reply was the sound of fire in the other room and a bottle popping dully somewhere in the heat. The room was all smoke, though he could see flame beyond the partially open door. "Over here. Come over here."

No reply.

With great effort, he managed to wedge himself and his air bottle into the tiny opening. A moment later he was half in and half out. He remained stuck in that preposterous position, legs kicking, until he flopped inside and found himself in a small room devoid of furniture and knee-deep in debris. The smoke seemed to have the texture of hot pudding. Crouching under the worst of the heat, he worked his way around the room, the broken window now providing the fire with an abundant supply of oxygen. A blanket of flame began to spread across the ceiling like angry marmalade.

"Hello. Anybody here?"

Flame nosed around the top of the partially open door to his right. Beyond the door everything was aglow. Under different circumstances it would have been beautiful.

Moving swiftly, he crawled around the perimeter of the room, one arm and leg brushing the wall, the other arm and leg stretched out toward the center of the room, searching the rubble but finding only knots of old clothes, a mattress, empty food packages, broken dresser drawers. Soon it would all burst into flame.

As he passed the door, he tried to close it, but the half-burned wooden panels crumbled at the touch of his heavy gloves.

He had no business being here without a hose line, but then, had he waited for a hose line, the victim's remote prospect of rescue would have been reduced even further. They'd already wasted too much time.

As he moved, the room grew noticeably hotter. His bunkers were fire resistant, but they weren't fireproof, and like potatoes wrapped in foil, firefighters could be and had been cooked inside their protective Nomex layers. Cordifis had died that way, and Finney was beginning to think he might, too. He figured he had thirty seconds to find the victim and make an exit, forty-five seconds at the outside.

He made one complete circuit of the small room without success. As he came around a second time, something moved under him in the debris.

"It's okay," he said. "I'm a firefighter. I'm going to get you out of here."

Now flames were crawling across the ceiling and banking down along the outer wall toward the window, sealing off their escape. It might already be too late.

The victim, whom he initially took to be a child, swatted at his face-piece and shrieked just once before going limp. This was no child. Too large. Too strong. It was a woman.

Half-carrying, half-dragging her limp body across the room to the window, Finney saw that the entire wall was now blocked by flame that had banked down from the ceiling. Fire lapped at his helmet, scalding his ears through the Nomex hood, roasting the back of his neck.

"Stay calm," he said. "I'm getting you out of here."

Then, as he gripped the windowsill with his gloved hand, he felt a water stream rush past his helmet from outside. He was instantly engulfed in it, the room boiling. A gallon of water produced 550 cubic feet of steam. It smothered the fire, but it also scalded his wrists and his cheeks around the edges of his facepiece. Even the helmeted figure outside backed away. Lord only knew what it was doing to the victim.

Finney did his best to shield her with his own body, but he knew his bunkers were hot enough that a mere touch would burn her. Moments later, as the heat from the steam subsided, he got up off the floor, picked up the victim, and passed her through the window. As her limp body plugged the tiny window, he knew that should the fire come back on him now he would be trapped. In rescues, the rule of thumb was to keep the victim from blocking the rescuer's egress, yet it was a difficult rule to follow in the field. He'd violated that rule and now his exit was blocked.

A hot, wet heat tightened the room down around him.

And then the victim was outside, taken away by the other firefighter. As soon as she had cleared the opening, he wedged his head and one shoulder through the tiny space. He could feel flame creeping up the trousers of his bunking pants. For twenty seconds he twisted and tried to swim through the aperture. Then, like a chunk of Crisco on a hot skillet, he began skidding on his stomach down the steep roof.

He thought surely something would arrest his slide, somebody would come to his aid, because if not, he was going to drop into the yard on his face. But he continued to skid with agonizing slowness, and then, just as the free fall was about to begin, his outstretched hands caught the gutter in front of him. The gutter creaked and he could hear the screeching of nails. Though he couldn't see the ground through the fog and smoke, he knew he was inches from a twenty-foot drop. Slowly, carefully, he turned around and got to his feet.

Traversing the roof, he reached the ladder a body-length ahead of the other firefighter, who was now struggling to carry the victim. Finney stepped onto the rungs and together they carefully transferred the weight of the still-unconscious victim onto his shoulder.

A minute later she was lying on a heavy canvas tarp at the edge of the yard.

When Finney set his helmet in the grass, tiny droplets of moisture on individual grass blades sizzled as they brushed up against it.

By the time he got his bottle off, he realized only one other rig had arrived. Ladder 1.

The firefighter who'd been on the roof with him was now in the yard, facing away, removing helmet, hood, gloves, facepiece. It wasn't until a mass of hair shook loose that he realized she was a woman. She turned around and met his eyes. Diana Moore. She'd obviously left her partner and gone to the roof by herself, the same as he'd done. She'd scrambled up the ladder and across the precarious roof lugging a charged hose line, no easy feat. She'd saved the victim and she'd saved Finney, too.

"That was kind of close," she said.

"Ooooh, yeah. Thanks for showing up. You saved my behind."

"McKittrick told me you were up there, but when I got up and saw all that flame, I didn't believe it. I couldn't even get close to that window."

"It didn't feel so wonderful from inside either."

She smiled and they continued to look at each other for a few moments. Without preamble, they both burst into laughter. Finney had had similar giddy communal moments throughout his career, yet now that he thought about it, always with men. She was good. She was damn good.

Except for disheveled knee socks and a sturdy pair of brown leather shoes that hadn't been touched by the ordeal, all the victim's clothing had been either burned off or melted to her skin. Her chest and torso were blackened and cracked, and other areas of skin were as pale as parchment, blood vessels visible underneath. Her charred face was burned into a grimace—long, crooked teeth exposed. Her hair had burned off, except for a wispy scrap that clung to the nape of her neck. Her eyebrows and eyelashes were gone.

Nothing moved except her eyes, which darted about the group, appraising each of them in turn. She seemed as horrified by the firefighters as they were by her. When her look fell on Finney, he felt as if he were being stared at by a mummy in a museum.

At least she was alive, he thought, as she continued to stare at him.

Sadler glanced at Finney but spoke to the others, as if he had another, private message to be delivered to Finney later. "How far away is that medic unit?"

"Medic Ten's delayed at the Sixteenth South Bridge with everybody else," said McKittrick. "There's an accident on the First South Bridge."

"Somebody put some O-two on her," said Diana.

Sadler used his portable radio to ask Medic 10 for an ETA. The reply: another ten minutes.

The driver of Engine 11, a short, stocky firefighter with a plug of tobacco under his lip, a man who'd been in long enough to have an attitude, put together a Laerdahl bag mask, connected oxygen to the mask, placed the mask over the victim's face, and began squeezing the bag.

She should have been breathing deeply now, with their help, but she continued to gulp like a landlocked fish. Engine 11's driver peered inside her mouth and down her throat with a flashlight. He tried again. Finney knew what was wrong. So did Sadler. The circumferential burns on her torso had contracted and hardened so that her lungs could not expand. They could pump in all the oxygen they wanted, but if her diaphragm wouldn't expand, they couldn't get air into her.

Sadler glanced at the others. "The medics won't be here in time."

"What do the medics do when this happens?" McKittrick asked.

Sadler held up his Buck knife.

Six minutes without oxygen and she would be brain dead. There was no telling where she was in the countdown.

"She ain't gonna make it," McKittrick said.

Finney could see the victim's eyes widen and react to the pronouncement. It was clear from the flicker of alarm that she didn't want to die in that yard any more than any of them did. It was also clear that she hadn't lost her cognition, not completely.

Sadler offered McKittrick the knife. "Uh-uh. I'm not trained."

"Don't look at me," said Sadler. "I'm no longer certified."

"You're a better choice than any of us," Finney said. As far as he was concerned, Sadler's refusal to do the deed was an act of cowardice. Until five years earlier Sadler had been a paramedic, but he knew, as did the others, that any time a public servant exceeded his or her area of certification, a personal lawsuit could result. On the other hand, it was obvious that if they continued to do nothing, she was going to die. Sadler stepped back, as if the problem were somebody else's.

Finney hadn't been trained in this, but he took the knife and knelt beside her. He didn't know how clean the blade was, but right now infection was the least of her worries. He carefully pressed the blade into her burned flesh and made a cut in the shape of a seven on her upper right chest, a reverse seven on her left. It was like cutting charred steak. If she felt it, she didn't respond, didn't open her eyes, didn't call out.

Once again Engine 11's driver placed the Laerdahl bag mask over her face and began squeezing the air bulb. For the first time since they'd removed her from the building her diaphragm rose and fell. Half a minute later she came awake and attempted to speak through the mask. Finney, who hadn't moved from his position beside her, motioned for the facepiece to be removed and leaned close enough to smell the sweet, sickening odor of cooked flesh.

"Water," she gasped. "For the love of God give me some water."

They gave her water and covered her with a burn sheet.

By the time the rest of the units arrived, the fire had punched a hole in the morning, flames jetting fifty feet into the fog. Standing in the yard in a daze, watching as the medics placed the victim on a stretcher and administered morphine, Finney felt dry heat from the fire. It wasn't long after Chief Smith arrived that the walls began collapsing inward.

Monahan was the one who found the two-wheeled cart near the back door, the handle melted, the cargo transformed to turds of char.

"Annie? Hey, was that her cart?" Sadler asked, when Monahan brought it around to the front.

"That was definitely her cart," said Monahan.

"It couldn't be Annie," said Finney.

"Yeah." Monahan held up the cart with one hand. "That was her all right."

# 21. THE HERO SYNDROME

At one end of the house a bathtub dangled by its plumbing. At the other end a broken chimney stood alone like a splinted finger. Most of the upper floor and roof had burned off or been pulled down by firefighters with pike poles, as they hunted out the last embers, and the house had spilled its contents like a broken egg; bits of smoldering cloth and burned garbage lay in the yard. They would wait to finish the overhaul until after Marshal 5 had sifted through the ruins and made a determination of cause.

Small rooms, a good toehold, lots of nooks and crannies, balloon construction, and careful preparation by an arsonist had made the fire almost impossible to stop. Because there was a victim, it was especially important to determine cause, yet there wasn't much left to sift through; the fire damage was massive. In Washington State an arson resulting in a fatality could be charged as murder and would be, if Annie died and if the SFD apprehended the culprit.

As they waited for Marshal 5 to arrive, Chief Smith located Finney in the rest area.

"Splendid job," Smith said, his face transforming into a mask of smile wrinkles. "McKittrick said he thought nobody could make it up there, but by golly, you did, John. You and Lieutenant Sadler. You two make a great team."

"Actually it was Diana Moore off of Ladder One. I probably owe her my life."

The chief, who may or may not have heard him, stooped and picked up Finney's helmet. SFD helmets were constructed of a tough, resilient plastic, and it was rare to melt one. Doing so was considered a totem of bravado, an announcement that one had gone where nobody else could. Finney's helmet was melted from the top down, the face shield dissolved onto the blackened shell like a slice of cheese. "I just wanted to let you know what you did won't go unnoticed. In fact, I'm going to submit you and Lieutenant Sadler both to the awards committee."

"It was Diana Moore. And I don't want an award. She should get one, though."

Chief Smith smiled. "Moore, huh? How the hell did she haul a hose line up there by herself?"

"Same way any of us would have. Muscled it up."

"Young woman surprises me sometimes." Chief Smith winked as he left, and said, "Sure is cute as a button." Or maybe he said, "Sure has a cute bottom." Finney wasn't sure which he heard. Both were true.

A few minutes later Gary Sadler approached, his coat open, a cup of hot cocoa hidden in his large fist. Drifting smoke mixed with the fog, so that except for the red flanks of two nearby fire engines, the neighborhood was blanked out.

Sadler's face was sweaty, his teeth and mustache peppered with soot. He looked around and, when he saw they were alone, said, "You have a problem following orders?"

The animosity in his voice surprised Finney. "Because I went for the ladder?"

"Because you left me alone inside. You have a problem?"

"My only problem is fiddle-faddling around while somebody is burning to death."

"I was waiting for *you* to go up those stairs with me. Were you scared?"

"The stairs were gone. I told you that. I told you I was going outside."

"It turned out the stairs were gone, but what if they hadn't been?"

"What kind of question is that? They were gone."

"I didn't know that at the time. I ordered you to stay inside with me. You and I both know we're in a paramilitary organization here. We have officers and we have firefighters. The last time I checked, the officers gave the orders. The firefighters followed them."

They stared at each other for a few tense seconds.

"You're saying I should obey your orders even if it costs a life?"

"What the hell do you think would have happened if Ladder One hadn't dragged that hose line up there and cooled your ass off? You were damn lucky you didn't both get incinerated, you and that old woman. And maybe Moore, too. She's a damned idiot, just like you."

Just as Finney was reappraising Sadler in light of his refusal to cut the old woman's chest so she could breathe, Finney could see in Sadler's nearly opaque brown eyes that he was wondering whether Finney had abandoned Bill Cordifis the way he'd abandoned him.

Finney's story about Leary Way couldn't be verified, and these days everybody in the department sized Finney up in terms of what they imagined happened at that fire. They saw Finney; they saw a dead partner. People connected the dots in different ways. It was as if Finney didn't have any other history, as if all those years he'd worked on Ladder 1 didn't count for beans.

"By rights I should write charges on you," Sadler said. "Insubordination at the scene of an emergency. You could get eight shifts off without pay."

"I'd gladly trade eight shifts off for that woman's life."

"Oh, that's cute. Make me look like the bad guy." Sadler stepped close. For a few moments neither spoke. In different circumstances, perhaps with a few drinks under their belts, they might have come to blows. They both knew it would be ludicrous for Sadler to write charges on Finney after a successful rescue, no matter what orders he'd disobeyed. It would only serve to spotlight Sadler's misjudgment and failure to reach her from inside the building. "When you came down to Twenty-six's three weeks ago, people told me you had an ego the size of Texas, that you had a problem following orders. I didn't listen because I like to size a man up for myself. But they were right. You're a freelancer. A loose cannon. You go off and do what you like. It's easy to see why Reese didn't promote you."

Sadler turned and walked away. When he was ten feet distant, he turned back and said, "I noticed your hand. You going to need stitches?" Finney had cut his hand through his glove sometime during the rescue, probably while breaking out the window. Someone had wrapped a roll of gauze around it; he couldn't recall who. "I'll get somebody to fill in so you can go see the doc."

"Sure." Although he knew in this instance it was true, Finney didn't like being called a freelancer. In the old days freelancers were highly valued members of the department, firefighters who could get things done without being told. But these days everybody worked in pairs and they worked to a master plan—a man walking the fire ground by himself was in danger of a reprimand from the safety chief.

A few minutes later Finney noticed Captain G. A. Montgomery and Robert Kub. As Marshal 5's unit administrator, G. A. rarely did fieldwork, so Finney was surprised to see him at a fire scene. Then again, they had a possible fatality.

G. A. took a couple of purposeful strides toward the house, surveying the disheveled firefighters in the rehab area. Clad in a fire department windbreaker, black slacks and dress shoes, a white shirt, and a tie that was so tight his neck veins stood out, G. A. Montgomery was hardly dressed to pick through a fire scene. Nevertheless, that's what he and Kub proceeded to do.

Ten minutes later they trotted back around the side of the house and met Finney as he was carrying his MSA backpack to the rig. They shook hands, G. A.'s grip like a gorilla's, not the least deterred by the dressing on Finney's hand. When G. A. doffed his small-brimmed orange investigator's helmet, his hair stuck out like bristles on an old brush, and his large, lined face grew serious.

"You guys first in?"

"Twenty-seven's was."

"But this is your district?"

"We were out of service on an aid run when the call came in."

Stepping close enough that Finney could smell cloves on his breath, G. A. produced a toothpick from somewhere and placed it in the corner of his mouth. "When you got here, you see anything?"

"Yeah. Fog."

"I was thinking along the lines of civilian activity, maybe someone suspicious hanging around?"

"Just fog."

"That's what your lieutenant said. He also said you two had a difference of opinion." He bobbed the toothpick between his fleshy lips.

"He wanted to make the rescue from inside. I told him the stairs were burned out."

"How did you know the stairs were burned out?"

"I knew where they were. And I could see the volume of fire in that part of the house. This is the house I was telling you about last night."

G. A. Montgomery raised his eyebrows. "We're on Riverside Drive? I guess we are. Hell of a coincidence. But then, coincidences are your meat and potatoes, aren't they?"

"What does that mean?"

G. A. used his tongue to relocate his toothpick. "You realize this is arson. No electricity. Nobody living here. There's a smell of gasoline around back."

"I said last night it was set to be torched."

Kub and Finney exchanged looks, and Kub turned to assess the building again, effectively removing himself from the conversation. It was a head-in-the-sand move that surprised Finney.

G. A. was holding a large clear plastic bag containing an article of navy-blue clothing. "We got lucky," he said, flashing a mirthless grin. "We went over to the ER on the way here and talked to the fire victim. She said somebody came up behind her and put a bag over her head, knocked her senseless. When she woke up, she was on the second floor in the smoke."

"She see who it was?"

"A fireman."

Finney paused. "She able to ID him?"

"Oh, she knows the jerk. Not his name, but she can pick him out of a photo lineup."

"There's always the possibility she's covering for her own screw-up," said Kub, without turning to look at them. "Say, she started a warming fire in there and it got out of hand. You know she was rambling. Some of what she said didn't make sense."

G. A. gave Kub a disapproving look. "She was in pain and on morphine. But she'll be a credible witness. People get burned like that, you get them on the witness stand, the jury wants to hang somebody real bad. And look at this," he said, holding out the plastic bag. "My guess is the perp took it off and forgot about it. People get so simpleminded." G. A. removed a jacket from the bag, and as he unfurled it, Finney realized it was nearly identical to one he kept in his clothing locker back at the station.

He started to say something, but stopped himself as the scattered events of the morning began rearranging themselves in his mind. An anonymous caller had set up a meeting an hour before change of shift. The assignation had left Finney loitering near the fire location, where, but for the fog, he would have been seen by any number of early morning commuters. As far as he knew, the only person to see him was Annie, but what if Annie thought he was the one who'd mugged her? It would certainly explain the terrified look on her face when she saw him after the rescue, a look that he now realized was more than just pain.

"You recognize this jacket?" G. A. asked, reaching into one of the pockets. He pinched a small green ticket stub.

"That a laundry ticket?" Kub asked.

Finney's mouth went dry. He'd had his jacket dry-cleaned just last week, and Emerald City Cleaners used green tickets identical to the one G. A. was holding. Finney scanned the right sleeve, and there it was, a tiny blemish where he had accidentally splashed a drop of bleach a year ago.

"Looks like mine," Finney said.

G. A. turned from the building and glowered at him. "What did you say?"

"That looks like my jacket."

"This is *your* jacket?"

"Looks like it."

G. A. glanced at Kub and then swung his gaze back onto Finney. "You running around setting fires on me, John?"

"I'm just saying that looks like my jacket." It *was* his jacket but he hadn't worn it in weeks. The last time he saw it, it was in his locker back at the station.

Kub said, "Could you have left it here the other day?"

Finney said nothing. He knew he hadn't been wearing it the other day.

"If it had been out in the elements, it would be damp," G. A. said. "Even if the fire had dried the top part, it was folded over pretty good and the bottom side would have been damp. It wasn't. This was left here today. This morning."

G. A. Montgomery and Kub both looked at Finney for several beats before Finney said, "You don't think I had anything to do with this."

"What I've learned over the years is that nobody's ever quite what you imagine they are. This is the property you told us was set to burn. Maybe you didn't think we were taking you seriously."

"You can't mean that. Even if by some incredible stretch of improbability I did do this—which I didn't—I wouldn't be stupid enough to leave anything at the scene."

"You're saying somebody else was stupid enough to leave your jacket here?"

"If I'd set this, why would I come back and drag Annie out?"

"Any sick son of a bitch can get a sudden attack of conscience. Or you mighta got bit by the hero complex. You see a chance for a medal and you go for it. You couldn't help yourself. I've seen that before. Maybe you even put her in there just so you *could* come back and save her."

"Someone took that jacket out of my station locker and planted it.

Somebody knew I was talking to you about this place, and they wanted to discredit me."

"I'd say you've been discredited."

"You told somebody," Finney said. "You must have given the address to somebody."

"Sure. I spoke to Charlie last night right after you left."

"Charlie Reese?"

"I called him at home. You think the chief of the department set this fire and framed you for it?"

"You tell him about my theory?"

"I told him. He said he was going to set up a committee to look into it. As soon as he found the time." G. A. rotated the toothpick around his mouth a couple of times. "I doubt he'll find the time now."

"This was not my doing."

"Put yourself in my shoes. You tell us about this building. Next day it burns down. At the scene, we find your coat, which you claim was stolen from your locker, a locker, I might add, that's in a secure fire station. You know the stairs are gone when nobody else seems to, and then you go off and make a lone-wolf rescue without telling anybody."

"I told Gary—"

"And now the victim tells us she talked to a firefighter on the street before the fire. I'll bet a nickel against a dollar you can't account for your whereabouts before you signed into the daybook this morning."

Across the yard two firefighters were yelling at each other playfully, some sort of joke concerning their nervous wait at the drawbridge during the drive to the fire. Finney knew if he told G. A. where he'd been that morning, he'd be in handcuffs before he finished the sentence.

"You were here, weren't you?" G. A. asked.

"I didn't set this fire."

"Everybody knows that mentally you've been all over the map since Leary Way. Now you get turned down for lieutenant. I don't blame you for getting a little pissy, trying to get back at the department."

"I didn't do this. You know me."

"Do I? Does anybody know anybody? A serial killer gets arrested. His neighbors show up at the trial as character witnesses. Did they know him? Not any better than I know you."

"This is a setup. Can't you see that?" He might have told them about the phone call last night, but then he would have had to admit he'd been here this morning.

"Maybe next time you'll listen when somebody tells you to stop poking around a fire that's already been investigated."

"What the hell does that mean?"

"It means if you hadn't had your head up your ass for the last few months, this might not have happened. Plenty of people warned you to get your act together."

"I'm sure John has an explanation," Kub said.

G. A. stared into Finney's eyes for a long while and then, bored with it, turned and strode away. Chewing gum madly, Kub palmed his skull and gave Finney a worried look. "Jesus, John. What the hell's going on?"

"I wish I knew."

"Did you light that fire?"

"No."

"And you didn't see that old woman this morning?"

"I didn't light the fire."

"It's beginning to look like you did."

"What he's got is circumstantial."

"Hate to tell you this, John, but most arson cases are *based* on circumstantial evidence. For your sake, I hope that old woman doesn't ID you. With the coat, the fact that you were talking about this place, your bad feelings towards the administration . . . Fact is, I could just about guarantee a conviction on that much circumstantial evidence. Unless you have a rock-solid alibi. You want my advice? Get a lawyer. Make sure he's good. When G. A. decides he's going to hang somebody, they usually swing."

# 22. A HUG FROM THE WIDOW

Finney headed down the dock toward his Pathfinder in the last of the afternoon light and spotted Emily Cordifis bustling along on a perfect collision course. She'd already seen him, so it was too late to hide. On the water there was no place to run from widows.

For eighteen years she'd been like a mother to him. Now when he saw her, all he could think about was her dead husband. Even though he knew the possibility that she would criticize him was almost nil, he flinched every time he saw her.

The woman striding down the center of the wooden dock was thinner than he remembered, grayer, her posture neither as tall nor as straight as it had once been. Her hair was still cut into a youthful bob, though now it was shot through with gray. Her long jaw gave her a thoughtful and distinguished look. Her eyes were as steady as ever and so dark they were almost black. They looked at you and did not blink and looked some more until you thought they were reading your mind. They came across as friendly, sincere, and interested, and they were. At times Bill had jokingly said he'd caught a doe in the headlights and then married her.

When he thought of Cordifis these days, Finney's mind flooded with Bill's last moments. Rarely his boisterous spirits or his raucous laugh. Rarely his storytelling or the pleasure he took in a practical joke. Never about the time he caught Balitnikoff napping and tied his shoelaces together, then hit the bell. Never about his knack of turning a bad day into one big joke.

Aside from everything else rotten that had come out of Leary Way, the event had erased the living Bill Cordifis from Finney's brain and replaced him with a corpse.

Virtually every weekend the clan had done something together—boating, camping, barbecues. The daughters with their boyfriends, and later their husbands and kids, would be there. So would Bill's cronies from the fire department. Guys who'd been alongside Bill when he coached his daughters' softball teams. Friends he knew from the Masons. The Cordifis household had been a clubhouse.

Bill was orphaned at an early age and afterward raised by a succession of indifferent relatives. Emily grew up with ten brothers and sisters. Coming from opposite poles, family was the one thing they both treasured above all else.

Sixty years old and as thin as a rail, built with the same wide bony hips, protruding ribs, and flat chest as her three daughters, Emily's dark eyes entertained a limpid look this afternoon.

"Emily."

"John, I know I should have called. I can come back if you're leaving."

"I was only going to the store. Nothing important. Come in. It's good to see you."

"I know. You, too. You don't come around anymore."

"No. I told you I wasn't going to. Things are just . . ."

"Sure. I know. But we miss you."

"I miss you, too."

"You've hurt yourself." She was looking at his bandaged hand.

"It's nothing." One of the pension doctors had put two stitches in the web of skin between his thumb and index finger. C-shift wouldn't be off until seven-thirty the next morning, but Finney was home on temporary disability leave.

Emily reached out and embraced him, the ribs in her back prominent under his palms. As always, she was spry and remarkably pretty.

Emily embraced him for a long time. "You are so tense, John."

"Am I? It must be the dampness from living on the lake."

Once they were ensconced in Finney's living room, he offered Emily a seat and a drink, both of which she declined. Dimitri eyed her warily from across the room, prepared to bolt at any sudden move.

"You've done a lot with this place. It's going to look nice," she said.

He glanced around. He'd taken the carpet up and hadn't replaced it, exposing a wooden floor scarred with nail holes and scratches. There were tools scattered in the corner, a skill saw on the floor behind the couch, and next to one wall, unpacked cardboard boxes. The trim had been removed from around the doorways and windows where he had yet to paint. "I'm a little behind schedule. It should look better in about . . . twenty years." He tried to laugh. It came out as half-burp and half-chuckle.

"No. I can see it's going to be quite nice." They were quiet for a few moments.

It was odd to be alone with her because the Cordifis clan had always done everything in clusters, the rowdy Christmas parties and the annual spring trip to Hawaii en masse. He could count on one hand the times he'd been alone in a room with Emily, mostly this past summer when they'd fallen into a reversal of roles, she striving to console him over her husband's death, he desperately inconsolable.

She'd aged. Her once-steady eyes had a haunted look. She'd given up whatever it was she'd done to keep her skin youthful, and her face was a skein of wrinkles, bags ballooning under her eyes. "How are you doing?" he asked.

"I still expect to hear his voice booming up from the workshop in the basement, 'When's the eats, Babe?' You know what bothers me more than anything? The house is so quiet."

"I wish—"

"I know you do, John, but he's in the Lord's hands." She sighed and let the silence widen around them like oil on a pool of water. After a few moments she said, "I've come to ask a favor."

"Anything you want, Emily. Anything at all. You know that."

Her eyes had a liquid sheen, seemed almost to glow in the dim light. "As a courtesy, I suppose, I was given one of the first copies of the fire department's report, which won't come out officially until sometime next week. I want you to read it, see if you can spot any inconsistencies, anything that doesn't make sense."

"Emily, you know I'd do anything for you, but I'm not sure—"

"They're talking about units taking lines here and there and hydrant pressure and vertical ventilation, and I try to put this together with the story you and others told me, and I just get confused." She pulled the report out of the tote bag she was carrying and handed it to him. It was the size of a small phone book, its heading in bold, black ink: SEATTLE FIRE, JUNE 7, 2000. "I need to know exactly how this relates to what you saw and remember, John. I need us to talk about this."

"Emily, I'd do anything for you, but I don't know if I'm the person you want for this."

"You're the *only* person, John. Bill said you had the best natural instincts of any firefighter he'd ever worked with. He told me if anything ever happened to him, I was to come to you for the truth. He said you would know."

"He said that?"

"Many times."

Finney wondered if Bill had had a premonition he was going to die.

He wanted to help her, but what was she going to think after he was charged with arson? And he *would* be charged. He couldn't tell her and he couldn't turn her down.

"I'll need some time."

"Just read it and get back to me when you've come to a conclusion. Maybe I'm being obtuse, but it all seems so artificial, like a huge construct. It should be a story with a beginning, a middle, and an end, and some sort of meaning, but it's just a bunch of loosely assembled facts that don't jibe. At least not for me."

"I take it you discussed this with G. A. Montgomery?"

"The report or my coming to you?"

"Either."

"We talked about the report."

"What'd he say?"

"Well . . . I'll be frank with you. He said it was basically your fault, but they didn't spell it out because that wasn't the fire department way."

"It was basically my fault? That's what he said?"

She nodded. "Don't worry. I don't believe that. If I did, I wouldn't be here."

"Thank you for your confidence."

They listened as a floatplane landed on the lake. Dimitri stalked across the room in the way that some cats have, walking so heavily you could hear his feet strike the floor like padded hooves. Finney caught Emily looking at a picture on the wall, a photo taken five years earlier of the crew of Ladder 1. The six of them were in their dress blacks lined up in front of the truck on the ramp at Station 10, Cordifis in the middle with a somewhat bemused look on his face and Finney to his right looking serious as all get out. "I miss him so much," she said.

"I miss him, too. He was a tremendous guy."

"You'd think thirty-odd years would be enough of risking your neck. Enough taking the chance of contracting hepatitis or AIDS from a patient. Or TB. Enough of getting up three and four times a night to put out a bed fire or pick up some drunk off the sidewalk. But every time I brought up the possibility of retirement, he got mad at me."

"He made that station a great place to work, Emily. Everybody there loved him. I'll read it and we'll talk."

She kissed his cheek, and he walked her down the dock to her car, gave her another hug, and watched her drive off in Bill's old Ford Bronco, the red IAFF union sticker in the center of the rear window.

The report was in binder form with three large flat staples buttoning it together along the left edge. Three-quarters of an inch thick, it was printed on regulation typing paper, eight and a half by eleven inches.

He began skimming the report while he ate dinner.

# 23. THINGS THAT DID NOT GO WELL

Oversized blue pages divided the report into sections: Table of Contents, Introduction, SFD Overview, Key Issues, Building History, FIU Report, FAC Report, Incident Overview, et cetera. The fire investigation unit report, G. A.'s investigation and determination that the fire had been accidental, as well as the Fire Alarm Center report that had been generated separately were included.

Within the Conclusion section was a page labeled THINGS THAT WENT WELL. Another page was headed THINGS THAT DID NOT GO WELL. Finney thumbed to the latter.

It was noted that the incident was short on manpower from the beginning. That heavy smoke in the vicinity obscured early reconnaissance of the buildings so that the first Incident Commander reported the building as being fifty by seventy-five feet, when in fact the warehouse portion alone was double that. The buildings on the north side of the complex contained the same approximate square footage. No other incoming units corrected Captain Vaughn's initial miscalculation, probably because they had the same visibility problems he had, so that all night calculations were based on the original figure. It was mentioned that fans were put up and then taken down, thereby wasting valuable time. Nobody mentioned the lack of visibility inside the warehouse that the fans would have cleared.

Although the wind was from the north that night, Engine 22 set up the command post on the south side of the building, so that officers and firefighters were immersed in clots of drifting smoke for almost an hour before the command post was moved.

Nobody ever did a walk-around to survey all four sides of the building. Had they done so, the IC would have known early on that there were other buildings connected to the warehouse, that those buildings were also involved, and that the crews of Engine 31 and Ladder 5 were actually fighting a fire in those smaller, older buildings while Vaughn thought they were supporting his efforts in the warehouse. After Ladder 5 opened holes in the older building, Vaughn couldn't figure out why the smoke didn't clear in the warehouse.

The report said Captain Cordifis shouldn't have split his crew and made a mistake ordering fans for ventilation. Supposedly, the early introduction of fans had fed the fire and made it larger before it could be located by hose crews. Yet, by all accounts, the fire started in the older buildings to the north and only spread into the warehouse later, probably after the wall collapse. When the first units arrived, the warehouse was filled with smoke, smoke that had leaked through from the older part of the complex. Finney still thought Cordifis's original plan was viable. Using fans, they would have cleared the warehouse in minutes. They would have searched it, realized the fire and possible victims were elsewhere, and been on their way. As it was, Ladder 1, Engine 22, and later Engines 5 and 25 lost precious minutes bumbling around in zero visibility.

Radio traffic had been problematical. Owing to confusion from the fires going on in the south end and to the fact that Leary Way was fought on channel 2 while the normal fire channel was channel 1, several units at Leary Way had been addressing the IC in the south end on channel 1 when they thought they were addressing Captain Vaughn. Quite a few of their transmissions either were not answered or were answered by the wrong IC. Even the dispatchers were confused.

Because several units had done their monitoring and broadcasting on channel 1, they missed key portions of Cordifis's search instructions and went into the complex without any notion of where to look.

The units that did hear Cordifis's transmission knew from what he reported that opening the door to his room would jeopardize his life, so these hastily organized rescue teams did not open any doors unless they swung out. Instead, using chain saws, they cut small holes in each door they encountered, a procedure that slowed the search to a snail's pace.

The older complex had a fire wall running along the spine of the building, north to south, with only two doorways in it. For reasons Finney had yet to discover, most of the searchers had been told to remain on the west side of the fire wall in the older complex; in reality, he and Cordifis had been on the east side. Only Reese and Kirby entered from the east.

The report said Finney was in the final stages of exhaustion by the time he tried to fight his way out of the building, that he and Cordifis should have taken a rest break after changing bottles, as if his exhaustion derived from not taking a break. What the report didn't indicate was how much criticism they would have drawn for taking a rest break while victims may have been dying inside.

Nowhere did the report implicate Finney in Bill's death.

Nowhere did it suggest that if he'd reacted differently Bill Cordifis would be alive.

Dozens of firefighters had told him it wasn't his fault, that he should consider his own escape and Cordifis's death as acts of God. Yet the unofficial accusation lingered in the air. G. A. had passed it along to Emily, and Finney knew others were uttering it.

After some minutes of skimming the report, he curled up on the sofa under a waterside window and, reading from page one, he used up the last of the afternoon light reflecting off the lake.

The part that disgruntled him most was Reese's statement, the same statement that had been clipped from newspapers, highlighted with yellow grease markers, and tacked to the beanery bulletin board in almost every fire station in the city: "We went in and within a minute we'd found one firefighter wandering around alone. He was in a panic and wasn't any help as far as indicating where his partner was. We guided him outside and then went back down the direction he'd come from, but there wasn't anything there. We searched as long as we could but were finally forced out by the heat."

The way Finney remembered it, they'd pointed him in the direction he was already headed and then turned their backs without even knowing if he could get up from his squat. Had Finney taken a misstep or collapsed in that last two dozen paces, Reese and Kub would hardly have seen him as they were chased out of the building by flame.

But he thought he also remembered counting exactly twenty-eight paces straight down the corridor from the small hole he'd hacked into the wall with his service axe. And he thought he told them as much, yet Reese said he hadn't been able to give them any help. If it was true that Cordifis was only twenty-eight steps away, they should have reached Bill in less than a minute with or without Finney's directions. He'd left his chirping PASS device outside the hole as a beacon. But maybe nothing Finney remembered after he left Cordifis was true. Maybe he'd been hallucinating the entire time.

The doctors said people with very high body core temperatures suffered debilitating weakness, hallucinations, seizures, and coma, roughly in that order. Finney had not escaped the hallucinations, which he knew he'd entertained in the medic unit and later in the hospital. But he could have sworn he was thinking straight when he spoke to Reese and Kub.

God, he wished he could keep from thinking about Leary Way.

Robert Kub was uneasy talking about the subject with Finney, obviously wanting to spare his feelings. The most Finney could get him to say was, "As far as I'm concerned, we all did our best. You could barely stand, and we were lucky to get out of there alive."

"If they'd only asked me in that medic unit I could have told them where to look," Finney told his brother, Tony, weeks after the fire.

"Not when I saw you," replied his brother. "When I saw you, you weren't making any sense at all."

In addition to a broken collarbone, heat exhaustion, and burns, Finney had so much carbon monoxide circulating in his system that one of the doctors at the Harborview ER told Tony he wasn't going to survive. And everyone knew one of the first effects of CO poisoning was confusion.

He'd still been confused at the funeral three days later.

When Finney was released from the hospital long enough to attend the funeral service, of which he recalled next to nothing, he remembered people saying they were sorry, which somehow was the last thing he wanted to hear. By the time Diana Moore approached, he had reached some sort of limit. "How are you doing?" she had asked.

"How the hell do you think? I've got enough Demerol on board to knock down a football team. I can't feel my fingertips. My neck hurts like hell, and I killed my partner."

"You didn't kill him," Diana replied quietly.

"Why don't you get out of my face?"

"You know you don't—"

"Just get the fuck away from me. And tell your shit-eating friends to stay away, too." The words had come out of a generic anger that picked targets at random, Diana the luckless target that day.

The next time they spoke was the day of his appointment with Reese, when he was turned down for promotion.

# 24. THINGS THAT WENT WORSE

irefighters went in from the north thinking they were fighting a fire in a group of two-story wooden buildings. Others went in from the south, thinking they were fighting a fire in a large concrete-walled warehouse. It was almost forty minutes before anybody knew the scope of the problem.

It was forty-six minutes into the fire before a crew reported putting water on the fire.

Cordifis's radio, still in working order, was found buried two feet under his body. Finney's radio, what was left of it, lay next to the body. A service axe was still strapped to Cordifis's waist. Another, Finney's, was found forty-five feet away in what had been another room. Cordifis's inactivated PASS device was still clipped to the belt of his MSA backpack. Finney's PASS device was found twenty-five feet from the body under a pile of rubble. It had beeped long into the night and was heard by dozens of frustrated and grieving firefighters outside.

The autopsy found Cordifis had died of smoke inhalation. Prior to death, he'd sustained multiple fractures of his tibia and fibula on both legs and a broken index finger on his left hand. What the report glossed over was that Cordifis died inhaling heat so hot it cauterized his lungs. Dying from smoke inhalation implies taking in smoke and losing consciousness. But Bill had died inhaling flames. Every firefighter who saw the report would read between the lines.

# 25. MAKING FRIENDS IN TAMPA

"We've got a CISD this morning at nine," said Lieutenant Sadler.

"It's such a waste of time," Finney said.

"Now don't get your briefs in a knot. You know it's mandatory for everyone who was on the alarm. There were probably some guys who've never seen a burn victim before."

A request for a critical incident stress debriefing from any member who'd been on an alarm spurred the department to convene one. One had been called after the Wah Mee massacre, where Seattle firefighters found thirteen patrons of an illegal gambling club bound and gagged and shot in the head. They convened one after the Pang Fire, where four firefighters fell through a floor to a fiery death. They held one after Leary Way. A CISD was meant to be an emotional analgesic, although in Finney's experience they only added more stress.

For Finney, the only positive aspect to having a CISD for Riverside Drive was that somebody might say something to shed light on his plight. It was tempting to believe Annie had appropriated his jacket after wandering into the station through an unlocked door, perhaps while they were out on an alarm. He could see the whole scenario: Annie steals his coat; a firefighter decides to play a practical joke with the phone call; Annie lights a warming fire, loses control of it, gets confused, and makes accusations; afterward, G. A. Montgomery comes along and flips happenstance into a full-fledged lynching. It could have happened that way.

The meeting was at the Four Seasons Olympic, arguably the ritziest hotel in Seattle, certainly one of the most venerable. After Sam Hoskins parked Engine 26 on Seneca, Gary Sadler and John Finney made their way through the sumptuous lobby, then upstairs to a thickly carpeted room off the mezzanine, where several dozen chairs were arranged in the shape of an oval. It was the same room they'd used for the debriefing after Leary Way, the same chairs, and Finney felt himself floundering in the same murky swamp of guilt and nervous anticipation.

Marshal 5 was building a case against him, and unless something extraordinary happened, he would be behind bars in a week. He would lose his job, and these people who'd once been his friends would abandon him without a second thought.

When all thirty-eight firefighters were seated, Finney saw G. A. Montgomery and Robert Kub station themselves near the door, arms across their chests like bailiffs. He had an uneasy feeling they were planning to arrest him in front of the group.

Just before the meeting came to order, Jerry Monahan popped through the door in his civvies and squeezed a chair into the oval next to Finney's. As contrary as Monahan could be in his private affairs, Finney thought, he was amazingly docile when it came to fire department dictums; he was there on his own hook.

The session was overseen by an African-American chief from the administration, Caldwell, a man who wanted nothing to do with field operations but who elbowed himself into the chairman's seat on any committee, always hustling to build his résumé. Finney didn't catch the psychiatrist's name, but in a room full of rough-hewn, aggressive firefighters, he stood out as a milquetoast.

The third member of the committee was, oddly enough, Marion Balitnikoff, who, although recognized department-wide for his firefighting skills, was just as widely known for being a jerk. Five years ago he'd been sent to Florida for a rescue and extrication conference and came back early behind a strongly worded letter from Tampa's police chief requesting Seattle never send him to their city again. Scuttlebutt had it that his offenses included an assault on two underaged prostitutes, wrestling in the street with a cabdriver, and urinating on a woman's pant leg, presumably while trying to urinate into a nearby fountain, this last performed in a hotel lobby full of tourists. After all this, the Tampa authorities had let him off without charges. You had to know Balitnikoff. Sober, he could be almost charming.

# 26. SAVING THE MAN IN THE HOLE

onversation in the room died down when Chief Caldwell stood up to announce the ground rules. Everything was to be kept within these four walls, said Caldwell. Nobody was to repeat anything heard in the debriefing, not to a spouse or a crew member or a pastor. It was, he explained, only under such a covenant that people would feel free to speak openly.

For five months people had been looking sideways at Finney, and today wasn't any different. They evaluated his neck for scars, stared into his eyes for signs of guilt, listened to his speech for indications of trauma, for substantiation of the persistent rumors that he was on the verge of retiring due to nervous breakdown.

During the meeting firefighters were instructed to announce who they were, how many years they had in the department, what rig they were working on the day of the fire, what they did at the fire, what they saw, and how they felt about it. Finney could see stress levels skyrocketing as each man or woman waited to address the group. Firefighters were a select denomination, chosen for physical abilities, brute strength, endurance, the knack of calculating on the fly, physical bravery, mechanical aptitude, a desire for public service. Nobody was selected for an ability to speak in front of a group or for the gift of soul-searching.

There was a preliminary overview of the basic facts given by Chief Caldwell—the time of the fire, number of units dispatched, the order of their arrival. Clearly Caldwell had done his homework. When he didn't mention that the house had been on their dangerous buildings list, Finney realized he hadn't heard the standard warning from the dispatchers during the alarm either. It hadn't occurred to him until now, but they should have fought that fire from outside, which was the procedure for handling any building on the list. He raised his hand and asked Caldwell about it, well aware that all eyes in the room were now on him. "Not on the list," Caldwell replied, curtly.

Finney and G. A. Montgomery exchanged glances, though Finney could not read G. A.'s face. Beside him, Monahan stared straight ahead.

They proceeded around the oval in the rough order in which the rigs had arrived at the fire location. When the members of Engine 27's crew told their stories, McKittrick stuttered and his officer got a case of dry mouth. Sadler told of their arrival, his orders to Monahan, McKittrick's notification that there was a victim, advising Finney they were going up the stairs, and discovering later that Finney had gone outside alone and put up a ladder. Sadler's disapproval was duly noted and Finney knew it would be passed around the city like a bad cold.

Monahan told a simple story of looking for the hydrant and nearly driving into the river in the fog.

Having paid scant attention to the others, G. A. swung his stern gaze onto Finney when it was his turn to speak.

"We went through the front door behind Twenty-seven's crew. None of us got in very far. Then McKittrick came and told us there was a victim. I got a ladder off Engine Twenty-seven, went to the roof, and found our victim inside the window. Moore brought a line up and cooled off the room while I got her out. After a while the medics showed up."

"That's a little sketchy," said Lieutenant Balitnikoff, the only facilitator who hadn't spoken until now. "I'm just trying to get us all on the same page here. What about the part where you left your partner?"

All eyes in the room turned to Finney. "I thought this meeting was supposed to be about our feelings."

"Just curious as to how you felt when you left him." The room grew quiet. People weren't stirring. Weren't breathing. "Don't you think you should have learned your lesson at the beginning of the summer? The way I remember it, this is a team effort. We work as a team." Balitnikoff looked pointedly at Diana Moore. It was clear he was including her in his critique. "We're all family or I wouldn't speak like this. I don't think I could bear it if anybody else got hurt."

Finney couldn't believe that under the guise of a brotherly admonition, Balitnikoff was publicly chastising him for both Leary Way and Riverside Drive.

"Maybe we'll think about our partners next time?" Balitnikoff said, to no one in particular.

Finney looked around the group and said, "If I hadn't done it, that woman would be dead."

A few people shuffled their feet under their chairs. More than one pair of eyes fell on Diana Moore, who was sitting on both hands looking at the carpet. Finney remembered the scene Balitnikoff had made at Cordifis's funeral, shouting in the foyer of the church until G. A. Montgomery escorted him outside. Finney never found out what it was about.

The psychiatrist dropped his pen, and from across the room Finney heard the soft sound on the carpet. He wondered if Balitnikoff had been chosen randomly as a facilitator at the debriefing. Generally the department chose from a pool of trained officers or firefighters not directly involved with the incident. While Balitnikoff's unit, Engine 10, had not been on the call, Ladder 1, housed in Station 10 with Engine 10, had. Finney would have thought that was enough to disqualify him.

Three years earlier, when Marion Balitnikoff transferred to Engine 10, he brought with him a thousand and one stories as well as a reputation for being strong as a bull on the fire ground. In firefighting, unlike many other arenas in life, aggressiveness was preferred over most other modes of action. Reactive was bad; passive was not acceptable. Quick, prompt, informed initiative was what the department wanted—and Balitnikoff had always been aggressive.

Finney's first real firefighting experience with Balitnikoff had been at an apartment-house fire. In a vacant room on the second floor they'd found a hole in the floor; the hazard had been marked off but nobody could see the warnings in the smoke. When Finney found a firefighter sunk up to his chest in the hole, about to fall more than two stories to the lobby, he threw his body across the man's arms, gripping his backpack, anchoring him. Now only the weight and friction of Finney's body prevented them both from sliding in. Finney hollered for help, and several pairs of hands pulled them out. The other man said nothing before, during, or after the incident, and he quickly disappeared into the smoke.

Later, Finney realized it had been Lieutenant Balitnikoff. "That was something, huh? That hole," Finney said to him afterward. "I thought we were going to lose you."

"You got the wrong guy." Balitnikoff turned and walked away.

The episode stumped Finney until he realized it had to do with machismo. Firefighters saved other people. A firefighter who needed saving himself was a rung down from the firefighter who'd saved him. That logic was a holdover from the days when neighboring engine companies raced at breakneck speeds so they could brag about being the first to put water on a fire in somebody else's district, from the days when only "weak sisters" strapped on air masks. Today, people wore masks and worked in teams. Today, safety was paramount, and today, crews worked together instead of against each other.

These days it was a job, not a way to measure your dick.

# 27. GET OUT THE TAPE MEASURE

The one thing Diana appreciated about stress debriefings was hearing about an incident from the perspective of each individual involved, viewing an identical scene from a *Rashomon*-like multiplicity of angles.

During the debriefing Finney seemed calm enough, but he was always unflappable. After his laugh, which erupted at the most unexpected times, it was what she liked best about him.

She recalled seeing him at a fire just off Denny Way, where a huge chunk of material sailed off a roof and landed squarely between Finney and a high-strung lieutenant named Gold who routinely took two or three months off every year to let his gastrointestinal ulcers calm down. Looking up and seeing a pair of rookies on the roof, Gold became furious and shouted that he was going to come up and write charges. "Leave this to me," Finney said, gritting his teeth in a Clint Eastwood grimace. "I'll fix them."

Not knowing Finney and fearing the worst, Diana had followed him up the various stairwells in the three-story house and then through a hole cut in the roof. There was no doubt Finney could make life difficult for the two rookies, who were nervously awaiting his arrival. Sizing them up, he spoke in a low voice devoid of emotion, "Next time you throw something off a roof, think big. Skip the lieutenants and captains. Go for a chief."

It was the sort of dry wit Finney and the rest of the men on Ladder 1 were famous for.

When the meeting finally broke up, just before lunchtime, Diana waited in the lobby.

Robert Kub and G. A. Montgomery emerged from the meeting room, Kub stopping to give her a hug. Montgomery, who had made a studied practice of ignoring her since her first day in the department, continued walking as if he hadn't seen her.

Kub, on the other hand, flirted with any female who didn't have a mustache and some who did. "Strange meeting," he said. "That poor old woman."

As they spoke, Gary Sadler bumped against Diana's shoulder and almost knocked her over. He tried to pretend it was an accident, but he wasn't much of an actor. She'd expected rudeness, had hoped for indifference, but outright hostility was a shock. Not many people were even aware that they knew each other, and Diana preferred to keep it that way.

"Hey," Kub said, as Sadler walked away. "What do you think you're doing?"

"Let it go," Diana said.

"That was awful goddamn rough."

"Forget it. Not to change the subject or anything, but I don't understand why you and G. A. came to this little soirée."

Kub's eyes followed Sadler out of the room, and then he looked away evasively. "Needed to talk to the entry team."

A group of firefighters from Engine 11 and Ladder 7 walked past, and one or two stopped to say hello. Then Finney appeared from a bank of phone booths down the hall. "Hello, John."

Finney nodded to Diana and then looked at Kub. "Robert, you get any leads on that fire yet?"

A pair of firefighters came by and slapped Finney on the back. "Great save. Congratulations."

"Thanks."

Kub gave Finney a beleaguered look. "You mean any *other* leads?"

"Yeah."

Diana realized something complex was transpiring between these two but didn't know what it was. They were quiet for several moments, outwaiting each other, the tension building. Finally, Diana said, "Was she living in that vacant house? The old woman?"

"According to the neighbors," Kub said, "nobody's lived there for the last eight years. No telling where she was sleeping. We had a witness once, rode buses all day and spent her nights at Sea-Tac. Always dressed up so people thought she was waiting for a plane. Nobody bothers you at the airport. Maybe she was living at the airport." Kub gave a little wave and left.

Diana took a deep breath. She was aware that since the fire on Riverside Drive her relationship with John Finney had changed. She'd proved herself to him, and there would be no more questions between them. She'd been thinking about this in a casual sense for the past two days, but now that he was in front of her, she plunged ahead. "John, you might think this is an awkward question, and it is, I guess, but are you seeing anybody?"

He looked as if he were trying to remember, then smiled. "Not right now."

"I feel silly even asking. I talked to Baxter, and he said the last he knew you were dating some college professor, but he didn't know if that was still happening."

"A community college English teacher. Her old boyfriend showed up."

"Sorry."

"Tell you the truth, I was kind of relieved."

"The reason I ask is I'm involved in the department's homeless children's charity, and we're giving a costume ball on Halloween. I have tickets, and I'd like you to be my date."

He took a deep breath, and for a moment she thought he was trying to compose a turndown. "That sounds like a lot of fun. I'll look forward to it."

"Look forward to what?" It was Marion Balitnikoff in his black dress uniform, hat pulled low to his eyes.

"Nothing," Finney said.

"Glad I caught you two together. I know I sounded a little rough in there, but I hope you both take it in the spirit in which it was given. We're all family, and I don't want to see anybody else hurt. I mean that. I couldn't take another funeral before I retire."

Diana said, "You were awful rough on him."

"Yeah, well, no hard feelings." Balitnikoff stuck his hand out to shake, first with Diana, then with Finney. "I just want things to go right from now on."

After Balitnikoff was out of earshot, Diana turned to Finney. "Don't forget Halloween. You'll need a costume."

"I'm not going to forget."

# 28. WHATEVER DOESN'T MAKE YOU STRONGER KILLS YOU

When Finney had left the conference room, Monahan was talking to another short-timer from Ladder 7 about investing in Asian markets, as if Monahan had any money to invest. He was still broke from importing two hundred kangaroos in a scheme to sell meat and hides. It turned out nobody wanted to eat a kangaroo, and after he had all two hundred of them in pens on acreage he'd paid too much for, he discovered he didn't have the heart to slaughter one anyway.

Monahan emerged from the conference room, took half a minute to get his bearings, then came downstairs and ducked into a public lavatory next to the Garden Room restaurant. When he still hadn't come out after several minutes, Finney knew he was in for a vigil. In the crapper at the station, Monahan often finished books, paid bills, made phone calls, wrote letters—and had been tardy for more than one alarm after his legs went to sleep.

"John?" Kub was suddenly beside Finney again, whispering. "I didn't want to talk in front of Diana."

Eyeballing the rest room door, Finney said, "What?"

"You know I can't act as your inside man."

"Why not? I'm getting crucified."

"I will tell you this. In a few days G. A.'ll show photos to that old woman."

"How's she doing?"

"Well enough to ID you. In a few days."

"He thinks I did it, why doesn't he just arrest me?"

"G. A. doesn't work that way. He likes to play. That's to your advantage if you use the time."

"I don't see any advantages here."

"The other morning he went to Riverside Drive and wrote down license numbers of people who routinely drive to work past there. He thinks he has somebody who might ID you. Course, it won't be as good as the old woman. You were there that morning, weren't you?"

"An anonymous caller asked me to meet him. Then he never showed up."

Kub took a deep breath and exhaled. "Christ, John. How did you get into this mess?"

"Forget it. I don't need your help."

"I wish I could help."

"Yeah, I wish you could, too."

A few minutes later Jerry Monahan rushed out the side door of the lobby.

Finney didn't catch him until he was at the corner of Fifth and Seneca, catercornered to the YWCA. Monahan was walking briskly, talking to himself, his hands in the pockets of his baggy, corduroy trousers. Under the cloudy sky his skin was gray, the smile lines around his eyes crinkled against the breeze that channeled down between the buildings.

When Monahan smiled, he tried to make it mechanical, but there was a warmth to his smile that he couldn't conceal.

"How are you?"

"I'm being framed for arson, that's how I am."

"What?" Monahan seemed incredulous.

"To start with, that house is not on the dangerous buildings list."

"Of course it's not. It burned down."

"It never was on the list."

"Sure it was. I put it on myself." Monahan smiled a concerned smile as if he'd just discovered Finney was mildly retarded and realized he had to be more diplomatic. "What makes you think it wasn't on the list?"

"Weren't you listening inside? Caldwell said it wasn't on the list."

"Oh."

"Why didn't you add that house like you said you would?"

"Well, I guess . . . Hmmmm. Now I'm getting confused. I don't know what happened."

"I'm not buying that."

"Okay, I screwed up. I'm no virgin. It must have slipped my mind."

"If it slipped your mind, why did you say you put it on the list?"

"I have a lot on my mind these days. My Elevator-in-a-Can is almost finished. I have a deadline— My wife says I'd forget my suspenders if they weren't attached to my belt." He smiled, striving to be cordial.

Was it possible he actually thought he'd added it to the list? Finney didn't think so. There was something else, too. Last Tuesday, Monahan had been far too excited about the department becoming tied up with all those alarms. It was as if he had known about it in advance.

"Jerry, you're screwing with me."

Monahan shoveled his hands into his trousers pockets and said, "What are you talking about?"

"You made that call Sunday night. You told me to meet you."

"What on earth are you—"

"You know where I was that morning, and you know why."

Like a crime victim trying to flee a robbery attempt, Monahan turned and began walking quickly up the street.

Finney followed and grabbed his arm. "Talk to me, Jerry."

"Geez-Louise, what do you *want?*"

"You took my coat out of my locker, didn't you?"

"Your coat? Now it's your *coat?* I thought you were talking about the dangerous buildings list?"

"You took my coat, didn't you?"

"Go get some help," Monahan said flatly. "Everybody said you were going to crack up after Leary Way, and now you have."

"There's a conspiracy, Jerry. You're involved. That house was involved."

Monahan looked at him intensely and said, "Don't try to tell me about conspiracies. I'm an expert on conspiracies. I can't tell you how many times I've thought there were conspiracies against me, when I found out later there weren't. Always when things go wrong, it feels better to believe people made it that way. It feels better to think you're not small and insignificant and wandering around an aimless universe like a bug that can have a big shoe snuff out its life at any moment. If there's a conspiracy and it's centered on you, then you're not insignificant. Somebody's watching. Somebody's paying attention. It's the conspiracy syndrome. I grew out of it. You will, too, John. And don't accuse me again, understand? I hear this once more, I'm going to the department, and after that I'm going to court to get a restraining order."

Monahan gave him one last mournful look, and walked to the corner, where he turned back. "They say, 'Whatever doesn't kill you makes you stronger.' That's not true. When trials come along, they make you weaker. The next trial comes along, *it* kills you. Listen to me. Get help."

# PART THREE

# 29. TWO MEN NOT FIGHTING OVER THE REMOTE CONTROL

His night at Station 26 had been bad enough that Finney was numbing himself with Katie Couric on the NBC morning show. He had tossed and turned until four A.M., when a heroin addict from one of the local biker gangs ODed in a cramped one-story apartment directly across the street from the station. By the time Engine 26's crew walked through the door, his pals had, adhering to street legend, stripped him and packed him in a bathtub filled with cold water and ice cubes. Finding a slow pulse but no respirations, Finney and Lieutenant Sadler fished him out of the tub and bag-masked him in a puddle of water on the floor. When the medics came, they tied him to a stretcher and shot Narcan into his veins. As usual with Narcan, he bounced back in seconds, cursing all involved for "fucking up" his high.

Finney wished he had somebody to talk this over with. He knew he had been surly and self-pitying in those weeks following Leary Way, growling at people who wanted to console him, going so far as to denounce God and the church to the department chaplain when he visited, making certain everyone knew he wanted to be alone.

For five months he had been alone.

What he'd known all along but seemed powerless to change was how Leary Way had turned him into the supreme egoist. He'd become a self-centered jerk, and what was worse, he didn't know how to change.

After making a few phone calls, he realized he couldn't confide in those he didn't trust, and he didn't trust the few he could confide in. Thomas Baxter, who was riding Ladder 1 with Finney the night of Leary Way, had turned to Jesus and now seemed to be breathing rarefied air from another planet. Finney didn't know whether his conversion was a form of self-hypnosis or a true immersion in spirituality, but whichever, it had propelled Baxter out of Finney's reach.

Finney was closer to his father now than he'd ever been, but he didn't want to put any more rocks on the wagon his father was pulling. His brother was supportive on the surface but continued to throw darts at him in small ways. His mother did not willingly take on problems, and rarely expressed an opinion that wasn't on lease from her husband. In the last five months he'd grown distant from all of his other friends.

There was no one else.

The doorbell rang, and as he scuffed his feet across the carpet, his loose wool socks becoming snug as condoms, he glimpsed himself in the mirror—unshaven, disheveled, eyes bloodshot.

His father was on the dock, nonchalantly puffing away on a cigarette.

Gil Finney was small, wiry, his face weathered from forty years of inhaling unfiltered cigarettes and Dumpster fires. Six months of cancer and a lifetime of quarreling with strangers about right-hand turn lanes and parking spots had given him a drawn look, as if he were made out of wire. He'd been showing up unbidden lately, a routine Finney had become rather fond of.

"Hey, John. Everything skookem?"

"Yeah, fine. Come in."

"I know you guys worked yesterday, but I thought you might want to shoot the breeze. I been up since five."

"Me, too. How're you doing?"

"Not so bad. God, last week I thought I was dying." He laughed and then coughed. Then laughed again. For reasons unfathomable to Finney, his father, who'd never seen much humor in life, now found hilarious almost everything having to do with death, particularly his own. For months he'd been unnerving people with jokes about coffins and cemeteries and had even threatened to play a gag on his pallbearers, who would all be chiefs, by having his casket weighted with six hundred pounds of lead. "Make their fat asses do some real work," he said, laughing until the phlegm rattled in his lungs with a wet, evil sound.

Using two fingers and a thumb, Gil Finney expertly flicked his cigarette stub onto the surface of the lake, where it sizzled for a fraction of a second and went out. A gull swooped down and swallowed it.

Sixty-two years of age, his father had lately become overly solicitous of the welfare of others, something Tony had once, after a couple of beers, theorized was a stunt to get people to think about him. Finney preferred to believe his father's illness had actually transformed him into a better human being, just as Leary Way had in many ways transformed Finney into a lesser human being. Or so he reasoned.

Finney and his father had endured many years when they were barely speaking, and one where they didn't speak at all, but time and circumstance had pretty much crayoned over the bad memories. These days Finney was glad for the visits and found, despite his own egocentrism, his father was often in his thoughts.

Gil Finney wore faded khaki slacks, deck shoes, and an old SFD windbreaker zipped to the neck. His wife, Finney's mother, had bought him a goose-down, Eddie Bauer ski jacket, but he preferred the worn and the familiar.

After stepping jauntily through the front door, Gil Finney sank onto the leather sofa, picked up the remote control, and, with the speed of a startled cat running across a piano keyboard, began flipping through channels. "What do you hear about making lieutenant, young man?"

Finney had hoped somebody else would be there to face the heartache in his father's eyes when he found out, but apparently, his old man's connections to the department notwithstanding, nobody had had the temerity to spill it. Now that they were in the same room together, he realized he couldn't do it either. At least not now. "All we can do is wait."

"Whatcha doin' now? Looks like you're lazing around the house like a three-dollar chippy."

"I would never ask for more than two dollars."

"What? You have a bad shift at Twenty-six's?" The TV remote in one hand, an issue of *Kayaker* magazine in the other, Gil Finney turned and looked at his son. His steel-gray, ball-bearing eyes squinted out from under caterpillar eyebrows. "Hey, you know what I just realized the other day? Reese was one of my boots. I remember him now. He used to walk around like he had his underwear on backwards." He laughed, and the phlegm danced deep in his lungs.

"I know. I came in with him."

"Thought I was going to have to pink-slip the little bastard, but then he had his first fire and didn't stain his shorts too bad, so I let him alone. Hey, somebody said they saw you with Diana Moore."

"Yeah."

"I'd stay away from women in the department. Women are genetic cowards. I told you that, didn't I?"

"I've heard your theory."

Gil Finney's bigotry had grown worse since his retirement. Finney guessed that all those years of being forced to pretend he was fair made him feel as if he had decades of hypocrisy to make up for. These days he rarely spoke of the department without bad-mouthing minorities, his most virulent harangues reserved for women.

"They aren't tough enough," he said. "They can't help it. They're bred to protect the nest. They hide with the young. God made 'em that way. It's the rooster who's out there fighting. It takes a cock to be a firefighter. And not a strap-on plastic cock."

Before his retirement, the old man had followed all the political dictates of a fire department in one of the most liberal cities on the coast, but privately he'd always believed the department of forty years ago was the only department worth saving—all white, all male.

"Maybe I should go down and rattle little Charlie's cage for you. There's no reason you couldn't be a lieutenant before the day is out."

Finney tried to sound casual. "I'd rather you didn't, Dad."

"You know I want to see this happen before it's too late."

"I know you do."

"By God, both you boys are going to end up battalion chiefs. Didja know Tony's already studying for the chief's test?" Finney knew it was another of Tony's falsehoods, but he had no intention of exposing him. "You're number one on the list. You'll be number one on the captain's list when you take that. This is what I've dreamed for you, John. You and Tony both. Ever since you were little. Remember when I used to take you down to Ten's and you used to scramble over Ladder One? 'Daddy, I be fireman.' " He sat back on the couch and reminisced silently for a few moments. "Believe me, John, a straight-arrow like you will fly through the ranks."

Fire department culture was odd, Finney thought. *Getting in,* they called it, an expression that typified how most firefighters felt about the job.

They were *in.*

Everybody else was *out.*

As a child, he'd been fascinated by the sense of danger, the sirens, the smell of smoke off his father's hair and clothing when he came home from work, the soot in his ears, the stories he told, the rough-and-tumble men who joked with him when his father took him to the station, the absurd confidence and astonishing resourcefulness with which they and his father attacked anything even remotely resembling an emergency.

Finney had been a sensitive boy, easily offended by his father's careless remarks. He'd tried college; his grades had been good but he'd lacked a goal. He'd worked on the assembly line at Boeing and then at Puget

Sound Paint, where he was bumped from one of the road crews to the front office after only nine months. He wanted to think of it as a lark when he applied for the SFD, but it turned out to be more.

"I got something for you off the news last night," his father said, holding a videotape aloft. "You know a man named Patterson Cole?"

"He owned Leary Way."

"Check it out."

A cheesy local gossip program had done a piece on Patterson Cole's ongoing divorce proceedings. The eighty-three-year-old Cole had been entangled in a much-publicized breakup with a woman forty-eight years his junior who'd been a waitress at Hooters when they met. She was disputing their prenuptial agreement, claiming she'd been coerced into signing it under false pretenses. Cole countered that she'd been married and divorced four times but told him she'd never been married at all, that she told him she wanted children when it turned out she couldn't conceive and knew it.

There was film footage of the couple in less litigious times, Cole, an unremarkable octogenarian, stooped, withered, his hair stringy and unkempt, invariably in a dark suit and rep tie; his cartoon wife a head taller, massively blond, massively busty, in high heels and tight skirts. In most pictures she clutched a cliché toy poodle, the dog's collar matching her outfit. Cartoons, both of them.

She claimed Cole had tried to kill her by pushing her off the sixtieth floor of the Columbia Tower, that he'd had her Mercedes torched, twice tried to poison her dog, sicced private investigators on her, bugged her phone, slapped her, and even tried to bribe her mother to marry him so he would be her ex-husband and stepfather at the same time, anything to upset her and ruin her life.

If even a fraction of what his wife was accusing him of was true, he was a reprobate, and Finney knew reprobates were capable of a lot of things, not the least of which was arson. As the show concluded, Finney got up to remove the tape.

"Your buddy is next."

"My buddy?"

Looking as sure of himself as a matador who'd just stabbed the bull, the chief of the fire department, Charlie Reese, was giving a short statement about Riverside Drive: "I've been working closely with my fire investigation team, and we've identified the culprit in the Riverside Drive arson. As soon as we're finished tying up some loose ends, we'll make an arrest." Reese fended off all questions, then added, "I can only say we were as surprised as you will be."

His father shut off the tape and began changing channels. "What does he mean by that?"

"I couldn't tell you."

"You must have heard something on the grapevine."

Finney shrugged.

"Reese—what a little shit!" his father said. "In the old days we would have made short work of him. You been to the Downtowner. Went in there on a bed fire once. Wrapped the mattress up in a tarp, me and a guy named Coghill, an old gummer. Had a heart attack about two years ago. Halfway down the hallway the tarp came unwound, and the mattress popped out like a spring and bounced off the wall. Fire and smoke everywhere. Coghill hauled that mattress by one corner and pitched it out a window. I think we were on the fourth floor. It caught some oxygen and flamed up like a meteor on the way down, landed on Chief Ballantine's car. Coghill and I just about died laughing. Chief Ballantine. Remember him? Used to write charges on people if their boots weren't polished? He's living in Mexico now with some little señorita." His father looked at Finney and held the look for a few seconds.

Ballantine had died of brain cancer a few months after retiring. Finney wondered if his father was purposely rewriting history or he'd actually forgotten. Maybe the cancer was eating away at his brain.

On his way out, Finney's father kissed him on the cheek, a throwback to a routine he'd abandoned when Finney was three but which had become standard operating procedure since the illness. Fists like talons, his father gripped his arms and said, "John, you took a big hit. You sat on the sidelines until your head cleared, and by golly you got back in the game. I've known a lot of good men who couldn't have done as much. I'm proud of you."

"Thanks, Dad."

"You're a good man, John. You're going to make a fine officer."

"Thanks."

After his father had climbed the wooden steps to the parking lot, Finney followed a gust of cool lake air back into the living room and stared out the window at the water. His father was so small and frail these days, and so lonely. Come to think of it, so was he, lonely.

# 30. MONAHAN'S MISSUS

Finney spent the next four days in Spokane and Coeur d'Alene looking for information on Patterson Cole, searching for irregularities concerning his properties. He learned that Cole owned thousands of acres of timber and most of one small sawmill town. He owned dozens of rental houses and apartment buildings in Coeur d'Alene and Spokane; one of the apartments had burned to the ground ten years earlier, a fire that had been judged accidental. Cole had collected a tidy little sum for a building he'd been having trouble keeping full. Finney was unable to contact either of the investigators. One had retired to Wyoming and the other had died in a car accident.

When Finney returned from Eastern Washington, one of his neighbors told him the fire department had interviewed him. By now G. A. Montgomery probably knew there was an hour Finney couldn't account for the morning of the Riverside Drive fire. The only thing G. A. still needed in order to put the noose around Finney's neck was for Annie or even a passing commuter to clearly identify Finney as the suspicious character outside the house before the fire took off.

On Tuesday C-shift worked a fairly typical shift. The chief in the Seventh Battalion gave them their monthly drill. Riding Engine 26 with Finney were Lieutenant Gary Sadler and Jerry Monahan. Their drill consisted of running a preconnect with supply and taking the hose line up a ladder to the roof of the station. The chief told them they'd done a good job and left while they were repacking dry hose and flaking the wet sections on racks for the hose dryer in the station. They cleaned up and went out to do building inspections before lunch. In the afternoon they fielded two alarms. One was to a single-family home where an infant's head was wedged between the rungs of an antique crib. They lifted the squalling baby to the center and gently spread the slats with their hands. The other call was a false alarm to one of the Boeing plants off East Marginal Way.

At five-thirty Oscar Stillman showed up at the back door, squashing his face with its gap-toothed grin flat against the glass. Stillman, a born comic, worked downtown as a confidence testing officer and parked his private vehicle at Station 26 every weekday morning, leaving his department car in the lot each night. His habit was to drop in for a cup of coffee on his way home, making him an ongoing source of information for the members of Station 26. Now that he thought about it, Finney realized it was probably Stillman who gave Monahan the scoop about his not being promoted.

Wearing crumpled gray slacks and his department blazer, Oscar Stillman punched the coded lock box on the back door and sauntered into the beanery. Of average height, Stillman was in his mid-fifties, stocky, and hirsute everywhere except for his head, which was shiny on top but for a few long gray strands crossing from left to right. As always, he was as playful and friendly as a Christmas puppy.

Displaying teeth the size of baby corn, he stepped close and pumped Finney's hand furiously. His glasses looked as if they'd been designed for a woman. His voice was deep and loud and cracked. "You really got *fucked* on that promotion, man. I don't mind telling you. Nobody around here's been *fucked* quite like that in a good while. Man, did you get *fucked*."

"Thanks," Finney said, trying to extricate his hand from Stillman's tenacious grip.

"No. I really don't know what he was thinking about. It's hard to say. You know, when a guy gets that far off track . . . I want to go up there and give him a piece of my mind, even though everybody tells me he'd screw me next time he got the chance. But hell, I been screwed before and you know what?" Stillman winked. "I kind of liked it." Stillman saw the look on Gary Sadler's face and said, "Is that a little too homoerotic for you, Gary? It is, isn't it? You know what your problem is? You're scared to death of homosexuals. What you need is a big fat kiss."

Stillman glanced at the others with a fiendish smirk, then started across the room. Sadler, afraid to run for fear he'd be chased, stood his ground and fended off Stillman's grasping arms. In the end, Sadler let Oscar grab his face and give him a buss on the end of his nose.

"There's nothing in the world warms my blood faster than a man in the throes of a full homoerotic panic," Stillman said, smiling broadly and standing back to appraise a job well done.

"That wasn't panic," Sadler said.

"Hell, it wasn't."

"It wasn't!"

"Maybe I should have given you a big wet one on the lips." Sadler flew out of the room, laughter chasing him up the hallway.

Turning back to Finney, Stillman said, "Oh, man, you got fucked. I still don't understand how Charlie scarfed up all that glory and that award for accomplishing basically nothing. Does that make sense? He goes into a building on a search, he comes out empty-handed, and they give him an award? Not to mention, three months later he's sitting on the big Kahuna's throne."

Leaving the room with Jerry Monahan, Oscar winked and slapped Finney on the back. "Don't worry, buddy. You'll think of something. Every dog has his day."

A few minutes later Gary Sadler poked his head out of the officer's rest room in the hallway. "He gone?"

"Talking to Jerry on the apparatus floor," said Finney.

"Christ, he's crazy. I'll be in my office till he leaves. Let me know when it's safe to come out."

Finney was washing spinach for the salad when another visitor appeared at the back door, Linda Monahan, Jerry's wife. Finney let her in, offering her a seat and a cup of coffee, then called Jerry on the intercom to let him know she was here. Whatever else Jerry Monahan had done with his life, he'd certainly married a decent woman. They were Mormons, at least she was, and she'd presented him with five children, all boys, the youngest still at home. She'd worked through all of her pregnancies and had bailed Jerry out of financial difficulties several times during their marriage. Finney knew of three occasions in the last twenty years when, single-handed, she'd managed to save their home after Jerry went broke and the bank threatened to foreclose.

"How is it out there?" Finney asked. "Traffic bad?"

Linda Monahan was ten or eleven years older than Finney, and had dyed her hair black to complement her milky complexion. Her eyes were hazel and flitted away from his nervously at unpredictable moments as she spoke. Dressed in a plaid business suit, she was trim and tidy, sitting with her legs crossed at the ankles, her purse in her lap. "It's so dark and gray out, that's all."

"It's going to be worse next week when Daylight Saving Time ends."

"Sometimes I wish for a whole year of sunshine. If we could have one year, maybe we could coast through this gray a little easier."

"It gets to me, too."

"Arizona was sunny. That's where I met Jerry. He was on his mission. He was four years older than me, and it was love at first sight."

It was hard for Finney to imagine Jerry Monahan inspiring love at first sight. But then, he did have that ingenuous smile.

"Jerry ever get that time off he needed?"

"Time off?"

"November seventh? Your anniversary?"

"We were married April twentieth. Whatever made you think it was in November? Jerry would never get that wrong."

"I must have misunderstood. Maybe it was a birthday?"

"We don't celebrate anything in November except Thanksgiving."

Finney's memory worked erratically these days, but he could have sworn Monahan told them he needed the shift off because it was his anniversary.

After Monahan showed up and walked her out to the parking lot, Finney went down the hallway to the officer's room and peeked in at Sadler. "I was just wondering if it would cause a problem if I was off on the seventh of November."

Tucking the phone under his chin, Sadler flipped open the captain's journal. "Jerry's already got it off. His anniversary."

# 31. PATTERSON COLE

Late Monday morning, after calling Cole's office for an appointment and getting the brush-off, Finney decided an impromptu visit was in order. He bluffed his way past a series of security guards in gray blazers, stepped off the elevator on forty-two, and glimpsed Cole and another man entering an office through tall glass doors at the end of the corridor. In person, Patterson Cole was a tall but stooped man who moved with the careful and precise gait of someone making his way through a room full of marbles.

The gold embossing on the office door proclaimed that the premises belonged to COLE ENTERPRISES, LTD.

Finney entered the waiting area through the glass doors, where he hoodwinked a receptionist and then in the next room, an assistant with hennaed hair and a short black skirt. It was amazing to Finney how far a suit and tie and a manila envelope with PATTERSON COLE—PERSONAL SIGNATURE REQUIRED typed across the front could get him. So far it had been a badge of entry at each checkpoint.

He stepped into Cole's gargantuan office just as the old man changed into a pair of ankle-high slippers.

"Pardon me?" It was Cole's assistant, a dark-haired man in a bow tie and horn-rimmed glasses, and a manner about him that quickly proclaimed his superiority.

"I need to talk with Mr. Cole," Finney said.

"And you are?"

"John Finney. I'm with the Seattle Fire Department."

"I'm not aware of any appointments this morning."

"It's about the fire on Leary Way last June."

The old man's gravelly voice entertained a slight quaver. "What about the fire?"

"I have a few questions."

"If you don't have an appointment, you need to be leaving," said the aide.

"Let him alone, Norris. I've always got a minute for the fire department."

Norris remained close to Finney, and Finney had the feeling Norris was not only an aide but a de facto bodyguard, that he'd had martial arts training, perhaps at one of the corporate antiterrorist schools. He was a head shorter than Finney and soft enough to use for a pillow, but that didn't mean he wasn't dangerous.

Patterson Cole walked behind his glass desk and sat heavily in a high-backed leather chair. A brace of windows on the side wall looked out over a sunny Elliott Bay. In one corner stood a glass sculpture of a naked woman crouched to throw a discus. The room had several other sculptures on stands, all glass, all nudes.

"What can I do for the fire department, young man?"

"Did you receive any threats against that building in the past few years? Any disputes with the tenants?"

"You know of anything, Norris?"

"Nothing."

"Any problem employees?"

"Only person holds a grudge against me is Bibi, my wife." The skin under Cole's chin hung like a paper bag with an apple core in it. He had penetrating, pale blue eyes that had probably made him handsome in his youth and a shock of white hair that needed trimming around the collar.

"I'm trying to figure out who might have had a motive to burn it down."

"Your own man showed me the electrical socket. Scorched all to hell. Cut it right out of the wall and showed it to me."

"I know there was an electrical socket. But supposing that wasn't the cause of the fire? Supposing it wasn't an accident?"

Cole glanced at his assistant. "We've already collected from the insurance. You want to go back over all this? What's the point?"

"How much was it insured for?"

"Who are you?" Norris asked, stepping forward.

Cole tipped his chair back and held the arms of the chair with a steely grip. "That's a good question. Who the hell are you?"

"John Finney. I'm a Seattle—"

"Yeah, yeah, yeah," said Norris. "You said all that. You got any ID?"

Before Finney could fish for his wallet, the receptionist burst through the door. "I'm sorry to bother you, Mr. Cole, but this man slipped past me. I thought he was delivering something for the divorce, but I called your wife's attorneys and they haven't sent anything over."

"That's okay, Doris," Cole said. "You can close the door on your way out. And call security."

"I've already sent for them."

"Good girl."

Norris placed himself squarely between his boss and Finney and said, "You'd better leave now."

"A man named Bill Cordifis died in that fire. He was my partner."

"I'm sure he was," Norris said.

Cole scratched the back of one hand, his fingernails as long as a woman's, his hands mottled with age spots. "What'd you say his name was?"

"Cordifis," repeated his assistant.

"I remember. We sent a wreath. I remember the night of the fire, too. That was the night Bibi told me she was seeing that bartender."

"Apparently the dead man was this man's partner," Norris said. "I suppose he's here for some sort of settlement."

"In this state, a firefighter dies in an arson fire and whoever set it is guilty of murder," said Finney.

"The fire was an accident, boy," Patterson Cole said.

"Maybe the building wasn't generating enough revenue? Or one of your other businesses needed an infusion of cash?"

"Out," said the assistant.

"I believe it was arson, and if it wasn't somebody with a grudge, it was you."

The old man's face darkened. "You're accusing me of arson?"

"If the shoe fits . . ."

Placing the knuckles of either hand on his desk, the old man rose ponderously. "Your own people called it an accident."

"You know anything about a fire in Tacoma ten years ago? Or another one in Coeur d'Alene twelve years ago?"

"Norris?"

"I assume he's talking about the Grapested Apartments in Idaho and the mill in Tacoma. Herb Jensen ran the mill for you. Remember?"

"But that place burned down in . . . I don't know. Must have been eight years ago."

"Ten," Finney said.

"You think because my properties had fires that I had something to do with this? I own a lot of property. All kinds of things happen. I fought fire in the Wenatchee National Forest when I was a youngster. Hardest work I ever did. The city's probably a little different, but I expect from time to time you see somebody die. You lost your friend, I'm sorry. But there's not much anybody can do now. You got a college scholarship fund for his kids or something, you tell Doris on your way out and we'll put our nickels in the jar. Happy to do it. Otherwise you just scoot on outta here. I don't know what you're saying to people, but you hear this and you hear it good. You slander me and I'll slap you with a lawsuit so severe you won't have a pot to piss in or a window to throw it out of."

Before Finney could reply, the tall oak double doors opened and three men in gray blazers rushed in, each with a portable radio in his hand. Keeping their hands on his shoulders, they walked Finney to the elevator.

In the hallway two more blazers joined the group, then on forty all six of them transferred to another down car. En masse, they walked Finney down the escalators to the Fourth Avenue entrance and told him not to come back. Ever.

# 32. DEMOLITION DERBY

inney's eyes had barely become accustomed to the sunshine when he spotted Jerry Monahan trudging up the steep Seattle sidewalk.

Monahan walked past without looking up, crossed Fourth Avenue, and entered the Columbia Tower through the southwest entrance. Finney might have followed, but two of the security personnel who'd walked him out of the building were still watching from the doorway.

The Columbia Tower was the tallest building in Seattle, standing nearly two hundred feet taller than the Space Needle. Monahan might have been there to see any one of hundreds of people. There were scores of offices, a private club and a restaurant at the top, public shops and an eating area on the lowest levels, and a multilevel parking garage below the structure.

It was almost one-thirty before Monahan exited the building and walked across Fourth, passing within twenty feet of Finney, who, by this time, had his face concealed behind a newspaper. He was about to follow Monahan when Chief Reese exited the building through the same exit, crossing Cherry and proceeding south along Fourth, probably headed to Station 10 on foot.

What were the odds Monahan and Reese hadn't been together for the last two hours? It seemed obvious to Finney they'd had a meeting of some sort in the very building where Patterson Cole kept an office. It was too much of a coincidence.

Keeping a good half block behind, Finney tailed Monahan down the hill and then under the shadowy Alaskan Way Viaduct and back into the sunshine on the waterfront. Monahan had parked at Fire Station 5 on the water. Finney hailed a passing cab and had the driver wait on Alaskan Way. Moments later Monahan's vintage station wagon pulled out of the cramped parking area alongside Station 5, and Finney followed in the cab as Monahan threaded his way to a set of buildings in the flat industrial area just south of downtown. When he parked, Oscar Stillman was standing on the sidewalk nearby.

This turn of events surprised Finney more than it probably should have; Stillman and Monahan had been friends for years. The two men spoke, then jog-trotted across Airport Way in front of some truck traffic and disappeared into the parking lot of an unmarked occupancy. From the street Finney could see three large warehouse-type buildings, most of the property hidden from view by a smaller, windowless structure in front.

Finney instructed the cabbie to wait a block away while the meter ticked and then, after thirty minutes, decided to return to his parked Pathfinder. When he drove back to Airport Way, Monahan's vehicle had not moved.

From where Finney parked one could drive miles in two directions and see nothing but industrial and commercial occupancies. Fifty feet above and behind him was an elevated portion of I-5, which had punched through the city's core back in 1960 at the time of the World's Fair.

A hundred years ago this lowland had all been tide flats, but millions, if not billions, of yards of fill had been carted in to stabilize it. Even now, when heavy trucks drove past, the ground seemed to rumble disproportionately.

From past experience Finney knew the woods sloping up from underneath the freeway harbored encampments of homeless men. Years ago, when G. A. Montgomery was working on Engine 10, G. A. had ordered his crew to wash out an encampment with hose lines after the occupants squabbled with him about dousing their campfire. Young, inexperienced, intimidated by G. A., his crew hosed down everything in sight—sleeping bags, tents, books, clothing. It had been the middle of winter. Finney knew he was only thinking up more excuses to hate G. A., but he didn't have to work hard. Plenty of people hated him.

As the afternoon wore on, workers left the complex in waves. Stillman left at five, and minutes later Monahan rushed out, patted down his pockets for his keys, and drove off in a haze of exhaust. Except for a couple of outside lights in the parking area, the buildings were dark.

When he thought enough time had elapsed, Finney walked across the street.

Behind the first tall, white, windowless building he found a large parking area where three vans marked MAKADO BROTHERS and a couple of dust-covered private vehicles sat.

He went back to his Pathfinder, fired up the engine, got the heater working, warmed himself, and drove around the block. It was a huge industrial block, almost half a mile in circumference, and by the time he got back to the front of the property, he was discouraged. Somebody was trying to put him in prison, and so far the only thing he knew was that Monahan had lied about the dangerous buildings list and about November 7. Yet he could be lying for all sorts of reasons. To cover up his own incompetence—maybe even to keep secret a surprise party for his wife.

Finney was back on Airport Way heading north when he saw a flash of winking red in his rearview mirror. He pulled to the side of the road and found an engine company closing in on him.

As he pulled to the curb, Finney looked in his mirror and realized the engine was in danger of sideswiping his truck.

He pulled his wheels onto the sidewalk, thinking if he didn't move, he'd get hit. It happened too quickly to think of much else.

The Pathfinder rocked wildly as the sound of metal on metal screeched in his ears. It was incredibly loud and seemed to play out in slow motion. His window dematerialized, and then it was in pieces in his lap. There was a second metallic scraping and then a loud crash. The engine had grazed the side of his vehicle. Was the driver drunk? Having a heart attack?

When his vehicle stopped rocking, Finney found his driver's-side door jammed. Shaking the glass off his lap, he climbed over the stick shift and out the passenger door. His face felt wet, but he was relieved to find sweat and not blood when he touched it. What the hell was going on?

Up the street he could hear the blatting of the Jake brake; fire vehicles were the only diesel trucks allowed to use compression brakes within the city limits. They worked off the engine and made a loud coughing sound when the driver eased off the accelerator.

It had all happened so quickly.

As he thought it through, he realized the driver might have felt Finney wasn't moving over properly and decided to teach him a lesson by coming close, then had misjudged. He knew how frustrating it could be to drive an emergency vehicle through city traffic. Few people actually obeyed the law and moved over. They ignored you. Or stepped on the gas trying to race you. They braked in the middle of the street. They stopped in the fast lane next to traffic that had already stopped in the slow lane, blocking the entire street. All sorts of stupid things.

As Finney inspected the damage to his vehicle, the engine turned around in the middle of the block.

The officer was probably on the radio right now calling for the safety officer, Battalion 1, and the police, informing the dispatcher that somebody else would have to handle the alarm they'd been on. Now the engine was facing him.

Finney began moving an instant after the driver floored the accelerator. The *exhilarator*, Captain Cordifis had jokingly called it.

Finney dove through the open passenger door, turned the key in the ignition, and pulled the Pathfinder forward so fast his tires smoked and the passenger door slammed shut with the movement.

Gusts of black diesel smoke thundered out the tailpipe as the engine accelerated toward him. His stomach was doing flip-flops. This guy was trying to kill him.

Finney steered for the concealment of a pillar, but the left wheels of his Pathfinder refused to negotiate the curb.

The engine had no such trouble; it bumped up over the curb and ran for fifty yards with two wheels on the sidewalk. For a moment they were on a collision course, and then Finney wrenched the wheel and the engine only nipped the left rear quarter panel of the Pathfinder. The jolt turned the Pathfinder counterclockwise so that it spun off the sidewalk and ended up in the street facing the direction the engine had come from.

The air horn on the engine had blown at the moment of impact; Finney's ears were ringing.

He watched the fire engine swing around in a lazy circle down the street. Try as he might, he could see no crew, no officer—nothing more than a silhouette in the driver's seat. This was crazy. In all his years in the department he'd never heard of an engine driver going berserk like this.

When he put the Pathfinder into reverse, the vehicle stalled. His front bumper was crumpled against one or both tires. He pushed down on the accelerator, and the Pathfinder made more noise and rocked and then settled back where it had been. Cold air blew in through the broken window onto his sweaty face. He couldn't back up. He couldn't drive forward.

And the maniac in the engine was coming back. Finney began to panic.

Like a man trying to rock his truck out of a snowy ditch, he shifted the transmission into first, gave it gas, slipped it into reverse, gave it gas. The fire engine began picking up speed, the wigwag headlights bearing down on him.

Once again, he shifted into first. Then reverse, where he felt something disengage. Suddenly he was racing backward across the street in a semicircle.

The engine swerved to react to his maneuver but caught only a part of the front fender. The crash shook Finney like a rag doll. The noise was horrendous, as if he were inside a garbage can being rolled downhill.

Five minutes later the first police cruiser arrived.

The officer's hair was chopped short and dyed beet red, and she approached Finney with a curious look in her dark brown eyes. "You got a story?" she asked, taking in Finney's Pathfinder. The engine had long since disappeared. Finney tried to make sense of it as he explained what had happened, but there was no sense to it.

"A fire engine?" she asked. "You sure?"

"I know what they look like."

The officer, who didn't like his sarcasm, took his license, radioed her superior, and ran Finney's plate. A few minutes later the sergeant on watch showed up and gave him a sobriety test.

After evaluating the scene for a few minutes, the sergeant spoke to the first arriving officer, whose name tag identified her as D. M. MANSON. "You call the fire department?"

"Yeah. No reported accidents."

"It was a Seattle Fire Department engine," Finney said. "It had the decals on the doors."

"You know which one?" Officer Manson asked.

"I didn't catch the unit number."

The two police officers made Finney feel as if he were standing in high-water pants with mismatched socks and flecks of a chicken TV dinner in his teeth. Clearly, they thought his story was fishy. They gave him a case number and told him to call later in the week.

"You're not going to check fire stations?"

The sergeant looked at Finney. "No point in making work. If the department had an accident tonight, we'll hear about it."

# 33. AIR 26

When Finney arrived at work the next morning and learned Hank Jovi was taking the shift off on dependent care disability, he quickly volunteered for Jovi's slot on the air rig. There were certain advantages to driving the air rig, advantages he could put to good use on this particular day. For one, he was exempt from Engine 26's alarms and had freedom of movement between stations. However, he would be responsible for routine delivery of air bottles to stations around the city and would be called to any fire where replacement air bottles were needed.

Finney had tossed and turned all night after the accident. But then, it was no accident. Even if the first pass had been accidental, the second and third charges had been deliberate. In order to avoid hours of scrawling out accident reports, a cagey driver might touch up a scratch on the rig with cardinal red or buff it out with automobile polish, but that only worked with minor scrapes. Last night's rig had to have some serious damage. If it was a fire department rig, somebody would know about it, and Finney aimed to find out who.

One possibility he was considering was that maybe one of the mechanics from the Charles Street shop, which was only blocks from the accident site, drank a few beers while working late and decided to go for a test drive. He wondered if it was possible one of the outlying fire departments had a unit that looked like Seattle's, although, unlike Seattle's traditional red, most of the outlying districts used lime-yellow paint schemes so they would be more conspicuous.

Finney couldn't decide if the hours he'd spent on Airport Way had anything to do with the attack or if the timing and location had been coincidental.

He'd telephoned the police that morning, but they didn't have any news. He called the Safety Chief, Stephanie Alexis, a cheerful, good-natured woman with forceful, often controversial opinions on how the fire department should be run, but Chief Alexis reported no vehicular accidents for yesterday's shift.

As much as he was plagued by Leary Way and puzzled by Riverside Drive, last night's attack bewildered him even further. More than bewildered—he was pissed. Some damned fool had tried to kill him. He couldn't believe how angry he was. Maybe he should have been this angry last night. Ever since Leary Way, things had taken longer to sink in, all things, as if his emotions had a blanket around them.

As soon as the housework was finished, Finney drove the air rig to Station 14. In back of the station he could hear the recruits in the current drill school hard at work, the shouting of orders, heavy-duty aluminum ladders rattling, the calflike bellowing of the prime pump on an engine. A bellowing again as some luckless recruit fought to get it right on his second attempt.

Fourteen's was a Spanish-style building with towers, a tile roof, and stucco walls. Its look hadn't changed much from the mid-thirties or from 1962 when Finney's father had been stationed there as a firefighter. The department's training division shared cramped space both upstairs and down with the living quarters for the crew of Ladder 7 and Aid 14. Years ago Engine 14 had been housed there, too, but it had been decommissioned long before Finney signed on. His father used to talk about how the drivers on Engine 14, nicotine and caffeine addicts to a man, would race to alarms full tilt over the railroad tracks a few blocks from the station and how, if they weren't braced for it, the men on the tailboard would be launched into the air, along with all the hose in the hose bed. More than one tailboard man had lashed his wrist to the rail.

During the twelve-week drill schools, training division commandeered the classroom at the northeast corner of the building as well as the mostly empty parking lot and seven-story training tower behind the station. About once a year recruits dropped a ladder on one of the parked cars belonging to a Station 14 crew member.

In Ladder 7's beanery they proudly displayed a photograph of one of the station's high-angle rescue team members sliding down a line tethered to the Space Needle, a photo that never failed to impress visitors.

Parking the air rig in front, Finney went inside and approached the building inspection file cabinets near the front doors. While two firefighters on a tall stepladder applied metal polish to the brass pole at the other end of the hallway, a female firefighter named Hedges began swabbing the floor around his feet.

"Whatcha doin'?" she asked, slowly painting him into a corner with her mop.

"Just looking up a phone number," Finney replied, ignoring her prank.

Every fire station in the city performed building inspections in its specified district. Meticulous records of each occupancy were kept, along with the disposition of each year's inspections and fire code violations, if any. Some of the records went back thirty or forty years. Included in the folders were the names, addresses, and phone numbers of the occupancies, as well as information about the owners. Using the map on the wall above the cabinets, Finney located the block number for the occupancy on Airport Way where Monahan and Stillman had met yesterday afternoon.

He pulled a thick folder out of the drawer and opened it on top of the cabinet. The occupancy name was MAKADO BROTHERS. Curiously, the last fire department inspection of the building had been done by Lieutenant Balitnikoff. Balitnikoff had not written up any violations, although the previous five inspectors had all penned Notices of Violation for various transgressions: extinguishers not tagged, fire doors propped open, cluttered aisles, illegal and improper use of extension cords.

Finney found it odd that Balitnikoff had inspected the building, but when he unfolded the small work schedule card from his wallet he found the day in question was listed as C-7, Balitnikoff's debit shift number. Firefighters worked seven debit shifts in addition to their regular schedules each year, approximately one every seven weeks, and most were worked outside the firefighter's normal station.

He flipped the file card and found the building was owned by Patterson Cole—not all that strange, since the octogenarian probably held the deeds to more property in Seattle than any other individual. It was with that thought that Finney riffled through the files and found two more occupancies on Airport Way owned by Cole, one of which, directly behind the Makado Brothers but addressed off Eighth Avenue South, had been listed as vacant three months ago.

After jotting down the pertinent information, Finney put the files away and was on his way out of the watch office when Lieutenant Balitnikoff and Michael Lazenby sauntered in. Outside, the tailboard of Engine 10 was butted up against the north stall door, facing the street for a quick getaway in case they received an alarm.

"Speak of the devil," shouted Balitnikoff, exuberantly. "We were just talking about you."

"Sure as hell were," said Paul Lazenby, pushing through the doorway behind his brother, Michael, who'd halted in his tracks. A fourth firefighter who didn't normally work on Engine 10 shouldered his way through the group and headed for the back of the station.

"Heard you had some magic mushrooms for dinner," Lieutenant Balitnikoff said.

"Extra special magic mushrooms," said Paul, smirking.

When Finney said nothing, Michael offered an explanation. "Thompson on D-shift is dating that cop. The little spinner? She told Thompson you claim you got run off the road."

Paul Lazenby and Balitnikoff burst into laughter. Michael, the only one of the three wearing his foul-weather coat, put his hands in his pockets and bit the inside of his cheek.

"What happened?" asked Paul. "You crash into a garbage truck and think it was your old rig?" All three of them laughed again.

Balitnikoff said, "You sure a deer didn't jump out in front of you on the way home from the bar?"

"Maybe you got hit by a beer truck," Paul said.

"Screw you," Finney said.

"Hey, you were off duty, man," Paul said, his voice growing more sympathetic. "Oh, wait a minute. You quit drinkin', didn't ya?"

Finney opened the door.

"No, wait, you guys," said Michael. "I want to hear this."

"Fuck all of you," Finney said, walking outside.

Michael followed him, zipping up his coat. "I don't know why they ride you like that."

"Because they're assholes?"

Michael chuckled. "Their main problem is they don't know when to quit."

Finney appraised Michael Lazenby for a moment. Though he didn't give a rat's ass for his older brother, Paul, he rather liked Michael, who had a boyish smile and a shock of blond hair that always looked as if it had just been rumpled. He seemed to take life as it came, while Paul tried to twist and force every circumstance to suit him. Both brothers were narcissists to the core, obsessed with building muscles and chasing women, but somehow Michael managed to make it seem like an amusing quirk, where it was just obnoxious in Paul.

"That wasn't a bogus rumor we heard?"

"Somebody tried to run me down."

"In a fire engine? For real?"

"That's right."

"Hey, if you find him and want somebody to help beat the crap out of him, I'm your man. People start using fire rigs for that sort of bullshit and we'll all get a bad name."

"Thanks, but that's not going to happen."

"Keep me on the shortlist if you change your mind. I always like to get in on a good beating."

"Will do."

# 34. HAZARDS OF THE PROFESSION

Diana and Blanchett had been working the chain saws for almost two hours, cutting through the heavy car-deck planking of the vacant pier until they'd uncovered the smoldering creosote-covered pilings where somebody, probably a lost tourist, had tossed a cigarette stub. They sawed and dug, stacking the heavy planks to one side after soaking the burned areas with a pressurized pump can. Ladder 1 and Aid 5 were the only units still on scene.

It was a three-story warehouse, longer than a football field and empty, just tin walls, a roof, and the pier below, some of which was paved and some not. Several weary firefighters sat on piles of car decking they'd torn out.

Before they were finished, Robert Kub arrived and, after inspecting the hole, removed himself from the immediate vicinity of the chain saws and lit a cigarette. A few minutes after Captain Moseby rotated personnel in the hole, Diana found Kub standing outside on the pier squinting listlessly into a southerly breeze.

"How you doin'?" Kub asked.

"I'm hot and I'm tired." Diana laughed.

"Now watch me throw this stub down here and start another fire." He snickered at the thought. "That'd be just like me."

"Robert, have you been in touch with Finney?"

"John? I've seen him."

"Is he all right?"

Kub exhaled loudly. "If you mean is he all right health-wise, he looks like shit. But if you mean is his life going okay, that's pretty much shit, too." Kub snickered again.

"The way Reese turned him down was crappy."

"Reese needs a new head."

"There's a rumor going around that G. A.'s after him for starting that fire where he brought out the homeless woman. Is that true?"

"It's true all right."

"That's so ridiculous."

"Until you start examining the evidence." Kub inhaled on his cigarette and peered up at the overcast sky.

Diana took off her heavy bunking coat and let the breeze cool her sweat-soaked SFD T-shirt. "What evidence?"

"I wish I could talk about it, but I can't."

"Any chance he actually had anything to do with it?"

Kub watched a quintet of gulls riding an air current thirty feet away. "I'll tell you this. When it looks like a duck, walks like a duck, and quacks like a duck . . . We came in together, me and John."

Kub withdrew a crumpled packet of Camels from his windbreaker pocket and, cupping his hands, set about the ritual of igniting another cigarette. In Elliott Bay a ferry steamed toward the dock from Bremerton. They watched in silence, while behind them the racket from a chain saw reverberated inside the tin-walled warehouse. The air smelled of cigarette smoke, salt water, sawdust, and from somewhere among the tourist shops on Alaskan Way, cotton candy.

"Does he seem different to you?" Diana asked.

"You mean after Leary Way?"

"He used to be so . . . I don't know . . ."

"Confident?"

"That's it."

"Yeah, well, one way or another, it'll work itself out."

"I wish I were that optimistic."

"You ever notice when a guy goes nuts—I'm not saying *he's* nuts—I was just thinking about this . . . you ever notice when a guy goes nuts, he's always the center of the universe? He's always the only one who can get the secret formula to the president on time. Ever notice?"

Whatever Kub was trying to say, it didn't make sense. "John's not nuts," Diana said.

# 35. THE KNOX BOX KEY

lthough nobody had made any requests, at 2100 hours Finney told Lieutenant Sadler he was taking Air 26 out to deliver bottles.

Sadler and Brinkley were draped in recliners watching a prizefight on cable television, Sadler making sniggering comments about the blond in the bathing suit who circled the ring between rounds holding up a sign. Jerry Monahan was half-asleep in the empty office near the front door, a book in his lap titled *Bear Attacks: Their Causes and Avoidance*. Finney still found it hard to believe he was involved in anything as sinister as arson. But then it was also hard to believe Monahan was a firefighter. Or that he'd made and lost several millions of dollars. Or that he'd been a semipro football player.

Finney picked up his hooded foul-weather jacket and went out onto the dark apparatus floor, where he stepped up onto the officer's side of Engine 26, opened the door, and reached across to an orange light on the dash. He unscrewed the plastic lens cap and disengaged the bulb so that when the current was tripped it wouldn't light up, then replaced the cap. He lifted the spring-loaded lid on the small metal box that he'd always thought would make a good rodent casket, removed the most valuable key any department rig carried, and closed the lid. With the dashlight disengaged, no one would be the wiser.

He was taking a calculated risk that Engine 26 wouldn't receive an alarm while he was gone, and if they did, that neither Monahan nor Sadler would notice the disabled light or the missing key. Probably because it had never happened, the department had not concerned itself with people stealing Knox box keys. The administration assumed that most people didn't know what a Knox box key was and wouldn't know where to find one if they did.

A Knox box was a small metal security box holding a building key, which could be installed by a property owner usually on a wall near the front door. Once sealed, a Knox box couldn't be accessed by the property owners or even the police—only the fire department. The department's assurance to property owners was to use Knox boxes only when lives or property was threatened, allowing emergency access without costly damage to expensive doors and windows.

Finney drove Air 26 to Airport Way past the Makado Brothers buildings and around the block to Eighth Avenue South. The buildings were dark. Below the freeway on Airport Way there was almost no traffic.

It was doubtful there was any kind of night watchman, but he pressed the doorbell twice anyway. When he'd waited long enough, he opened the Knox box with the stolen master key, removed the property owner's key, and unlocked the front door. Then he replaced the building key in the Knox box.

Uncertain what he was looking for, he followed the small cone of light from his flashlight through the offices and down the causeway into a warehouse. Fifteen minutes later he was back in the truck, no wiser than when he'd gone in.

The first warehouse area had contained rows of shelves, thousands of small boxes stacked on them. A smaller building was filled with various machining tools. He'd found three Rolodexes in the office area, but none of the names meant anything to him. Could it be that Stillman and Reese were investors, and this company was being solicited to put Monahan's high-rise rescue contraption into production?

The wreck last night, the frame-up, Leary Way, Monahan's peculiar actions the past few days—all of it had the feel of a jigsaw puzzle he'd been asked to assemble blindfolded.

As he considered the possibilities, his gaze wandered across Eighth Avenue toward an enormous lot with two large, interconnected buildings, the only other piece of property Patterson Cole owned in the surrounding area. There were no lights, just an empty parking lot and a lone Dumpster. Finney knew from the inspection cards these buildings were vacant.

In the distance a disposal truck worked its way up Eighth Avenue. Finney watched as it stopped at various occupancies, the clatter of falling glass, metal, and rubbish clashing in the night. The driver emptied the Dumpster across the street, rounded the corner, and disappeared without seeming to notice Finney. It occurred to Finney that if the buildings across the street were vacant, the Dumpster should have been empty.

Finney found the building key inside the Knox box bolted to the concrete wall near the front door. Moments later he was exploring the office areas, all empty except for a broken desk and a chair shoved into a corner.

The bathroom smelled as if it hadn't been aired out in months. When he opened a third door, the light from his flashlight was dwarfed by an immense warehouse, vacant except for a workbench and a tall, portable screen in the far corner.

As he approached the workbench, he sniffed the odor of fresh paint and lacquer thinner. The screen was twelve feet high, thirty-five feet long. On the near side stood a red, cabinet-style tool box, open and promiscuous with tools.

On the other side of the screen he was both shocked and relieved to find a fire engine—large, red, damaged, and presumably the one that had run him down the previous night. "Damn," he said.

He circled the vehicle slowly and saw where they'd already patched the fender, sanded and buffed it in preparation for the red spray cans of enamel lined up on the floor on newspapers.

Across the grille were large red numerals: E-10.

Twice he circled the vehicle looking for any subtle detail that would convince him this wasn't an official Seattle Fire Department apparatus. It had decals on the doors, a map book in the cab, and every other piece of equipment one would expect to find on a Seattle rig. Yet he'd seen Engine 10 only hours earlier while making his air deliveries; it hadn't had any front-end damage.

This was a clone.

He climbed up into the high driver's seat, trying to figure out what it meant.

The glove box contained an elevator key and an air gauge, assorted paper clips, a couple of ink pens with teeth marks, and ear plugs in their cardboard envelopes. He found official fire department Notice of Violation forms and Form 20Bs for aid runs, one of which was arranged on a standard brown SFD clipboard the way it would be in a working rig—ready and waiting for the next patient. The radio bracket on the officer's door held a portable radio, and when he turned it on and switched it to channel four, he heard fire department dispatchers sending Engine 39 on a call. There was a prefire book for the Columbia Tower along with a standard department map book of the city, marred by smudges and thumbprints, as if it had been in use for years.

This was the rig that ran him down last night.

He wondered how he was going to report this to the police without getting arrested for breaking and entering. The only windows in this part of the building were thirty feet off the ground, so he couldn't say he'd seen it through the window.

He was pawing through the drawers of the tool box when his pager went off, a full response to Eighteen Avenue Northeast, a residential neighborhood just a few blocks north of the University of Washington.

"Air Twenty-six responding," Finney said, after the dispatcher asked for confirmation.

The first unit was already on scene, reporting heavy smoke from the basement of a two-story house. The fire had started in the kitchen in a basement apartment and spread through heating vents. Nobody was hurt, but they lost most of the basement, along with several rooms on the first floor.

Ninety minutes later, when he was released from the scene, Finney drove Air 26 to Robert Kub's house on South Ferdinand Street. A shiny black BMW with custom wheels stood in the driveway next to a battered gray Ford Tempo. Finney didn't recognize the Ford, but the BMW was Kub's.

# 36. OH, IT'S GOOD ALL RIGHT

"This damn well better be good," Kub said, as he climbed into Air 26. "Trust me."

He had no hypothesis, just the splash of excitement that told him he was on the fringe of something big. The phony engine must have cost a couple of hundred thousand dollars, to think nothing of the incalculable trouble somebody had gone to in replicating Engine 10 down to the last detail.

"Drag me outta my home, away from a woman I been thinking about for two years. Sweet Jesus. She better be there when I get back. Lavernia. You see her?"

"This is important."

"At least tell me where we're going."

"Just down the hill here. I'll have you back in twenty minutes."

"Before she gained some of that weight, Lavernia was in *Jet* magazine. I got close to poking her once, but she started thinking about the Lord and feeling guilty. This'll probably be just enough time to get her feeling guilty again. You probably read about her husband. A Baptist minister, one of those righteous political activists who keeps Jesus in his back pocket." Kub smiled, his teeth gleaming in the light from the dash. "Know what's going on tonight? She caught him playing around. Guess what I am. The revenge fuck."

"I'm going to need advice. This place I'm taking you to . . ."

"I get back and she's gone, I'm going to be pissed. I never been a revenge fuck before."

"I know," Finney said, stopping on Eighth Avenue.

It was almost midnight and cold. Finney went through the ritual with the Knox box while Kub watched. "Come on, Robert." Finney pushed the front door open with his fingertips.

"Not unless you own this place."

"I hear an alarm. Let's go investigate."

"There's no alarm. No way."

"We're on a street that probably won't see another vehicle until seven in the morning. There's something in here you have to see to believe."

"What?"

"Like I said, you have to see it." Clad in slacks, a dress shirt he'd hastily buttoned, loafers, and no socks, Kub was shivering. He glanced up the vacant street in both directions.

"What the hell!" He hopped up the four concrete steps and followed Finney inside and across the expanse of unlit, empty warehouse floor to the portable screen. "This better be good," he said, cantering along several paces behind the beam from Finney's flashlight.

"Voilà!" Finney said, stepping around the tall screen and raising his light.

Kub poked his head around. "What?"

They were gone—the engine, the newspapers, the tool chest, even the paint cans. Finney had been away only two hours.

"Okay, John. Quit dickin' around."

"It was here."

"What the hell you talkin' about?"

"They must know I found it. That's the only explanation. Come on. Let's talk outside."

"Not until you tell me what we're supposed to be looking at."

"It was a mock-up of Engine Ten."

"Say what?"

"A perfect replica of Engine Ten. Exact right down to the greasy rag under the driver's seat."

"You're talking 'bout a plastic model?"

"Full size."

"Out of cardboard, or something?"

"Steel and Fiberglas. You wouldn't have known it wasn't Engine Ten."

"You kidding me?"

"Last night about half a mile from here an engine ran me off Airport Way and almost killed me. Tonight I found it right there."

"So where is it?" When Finney didn't reply, Kub said, "I don't know which is worse, what you're telling me you thought you saw, or the fact that you're telling me you thought you saw it."

"It was here. I swear."

"Maybe they're out on an alarm."

"Not funny."

Kub's laugh echoed off the walls in the empty warehouse. "I think it's hilarious. But let's assume you saw it. It was probably some rich collector building a model so he can drive around in parades. God knows there're enough firefighter freaks out there, and now with all these Microsoft millionaires running around . . ."

"I don't believe that."

"Maybe the building has a silent alarm," Kub said.

"All I saw when I came in was the fire panel."

"The best burglar systems, you don't see them."

At the front entrance, Finney turned off his flashlight and peeked out through the tall, narrow window alongside the door. They stepped outside and Finney pulled the door shut just as a brilliant light swept across the wall next to him. "You guys need help?"

"SPD," Kub whispered. "Shit fuck shit! I can't believe I let you talk me into this."

Finney couldn't see a squad car or the woman speaking or anything else except the light.

Traditionally the police and fire department in Seattle were amicable. Cops came into fire stations to use the telephones or the rest room, to write reports, and to bullshit, and if a traffic cop pulled over a firefighter for speeding, more often than not the firefighter was let off with only a warning. Until thirty years ago their unions had even negotiated city contracts together.

"I'm commissioned," Kub said. "Marshal Five."

"Hands on the wall. Step back."

"I'm commissioned," Kub protested.

"You heard me."

They were frisked by two uniformed police officers, one male, one female. Though he couldn't see much of her in the glare of the spotlight, Finney recognized the voice of the redhead who'd taken his accident report the night before. Kub knew them both.

"What's going on, Robert?" the woman asked.

"We were out driving when we heard an alarm. Thought we'd investigate before the dispatchers sent out a full response."

The male police officer said, "Monitoring company said somebody was on the premises."

The female stepped to the front door while the second police officer kept his eye on them. The officer cupped her eyes against the dark window and tried the door handle. "Okay," she said, turning around. "You two be careful. Some officers would get real jumpy seeing two guys in the dark like that." She looked at Finney closely. "Ever find your fire truck?"

"Nobody reported an accident."

A minute later when they were alone, Kub said, "Fuck you and the horse you rode in on. They got here two seconds sooner and we'd be in their backseat sitting on our hands. I would have lost my job."

"Sorry, Robert."

"Turn on the damn heat."

After they'd driven a mile, Kub said, "You really saw an engine?"

"I know how weird it sounds."

"Do you? Somehow I don't think you do. Goddamn! Lavernia better be there."

The Ford Tempo was still in the driveway when they got back to Kub's house. Finney said, "Do me a favor?"

"What now?"

"That night at Leary Way when we bumped into each other?"

"Not this."

"I was changing my bottle. You were on the other side of the rig. Bill was over there talking to Stillman."

"I don't remember what they were talking about. Whatever it was, it was just talk. Bill went into the building and the next time I saw him he was dead."

Loud music drifted from the front door as Kub disappeared inside.

# 37. WE HAD THE BASTARDS FALLING OUT OF THE SKY ON US

Still clad in his department T-shirt and uniform trousers, Finney circled Engine 10 until he was certain it was the original, then reached into the rear wheel well on the officer's side and used the tip of his Buck knife to nick his initials into the thick red paint above the duals. It wouldn't be visible without squatting and then probably not without a flashlight, but he would be able to feel it anytime he wanted.

"What the hell do you think you're doing?" Paul Lazenby asked, his voice a low growl. Sheathing the knife, Finney wondered how long Lazenby had been watching.

Lazenby's thick hair was mussed, his face puffy. He wore a sleeveless T-shirt with an SFD logo across the chest, the veins in his forearms and biceps as prominent as the noodling on his neck.

Diana appeared behind Paul, her chestnut hair plaited and trailing down the center of her back. Paul gave her a sour look and left.

"He seems a little on edge," Finney said.

"The fire this morning didn't go well for them." It had been in a small, two-story office building located in a strip mall. Someone left a coffeepot on all night, and it caught the wall on fire and then spread to an attic space. Finney was there on Air 26, but he hadn't spoken to anybody. "Michael made a mess of the hose at the front door, and when Paul charged it, it turned into a giant knot. Engine Thirteen marched right past them and tapped the fire. They were all whooping it up."

"That's what Paul and Michael do when they take a fire away from Thirteen's."

"They don't like it so well when the shoe's on the other foot. Paul's furious at Michael for messing up the hose, and Michael blames Paul for charging it before he was ready. Balitnikoff says they're going to drill all next shift."

"What'd you guys do?"

"Put up a twenty-five and opened the roof. Haven't done that in a while. Baxter and I cut the hole, and then Ladder Three shows up and cuts another one right next to ours, upwind. We were all wearing masks, but if there'd been any heat coming out, it would have been an ugly situation."

"Why'd they cut a second hole?"

"I don't know. In the beginning I thought they were racing us. They got off their rig and ran to the building. None of them had anything in their hands."

"Violates one of the first rules of truck work. Never go to the building empty-handed."

"When they tried to use our stuff, we told them to go get their own."

"Second rule of truck work. Never give up equipment to another crew."

She thought about it for a moment. "Used to be, every fire the truck went to the roof. Now we're using those fans about eighty percent of the time. I kind of miss it. Going to the roof was part of the adventure."

"I'd give anything to be back on a truck."

"There'll be a spot on Ladder One soon. Baxter's going to retire this year. Now that his divorce is final, he wants to go back to Tennessee."

Finney knew that even if Reese didn't block a transfer, he could never work at Station 10 again. The memories were too painful and always would be. It was ironic that Reese, who had never much cared for the physical act of firefighting, would endeavor to punish Finney, who loved it so much, by placing as much distance as possible between him and any real chance to fight fire.

Before they could say anything else, Paul Lazenby came around the front of the rig again, opened the cab door, and began swabbing out the floorboards with a damp rag. It was clear that the floorboards didn't need swabbing.

A moment later Michael Lazenby sauntered around the front of the rig with a dirty pike pole and behind him, Lieutenant Balitnikoff. "What the hell are you doing?" Balitnikoff asked, when he saw Finney.

"Came for the station tour. You out of coloring books?"

Balitnikoff glanced from Diana to Finney and back again, as if seeing the two of them together confirmed some pet theory of his. "Well, why don't you just take your *tour* somewhere else?"

"Ease up," said Diana.

"Ease up? What the hell does that mean? Ease up. Jesus!"

"Hey," Finney said. "You guys are tired. Go home and kick your dog. Leave her alone."

"You think you're hot shit because you saved some old dame? Both of you? Is that what you think?"

"Come on," Michael Lazenby said, stepping close behind his officer and placing a hand on his thick shoulder. "John's right. Let's go home and get some sleep."

"Bill and me were eating smoke before you were out of fuckin' diapers, either one of you," Balitnikoff said. "Hell, at the Ozark we had the bastards falling out of the sky on us. Back in them days we fought more fire in a year than you'll see in your lifetime. Bill was a good man. He was a friend of mine."

"He was a friend of mine, too," Finney said.

"Then why did you let him cook?"

"Come on," Diana said, tugging on Finney's arm. "Let's go."

"If you'd been a real firefighter, you mighta had the balls to drag Bill out of that room instead of just crawling off to safety and saving your own ass."

The five of them lapsed into silence. Even Balitnikoff seemed in wonder at what he'd said, the words that until now nobody had dared utter, the words Finney knew were on everyone's mind, just as he also knew that by noon Balitnikoff's outburst would be quoted and discussed and dissected in every station in the city.

Finney was so angry he couldn't breathe. It was ironic that Marion Balitnikoff of all people would be the one to say it, because he'd once rescued Balitnikoff, though the wily old bastard would never admit it. If it hadn't been for Diana's gentle tug on his arm, he probably would have taken a swing at Balitnikoff.

"That was uncalled for," Diana said. "You don't know what happened in there."

"Nobody knows," Michael said. "Come on, lieut. Nobody knows. Lay off, will ya? Bill was your friend, sure, but the fire killed him. Come on. It coulda happened to any of us. You know that. Lay off."

Balitnikoff stalked off.

Michael Lazenby said, "We had a long night."

"No, he was right," Paul Lazenby said. "What sickens me about the whole thing is this dude comes out and pretends he can't remember."

"What's wrong with you guys?" Diana asked, tugging Finney to the rear of the apparatus floor.

As they left, Paul muttered under his breath, "Can't understand normal thinking."

Diana walked over to the workbench with the service axe she'd been carrying, sprayed the gummed-up blade with WD-40, and began scrubbing nubs of tar off the metal.

"What was that last?" Finney asked.

"It's an acronym."

"Christ. That sorry bastard."

"Don't worry about him. Being a jerk is its own reward."

It wasn't Balitnikoff's diatribe that had stung so much as it was the self-assured look on Paul's face as he'd watched Finney's reaction. He hadn't been there to clean Engine 10's floorboards. He'd gotten wind that Balitnikoff was going to tee off on him and had shown up for a ringside seat.

Finney took a few deep breaths and watched Diana polish the axe. "Engine Ten lose a map book recently?"

"I know they have a new one. They get beat up. You know how that goes."

"What about a prefire book?" There had been only one oddball item on the mock Engine 10, a prefire book for the Columbia Tower.

"You know they don't carry prefire books on board."

"I thought maybe the station captains had changed the policy for the Columbia Tower."

"No, we still keep that in the watch office," Diana said. After a few moments, she continued, "All ready for tonight?" It took a few moments for Finney to realize what she was talking about. This was the thirty-first of October, Halloween. The costume party. "You can't come?"

"No, my truck. I was in an accident. I don't have anything to drive. I mean . . ."

"I'll pick you up. A little before seven?"

"I'll be ready."

They both knew he'd forgotten all about it. Her gray eyes registered disappointment for a fraction of a second, but she was nice enough not to mention it.

# 38. THE CAT IN THE HAT

Finney's day had been more tawdry than a two-dollar toupee, and although at first he'd regretted accepting Diana's invitation, he found himself looking forward to the party as the day wore on.

Paddling off across the lake in the morning sunshine, he realized he'd become the houseboat equivalent of poor white trash, the neighbors dubious and gossiping as to when his remodel would be finished. It was hard to believe he'd drifted into this bog of neglect and procrastination, his days encompassed by one snafu after another, an endless mind-robbing syndrome of doubt and worry. He recognized in himself something he'd seen in the street people he assisted on the job: the beginning of a downward-sloping path toward the fringes of mental illness, toward total loss of self; and there wasn't a damn thing he could do about it.

He paddled his kayak along the periphery of the lake and performed a series of sprints, trying to burn off his anger. Between efforts he basked in the sunlight glinting off the choppy water. He couldn't help replaying Balitnikoff's words. For months he'd lived in dread of an accusation like that, yet, amazingly, at the crucial juncture, he'd found himself unable to respond. Bobbing along in the lake, a thousand snappy comebacks sprang to mind, pencil-sharp rejoinders that had eluded him on the apparatus floor. Diana had been supportive and appropriately silent afterward, which somehow helped staunch his venom.

He couldn't help thinking his ex-wife, Laura, never would have defended him the way Diana had. In his late twenties Finney had fallen in love with and married a woman several years his junior who, over the course of three years of matrimony, slowly dressed herself in the notion that she was born to be a citizen of the world, that life in Seattle was too restrictive and parochial, that her spirit needed the nourishment of travel, the taste of life in Europe or Russia, where she would write a novel or pen poetry or even compose music—although she'd never shown any inclination to write and everyone knew she had a tin ear.

Nothing he said dissuaded her, and after their divorce she made various sojourns abroad, eventually settling in Sweden. To date she'd penned six unpublished novels, sending each to him for his evaluation. Though he tried to be encouraging, they were uniformly horrid. She was living with a widowed proctologist who had six children, and she claimed she'd never been happier.

Late that afternoon Finney tried to nap, but after twenty minutes on the sofa, he gave up and made a telephone call to his auto insurance company and then to a couple of body repair shops. An hour later, the insurance adjuster arrived and snapped pictures of the Pathfinder.

Shortly after six Finney shaved and showered, climbed into his costume, and abruptly fell asleep on his face on the kitchen table. The house and sky were dark when he woke to the sound of knocking. It took a few moments to realize where he was.

Diana was dressed in a form-fitting black skin suit and wore a tall, red-and-white-striped hat, a floppy red silk bow at her neck, and four-fingered white gloves. Her cat whiskers twitched beguilingly when she smiled at Finney. Who would have thought the Cat in the Hat could look so seductively sexy? As far as Finney was concerned, this was Dr. Seuss's finest hour.

"Listo, señor?"

Finney waved his black Zorro cape. "At your service, señorita. You look terrific."

"You look suitably dashing yourself."

"I hope I don't cut myself on this sword."

"I hope I don't let all the little cats out of the big hat."

"Wasn't that Bartholomew Cubbins?"

"You might be right."

"Nice houseboat," Diana said, stepping inside.

"I'm remodeling."

"So I see."

Her Jeep, she explained as she drove, had taken her through college, several summer jobs, and twice to Alaska. It was now one year older than she had been when she bought it, a virtual relic on Seattle's streets filled with shiny new SUVs and lightweight trucks.

Although the day had been clear and sunny, an evening chill had brought a dense fog that was beginning to trap airborne pollutants; the fog left a vaguely metallic tang in the back of Finney's throat.

Seattle was experiencing an autumn inversion, one of several in succession in the past month, where warm air stagnated in the basin between the Olympic Mountains to the west and the Cascades to the east, trapping cooler air over the city. In the daytime the air warmed up enough to lift the ground fog, but at night it all came crashing back down like an intermission curtain. Ordinarily the pollution would be blown out of the region by southern winds and autumn rainstorms, but this year the wind and rain were absent.

They were headed for a Holidays for the Children charity ball, a benefit that was sponsored in part by the fire department. As a volunteer coordinator, Diana was invaluable not only as a hard worker but because of her family's social connections throughout the Puget Sound area. In its seventh year, the event was becoming an institution in Seattle.

The party took up the entire seventy-fourth floor of the Columbia Tower. The event didn't officially start until eight, but already several dozen people stood around admiring the decorations or gazing out the windows at the fog. Another half-dozen people scampered around on last-minute errands. On the floor were artfully arranged tableaus of brilliantly colored autumn leaves, cornstalks, sheaves of wheat, and candle-lit carved pumpkins of all sizes.

"Okay," Diana said. "I need to make sure everything's set. Back in ten minutes. Food's over there."

"Do I look that hungry?"

"Ravenous."

"I get you anything? Green eggs and ham, perhaps?"

She laughed and disappeared.

Outside, only a few pink and purple vestiges remained from the sunset. The jagged ridges of the Olympic Mountains defined the horizon. Lights blinking, a helicopter cruised across the city.

Finney bought a hundred dollars' worth of raffle tickets for a Dale Chihuly glass sculpture, knowing his cat, Dimitri, wouldn't suffer a Dale Chihuly in the house for twenty minutes before knocking it over.

At the far end of the room the band was tuning up, each member made up like a famous musician from the fifties or sixties. Perfect for this crowd, Finney thought, mostly middle-aged, affluent, and nostalgic. First up was a Frankie Valli tune.

When Diana found him, she said, "I should have taken yesterday off. I'm beat. There were supposed to be two of us making all the last-minute preparations, but Angie's suffering a personal crisis. Last Wednesday her fiancé announced he's gay. I guess I shouldn't have told you that."

"I don't even know Angie."

"No, but she gets embarrassed for anybody to know. She thinks it's a personal failure on her part."

"Is that why you didn't have a date until late?"

"Because I was afraid you would turn gay on me?"

He laughed. "No. Because you were jammed up doing the work of two people?"

"Yeah, I guess that's why. Last year I didn't have a date. It was a mistake, because once this thing starts, it more or less runs itself, and I found myself standing here gabbing with a succession of elderly married couples. Almost no singles come." They were quiet for a few moments, unable to do anything but eavesdrop on a shrill conversation nearby. "You forgot about the party, didn't you?"

"I'm afraid I did." He smiled, discomfited by her candor. "You always just say what you think?"

"Usually. I do what I want, too." She stepped forward, cupped his face in her hands, and kissed him on the lips. It startled him enough that he didn't fully participate until it was nearly over, a mistake of timing he regretted immediately.

"What was that for?" he asked.

"The good-night kiss."

He smiled. "I don't get one later?"

"Who knows?" She laughed and glanced around the room. "I think we're going to have a pretty good crowd. We had a lot of volunteers from the department this year."

"What about Oscar Stillman?" Finney asked. "Or Jerry Monahan? Either of them take any interest in this? Reese?"

"Are you kidding? Reese's contribution will be to show up just long enough to circle the room and allow everyone to shake his hand and congratulate him on becoming chief. I don't think Jerry Monahan's ever spoken to me, and Stillman's favorite charity is the tip jar at the Déjà Vu." The latter was a strip club just off Aurora in downtown. "Why do you ask?"

"No reason."

# 39. TRAMPLING THE ELDERLY, THE INFIRM, THE HANDICAPPED

lowly the room filled with body heat, music, and chitchat. Waitstaff in Mickey and Minnie Mouse costumes waded through the assemblage, balancing trays and dispensing hors d'oeuvres. People had come dressed as Marilyn Monroe, Abraham Lincoln, Batman, the Mario Brothers, Madonna, Jesus, the Pope, Ty Cobb; there was even a man in a Bill Clinton mask sporting a SLICK WILLIE tattoo. There was a couple dressed as Laurel and Hardy and another costumed as firefighters. Finney was glad he'd come. It was just the sort of well-meaning diversion his life lacked.

Diana was only a few inches shy of Finney's six feet, and when they danced he couldn't help noticing they fit together like a hand and glove. He'd had a lot of surprises recently, few as pleasant as the kiss she'd given him earlier. There was something vaguely adolescent in the way he couldn't stop thinking about it.

"So, you're house-sitting, did you say?"

"My parents took their motor home to the Southwest so they could use up the last of the country's petroleum supplies. Mom's always wanted to see the high desert in the autumn. I'm sitting with eight parakeets, two hundred houseplants, and an answering machine that fills up twice a day. I swear my mother is the most gregarious woman on the face of the earth."

"You are indeed a dutiful daughter."

"It's the least I could do to make up for all the grief I've given them." She laughed. "No, really, two of my brothers live out of town, and the other one works fourteen-hour days and barely ever sees his wife and kids. It was me or a professional house-sitter, and I couldn't let that happen."

"So you grew up on the Eastside?" he asked.

"Want to hear my sad tale, do you?"

"I do."

"I wish it was sordid. At least that would be interesting, but I was a typical spoiled Eastside brat, raised on Pickle Point just off Meydenbauer Bay in a house almost as large as Ten's. We lived about sixty feet from Lake Washington in a neighborhood of disgustingly conspicuous wealth. I had a stay-at-home mother with a master's degree in English, who thinks all little girls should grow up to be just like her, and a father who is one of the founders of a law firm with offices in Seattle, Spokane, and Portland. I had three brothers who treated me like a boy until I was sixteen, which was how I wanted it." She laughed. "Now for the sordid part. I had it all: private schools, tutors, my own pony at age three. We grew up with a full-time housekeeper and a summertime grounds-maintenance team." She rubbed her nose against his cheek. "I broke this playing football when I was twelve. I broke it again when I was fourteen. My parents were apoplectic when I refused cosmetic surgery."

"Ever regretted it?"

"Not for a minute."

"It's cold."

"That's why I'm warming it up on you. Did you know cats live their lives through their noses?"

"I did know that. And congratulations."

"On what?"

"On breaking it twice. I haven't even been able to get my nose to bleed."

"We were soooo spoiled. I was chauffeured everywhere by my mother in a Mercedes. Ballet, piano, ski, gymnastics lessons. In high school my parents gave me an Alfa Romeo. Were they ever teed off when I traded it in for that Jeep. Except for that and being a tomboy, I was an exemplary child until I dropped out of Pepperdine five credits shy of a degree."

"Why'd you do that?"

"I don't know. I guess it was a pinch of postadolescent rebellion."

"Then what'd you do?"

"Social work with kids, counselor at a summer camp, clerk in a Starbucks shop, and training for triathlons. When I eventually joined the fire department, my mother told me firefighters were tobacco-chewing rednecks or lesbians with crewcuts. I said, 'No, Mother. The lesbians chew the tobacco and the rednecks have the crewcuts.' Mother still talks about my completing a degree in communications and perhaps turning out a novel. Mother has two half-finished novellas tucked away in a dresser drawer."

Finney didn't mention his ex-wife's ambitions in that direction.

"That's enough about me. What about you?"

He told her about his childhood trekking around the West Seattle Golf Course with the steel mill kids, polishing used golf balls to resell to their former owners, about getting thrashed by the older boys at Cooper

Elementary. He'd been small for his age and until high school had suffered for it. He'd had a paper route and a love-hate relationship with his father who'd been a harsh disciplinarian and a worse critic. "Tony and I never quite measured up—me even less than him. I always resented my mother for not sticking up for us, but now I realize she was barely holding her own. I didn't realize the dynamics of our family until just a couple of years ago. In those days the department didn't pay like it does now, and my father used to work a second job down at the steel mill in West Seattle. He had little patience to start with and less when he was tired. And he was always tired.

"In school I never did more than okay unless I really liked the class. I was a second-stringer on the basketball team. I wrestled and ran track. After high school I tried college, but my heart wasn't in it. I worked at Boeing, then got a job with a paint company. I thought I liked it until one morning I woke up and realized I needed to get into the department. It shocked the hell out of my father. I wish we hadn't wasted so many years yelling at each other."

"In our house we never raised our voices," Diana said. "You know what I like best about this job? I like when we're downtown and some businessman in a three-piece suit sees me on the rig and realizes he's looking at a woman. The double take. I love it."

"I love the way little kids go crazy when we drive by."

"You want kids?"

"If I ever get married again. You?"

"I think so. In a few years."

They were quiet until she said, "So. You ever going to tell me why you carved your initials in the wheel well of Engine Ten?"

"You saw that?"

"Don't worry. Nobody else caught it. Tell me what's going on, John. Tell me why G. A. thinks you set the fire on Riverside Drive." He was quiet for a few moments as they danced. "I want to help you," she whispered into his ear.

Until now, he hadn't trusted anybody with the full catalog of his suspicions, wasn't sure he wanted to. "I'm being framed," Finney said. "You really want to hear this?"

"Yes."

The story took two slow dances and the better part of a fast number which they stood out, gazing out over the fog. From time to time they could see the blinking red lights atop a neighboring skyscraper, but mostly what they watched were the reflections of dancers and candlelit pumpkins in the dark windows. He told her about the dangerous buildings list, about following Monahan, about the counterfeit fire engine, the attempt on his life. When he paused, she said, "I saw Paul and Michael taking pictures of Engine Ten one day."

"I'd like it better if you saw Jerry Monahan taking pictures of it. Paul and Michael probably carry snapshots of the rig in their wallets to show people next to them on airplanes."

"Actually, I believe they do."

He recounted the rest of it, and she listened sympathetically.

"There's been speculation an arsonist was working last June," Diana said. "Earlier this week Reese even set up a committee to look into it."

"I'd hoped that was coming."

"The committee was disbanded almost as soon as it was put together. Reese said their preliminary findings indicated it was a waste of time."

"And the committee agreed?"

"I don't know. I could ask Oscar Stillman. He was the chairman."

"Don't bother." He hadn't told her about seeing Stillman with Monahan on Airport Way.

When the band announced a short intermission and the dance floor began to clear, a man dressed as Abraham Lincoln accidentally clotheslined his stovepipe hat off on a mobile of witches and goblins, only to have it caught in midair by a man in a Superman outfit, much to the entertainment of the bystanders. People mingled, ran into old friends; the conversations grew almost as loud as the band had been.

"Somebody's trying to frame you . . . ?" Diana said, thinking aloud. "Somebody was responsible for Leary Way, and they think you'll expose them? That's what's happening?"

"Patterson Cole owned Leary Way. He also owns the building where I found the engine. That's too much of a coincidence to be a coincidence."

"Patterson Cole owns property all over town. He owns vacant lots in Medina that the city's been trying to get hold of for twenty years. He owns this place."

"The Columbia Tower?"

"Bought it over a year ago. He has an entire floor on forty-two."

"I knew about the office, but I didn't realize he owned the building. I guess it stands to reason."

Diana said, "An engine has to cost close to three hundred grand. Why would anybody invest that kind of money?"

"I can't even guess what they're planning to do with the engine. But they want to tie up the fire department bad. They want to get us running around until we're so busy they can set fire to whatever they want and nobody will be there to stop it. They want a conflagration. You know as well as I do, once you get a block or two going, you get a firestorm—and nobody and nothing can stop one of those. They're going to burn down something, and it's going to be big. The phony engine was carrying a pre-fire for this place."

"There are four or five thousand people here in the daytime," Diana said. "Knock out the elevators, which the alarm system does automatically, and there are only two exits, both down narrow stairwells. One of those stairwells would be reserved for firefighting. Can you picture five thousand panicky people trying to get down the other one, walking forty or fifty stories probably in the dark?"

"This place will be full of smoke as soon as somebody opens a door onto the fire floor, which you know will happen."

"We did a prefire here a few months ago," Diana said. "The system has backups out the ying-yang. Television cameras. Sprinklers. Fire walls. Fire pumps to assist the department in raising water to the upper levels. It even has a water tank upstairs that holds thousands of gallons for fire suppression. This wouldn't be like Leary Way, where they didn't even have a night watchman. They'd be tangling with the best in technology here."

"The First-Interstate Bank building in L.A. had the best in technology, too," Finney said. "And that fire took rotating crews and four hundred firefighters to tap. Even so, it almost got away from them. Seattle's only got two hundred firefighters on duty at a time."

"So we'd start out with half as many people as needed, and the rest of the city wouldn't have any coverage at all."

"No. The Columbia Tower wouldn't have any coverage at all."

They both thought about that for a moment. She said, "I read something recently about this place, but I don't remember what. It didn't have anything to do with what we're talking about though."

He took her white-gloved hand as the band began playing again, and they danced. He couldn't stop thinking about the possibility of a fire in this building. Once in the stairs, anybody who was handicapped or elderly or infirm would be in serious trouble. Seattle's aerial ladders might reach to the sixth or seventh floor, but no higher. They didn't have air bags for people to jump onto, and even if they did, a seventy-story jump onto an air bag would be lethal.

# 40. THE MAKE-OUT ARTIST

t was after one A.M. when Finney spotted Charlie Reese and his wife entering together on the heels of several Supersonics still high from a squeaker at Key Arena: Sonics, 101; Utah Jazz, 100.

Chief Reese began working the room, shaking hands with firefighters, politicians, and anyone else who might be useful. His wife seemed a reluctant participant. Finney remembered having thought when he first met the two, eighteen years before, that they were a strange couple—Reese particularly handsome and she notably unattractive in a way that she had to work at, letting the hair on a mole on her chin grow an inch long, not shaving her legs, wearing ill-fitting, unflattering clothes. Finney noticed her once at the department picnic, where she sat alone all day, immersed in a romance novel. Charlie had alluded to the murky origins of their relationship during lunch at drill school, something about a sleazy affair he'd had with her married sister before dating her. In recent years, Reese had become a stalwart churchgoer, while his wife was a self-proclaimed atheist.

Finney watched Reese circumnavigate the room and wondered what kind of reaction the chief would have when he came to Finney and Diana. He glanced at Finney's mask. A flash of recognition crossing his features, he turned away, striding deliberately past both Finney and Diana to shake hands with one of the D-shifters from Station 6.

"That was awful blatant," Diana said. "He always snub you like that?"

"This is the first time I've run into him since he screwed me over."

"Come on. Let's go. This thing is winding down anyway. Or do you want to stay?"

"Let's go."

Around the corner near the elevators the odor of roasted pumpkin from the candles in the jack-o'-lanterns was particularly pungent. They pushed the down button and waited, Diana staring at him as the music and noise spilled around the corner. He was remembering that goodnight kiss she'd given him hours earlier.

Without thinking about it further, Finney leaned forward and kissed her. Her arms melted around his neck. On the descent to forty they resumed their kiss as soon as she'd punched the down button.

Outside, the fog had thickened, visibility reduced to a hundred feet.

When they pulled into the parking area near the dock, it was almost two. Finney was exhausted and knew Diana was as well. Shutting off the Jeep engine, she pulled the emergency brake and turned to him.

"You want to come in?" he asked.

"That would be nice."

"I can barely stand."

"You want me to carry you?"

He laughed. "No, I think I'm better off than that."

"Because I could."

"I know you could."

"I had a wonderful time tonight, John."

"So did I. Thanks for inviting me."

Their footsteps echoed on the wooden dock, his porch light showering a halo of yellow over them in the fog as he unlocked his front door. Inside he took off his hat, cape, and sword. He turned to find the Cat in the Hat stepping into his arms, kissing him repeatedly across his face, backing him up until they both tumbled onto the couch in his living room. He hadn't had time to turn on a light. After a moment, there was a noise in the dark and their kisses slowed and then ceased altogether.

"You have a roommate?" she asked.

"I guess I should have told you about him."

"You guess you should have." She sat up. "This could have been embarrassing."

"Dimitri likes to watch. Don't worry. He won't say anything."

The noise came again and Diana grew utterly still. Finney reached up and turned on a lamp. His tailless cat sat four feet away, staring at them from the seat of a wooden rocking chair that tipped back and forth slightly as the cat balanced. "Diana, meet Dimitri. Dimitri, Diana."

She laughed, and when she flung her hat across the room toward the hat rack—a perfect landing in the shadows next to Finney's Zorro cape—Dimitri ran for his life. Diana took off her four-fingered gloves and snuggled against him. After a while, Finney reached up and draped the afghan from the back of the couch across them. He couldn't recall when he'd felt so contented. "Umm," Diana said, "I don't want to drive home in this soup."

"I don't want you to."

"You don't mind if I stay until it lifts?"

"I hope it doesn't lift for weeks."

She kissed him again and said, "I bet you did this all the time when you were a kid. I bet you were the make-out king in high school."

"I was too shy for that."

"Why do I find that hard to believe?"

"I don't know. I was."

"Um, hmmm."


The knocking had been going on for some time before it turned to banging. It took Finney a few moments to awaken fully.

"Open the door. I've got a warrant for your arrest. John Jacob Finney! Open this door. I've got a warrant."

"Oh boy," Diana murmured, half-asleep. "What time is it?"

"Just after three."

"Why would they . . . ?"

"Probably want to take me by surprise."

"I'll call a woman I know in my father's law firm. She'll have you out by noon."

She might bail him out, he thought, but she couldn't keep him out.

Finney climbed to his feet, opened the door, and confronted a man pounding the door with the heel of his palm. "Open up, you bastard! Open up in the name of the law."

"For Christ's sake, Gary. What the hell are you doing?"

Gary Sadler was half a six-pack on the wrong side of sober, eyes bloodshot, breath reeking of beer and cigarettes. His hair was jeweled from the fog. "Came to arrest your sorry ass," Sadler said. "Came to take you in for arson. Whaddya think? Arson or stealing my girl. You choose." Sadler couldn't stand without constantly resettling his feet, as if he were in a small boat. He tried to look past Finney to see who was with him. "That ain't your Jeep out there, John boy. Motor's still warm. Got a union sticker in the window. Did I interrupt something? Garyius interruptus?"

"Shut up, Gary. And go away."

"Can't go away. Can't go nowhere."

"Why not?"

"Too drunk."

"You didn't drive here?"

"Yeah, I did. But I ain't driving home. Friends don't let friends drive drunk, do they?"

"What do you want?"

"Came to warn you."

"About what?"

"Secret stuff."

Finney felt Diana behind him, her hand on his shoulder. She gave him a peck on the cheek. "I'm going now."

"Diana," Sadler said, stepping back in an exaggerated gesture of gentlemanly courtesy. He stumbled and caught himself. "Didn't mean to break up your tête-à-tête. Damn, woman. That's some outfit. How come you never wore anything like that when we were going out?"

"We never went out," she said, vanishing into the fog.

Finney pulled Sadler into his living room so the neighbors wouldn't overhear. He switched on a lamp next to his bookcase. "What do you want, Gary?"

"Came to tell you something you need to know. Mind if I sit?"

"Go right ahead."

Sadler collapsed in a heap on the floor. "I'm okay." He put his index finger to his lips and made a shushing noise. Dimitri was sitting on top of the sofa, staring at Sadler. "That your cat?"

"Be careful. He doesn't like lushes. Cut to the chase, Gary."

"Got a visit from G. A. Montgomery and his little stooge, firefighter slash law enforcement officer Robert Kub. G. A. did all the talking. Said you lit that Riverside Drive fire."

"I didn't."

"I know that."

"How do you know?"

"Because if a firefighter set it, it was Jerry Monahan. Tell you why. Couple of things. You wanted that place on the dangerous buildings list. He didn't. And he didn't put it there. Why didn't he put it there? He didn't want to attract attention to it. Also, we parked on that same block two weeks before the fire. You weren't working that day. Me and Greenleaf came back to the rig and found Jerry all dirty. When I asked what happened, he said he was messing around down by the river and fell over the bank."

"Without going into the water?"

"Exactly our thoughts. He was inside that house. But why lie about it?"

"Why set a fire?"

"Who knows? G. A. says the phone line at the station will be tapped by the end of the week. They're getting a court order. Even wanted me to trick you into revealing complexity in the arson."

"Complicity?"

"Yeah, that's it."

"What'd you tell him?"

"Told him Jerry's crazy as a bedbug with a snootful of kerosene. Told him you might be a fuckup at a fire, but you're no criminal. And that old woman? Hell, you were the only one in the station didn't run when you saw her coming in for a BP."

"Thanks for telling me, Gary."

"You watch out for that female type just left."

"Don't warn me about her."

"Oh? Somebody already warn you?" He laughed. Then he saw something across the room, something visible only from his vantage point on the floor. He crawled across the carpet and pulled a large piece of plywood from under a table—the plywood base Finney had used to build and replicate a miniature Leary Way: the buildings, the fire engines and ladder trucks, each painted with the appropriate numerals, and the firemen, with yellow helmets for the firefighters, red for lieutenants, orange for captains, white for chiefs.

"Mother of Mary," Sadler said. "This is like something out of *Gulliver's Travels*. You build this?"

"Yeah."

"Why the hell'd you do that?"

"I was trying to understand."

"Jesus H. I was thinking about asking you if I could stay the night, but maybe I should crawl into a cab. This is spooky."

# 41. EMILY CORDIFIS

It was a modest little house in Wedgwood, a quiet neighborhood north of the University of Washington. Erected on a small hillock in a neighborhood of identical houses on similar hillocks, it consisted of a tiny living room, a tinier kitchen, two small bedrooms, and a single bath. Finney had been here so many times he knew where the girls had buried their pet turtles in the backyard.

Bill Cordifis and his bride had purchased the home the year after he'd joined the fire department, which meant they had been there thirty-five years at the time of Bill's death. The thought precipitated a sudden picture of Bill Cordifis's charred body, his arms stumps, the fat on his torso boiled off, his face blackened to the bone, Nomex bunking coat burned as brittle as tissue paper. Finney hated that these images of Bill's last few minutes ambushed him everywhere: in line at the grocery store, driving on the freeway, dancing last night with Diana.

"Hello?" Emily Cordifis gazed at him like a wobbly animal that had been grazed by a car, her elegant outline blurred by the screen door. "Oh, it's you, John. I guess I forgot you were coming. I've been cleaning."

"May I come in?"

"Of course." She unlatched the screen door and swung it open. "I don't know where my manners are. You've read the report, you said?"

"I've read it."

"Good. I'd like to hear your thoughts."

She led him around the corner into the small kitchen. He set the report on the table. "Coffee?" she asked.

"Thank you, but no."

The phone rang and she spoke over her shoulder as she moved toward it. "Have a seat. This won't take a minute."

Finney sat at the chrome-and-Formica kitchen table, the pale light from the window cascading in over his shoulder. The house had always been filled with the smell of coffee and nicotine, though now that Bill was gone, the odor of cigarettes had faded.

Hanging up the phone, Emily Cordifis turned to him and said, "Sure you won't have some coffee?"

"Okay. It smells wonderful."

Emily wore a simple black pullover and trousers that ended at mid-calf. She filled two cups and sat across from Finney, folding her hands on the tabletop. The afternoon light from the window emphasized the lines in her face.

"G. A. has been good about this. I know Bill had high regard for him. He's answered all my questions and been patient, but for some reason I still can't grasp what happened. Bill went here. Bill did this. I hear the words, but I can't see the picture."

She was lucky, Finney thought; he could see the picture.

"The bottom line is I'm to blame. I tried to get him out. I failed."

"But you had a broken shoulder."

"Collarbone. Doesn't matter. I should have saved him."

Her unblinking eyes stared at him. He could tell she was determined to be the best listener she could be, and that she'd vowed not to cry. He could tell she didn't blame him. It was the immediate and unquestioning nature of her unspoken blessing that made it worthless to him. She gave it not as if she'd carefully considered all the opposing arguments and come down on his side, but as if she had no choice.

"To understand what happened at Leary Way, you need to understand how Seattle fights fires. You probably know most of this already, but I'll start at the beginning."

He told her that less than ten years earlier the department had adopted an incident command system that had been and still was in widespread use across the country. The idea was that no matter what the emergency, large or small, the structure of command for handling it would be the same. Instead of having everyone on the fire ground swamp the IC with information, division and sector commanders would be appointed so no one person had more than seven people reporting to him, optimally no more than five. The incident commander would label himself so as to distinguish that incident from others taking place in the city.

Captain Vaughn called himself "Leary Command."

"Even though they were both captains, Bill had been senior to Vaughn, and by rights could have claimed the post of IC for himself when we arrived."

"But he didn't do it?" Emily asked.

"No. If there was action anywhere, Bill wanted to be there. He split the crew and we went in."

Finney had to marshal his thoughts before he continued. In contrast to his own mental health, which he realized was spiraling downward like a maple seed, each time he saw Emily he was stunned at how much more significantly recovered she was than the last time he'd seen her. He admired her strength and wanted to tell her so.

Instead, he said, "Visibility was hampered from the minute we went through the door. Bill sent one member to get a fan. Had she been allowed to set it up, the air in the building would have cleared in short order—"

"That was such a huge building. The news made it look like an airplane hangar."

"Still, those fans would have cleared it out in a matter of minutes. They're pretty amazing. Without fans, you're talking about searching a building in twenty to forty minutes. With fans, in five."

"So why did Vaughn take them down?"

"He was following rules. The rule is to not put up a fan before an engine company gets a line on the fire. Trouble was, without the fans, they couldn't find the fire. Bill did what worked. He knew most of the folks outside telling us we couldn't use fans were people who hadn't crawled into a fire in years."

"Okay. Fine. Bill made a call. Vaughn countermanded it. But if Bill had seniority, why didn't he tell Vaughn to go fly a kite?"

"I don't know."

"You mentioned a woman firefighter. Bill's said a few things over the years . . ."

"Moore is one of the best firefighters in the department. I'd put my life in her hands."

"Would you really?"

"In a heartbeat."

"That's good enough for me. Can you go on?"

"The system requires a lot of people to set it up adequately, and we didn't have them. Each incident has a base area where rigs park. One person is in charge of setting that up and making sure rigs don't block the streets. Then there's a staging area where firefighters and equipment are gathered and where crews wait to receive assignments. Another person is in charge of that. The fire building will have division commanders, probably four of them, and if need be, the division commanders will assign sector commanders under them."

"How was Bill faring when you went back in the second time?"

"Why do you ask?"

"He would come home after you guys had a fire and lie on the couch all day. Totally bushed. I'm wondering . . . did you ever think about not going back in with that second bottle?"

Finney had to think about how he was going to word this.

# 42. LIKE TAKING A NAP

"To be honest, Bill and I didn't think about anything except finding those victims."

"That was just like Bill."

"Yes, it was. While we were inside on our first bottles, Engine Thirty-five showed up and then Engine Ten and Engine Five. Engine Ten ended up taking a line inside the warehouse. We saw their line, but we never saw them. Twenty-two's crew got a supply line from a hydrant to their rig and followed Ten's inside with a secondhand line. They never found any fire either. Thirty-five's showed up at the north side of the building, where a large volume of black smoke was pouring out the windows and rolling down the street. Visibility was so bad they were afraid they'd crash into another rig if they continued driving, so they stopped right there, assuming they were at the location."

"Without any other units, where did they think everybody was?"

"Good question. The incident commander didn't hear the announcement that they were at the location, but the incident commander from another fire going on at the same time mistakenly believed they'd arrived at *his* fire. He told them to take hand lines to the front of his building and wait for a second crew who would help them hold the exposures. Nobody caught the mistake.

"Thinking they were at the front of the building, Thirty-five's crew stood with a dry line for almost twelve minutes while the fire continued to build. There weren't any exposures to protect, and although they couldn't see anybody inside, they thought fire crews were working their way through the building from the other side and that the IC was telling them not to push the fire onto those crews. They tried to get a clarification of their instructions, but channel one was completely jammed, three separate incidents using it by that time."

"I thought your fire was on channel two?"

"It was. They were on the wrong channel. Meanwhile Ladder Five arrived and went to the roof, where they opened two holes on the older buildings. They found no fire and stalled two chain saws in the hot tar on the roof and then an XL-98. That's a rotary saw. By the time they were brought down to help with the search, they were exhausted, and even though they'd cut three good-sized holes with their axes, the building still wasn't venting.

"Three more engines arrived. Engine Six. Engine Seventeen. And Engine Twenty-one. They were put to work laying supply lines to hydrants and taking hose lines into the interior from the south side of the warehouse, where they had almost no chance of reaching the fire. By now there was more smoke buildup, and the holes Ladder Five had cut earlier in the roof were beginning to produce flame.

"By this time the crew of Engine Thirty-five was frantic. The officer, a firefighter acting as a lieutenant, took matters into his own hands and entered the building with his team. Soon after, Engine Twenty-four arrived and went in behind them. This was the correct side from which to attack the fire, but it was too little too late. By now, the old, wooden buildings were raging. Engines Thirty-five and Twenty-four got less than thirty feet inside the door.

"Meanwhile, Bill and I searched the warehouse and started on our second bottles. We made our way across the courtyard and into the older buildings to the north. Eventually we found the room the band rehearsed in. That's where the wall came down on us."

"You must have thought you were about to die."

"I didn't think either one of us was going to die."

"Not even when you were wandering around?"

"I don't remember all of it. My recollection is that when I ran into Reese and Kub I told them exactly where to find Bill. The problem is, when you're that tired and you've taken as much smoke as I took, just about anything can come out of your mouth."

"They said you didn't give directions. But like you said, the smoke and . . ."

"I don't think anybody found the door we'd used. On the north side in the older buildings they finally knocked down some of the fire and searched there, too, but they were on the wrong side of the fire wall. Then when the roof started to collapse, they called everyone out. Flame had gotten into the warehouse by then and ignited hot gases that had been collecting near the ceiling."

"So they pulled out and watched Bill die?"

"If they hadn't, they would have lost more people. Bill wouldn't have wanted that."

"No."

"Anyway, judging from the time line and the amount of smoke, Bill died before they pulled out."

"Are you sure?"

"Nobody's sure. His last radio transmission was at zero-three-fifty-one. They pulled everyone out at zero-four-oh-two. I don't think he lived to see four o'clock."

Emily's eyes watered over for the first time. "A fire wall? What's that?"

"An extra-thick wall built into a building to keep a fire on one side or the other. A paint company, say, might use it between the warehouse and office. It was an old wall, put in there God only knows how many years ago when the place sold lumber. It was a two-hour wall—built to keep flame out for two hours. The biggest portion of the older buildings was put up in 1919, added onto later. Bill and I entered that section on the east side of the wall. Chief Reese and his partner were the only ones on our side."

"I just . . . can't help thinking how . . . horrible it must have been."

"If it's any help, Milt Halpern got trapped in a fire a few years ago. Fourteen-hundred-degree temperatures down to the floor. He got tired and couldn't move, and then he lay down. He said it was like taking a nap. He got burned pretty good, too, but he didn't feel it. You wear those bunkers, you get cooked. It's different from what you'd think."

"What happened to Milt?"

"A firefighter just happened to be standing fifteen feet away in a doorway, blacking out the room with a two-and-a-half. A guy named Gary Sadler. He spotted Milt and dragged him out."

"He didn't feel anything?"

"Like taking a nap."

The phone rang, and as Emily stood up to get it he wondered what it would be like to lose a spouse of thirty-five years. He was hurting, but he didn't have to give away Bill's fishing tackle or find a home for his hunting dogs. He didn't have to figure out what to do with Bill's tools or his shotguns or his fire department uniforms. Or the folded flag from his coffin.

"Okay," Emily said, hanging up the phone. "Why didn't Reese and Kub find him?"

"It was a big place. Lots of smoke. Reese says they searched until the fire chased them out."

"How far away was Bill when you met them?"

"About seventy-five feet."

"I suppose they searched as long as they felt they could."

"That's my understanding."

She looked at him with her wide doe eyes. As she walked him out of the house, Emily Cordifis detoured into the room Bill had converted to a combination den–sewing room after their youngest daughter moved out. "Some papers I found. Mostly department stuff. I haven't really had the heart to sort through them. I would appreciate it if you would return anything that needs to be returned."

He took the envelope from her, and said, "Emily I have to tell you something."

"What is it?"

"I was lost."

Emily stepped forward and, without uttering a word, kissed Finney's cheek. "Of course you were. Who wouldn't have been? John? Next month would have been our thirty-sixth wedding anniversary. The girls and I have decided to hold a celebration of his life, and we want it to coincide with our anniversary. Everybody's going to be here. Marion, the whole gang from Station Ten. G. A. Montgomery. Chief Reese has promised to make a speech. Say you'll come. It wouldn't be complete without you."

"I'll be here," he said, though he didn't know how he could ever celebrate with that bunch. Anyway, he'd probably be in jail by then. He kissed her brow and left.

# 43. THE DEATH ROOM

inney was driving his father's 1948 Universal pickup truck, the same vehicle he'd borrowed as a teenager, the truck he'd parked on the West Seattle golf course on so many frustrating Friday nights with Sally Morrison. After high school Sally, still a virgin, went on to Western Washington University in Bellingham. Rumor had it that she'd married a podiatrist in San Bernardino and had two kids, a Great Dane, and an artificial hip. Finney had dated only two girls in high school, a statistic that had caused his older brother to label him a "social retard."

With the mist-covered Lake Union to his left, he drove past Gas Works Park to Thirty-sixth and then to Leary Way. The fog was slowly crawling up from the lake, the streets dark enough now that alert drivers had turned on their headlights. The area was a mixture of residential and industrial blocks.

The ruins on Leary Way were much as the fire department had left them, the fire ground encircled with fence poles anchored in concrete blocks and holding up Cyclone fencing that well-wishers had decorated with flowers, cards, handwritten notes, and along one section, teddy bears and stuffed animals.

Little had been removed from the scene. The day after the fire Bill's body was taken away, and then two days later the melted junction box G. A. said had caused the fire was dug out of the wall and taken downtown where it was displayed for months atop G. A.'s desk. The rubble from the fire had been pushed into piles along the remains of the interior walls. In some spots the rubble had sunk into what remained of the basement, so that it looked like an enormous swimming pool filled with sludge.

Finney came here only at night and found it looked sinister in a way that the actual fire in June had not. He rolled to a stop in a cul-de-sac, parking the old pale green pickup on the north edge of the ruins, where Engine 35 had parked that night. Over the summer, a fast-growing thicket of blackberries had woven their way into the fencing and formed a screen that obscured his parking spot from motorists.

Finney stepped into his fire department coveralls, put on a pair of

Ranger Firemaster rubber boots he'd worn for years on Ladder 1, a helmet with a lamp on the front that he'd bought at Safety and Supply, and made his way through a wing in the Cyclone fencing into the labyrinth. Twenty feet inside the fence, he lifted a set of charred planks and removed a D-handle shovel and a long, steel bar. He put on a pair of work gloves and carried the tools along a well-trod path in the rubble.

He entered from the north and walked through the remains of the first three rooms, heaps of bricks, mortar, and broken boards forming irregular igloos of trash.

The crew of Engine 35 had reported the hottest part of the fire had been in the room Finney was now working in, sixty to eighty feet inside the northwest doorway. Wind had blown the flames through the complex, and then, later, through the high windows into the adjoining warehouse.

Finney scrutinized the area at his feet in the dim light from his helmet and began shoveling. A week ago he'd worked until almost three in the morning, had cleared three-quarters of the room.

Tonight he scooped up the rest, using the bar to lever out the larger chunks. Finney turned his handheld flashlight on and began searching for burn patterns on the floor. Pawing through the pile behind him, he thought he detected the faint aroma of gasoline on two boards. Oddly, when gasoline was used as an accelerant, the odor oftentimes remained long after the structure burned, especially if it had seeped into cracks in the floor or woodwork. Had they used dogs during the initial investigation, they might have found this, but G. A. Montgomery had nixed the idea of using another agency's accelerant-sniffing dogs—Seattle had none of its own.

It was the second time he'd found the odor of gasoline. Last month he'd detected it in a room adjoining this one. It was possible the gas had been in a container that melted in the heat, that the odor had been produced after the fire started, not before, but Finney didn't think so. Still, his findings would never hold up in a court.

G. A. would say Finney had spilled the gas himself.

Minutes later Finney found himself in the room where Bill Cordifis died. The room had been scoured down to the floor. Anything he wanted to learn from it was either in the official report or in the sixteen-foot-high debris pile they'd built alongside it, and he'd already sifted through that piece by piece. In the process he had moved it thirty feet to one side.

It had taken over a month, and he'd found dozens of artifacts, including the melted remains of a drum set, a wristwatch, parts from an electric guitar, components from a sound system, and one heat-congealed condom still in its foil wrapper.

He'd been here many times since June. He knew it was a fluke the wall had trapped Bill instead of him. He also knew that had their fates been reversed, Bill wouldn't have had the strength to chop through the wall, that the two of them would have died here together. He looked down. His hands were trembling.

Until Leary Way he'd never been afraid of death. He'd always thought of it as an event somewhere in the distant future, an event he didn't need to contemplate. These days, he pondered death constantly. Bill's death. His father's death. His mother's. The deaths of everyone he knew or had known or ever would know. It wasn't healthy, but there was nothing he could do to stop it.

What made this gloomy meditation so ruinous was that Finney had also discovered he no longer believed in God. Heaven, he now surmised, was a human invention to alleviate the universal fear of death. He'd become convinced on a visceral level that when you were dead, you simply ceased to exist, that in some ways it must be like a very deep sleep.

A deep sleep. Wouldn't that be nice? he concluded. He hadn't indulged in genuine all-night wake-up-and-wonder-where-you-are sleep for half a year.

The band room was clear now, just four walls, or what was left of four walls, a rectangular patch of flooring. In spots the linoleum was intact. On the north side of the room there had been a corridor, and it was along this corridor that much of the smoke and flame from the initial fire had traveled, gradually eating into the north wall, weakening it until it collapsed on them.

Tonight Finney was determined to retrace his escape route from the room.

It was only the second time he'd had the gumption to attempt this.

It took a while to find the place where he'd hacked through the wall with his service axe; most of the wall was gone now, either destroyed by fire or dismantled by work crews. Once again, he marveled at how it was narrower than he remembered.

He'd squirmed through the wall and turned right, found himself wedged up against a large diesel motor. He'd turned back past the exit hole and gone through a doorway into a room that was approximately twenty-five by forty and shaped in the form of an *L* so that, given the machinery on the floor and the smoke, it was easy enough to see how he'd become disoriented.

He'd been here when Reese and Kub opened the door on the east side of the building, when the fresh air from their entrance fed the overhead gases and caused them to ignite. Had they come in quickly and sealed the door behind them, there would have been little change in the atmosphere, but they left it open, so that gallons of cool air supplied the starving fire with the oxygen it had been craving.

Had he not had his face pressed to the floor in an effort to suck up every last lungful of good air, he would have been burned alive.

Eventually, he'd made his way out of that room via a doorway at the south end. It was cooler in the next room, and he'd stood up for the sake of speed, keeping the wall to his right. It was here that he counted his footsteps from the PASS device, having returned to the point at which he'd started.

Twenty-eight paces.

He remembered that much.

Retracing his path, he made the count again—twenty-six, twenty-seven, twenty-eight—and found himself stepping across a pile of one-inch steel pipes under the debris.

The pipes were ten feet long, eighty or a hundred of them. He had no idea why they'd been stored in the corridor. They had made a horrible racket just as he met up with Reese and Kub, a hundred steel pipes weighing hundreds of pounds falling to the floor.

It was clear that had he been a few feet farther back, the pipes would have killed him.

He met Charlie Reese and Robert Kub, gave them directions, or thought he did, then proceeded along the corridor, at the end of which he was later found muttering to himself, making no attempt whatsoever to exit the building.

Now at the entrance to the building, he turned around and retraced the route Chief Reese and Robert Kub had taken. According to their report, they searched one small office before proceeding west along the corridor. Stepping it off, Finney calculated they traveled eighteen paces into the building before they met him.

Finney remembered telling them to listen for the PASS device, which other firefighters later reported hearing as they shot water into the interior. He remembered telling them about the hole he'd chopped. He remembered repeating the number twenty-eight. He remembered it, but even as his memories replayed that night, he didn't know if they were dreams or memories.

The pair said they'd explored for as long as the heat allowed, and by accounts of independent observers, they were inside ten or eleven minutes after Finney met them.

Finney placed himself at the spot in the corridor where he'd met Reese and Kub. To his left was another, smaller corridor. Kub had told him it was where they'd spent most of their search-time before being chased out of the building.

But the corridor to the left had had a steel gate across it. Finney knew that, because he'd run up against the gate himself on his way out. Others had spoken of it during the cleanup. Finney had seen the gate in a stack of debris in the parking lot, but he'd never examined it.

It was dark now, cooler, visibility down to a quarter mile. A boat horn sounded off in the Lake Washington Ship Canal. The cold fog penetrated his clothing.

It took twenty-five minutes to free the wrought-iron gate and drag it clear. On the left side were heavy hinges; on the right a latch and a locking throw bolt that had been cut through, probably with a circular saw. Had it been sawn through before or during the fire, the newly sliced end would have been discolored by heat and smoke. But it hadn't been cut during the fire—it was shiny.

During the fire it had been locked.

Which meant the only avenue Reese and Kub could possibly have explored was the corridor Finney had come down.

They must have gone past the chirping PASS device and the exit hole he'd chopped. How long could they have lasted that deep in the building? It was possible they'd passed the device, each thinking the chirping was coming from his partner's PASS. One of the troubles with the PASS was that it gave off so many false alarms, people didn't pay attention. In any large group of working firefighters at least one of their devices was sure to be sounding off, which was the primary reason so many people broke the rules and didn't switch them on at all.

It was thoroughly dark when Finney hid his tools. He was opening the pickup's door when he spotted a young woman in blue jeans and a yellow raincoat stealthily threading a bouquet of asters through the Cyclone fence. "Oh," she said, startled.

"I didn't mean to scare you. I'm with the fire department."

"These flowers—it's okay, isn't it?"

"Of course."

"Are you . . . ?"

"Just doing some work."

"I was here that night visiting my friend up the hill. The guy who died? I heard he got all burned?"

Finney nodded.

"Was he a pretty nice guy?"

"About the most decent human being I've ever known."

"Wow."

# 44. THE CREAKING OF CEDAR LOGS

When he sat down to examine the papers Emily Cordifis had given him, Finney heard the subtle creaking of the cedar logs under the floorboards, evidence that a large craft had plied the east side of the lake while he was in the shower.

Visiting Leary Way was invariably an ugly booster shot to the melancholy and sorrow he'd been nursing since June, and it was worse coming on top of his visit to Emily. He wouldn't eat anything tonight and would be lucky to sleep. Hell, he didn't need food or sleep. What he needed was absolution.

Purring, Dimitri jumped up on the recliner as Finney spilled the contents of Emily's envelope into his lap. Finney saw his own phone number on the back of a receipt for a pair of hunting boots. Bill wasn't in the habit of memorizing phone numbers. He knew Bill jotted messages to himself on just about anything that came to hand. Finney knew of one occasion when there was so much scribbling on the back of his paycheck that the bank refused to accept it. For a couple of weeks in May, Bill had been coming over to help on the remodeling of the houseboat, but he couldn't recall the last time they'd spoken on the phone.

He found an outline of a battalion-wide drill Bill had been organizing, a simulated mass-casualty bus accident in the Metro bus tunnel deep under Seattle's downtown streets. Teenagers from the SFD's cadet program had been slated to wear moulages and pretend to be injured. It was heartbreaking to see Bill's diligently prepared notes for a drill that never took place, the names and phone numbers of all the people he'd never called back.

On a piece of junk mail Finney found a large four-digit number scrawled across the top, along with a series of what appeared to be phone numbers down the right side. Six names, a phone number alongside each of the first three:

Montgomery
Balitnikoff
Monahan
Stillman

Kub?

Finney?

Staring at the tall digits at the top of the page he knew he was looking at the street number of the Leary Way complex—4400. There was no street name, just the number, the digits highlighted and underlined, adorned with curlicues and squiggles as if Bill had stared at and played with them for a good long while.

Flipping the page over, Finney saw that it was a solicitation from a refinancing lender in Reno, Nevada, the envelope postmarked June 3. Leary Way had occurred on the morning of June 9. They'd been at work all day on the eighth, so he'd probably opened the mail and used it for scratch paper on the seventh.

Montgomery, Balitnikoff, Monahan, Kub, Finney. Cordifis had hunted and fished every year with Montgomery and Balitnikoff. He'd known Jerry Monahan before they got into the department during a phase when he and Emily had entertained the notion of joining the Church of Latter-Day Saints; and they had been firefighters together twenty-five years earlier on a now-defunct Engine 19. There was no telling how well Bill had known Kub.

There were three Finneys in the department. Finney's father worked with Cordifis when they were both lieutenants together at Station 18 in the heart of Ballard—Bill on Ladder 8, Gil Finney on Engine 18. Bill had been one of Tony's instructors when Tony came through drill school. And, of course, John had worked with him eighteen years on Ladder 1.

Had Bill Cordifis known there was going to be a fire on Leary Way? Why else would he have written down the address? Or had the number on the paper been a coincidence? If so, it was a hell of a coincidence. And what connection did the six names have to the Leary Way address?

Finney was asleep in the chair when a light tapping at the front door woke him. At first he thought he was having a heart attack, but then he realized Dimitri had stretched out on his chest, eighteen pounds of purring weight. "Come on," he said, lifting the cat off his torso. "Up you go."

Finney opened the door and slowly accustomed his eyes to the blinding sunlight off the lake.

"There someone here? I thought I heard you talking to someone." It was a woman's voice, a husky sound from an individual who'd never smoked but who'd been hit in the throat with a baseball when she was thirteen.

"The cat. I was talking to the cat."

"Did I wake you?" Diana asked. "I called last night and then again this morning. When you didn't answer I thought . . ."

"Maybe I was in the slammer?"

"I thought I should check."

"What time is it?"

"Ten."

"Come in. God, I must look like hell."

"You look . . ."

"Like something that's been sitting at the bottom of Santa's sack all summer?"

Diana laughed. He liked that she laughed at his jokes. "I admire men with rumpled hair and only one sock," she said affectionately. Finney looked down at his feet. He had two socks on. She was kidding him. Diana walked into the interior of the houseboat and stood with her back to him. She wore blue jeans and a light blue fleece vest over a T-shirt, a baseball cap over a ponytail. The chill air off the lake blew into the houseboat and mingled with the fragrance of her perfume. He opened the drapes, and the sunlight made him wince.

"Sorry to bust in on you like this," she said.

"I'm glad you came."

"I wanted to explain about Gary."

"Don't even think about it. He was drunk." Still, he was curious about her and Gary. Had they had a relationship? It seemed hard to believe, since by his own admission Gary specialized in women he referred to as trailer-park trash, but you never knew.

"He's got this thing about me. We went to some movies together. The Seattle Film Festival this last spring. I usually have tickets for the festival, but this year I didn't and he did. He told me he'd been planning to see most of those movies with his sister, but she finked out on him and went back to Minnesota to be with her ex-boyfriend. He asked me if I'd go with him."

"You don't have to explain any of this."

"I want things to be out on the table with us from the start."

Despite Friday night he hadn't thought of the two of them in terms of *us*. Until now. That prospect sent a whisper of hope into his life. Her proximity also sent a low shot of voltage down his spine. He was going to have to get used to that voltage because it seemed to return every time she did.

"He had a horrible crush on me. Not that I gave him any encouragement. As far as I knew, we were just friends who both happened to like films. One night after this Brazilian comedy he started coming on to me. I told him no, and then we had a wrestling match that ended with him on his back on the floor. I ever tell you I had four years of judo?"

"No, but thanks for the warning."

"That's when he started driving through my neighborhood on Capitol Hill at all hours. I thought I was rid of him until the other night."

"Gary's a jerk."

"Now he claims he's trying to bring me to Jesus." The phone began ringing. When Finney didn't budge, she said, "You should answer it."

He didn't. He didn't want anything to spoil these minutes with her. It was his brother, Tony, speaking on the answering machine. "John? Pick up if you're there. I've been callin' all night. I left a message. Damn it, John, where are you? I hope you're out gettin' some tail, 'cause it might be your last. There are all sorts of rumors. You need to stop asking people about Leary Way. You were lookin' nuts before, but now with this rumor that you'll be arrested . . . Damn it, you're my brother. I know you didn't do this. There's even talk that you've been committing arson for years and the old man was covering for you. John, take my advice and stop askin' questions. Give me a call when you get this message. I love you, guy."

Finney collapsed into the recliner he'd spent the night in. The sudden movement frightened Dimitri, who scampered out of the room.

"What's going on?" Diana said. "What's changed since Friday?"

"You don't want any part of this."

"Yes, I do. I want to help." She knelt on the floor in front of him and took one of his hands between hers. "I mean that."

Reluctantly, Finney told her about his excavations at Leary Way, about the gasoline odors he'd detected, his belief that it was an arson, not an accidental fire, about his inability to explain Reese and Kub's failure to find Bill Cordifis. Before he knew it, he was showing her Cordifis's note.

"I guess I don't get it," she said.

"Look at the number at the top of the page." She looked again at the note and her brow furrowed. "Forty-four hundred. Isn't that the street number that came in for Leary Way? This was written before . . . well, obviously it was written before the fire. Are you sure this is Bill's handwriting?"

"Yes."

"So Bill knew something about Leary Way before it happened?"

"He must have."

"But surely he didn't think it was going to burn down? He would have told somebody."

"Not if he didn't really believe it. Think about it. You have some friends who you trust implicitly, and somehow you come up with the idea they're going to set a fire. Would you believe it?"

"You mean those names are the friends?"

"That's my guess."

"Your name's on the list."

"I know it."

"I wouldn't believe it. You're right. He probably didn't believe it until it happened. So . . . was it a coincidence he died there? Do you think? You don't think somebody pushed that wall over on you guys, do you?"

"No, of course not."

"Did they know he knew?"

"He got in a screaming match with Oscar Stillman right before we went back in the second time."

"Stillman's name is on the list."

"Yes."

"Let's tell somebody."

"Who's going to believe us? No. Don't answer that. I know who. Nobody. Besides, the minute I mention any of this out loud, G. A. will arrest me."

"What makes you say that?"

"He's on the list."

She came around the chair and began massaging Finney's shoulders at the base of his neck, working her thumbs and fingers deep into his trapezius. "Buddy, you are tight as a banjo string. Why don't we go do something? Take our minds off this for a little while. Take me out in a kayak? I've been dying to try it."

"Are you kidding? They're probably on their way to arrest me right now."

She leaned over and looked upside down into his face, her gray eyes inches from his. "Come on. I bet you can launch a kayak right from the dock outside."

"Closer than that."

# 45. MAXIMIZATION AND MINIMIZATION

Diana sat in the rear cutout of the double kayak, paddling in perfect synchronization with Finney, who was in front working the rudder pedals. Other than explaining how to put on the splash apron and how to get in without capsizing the vessel, she hadn't needed much instruction. "It's so low in the water," she said, like a child with a new toy. "Everything looks different from down here."

He heard the familiar slap of the lake water on the thin hull, felt his muscles filling with blood and warmth as he wielded the double-bladed paddle in a steady rhythm on either side of the kayak, muscles made powerful from kayaking thousands of miles over the last ten years.

He'd selected one of his three kayaks, a double, and dragged it through the missing outer wall of his spare bedroom. As he plunked it into the water, he said, "Sort of like Ma and Pa Kettle's houseboat, huh?"

"I like it."

"You don't really?"

"I do. But maybe you should get it buttoned up before winter."

"I was thinking about that."

"I bet kayaks are great for impressing women. I know I'm impressed. Who do you generally take out in this?"

"My mother."

She laughed. "No, who? Really?"

"The usual. Michelle Pfeiffer. Courteney Cox. Jewel."

"Okay, so you're not going to tell me. Fair enough. I'm not going to tell you about the time Matthew Perry tried to pick me up."

"Really?"

"Yeah, he really did."

"I don't blame him," Finney said. The craft skittered across the mirrored lake water like a four-legged bug. When the light was at the right angle, they could see deep into the gray-green water. From time to time a sloppy stroke from behind would splash the back of Finney's arm. He found the thrill of being out on the water with Diana a studied contrast to the rest of his life. He'd almost forgotten how much speed two people who were willing to work could generate; the feel of the wind, the sunshine on their backs was exhilarating. It was clear that Diana was one of the strongest kayakers he'd ever doubled with, male or female, and he wished this little excursion could last forever.

Hugging the shoreline, they traveled north past berthed ships, small marinas, and various businesses.

When he turned around to see how she was doing, she was looking at Gas Works Park, where a man was trying to fly a kite in the windless sky, a woman tagging along behind with a pair of toddlers and a dog on a leash, a plastic bag tied around the dog's collar for his business.

She caught his eye and said, "Remember I told you I thought I'd read something recently about the Columbia Tower?"

"No."

"I told you Friday night."

"Oh, yeah. Sure." But he didn't remember. These days his short-term memory was a sieve. It was more than bothersome. It scared him. Could early Alzheimer's be brought on by smoke inhalation? Or was it just all the tension in his life?

"I hate to mention this when you're just starting to relax, but when I got home I looked it up on the Web. Get this. Apparently during a pretrial hearing for Patterson Cole's divorce, his wife claimed he was mismanaging the Columbia Tower, said it was underinsured."

"Underinsured by how much?"

"There's some dispute over the worth of the building, but it seems to be short by somewhere between fifty and a hundred million."

"So he'd lose his shirt if it burned down."

"Right."

"Then something else is going to burn down."

"John, I've been thinking about your predicament. G. A. thinks you set the fire at Riverside Drive. *You* didn't, but *somebody* did. They say there are seven reasons people set fires and almost any arson falls into one of those seven categories. Maybe it would help if we thought about it that way."

"I can't even remember all seven."

"Well, let's see. The first is revenge. And then two would be the sex-thrill thing. Along with vandalism."

"Three I guess would be to cover up another crime."

"Four would be the insurance fraud we were talking about."

"Political terrorism and social protests."

"Along with riots and all that—five. Six is the hero gig. Somebody lights a fire so they can save people and look important."

"That's what people are going to think I did. To make up for my failure at Leary Way. They'll say I placed Annie Sortland in the building so I could save her."

"Ridiculous."

"It won't sound that way after G. A. puts his spin on it."

"What's left? We were at six, the hero gig."

"Morons and madmen. Irrational pyromania."

"That's seven. Riverside Drive doesn't fit any of them," she said. "Does it?"

"Maybe it was done to frame me. No other reason."

"People don't usually murder someone in order to frame someone else."

"Maybe they were just going to light the place and the old woman stumbled onto the perp while he was doing it, and he was afraid she'd tell the police it wasn't me."

"And then they put your jacket on the back porch?"

"They were probably planning that all along."

"Did you recognize the voice on the phone that night?"

"Nope."

"I guess if there were eight reasons, number eight would be framing another person to get them out of your hair. You find this house prepared for arson. The house is evidence. The house burns down, the evidence is gone, and you're discredited and removed from the picture because you're the prime suspect. What I don't understand is why G. A. is so determined to get you. There's a good chance any other FIU investigator would have handed you that jacket and said, 'Here, you forgot this when you were here the other day.' He started building a case right away."

"He and I have been butting heads over Leary Way."

"So he had a grudge against you before the fire?"

"I would say so."

Keeping close to the beach, they circled Lake Union, paddling slower when there was something Diana wanted to see, faster during the open stretches. They passed the Lake Washington Ship Canal Bridge with the freeway running atop it and then headed west, paralleling a former rail line that had been converted into the Burke-Gilman jogging trail. Two in-line skaters paced them for a few blocks.

On the west side of the water they doubled back and passed under the Aurora Bridge and Highway 99. Finney knew Diana was an active athlete, but still he was surprised at the depth of her competitive spirit. Nobody had ever outpaddled him from the backseat, and only a few of the strongest had been able to match him stroke for stroke the way she was doing. On the west side of the lake they got into a playful contest to see who would quit paddling first, their speed gradually picking up. "You're welcome to take a rest anytime you want," he said.

Breathing hard, she said, "Yeah, so are you."

They were both arm-weary by the time they began closing in on the houseboats off Westlake Avenue, by the time Finney noticed a man standing on the dock in slacks and a navy-blue fire department windbreaker. Captain G. A. Montgomery. Oh, God, Finney thought, the bastards have come to arrest me in front of Diana. Robert Kub and Chief Reese loitered in the shadows farther along the dock. As expressionless as a bum requesting spare change, Montgomery waited while Finney held the kayak snug against the wooden dock and let Diana climb out. Kub met Finney's gaze as Finney climbed out and held the bow rope. Reese folded his arms behind his back.

"What do you want?" Finney asked.

G. A. moved forward, and an angled sunbeam spotlighted a patch of beard his razor had missed. "This would be better if you and I were alone," he said, giving Finney the full effect of his intimidating stare.

Mirroring his cocky demeanor, Finney said, "Why? You afraid of witnesses?"

"John, go easy on the insolence. I just wanted you to know we went through that jacket one more time. Don't know how we missed it earlier, but there was a ticket stub in one of the pockets. Want me to tell your friend here what it was for?"

"There's no other reason for you to find a stub you couldn't find earlier except to frame me."

"I'll ignore that. You go to the movies?"

"Not for about a year."

"How about a movie the night before Riverside Drive?"

"I was with you that night."

"After we spoke you went to a flick. One of those artsy-fartsy theaters in the U District. We have the stub."

"I haven't been to any movies."

After several beats, G. A. continued, "You want me to explain to your friend here the significance of this?"

"The significance is that you're a liar. I know what you're doing. You're going to introduce the jacket in court. I'll say it was stolen from my station locker and you'll say it couldn't have been because I was wearing it the night before."

"We can prove to the jury you were wearing it the night before."

"If I wanted to torch that house, why would I tell you it was set up for arson the night before I did it?"

"A man who plays with fire knows how it starts, but not how it ends. You assumed Engine Twenty-six would be first in and you could run upstairs and save the old woman and get yourself a medal. You weren't counting on catching that aid run just before the fire was called in."

G. A. and Finney stared at each other. They both knew he hadn't been to a movie. It was bad enough that incriminating details were piling up against him by accident and that somebody had tried to frame him.

"I don't understand why you feel the need to falsify evidence," Finney said.

"Be careful, or I'll sue you for slander while you're away getting your education. Don't think I won't do it either. And don't forget, when that old woman dies, and she will die, we're going to call you back and tag you with murder. My advice is to make it easy on yourself. Cop to a plea, and we won't press for the death penalty."

The death penalty? It hadn't even occurred to Finney. Was this guy nuts? He had to know Finney hadn't set that fire. Or had he convinced himself Finney had gone off his nut? The death penalty! This was all just too . . . bizarre. It all came into focus now. G. A. was part of the group setting the fires. Of course he'd investigated Leary Way himself. He'd probably set it himself, too.

"Hell, I can think of a million reasons you didn't mean for anything to happen," G. A. continued. "You told me about the house, said it was ready for arson, but you knew I didn't believe you, so you decided to cross the line. I bet you didn't even know that old woman was around. That wouldn't be murder; that would be an accident. Lighting a match is a pretty small act in itself. You've been under duress. I think we'll be able to convince a sympathetic judge to be lenient. Keep denying this and we're going to end up throwing the book at you."

"What did you and Bill talk about the day before he died?"

Nothing Finney had said until now had fazed G. A., but this seemed to stop him like a .300 Magnum slug hitting a bull elephant. Or maybe it was just the fact that it was a non sequitur. "What are you talking about?"

"We worked on the eighth of June. Bill died early the morning of the ninth. He called you from home on the seventh, didn't he?" He was stabbing in the dark. Finney was guessing that because Bill Cordifis had written down those three phone numbers he'd called them. Maybe he had. Maybe he hadn't. He certainly hadn't called Finney. Maybe he'd phoned his father. He was flailing, but right now flailing was all he could do.

"We talked all the time."

"Emily had some notes he'd written. There was a list of phone numbers. One of them was yours. On that same piece of paper was the address of Leary Way. Why did he have the address of a fire that hadn't happened yet? And why call you about it?"

"I didn't say he called me. And Emily never told me this."

"She doesn't know."

"She doesn't know? That's convenient. Who knows? Just you? Of course, just you. Anybody can get a pen and write some crap on a piece of paper. You did that yourself. Man, you're really stretching here. You're just . . . pathetic."

G. A. gave Finney a long look, swiveled around on his heel, and strode up the dock past Robert Kub and Chief Reese. Maybe that was what Finney should have done when G. A. accused him, turned around and walked away without a word. It was effective.

As soon as G. A. was out of earshot, Robert Kub approached, but before he could speak, Finney went on the attack. "You really see him take a ticket stub out of that jacket pocket?"

"Sorry to say that I did."

"There's no way he could have been the one who put it there?"

"G. A. wouldn't do that."

"Who would?"

"You're telling me Annie Sortland isn't going to ID you?"

"I don't know what she's going to do."

After Kub left, Diana touched Finney's shoulder and said, "I've been up to visit her, but they won't let anybody in. G. A. was on the ward, too, arguing with one of the doctors. I think he was trying to get in to see her."

As she spoke, Charles Reese stepped within hailing distance, a crooked smile on his face. He stared past Finney as if he wasn't there. "How are you doing, little lady?"

"Fine, Chief. You?"

"I'd feel better if your boyfriend would listen to reason. They tell me the case against him is rock solid."

"It doesn't sound like it to me."

Watching the sun gleam on Reese's dark hair, it occurred to Finney why he wasn't behind bars. After boasting to one and all that he had a witness who would finger Finney, G. A. was afraid Annie Sortland would come out of her drug-induced stupor and name someone else. Even if G. A. wasn't conspiring to frame him, he might have guessed Finney hadn't left his jacket at the fire scene and he should have known Finney had gone to him in good faith the night before the fire. He certainly knew Finney had not purchased that movie ticket stub. What he didn't know was whether or not Annie Sortland would ID him. If she ID'ed someone else, G. A. would end up looking like a boob, since he'd already told half the department Finney set the fire.

Because Finney had chatted with Annie that morning, he, too, had assumed she would name him. But there was at least one other person she might finger: the arsonist, whoever that was.

"I can see why G. A. would want to harass me," Finney said. "But you've already done your damage."

Reese was smiling with just the left side of his face, the right side dead and wooden. "What we got here is a public relations nightmare. Much as I hate to admit this, losing Bill Cordifis last summer was about the best public relations coup the department has had in a while. You are going to single-handedly put us back to square one, the son of a former chief indicted for arson."

After Reese left, Diana said, "Why did they come?"

"They're trying to turn the screws. G. A. thinks he can get me to crack. Kub told me he does that with people he's building a case on."

"You catch the game G. A. was playing? First he exaggerates how bad it's going to be for you. The death penalty—he's maximizing there. Then he pretends he's on your side. That's where he minimizes. You didn't really mean for anybody to get hurt. You were just lighting a match. Maximization and minimization. Cops have been using it ever since the rubber hose was banned."

"I don't know," Finney said, putting a stupid look on his face. "I think it was working. I almost confessed." She stared at him a moment before he burst into laughter.

Laughing together, they hauled the kayak out of the water.

# 46. HAPPIER THAN A DEAD PIG IN THE SUN

Sadler was so pissed off he could barely see straight. He'd run into the Kmart off Delridge to buy a pair of mats for the new truck, and came out less than five minutes later to find a big dent in his driver's door. Hell, he hadn't even turned off the motor. It was a beautiful truck, spruce-green with chrome running boards, an extended crew cab, and tires bigger than some third-world countries. Hell, it was brand-new. He'd picked it up two weeks earlier from Midway Motors in Fife for just under twenty-nine and a trade-in on his three-year-old Firebird.

Three errands to run while he was in Seattle, and already one of them had gone tits up. Some asshole had put a perfect pie-sized dimple in the driver's-side door, probably with a boot, some self-righteous parking lot Nazi who'd taken issue over his being in the LOAD ONLY lane.

When Sadler pulled up to the house on lower Delridge Way, the old man was out in the driveway monkeying around with the Pathfinder Sadler knew belonged to his son. Somebody or something had knocked the hell out of it.

"How you doin', Chief?" Sadler said, startling the old man, who'd been kneeling beside the Pathfinder with a pair of pliers. Sadler was shocked at how much weight the chief had lost, at how drawn and shaky he was.

"Oh . . . hello, young fella."

"Sadler. Gary Sadler. I worked at Thirty-six's when you were in the Seventh."

"You're the one had that girlfriend broke a pie plate over your head."

"It was a turkey platter. And I deserved it. I was a terrible drinker in those days."

"What brings you to this neck of the woods?"

"I was talking to your son the other day, and I thought I'd drop by and see how you were doing."

"Right now, I'm happier than a dead pig in the sun. My grandfather used to say that. It won't be long, I *will* be a dead pig in the sun." The old man laughed, which set him on a coughing jag.

"I doubt they'll leave you out in the sun," Sadler said.

The old man laughed harder at this. Gary could only conjure up a smile. "I guess there's some of us don't figure out how to live until we're about done doin' it. Don't mind telling you, I'm one of them. Family and friends. That's what it's all about, Gary. Don't let anybody tell you any different."

"Yes, sir."

"Goddamn lung cancer. Spread to my bones."

"Sorry to hear that."

"Too many fires without a mask. You stay out of the smoke."

Sadler produced a pack of cigarettes and lit one. "Too late for that."

"It's never too late." As if by mutual agreement, they both stood back and surveyed the Pathfinder, sharing cigarettes from Sadler's pack. "It's Johnny's car," Chief Finney said, running his fingers over the dents.

Sadler inhaled and blew smoke out his nostrils. "What happened?"

"A fire engine hit him. He didn't tell you about it?"

"No."

"You work with him. You two ain't getting along?"

"He's not exactly first in line to be best man at my wedding."

"Sorry to hear that. He's a good kid. How's he taking not getting promoted?"

"You knew that?"

"Word gets around. He doesn't want to talk about it with me, so we don't talk about it."

"He's got worse problems than not getting promoted."

"You mean that house fire?"

"That's one reason I'm here. I've got my own suspicions on that. There's another guy on my crew showed some unnatural interest in that house before it burned."

"Who would that be?"

"Jerry Monahan."

"That old corn dog ain't retired? You woulda thought what happened to Cordifis would have been a wake-up call to all those old dinosaurs. Fighting fire is a young man's game. Soon as I made chief and couldn't go inside anymore I realized I'd been going in way too long." He coughed, the phlegm rattling in his lungs. "That's what happens when you fight fire all those years. Hell, in Denmark they only leave you on the pipe for five years. After that, you get a job that keeps you out of the building. So you think Monahan might have set that fire?"

"He's just crazy enough."

"I remember once when we were both firefighters Jerry asked to borrow three thousand bucks. Hell, I didn't have a dime to spare, was working down at the steel mill off shift, but a guy named Shimkus did, and when he still hadn't gotten a nickel back after eight months, he took Jerry out behind old Station Nineteen and knocked three of his teeth out. Jerry gave him the pink slip to his car and took the bus to the dentist the next morning. That was how Jerry got interested in karate."

They chatted for another half hour, recounting good times and bad. As he listened, Sadler wondered how such a spindly man had ever carried his reputation as a fire-breathing, door-busting, get-out-of-my-way smoke eater. He'd worked on Engine 14 and then Engine 7, and they always said nobody could take more smoke or stay in a fire longer. When Gary entered the department twenty years ago, all the older chiefs talked about Finney, a captain at the time. Those chiefs were all dead now. Rutgers, Mortimer, Stallworth. Heart attacks and cancer, mostly cancer—the number one item in the firefighter's retirement portfolio.

"I could be wrong about this," Sadler said. "So I'd appreciate it if you didn't mention it to anyone."

"Sure. What's that you got around your neck? That a cross? You ain't gone Jesus on me?"

"Yes, sir. Not that I'm perfect, mind you. I guess Jesus is why I came by today. He told me to ask if there was anything I could do to make you more comfortable."

"I figured when I got sick, religion would grab me by the nads, but it didn't. I still think it's for suckers. But you can do one thing for me. Would you try to make things work with John? Even if he don't know it, Leary Way's eating a hole right through him. He needs every scrap of understanding he can get. That's what you can do for me, Gary. Be a friend to John. Look out for him."

"I'll do that."

"Thank you." The old man shook hands with Sadler, his grip weak, his palms sweaty.

Driving across the West Seattle viaduct toward I-5, Gary couldn't help thinking about the night of the Leary Way fire. Gary had been on Engine 26, the only unit in the south end not at an alarm at four in the morning. The three of them had been in the watch office—Sadler, Monahan, and Jenkins.

A worried dispatcher had called on the main phone and told Sadler they'd been out of contact with Chief Finney for nearly an hour, that he'd disappeared from a fire in the Fifth Battalion. They'd used the radio, they'd paged him, they'd called on his cell phone. Even though he wasn't supposed to be at Station 29 where he was stationed, they'd hit the bell there repeatedly. The vanishing act had begun a few minutes after the dispatchers told him they'd tracked the distress signal at Leary Way to his son's radio. Nobody realized until later that Finney had left his radio with Cordifis.

Monitoring channel fourteen, the channel reserved for ordinary department business, Sadler and the crew on Engine 26 climbed onto the rig and began driving the south half of the Seventh Battalion. Just before dawn they found him parked on the grass in a small park, Riverview play field, where he had a somewhat obstructed view from the promontory that looked out over Harbor Island, downtown Seattle, and beyond that, Queen Anne Hill. The red Suburban's motor was running. In the distance he'd been watching the glow in the sky from Leary Way.

Even after they told him his son was alive, he didn't snap out of it.

They ended up driving him home, Sadler and his crew sitting with Chief Finney in his living room, his wife beside him in a nightgown, none of them knowing quite what to do until the medics got there.

Two weeks later, Chief Finney retired.

# 47. THE LAUGHING FIREFIGHTER

When the bell hit at twenty minutes before midnight on Monday, November 3, the overhead lights came on automatically with the alarm, just as they always did. Finney found himself laughing. He wasn't sure why, perhaps because he'd been awakened from the first truly deep slumber in recent memory, perhaps because he'd been dreaming about the good time he'd had with Diana the other day. They'd spoken on the phone at work, too, just before going to bed. As he pulled on his socks and stepped into his rubber boots and bunking trousers, the dispatcher's urgent voice awakened him fully.

"Time out: twenty-three forty hours. Engines Eleven, Twenty-six, Thirty-six, Twenty-seven; Ladders Seven and Eleven; Battalion Seven; Aid Fourteen, Medic Ten, Safety One; Air Twenty-six: West Marginal Way Southwest and Southwest Michigan Street. Channel one. Engines Eleven, Twenty-six . . ."

After the dispatcher gave three rounds of response information, she added, "A large volume of smoke reported from Bowman Pork Products."

On the apparatus floor, Jerry Monahan wore a sleepy grin, his gray hair erupting from the sides of his head like whipped cream. They'd barely exchanged ten words all day—Monahan had been secreted away in the spare room working on his invention—and now this ingenuous grin. Finney couldn't figure him.

Finney climbed into the crew cab on Engine 26, buckled the snaps on his coat, turned on his portable radio, and switched it to channel one. Then he slid his arms into the straps of the self-contained breathing apparatus stored behind the seat. He couldn't help it. He loved this shit. Getting up in the middle of the night to do who knows what. It was the most interesting job in the world. Anything could be out there waiting for him. Absolutely anything. As they pulled out of the station, he put the strap of his rubber face mask around his neck, screwed the low-pressure hose onto the regulator at his waist, then reached back with his right hand and opened the main valve. The warning bell chattered momentarily as air blew past and freshly energized the system.

Two minutes later they arrived at the location next to the Duwamish Waterway, where the foul-tasting odor of smoke hung in the chill night air. They were definitely about to fight some fire. Good, Finney thought. Love it.

The property was flat, as was all of the land for a couple of miles to the east. Behind them was a huge wooded hillside, West Marginal Way, a little-used four-lane road running along its base. Moments earlier the lieutenant on Engine 27 had taken charge on the radio, giving himself the title "Marginal Command," an unfortunate choice of words. Engine 27's driver worked the pump panel, and the third crew member occupied himself dragging a fifty-foot length of four-inch hose toward a hydrant.

"Stick with me!" Sadler said, pointing a finger at Finney as he climbed off the rig.

"Of course."

Sadler opened a side compartment and began slinging his mask while Finney surveyed the buildings. There were two main structures: an older, smaller building to their left, with concrete walls and a flat roof; a newer concrete structure to the right. There was nothing pretty about either building, and the situation was strangely reminiscent of Leary Way, though they weren't going to be shorthanded here. There were already three engines on scene, and Finney could hear more sirens down the road.

Between the buildings and almost directly in front of Engine 26 was a small parking area with a loading dock, two cab-over trucks parked inside the gate. It was in front of this loading area that Engine 11, Engine 27, and Engine 26 had clustered like bees around a concrete chrysanthemum.

Flame licked the inside corner of the building on the loading dock, black smoke crawling up the walls. Like a paste-on eyebrow dangling off a drunken actor, one melted rain gutter hung loose. Two firefighters from one of the other units charged toward the building hauling a line that was rapidly filling with water and would soon slow their progress to a crawl.

Around the eaves of the larger building, dense, black smoke puffed into the night sky. In places it crept out like a wraith, but in others it blew out under pressure as if from an exhaust pipe. It might have been coming from the fire near the loading dock, or it might have been indicative of something worse. "Bowman Pork Products," Finney read off the side of one of the trucks. What could be burning except machinery and bacon fat?

Followed by a small man in a puffy gray ski coat, Lieutenant Parkhurst strode over to them. He'd established himself as incident commander and would be giving orders and assignments until a chief arrived.

"Gary," Lieutenant Parkhurst said, stopping in front of Lieutenant Sadler, who was belting himself into his backpack, "this man says there's a family inside."

"Back of the warehouse," said the man, nodding briskly. He was on the underside of forty and wore baggy black trousers, his ski coat zipped low enough to reveal a bow tie. A tri-colored ski cap covered his brow. "Whole family. I haven't seen them. Not since eight o'clock."

"Okay. Come on," Sadler said, tapping Finney on the shoulder and walking in front of Parkhurst and the civilian. "Let's go."

"How many?" Finney asked, turning to the civilian, who looked vaguely familiar.

"Five. No." He held up six fingers. "Six." His mouth was dry. It sounded like *sex.*

"Where?"

"Back. Way back." He waved at the building. It was obvious he was too wound up to think clearly.

"That's a big place. Where in the back? This end? Where?"

He stepped around in front of Engine 26 and stared at several hundred feet of blank concrete wall. "They're in there," he said, motioning hopelessly.

Together Finney and Sadler shouldered two hundred feet of line from the rear of Engine 11 and dropped a trail of zigzagging hose behind them up a short flight of concrete stairs opposite the loading dock. When Sadler used the heavy, rubber-tipped nozzle to break the glass out of a door, smoke enveloped them.

The smoke wasn't particularly hot, which meant there would be a lot of survivable spaces inside.

# 48. NITWITS

inney tightened the straps on his facepiece, opened the low-pressure valve at his waist, and felt the cool air wash over his face. Believing the fire was nowhere nearby, Gary Sadler dropped the nozzle in the doorway so they could search quickly and without the burden of dragging that heavy hose around corners; they would come back for it later.

Six people living in a factory, probably a family of immigrants, perhaps boat people from Southeast Asia. That hose could slow them down immeasurably, and Finney was glad they'd decided to leave it. A house fire would be one thing, but this place was huge. Their two hundred feet of hose line probably wasn't even enough to reach the fire.

On a bulletin board in the hallway, leftover Halloween decorations had curled in the heat. The smoke quickly became so thick they couldn't see the walls, much less the overhead lights. By rights they should have been crawling, but the building was immense, and if they were going to search it in time to do the inhabitants any good, they needed to move quickly.

"The witness said they were in the back of the building," Finney said, probing the murk with a nine-volt battle lantern.

Intent on doing it room by room, Sadler ignored him. There was no point in quibbling. Sadler wasn't going to listen, and Finney wasn't going to break up their team. They quickly passed through several offices, a lunchroom, and what appeared to be a changing room with metal clothing lockers against the walls. The smoke was lighter in these rooms.

They searched a pair of small storage rooms, and when Sadler broke out two windows, the smoke didn't dissipate.

On the main floor Sadler reached the door to another room and said, "You're the outside man. I'm going in."

Though they hadn't discussed which search technique they would use, they both knew this one: the would-be rescuer posted a second firefighter in the doorway—the idea being that while he moved around in the room, he would maintain his orientation by the sound of his partner's voice in the doorway. The protocol was that Finney would search the next room and Sadler would be the doorway man.

When Sadler came out of the first room, he shouldered Finney out of the way and proceeded into the next room—alone. For some reason he was bent on treating Finney like a recruit. "Shit!" Sadler yelled.

Finney stuck his head through the door, but he already knew what he would find. The hose line at his feet was a dead giveaway. They were at the door they'd used earlier to enter the building. They'd come full circle, and Sadler had stepped back outside. To make matters worse, another team had appropriated their nozzle and taken it inside.

Moving more quickly than ever, they followed the team that had their nozzle up a flight of stairs and into a loft area where a pair of helmet lights moved through the smoke on the far side of the room. Sadler turned around and headed down the stairs. "They're jacking off. Let's go."

On the main floor they found a corridor that led toward the newer section and after a dozen yards encountered a set of locked doors. They took turns kicking them until they gave way.

It was smokier in this part of the building, and hotter, and after twenty feet it got so black Finney had to hold onto the back of Sadler's bottle to keep track of him. Heavy hose streams thrummed on the outside walls.

On their right was another door leading to what Finney assumed was the loading dock area where they'd originally seen fire. The golden rule in firefighting was to not pass up any fire, to put it out as you came to it, and through the crack in the door he could see a sheet of solid orange, the metal push-plate on the door hot to the touch. Should the fire breach these doors, it could cut off their escape. Going forward was risky, but going back for a line would mean depleting much if not all of their air. Finney would have gone back for a line, but he wasn't making the decisions.

When they encountered a large, walk-in freezer, he was again assigned the task of doorkeeper. Gary was babying him, and Finney didn't like it, in fact, was getting pissed off. Still, there wasn't anything he could do about it. He knew he was in better shape than Sadler, and he knew that if one of them was to stand and wait, it made more sense that it should be Sadler. As Finney waited, a pair of firefighters approached from the general direction in which he and Gary had been traveling.

They told him they'd found a pair of victims upstairs on a mezzanine not far away and their portable radios weren't getting out of the building, that they were going for help. They gave Finney directions to the victims and said they would stay but they were almost out of air. As if to underscore their plight, one of their alarm bells began ringing. Before

Finney could ask why they hadn't simply brought the victims out with them, they vanished into the smoke.

It occurred to him that they hadn't mentioned the condition of the victims. If they were unconscious or dead, they might have told him. He had to assume they were at least unconscious, or they would have followed them out of the building. If they were dead, it would have explained the lack of urgency in their demeanor. In a body recovery, the investigators usually wanted to see the corpses where they lay.

When Sadler came out of the freezer, Finney said, "Somebody came by and told me where they are."

"Why didn't they stick around?"

"Out of air."

"Okay, let's get going, man. I don't want to be breathing through my T-shirt."

"Me neither." Finney felt his way through the smoke for another fifteen paces and, just as described by the firefighters, found a set of wooden steps running alongside a wall.

They were halfway up the stairs when the abandon building sequence went off on their portable radios. The *hi-lo* signal meant fire tactics were being switched from an interior to an exterior attack, that any and all firefighters inside the building were to exit forthwith.

"Jesus," Sadler said. "They're bailing out." He grabbed his portable radio. "Marginal Command from Engine Twenty-six. We're in what appears to be the east end of the factory. We have a confirmed report from other firefighters of victims. We're going to complete our search."

Seattle's portable radios made a high-pitched clinking sound at the beginning of a successful transmission, a lower-pitched *bonk* to signal a blocked transmission, but Sadler's radio had made no sound whatsoever. It was possible the concrete walls of the building were obstructing the signals. Or that the amount of fire traffic had made it difficult for the repeater tower to pick up their message and relay it. Sadler tried twice more with no better results.

"You want to keep on?" Sadler asked.

"Absolutely."

"I don't know why those assholes walked out. When I find out who they are, I'm going to break their balls."

The higher they went on the stairs, the hotter the smoke. By the time they reached the top of the stairs, they were on their bellies.

Thrusting their feet and free arms toward the center of the room, they proceeded along the right-hand wall.

"You sure this is where they said?" Sadler asked.

Finney was about to reply when Sadler slapped at his arm, kicked his helmet hard, and then pulled on him. At first he thought he was being assaulted, but Sadler was thrashing about the way a drowning man thrashed about. In order to not be pulled off balance, Finney reached out and grabbed some smoke, then finally grasped a metal bar on the wall. He held onto the bar on one side, Sadler on the other. A few moments later Sadler regained his balance and let go.

"Jesus Christ!" Sadler said.

"What happened?"

"Look at this shit."

Finney couldn't see anything but smoke. He placed his face within a foot of his battle lantern and discovered they were on a balcony. Though he couldn't see the ground floor in the smoke, the drop-off was fourteen or fifteen feet.

"I almost went off!" Sadler said. "There's no goddamned rail! Come on, let's get out of here."

"What about the victims?"

"Fuck the victims! They're dead. Hey, anybody here? Hey, you assholes? Where are you? See? There's no people. We're getting our butts kicked for nothing."

Fueled by fear and adrenaline, Sadler turned and headed back the way they'd come.

"We can't leave," Finney said.

Sadler spoke clearly and succinctly. "I'm going out. You coming with me?"

"I'm coming."

# 49. THOUSANDS OF PIGS' FEET

Moving with a recklessness he hadn't displayed earlier, Sadler plunged down the stairs, and then, instead of hugging the walls, he proceeded directly through the open space toward their entry point. Finney couldn't decide whether Sadler was angry or scared. Maybe both. He didn't have time to think about what he was feeling, but he knew he was some kind of upset. They'd just left at least two people to die up on that mezzanine.

In short order they passed the door that had fire behind it and ran headlong into the two doors they'd kicked in to get into this section of the plant.

"Sombitch," Sadler said. "Goddamned stupid sombitch."

"What's wrong?"

"Look at this bullshit! Sombitch door's jammed."

"It can't be. We broke the lock."

"Yeah? You try it." The doors were as solid as if they were anchored on the other side by a large truck.

"Maybe these are the wrong doors?" Finney said.

"Not a chance."

Had he been riding a ladder company, Finney would have used the axe on his belt to chop through, but he didn't have an axe. They were rapidly running out of air, fire was eating its way through a door thirty feet behind them, the space they were in was superheated, they couldn't see anything, and their original entrance point was locked.

In another minute they would be trapped by fire in this corridor.

Sadler continued pulling at the doors.

Then they both kicked at them, their feeble efforts a testament to how much strength they'd lost in the heat. "What happened?" Finney asked.

"I don't know," Sadler said, gasping for breath. "Something locked them after we went through."

Sadler tried his radio but couldn't get through.

Arrows of flame were already darting out over the doors behind them. Instead of taking the left wall as they had before, Sadler said, "This way," and took the right. Finney couldn't get over how Gary was mothering him.

The fire leaked quickly through the doors behind them, and began riding the wall above their heads, moving in great, screwlike twists toward the ceiling. As the amount of flame in the area grew, visibility got better.

When Finney spotted an unlocked door to their right, they entered a thirty-by-forty-foot room with a ceiling almost as tall as the room was wide. Smoke filled the upper portions of the space, but from five feet above their heads to the floor it was surprisingly clear. They spotted an exit on the far side of the room, a single door set into a heavy brick wall, locked and nailed shut.

Finney found a small bar on a workbench and began prying. After he'd worked fifteen seconds, Sadler took the bar out of his hands, his impatience signaling a reservoir of anxiety he never would have admitted to. Finney decided right then and there he was not working with Sadler again. He would transfer out of Twenty-six's—if it took an act of Congress, he would transfer out. Sooner or later Sadler was going to get him killed. The thought occurred to him that if he did transfer, he might do it directly to the King County Jail.

It took Sadler sixty seconds to pry open the door.

Finney assumed from the amount of smoke on the other side that they were returning to the main warehouse. It was hotter after the relative calm of the closed room, and once again they could hear water streams beating against the outer walls.

For a split second Finney glimpsed a door on the wall directly behind Sadler in the smoke.

"Over there," Finney said, walking forward. As he proceeded, Sadler ran not for the door, but directly at him, reaching him in two large strides, knocking him backward.

Finney tumbled back through the doorway, his bottle clanking on the concrete floor, the wind knocked out of his lungs, his hip and one elbow numb with pain. For a moment he felt as if he'd been struck by a bus.

"Goddamn it, Gary!"

Rolling onto his hands and knees, he took a moment or two to regain his senses before he realized Sadler was under a pile of burning debris. He felt the heat on his wrists as he frantically pulled the burning materials off his partner.

Several boards and one timber had fallen from somewhere above. They might have killed an unsuspecting Finney if Sadler hadn't knocked him out of the way. When he turned and saw a pile of burning lumber teetering on a mezzanine over their heads, he half-carried, half-dragged Sadler out of the way. A hose stream from outside burst through a high window, forcing steam down on them. As the heat came down, Finney slipped and fell beside Sadler.

He became aware that he was lying on something, a lot of little somethings. Like ball bearings. He felt around with his gloved hand and then turned on the small flashlight on his chest strap—pigs' feet, hundreds, thousands of pigs' feet.

"Come on," Finney said, receiving no answer. "Lieutenant?"

There was nothing more cumbersome than a man in full bunkers carrying another man in full bunkers. Sadler weighed 230 plus his 50 pounds of equipment. Finney knew it would be hard to drag him, next to impossible to carry him, but still he knelt and pulled him to a sitting position. When he had him almost standing, he threw his shoulder under his hips and folded his limp body across one shoulder. For a moment he thought rising from this half-crouch wasn't possible, but with a great effort, he finally succeeded.

Breathing like a racehorse, he walked slowly, shakily, toward the wall where he'd seen the exit. At each step his legs threatened to buckle. How the hell did I get in this fix, Finney thought, as he tried to calm his breathing. I go to a big fire, the world caves in on me. Is it just me? Even as he had these thoughts, things began to get better. As it happened, he walked almost in a direct line to the outside door.

After he'd put Sadler down, he looked up and saw two firefighters nearby, both wearing backpacks and masks. He made sure they saw Sadler against the doorjamb and waited until they were approaching. Just before they reached him, Finney stepped back inside and lost himself in the smoke.

# 50. AN INCH OF COOL AIR

A larm bell ringing, he made his way on rubbery legs across the warehouse space. His bottle would soon be drained of air, but unlike a lot of younger firefighters, Finney had entered the department under a regime when firefighters rarely masked up for anything, so he knew from brutal experience he could force himself through almost any amount of smoke.

Together with the conviction that they'd been within a few feet of the victims, frustration and anger nudged Finney back into the depths of the warehouse and beyond the immediate sounds of hoses and running pumps and shouting men.

He was dizzy and hot and still shaky from carrying Sadler, and even though he didn't want to admit it, he was scared.

What he couldn't have foreseen was the astonishingly quick buildup of heat in the building. "Christ," he said to himself.

He reached a wall and followed it to the left. He'd lost the battle lantern and now had only the small, department-issue flashlight, which he could use to see at arm's length in some places, not at all in others.

Locating a set of wooden stairs, he decided they were the same stairs he and Sadler had used earlier. As he crawled up into the heat, the sweat inside his bunking clothes began turning to steam and scalding him. He thought he saw orange licking across the space directly above, but when he tipped his head back to get a better look, there was only blackness and a burning sensation at the back of his neck where his collar touched him. The void in front of his eyes might have been thirty millimeters distant. Or thirty miles.

He reached the top step, dropped to his knees, and crawled alongside the wall, the ringing bell a constant reminder that his air was nearly depleted.

The space turned out to be empty. He was disappointed and somewhat surprised.

As he was mulling over his options, the bell on the back of his belt stopped clanking and he felt a sensation similar to sucking on a snorkel with a hand over the end. He ripped his mask off and scuttled down the wooden stairs on his stomach, trying not to breathe until he reached the shallow layer of relatively good air an inch above the concrete on the main floor.

Perhaps there was another set of stairs. Perhaps the firefighters who'd given him directions had been confused. Or maybe *he* was confused. Inhaling shallowly, he continued on his hands and knees along the wall, heading toward what he guessed was the east end of the building. He had no idea where the exit was.

It was always this simple. Leary Way had been this simple.

One small misstep. Nothing portentous. This was how it started. The margin for error was always minuscule. You screwed up one step at a time; pretty soon you were in trouble, and a while after that, not too long after that really, you were dead.


He was still crawling when he heard the sounds an MSA mask makes as somebody at rest inhales and exhales. On his MSA backpack belt he carried, as did all Seattle firefighters, a PASS device, which he now held in his hand.

The PASS was the size of a double-thick cigarette pack and had two settings—one designed to emit a piercing whistle after twenty-five seconds of motionlessness, so that others could home in on a downed firefighter, the other a manual mode to whistle regardless of movement. He switched his to manual.

He saw a fuzzy light and realized they were within twenty feet of him, moving closer. He tried to stand and holler, but the heat knocked him to the floor.

It didn't take a whole lot of carbon monoxide to get your brain swimming. He was dizzy. Nauseated. Sleepy beyond all expectation. His temples throbbed. His face was flushed and hot. His eyes dry. He was beginning to lose track of time. The sense of déjà vu became almost overpowering. This was so similar to Leary Way. But then, smoke was smoke. He could have been anywhere.

They were closer now, his rescuers. Wanting to be able to listen, he fumbled with the noisy PASS device until it was off. Now there was only the low, crackling symphony of whispers from the flame overhead.

"Hey," he shouted. "Over here. Seattle Fire Department." But they were gone.

Then he saw an opening, a doorway with lights and noise and people and activity; it was all so close he couldn't believe his luck. As he crawled toward the light, a woman stepped into the doorway, her hands in the pockets of a long, gray raincoat that reached her ankles. For a moment he thought it was . . . it was—Diana. He couldn't figure out why she wasn't in full bunkers. When she took her hands out of her pockets she wore no gloves; her hands were as bare and smooth as milk.

She was blocking the doorway, and for some reason, as he looked up into her gray eyes, he no longer felt any urgency to get outside. "You been in there killing old ladies, John?"

"What?"

"You realize sooner or later you're going to have to explain yourself."

"Why aren't you suited up?"

"We're talking about you, sweetie. Not me. We're talking about your criminal career."

He tried to move closer, but moving made him dizzy. He staggered. Hands on his knees, he put his head down and let the blood run back into his brain. It felt as if someone were beating on his skull with a mallet.

When he looked up, he was alone. No Diana. No doorway.

He spun around in a circle trying to figure out where she'd gone, or if she'd ever been there.

He'd been within ten feet of an exit, and sure, maybe the smoke got heavier and obscured it, but if he stood still long enough, surely the smoke would lift and the door and the woman would reappear.

He saw something. He wasn't sure what. A movement. A sliver of light. He moved toward it.

He felt a hard shove from behind and dropped to keep from stumbling, striking the concrete hard with his knees. When he put his hands out to push himself back up, he realized he was on the lip of a deep shaft, a shaft somebody had tried to catapult him into. He rolled to the side and crawled along the edge of the shaft in the blackness.

Switching the PASS device on, he flung it across the floor. Twenty-five seconds later the device began emitting a high-pitched wail. He heard movement, scuffling boots heading in the direction of the PASS. A burning timber crashed nearby, and when sparks flew off, he saw two helmeted figures in full bunkers. He couldn't tell if they saw him or not.

———

After some time he realized he was staring at the ceiling light in a medic unit. The firefighter paramedic, an intense woman in a white shirt, was bending over him asking questions.

Naked except for a pair of wet boxer shorts and socks, Finney lay on his back under what felt like a giant sticky spiderweb. An electric fan somewhere blew air across his torso. He was thirsty, his teeth as dry as pebbles in the desert.

For some reason he knew he was still on scene. Put an address on it, he thought, straining to make his mind function, but he couldn't come up with the day of the week or even the name of the president when they asked him. He couldn't identify the unit he'd been riding or his partner. "Bill Cordifis," he finally muttered, when they asked, but even as he said the words he knew he'd flunked the quiz.

He was drifting in and out of his own life.

Although he realized even as he was speaking that he wasn't making sense, he felt he had a story to tell, one they needed to hear. He found himself jabbering about victims, female firefighters in raincoats, unknown assailants; even as he tried to get the tale out, he knew the odd-shaped lumber in his sentences was not building a structure that would stand. He knew his words conveyed nothing but his own befuddlement, and the worst part of it, now that he'd begun talking, was that he couldn't stop. And when he did stop, he couldn't start again.

Determined to compose a single sentence that would convey all of his desperation, he fell silent, straining to muster the right sequence of words. The faces over him were as somber as if they were peering into a casket.

When he moved his head from side to side ever so slightly, it seemed as if the entire medic unit tipped. The effect was so bewildering and wondrous he continued rolling his head back and forth for some minutes.

The medic who'd been working on him, a short-haired, broad-shouldered woman with a chest that, from Finney's angle, all but obscured her face, stood up straight and, with a certain amount of deference, addressed someone at the rear of the van.

"We're putting ringers into him, Chief. This is our second bag. When we got him, he had a rate of one fifty-eight and his blood pressure was eighty palp and falling. We cut everything off and put this damp sheet over him, but he's not cooling down. We didn't think to take his core temperature until maybe ten minutes into it. It was a hundred six. Hallucinations start at around a hundred five. You want to talk to him, fine, but he's not making any sense. Right now we need to get more fluids on board and stick him in a hyperbaric chamber."

"John? How are you, old pal?" The voice was directly over him, deliberate, cool-headed, and noticeably more affable than it had been with the medic. This was a man who knew what he wanted. "John?"

Finney stopped rocking his head and peered down between his feet through the open back doors of the medic van. Beyond his feet he saw a wall of rippling orange.

"John, we need to know what happened. We need to know. Where's your partner? We've got a man missing, and you're the only one who knows where he is. John, this is Chief Reese. Your old friend, Charlie. Stop and think and try to make sense. John, where is Gary?"

"I carried him out."

"You couldn't have. You could barely walk when they found you."

"Before they found me. Left him with a couple of firefighters in the doorway."

"John? Don't go to sleep. Where'd you leave Gary?"

Finney could hear voices, but he couldn't get his eyes open.

Reese barked out orders. "Get somebody to check all the doorways. Get moving. And don't let those newspaper people know what you're doing."

It was then that a bulky figure in a dirty yellow bunking suit parted the white-shirted workers, an older man with a fleshy face and ruddy cheeks. It wasn't unusual for Finney to see Bill Cordifis. He was dead, obviously, but Finney saw him once or twice a week. Sometimes in the visage of an old man collecting aluminum cans behind a supermarket. Sometimes he was a utility truck driver, or a face on a passing bus, a man in the passenger seat of a motor home on the freeway.

Leaning close, Cordifis said, "Bet you thought you were rid of me, huh, Sport?"

"I tried to get you out," Finney whispered. "I tried my best."

Unbuttoning his bunking coat, Cordifis said, "See what you did?"

From deep down in his stomach, from somewhere near the base of his spine, Finney could feel the scream coming even as he tried to staunch it. Although he'd lost most of his voice from the smoke, the sound he made was hideous. Hands struggled to hold him down, and as he screamed he knew he sounded like a gut-shot dog. The knowledge did not arrest the howl coming out of him. He screamed and screamed again.

# 51. JERKED OFF BY A MORON

Tuesday morning Oscar was forced to park nearly a half mile away from the site. Besides the gawkers who mobbed the intersection near the smoldering ruins, there were hundreds of firefighters who'd come to mingle in the smoke and early-morning fog. With one man missing and another possibly dying in the hospital, the mood was distinctly gloomy. Intermixed in the crowd were a few female fire groupies, but mostly male wanna-bes with bulging muscles and military haircuts, or fire-buff types, pocket protectors swollen with pens, medical flashlights, EMT cheat cards, and chief's badges they'd bought mail-order from the back of *Firehouse* magazine. What a circus, Oscar thought.

Nearly every civilian vehicle passing through the intersection slowed as the occupants stared at the ruins. Some of the passersby rolled down their windows and shouted questions at the traffic babe under the light. Others turned on their headlights or pushed flowers out their windows onto the roadway—which by noon was carpeted with crushed roses and carnations, the sweetness blending with the bottom-of-the-shoe odor of last night's fire.

Oscar wished he had a nickel for every time Finney's name was invoked.

It was a bad time for the fire department. The medics said they'd be surprised if Finney survived, and even though he was officially listed as missing, everybody knew Gary Sadler was dead.

It was all so needless, Oscar thought. For Christ's sake, a fellow who five months ago had been as badly injured as Finney, you'd think he would do anything to avoid Operations Division. Yet the dumb bastard couldn't get back into combat fast enough, clearly a man who couldn't stay out of trouble. Look at that mess on Riverside Drive.

Everybody knew barking dogs got shot, and it surprised Oscar that a man as intelligent as Finney could get himself into this kind of bind.

The newspapers were bound to regurgitate the Leary Way story. Last summer both Seattle papers had run multiple features on Leary Way, the Seattle Fire Department, and firefighting in general. Oscar remembered some of the press clippings: FIRE CHIEF'S SON NARROWLY ESCAPES BLAZE.

CAPTAIN DIES, CHIEF'S SON LIVES. FIREFIGHTER'S BEST EFFORTS UNRE-
WARDED. Nor would the media pass up a chance to rerun last summer's
photos of Reese and Kub emerging from that flame-shrouded doorway.
Nobody was going to overlook the fact that John Finney had been a key
player in both debacles. Oscar hated to see a firefighter go to the grave
with that sort of stain on his reputation, especially a firefighter as likable
as Finney.

It would be better if he died. They would give him a hero's funeral,
shed a few tears when the bagpipes played, start a college fund in his name.

Media mavens had flown in from as far away as L.A. and San Fran-
cisco, and Oscar knew that as long as the story remained ongoing, as long
as Gary Sadler was missing and the outcome of Finney's hospital stay remained in question, there would be hourly updates. Breaking news, they
called it. Chief Reese milked his minutes in the limelight, joking with the
large-jawed news lady from KSTW-TV in Tacoma as if she were an old
girlfriend, or as if he wished she were. Reese knew that once Sadler's
body was recovered, the media would stop focusing on the minute-by-
minute events and begin digging into why it happened. When it came to
that business about not promoting Finney, Reese was going to look
damned near prescient.

At noon Oscar tucked his shirt in and wandered over to the traffic
enforcement babe under the light at West Marginal and Michigan, a
dishwater blond with a thick waist and an officious air about her that
amused Oscar. They chatted for five minutes, and when he asked for her
phone number, she pulled her lips into a thin smile and informed him
that she *had* a boyfriend. Oscar said her having a boyfriend didn't bother
him in the least. Unlike a lot of Seattle males, Oscar Stillman wasn't
afraid of women. He told her so, said he'd grown up with six sisters and
four aunts, had three daughters, and had been married and divorced
three times. He liked women and they liked him, too.

He was still talking with her at 1300 hours when John Finney turned
up. He was supposed to be dead, or close enough you couldn't tell the
difference, so Oscar was as surprised as anyone. Finney wore combat
boots, hospital greens, and a pale blue woman's cardigan sweater that
was too small, most of the buttons in the wrong holes. The getup made
him look like a mental patient on furlough. It was obvious he shouldn't
have been released from the hospital. He had bloodshot eyes, and his

posture, which had always been erect and proud, was slouched and hunchbacked. He moved with the left-slanting gait and wobble of a dying goldfish swimming across the bowl, at times leaning on Diana Moore's shoulder.

No matter what delusions he was harboring, no matter what crimes he might be guilty of, here was a fellow firefighter in obvious physical and emotional distress, and Oscar knew, no matter how many others kept their distance, the Christian ethic was to be friendly. It was Oscar's practice not to abandon the Christian ethic unless there was some profit in it.

"John. John, how the hell are you?" Oscar said, approaching the duo as they made their way through the mute clusters of firefighters. Stillman had to step in front of Finney to get his attention. "Hey. Hey, how are you doing, guy? Aren't you going to talk to your old buddy?"

"They find him?" Finney asked, his voice thick.

"You took a hell of a beating in there. We're proud of you, boy."

Finney, who had been staring into space as the crane removed a huge slab of concrete from the rubble, turned to Oscar, his eyes moist from the wind. "You're what?"

"We're proud of you."

"You don't even know what happened," Finney said, brushing past him in a clear dismissal.

Oscar molded his lips into a smile as Diana Moore came abreast and gave him an apologetic look. Nothing like getting jerked off by a moron, Oscar thought. God, she was pretty for a firefighter. Up close her skin was flawless. And the gray in those eyes was something you could look into forever, like a lake you'd discovered up in the mountains that no one else knew about. She was a work of nature, all right.

As did many of the others during the afternoon, Oscar kept an eye on Finney. Diana Moore remained at his side, as silent and loyal as a guide dog. Oscar wondered if standing around in paper clothing for hours in the November chill bothered Finney; if so, he showed no sign of it.

It was that type of focus that worried Monahan. In fact, it was Jerry who'd paid some drunk he'd found at a bar out on Pacific Highway South to make the phone call about Riverside Drive. G. A. had done his part, too, although by rights he should have arrested Finney a week ago. Had he been in the slammer, last night wouldn't have been necessary.

Finney's discovery of the engine had made all this inevitable. And of course, he never would have looked for the engine if that idiot Paul hadn't tried to run him down in it. Nobody had okayed that. He'd done it on his own. It didn't matter now. Dead or alive Finney would no longer be the loose cannon. Jailing him would erode his credibility.

By now everybody knew Finney thought he'd spoken to two firefighters inside the Bowman Pork building, even though nobody else had been in that part of the building. They'd heard about his screaming, too. Everybody'd heard about his screaming.

Just after four o'clock word percolated through the ranks that the search teams had located a body. Blind luck, Oscar thought, having privately figured it would take three or four days to ferret out the corpse from under those massive chunks of concrete and ceiling beams.

The state investigators, along with a federal team from Alcohol, Tobacco and Firearms, spent almost an hour excavating the area and snapping pictures of the corpse. During the wait small bits of trivia were passed down the line like buckets of water along a fire brigade: his body was unrecognizable; both hands were burned off; he'd been found under a piece of machinery; the gold in his teeth had melted out of his head and had wrapped around his skull like strands of a spiderweb. A second PASS device had been found several feet from Sadler. ATF quickly identified this as the missing PASS from Finney's backpack. It was easy for those with no imagination to guess what had happened. Sadler had gotten into trouble and Finney had left his PASS with him and gone for help, just as he had with Cordifis. Of course, that didn't match anything Finney said. Oscar knew it didn't match what happened either.

Oscar smiled. It almost didn't matter that Paul and Michael Lazenby hadn't been able to kill him last night. Anything Finney said now would be discredited before it was out of his mouth.

# 52. PARANOIA IN BED

At seven-thirty that evening Diana put John into bed, then took a shower and changed into fresh clothing she'd brought in her gym bag. All day she'd been posing as nurse and nanny. The doctors had told her to call if he showed signs of irrational behavior, ischemic attacks, a loss of consciousness, or anything else that wasn't normal. They were clearly scared to death that he was going to collapse outside their care.

When someone was exposed to smoke, the carbon monoxide in the smoke bonded with the hemoglobin at a rate two hundred times faster than oxygen did, displacing oxygen in the heart, lungs, vital organs, and brain. To make matters worse, the half-life for CO in the blood was five to six hours, which meant concentrations took a long time to dissipate.

The carbon monoxide in Finney's blood had been measured at a level that could easily have proven fatal. Several hours in the hyperbaric chamber on one hundred percent oxygen had brought it down, but the doctors were still worried.

Against medical advice, John had found some scrubs to wear, signed the release form, and walked out of the hospital into the cool morning air as if he actually knew where he was headed. Outside the hospital, where Diana caught up with him, he looked disoriented and helpless.

"You know where you are?" Diana asked.

"I guess I don't."

"Let me drive you home."

"They find Gary?"

"I don't think so."

"Let's go there."

"Come on. I'll show you where my Jeep is."

Diana knew smoke inhalation produced various side effects, including short- and long-term memory loss; the doctors had warned Finney of the potential complications, stressing his need for continued treatment, constant monitoring, and lots of fluids. In the hours since driving him from the fire site to 26's to pick up his things, and then to his houseboat on Lake Union, Diana had forced copious amounts of juice and water down him. Short of hog-tying him and dragging him back to the hospital, she'd done all she could.

Diana turned the lights out and went into the living room where she climbed into his recliner and pulled a quilt over herself. She watched the running lights from a cruiser easing quietly past the window.

She listened to his answering machine take another call, this from a local country-western radio station brazenly asking Finney to drive to their studio tomorrow morning for a chatty interview during the commute hour, as if he was in any condition to talk, or to drive. Or to be chatty.

Sadler's body had been recovered under a stainless-steel tub. Hiding under a tub of pig guts didn't seem like a good way to die, but then there was no good way to die in a fire.

Diana was washing dishes in the kitchen sink, up to her elbows in the hot, sudsy water when Finney called from the other room. Although his bedroom was not particularly warm, he was sitting up in bed, sweating heavily. Avoiding the postage-stamp burn on his neck, she touched his bare shoulder reassuringly. "Something to drink?"

"I've been lying here trying to think it through. I'm confused."

Diana sat on the edge of the bed. "You went to a fire on Engine Twenty-six, down off West Marginal Way. You and Gary went inside searching for victims. Gary never came out."

"No, that's Leary Way. I'm talking about last night."

"That was last night, John."

"But I brought Gary out."

Last night nobody believed him, and now she didn't know if she believed him either. She didn't think he would lie, at least not deliberately, but even after coming out of the hyperbaric chamber he'd been about as confused as a man who wasn't drunk or on drugs could get.

"Where did you take him when you brought him out?" she asked.

"I don't know. Two firefighters came over, so I went back in."

"Earlier you said a doorway. Which doorway?"

"I don't know."

"John, why didn't you talk to somebody when you came out? They would have told you the search had been called off."

"I'd just spoken to two firefighters who said they'd seen victims."

"Okay, what if he went back in himself? Isn't that possible? Could he have been looking for you?"

"I saw somebody inside later. It might have been Gary. Did you know he saved my life? That's the second time this month somebody's saved my life."

"John . . ."

"I was hiding from them. I thought they were trying to kill me. I guess I was hiding from Gary."

"They found your PASS device near Gary's body. Do you know how it got there?"

"I'm sorry. I really can't remember."

"John, nobody's going to blame you for not recalling details the day after a fire."

"You gonna be here in the morning?"

"I was planning on it. If that's all right." She handed Finney a drinking glass half-filled with water, then leaned over and kissed his forehead. "Go to sleep."

"I need to tell you something."

"Not now."

"No, I need to say this. It's about Leary Way. I have to get it off my chest. Bill called me over to look at the wall. When I saw it was coming down, I ran like a scared kitten. I can still feel the panic when I talk about it."

"You did your best. You—"

"No, I didn't do my best. I didn't try to save him. I just ran."

"There are times when all you can do is run."

"I don't think that was one of them."

"Okay. Say you hadn't. Where would that have put you? Under those bricks with Bill. What good would that have done? You did the right thing. It's the same reason the airlines tell us to put that oxygen mask on ourselves first. If you'd slowed to help Bill, you would have both been trapped."

"But the only thing in my mind was getting out."

"As it should have been. You're saying you feel guilty for running away from that wall?"

"Yes."

"Okay. You want to hear my confession? At Leary Way when your mayday came through, we were in the basement. Our radios weren't picking up anything. That's why we didn't have time to do much of a search. We weren't supposed to be down there. We screwed up."

"We searched the basement."

"I know. We saw the tape on the door after we came back up. Maybe we could have found you and Bill if we hadn't been messing around down there. Bill would be alive today. We never even looked at the door on the way in. We forgot to check it for tape. You think I don't feel bad about that?"

Diana was still asleep in the easy chair when Finney's parents showed up Tuesday morning and let themselves in with a key. It would never have occurred to her that nodding off in Finney's living room would be awkward. There was some chitchat, a few avoided looks, a good deal of fidgeting on the part of Finney's mother.

Looking weak and pale and grasping a morning newspaper, Chief Finney spoke gruffly. "How's he doing?"

"Last night, not good. I haven't seen him this morning."

"He should be in the hospital."

"I agree. He took a lot of smoke. It could take weeks for it to purge from his system."

"If he ever purges it. Is he making any sense?"

"Well . . ." Even as she spoke, she regretted the bluntness of her statement. "He's spinning fairy tales. He doesn't know what he's saying. He thinks he does, but he doesn't."

"He usually tells a pretty solid story."

"Last night he was all mixed up. I found it hard to believe anything he said."

When the room grew quiet, Diana realized Finney was in the doorway in a robe and bare feet. It was easy enough to see he'd been standing there long enough to overhear her comments. He was staring at her, through her. This would be a good time, she thought, for the floor to open up and swallow her. She'd been defending John at every fire station she worked at, and the one time she was caught off guard and said something denigrating, he'd overheard it. "John. I'm not awake yet. I didn't mean that."

"Thanks for coming over, Diana."

"I really didn't—"

"Thanks for coming."

She glanced at his parents and said, "I'll get my things."

On the way down the dock she passed a man lugging a television camera and a coifed woman in a long overcoat. They would have detained her if they'd realized she was a firefighter, but in civilian clothes with her hair down it never occurred to anyone.

# 53. POPPING MOTRIN

G. A. stood in the backyard popping Motrin and staring at the mountain of debris the firefighters had hauled out of the house. There was enough garbage here for an entire apartment building. The pile was sopping wet, mostly clothing—but there were also stereo components, mail-order catalogs, pieces of a television, hunks of broken furniture, books, magazines, old shoes, wallboard, and ceiling tile.

Typically an overhaul was performed to make certain the fire didn't rekindle after firefighters left; anything that might spark up and start another fire was removed from the building, placed in the yard or on the street, and hosed down.

G. A. knew the building owner was planning to tell the insurance adjuster this junk had been in mint condition before the fire.

When the owner sauntered around the corner into the backyard, G. A. pulled his handcuffs off his belt and cuffed the man's hands around either side of a vertical support of the porch. The owner, a man named Yassar Himmeld, made a face that implied he was guiltless and said, "What for is this? I do nothing."

Yassar was short. He wore a suit and a starchy white shirt without a tie, and G. A. knew he owned two jewelry stores over on Jackson, as well as eleven houses spread throughout the Central Area. Yassar wore a Rolex and four gold rings. Gold necklaces clanked at his throat as he made futile efforts to free himself from the handcuffs. G. A. didn't like anything about him.

"For what is this?"

"I'm going to make it simple for you, Yassar. You got a nice little duplex here. A day-care upstairs that your wife runs."

"Dar is my sister-in-law. My wife is back in our country."

"Sure. Whatever. You have offices downstairs. You have a safe that you say was robbed by the firefighters who extinguished the fire this morning. I'm going to let that one pass. You have this stack of shit here in the backyard."

"Firemen do that. Firemen wreck my house."

"No, Yassar. You wrecked your house." G. A. lowered his voice. It was getting dark, and Yassar was shivering. "You set fire to this place and you trashed it."

"I no set fire. How you say I set fire? Is accident."

"Sure it was, Yassar. It was an accident just like the one you had three months ago over on Sixteenth. What you did here was, you splashed some flammable liquid around the basement, left the door open, and tossed in a match. I don't mind that so much. The problem I have is that you did it while your sister-in-law was upstairs taking care of fifteen children, six of them in diapers. But never mind that you set this fire while those babies were upstairs. What bugs me about this whole thing is how greedy you are. It isn't enough to collect for this house so you can re-model with the insurance company's money, but you have to haul in a bunch of clothing from somebody's rag bin so you can collect even more."

"No, I no—"

"You're going to prison, and when you get out, you'll be deported."

"I have not done this. What you say, I have not done. I swear."

"We got a piece of the wallboard with gasoline on it. We got a witness saw you with a gasoline can just before the fire."

Yassar Himmeld hung his head and collapsed against the support. G. A. looked up and saw Robert Kub gazing down on them from the back porch. "Wait out by the car, would you?" G. A. said.

"You going to beat me?" the handcuffed man asked, after Kub left.

G. A. spit into the wet grass. "Why should I bust my knuckles? They love you little Arabs in prison. You're going to have a good time, Yassar. You get out, you'll be wearing mascara and a padded bra."

"I no do this."

"What really pisses me off is that you did such a crappy job. You might have gotten away with that fire over on Sixteenth, but there was no way you were getting away with this. Even an imbecile insurance adjuster would be suspicious."

"I can pay you."

"Pardon me? I didn't quite catch that." G. A. put a hand behind one ear.

"I can pay."

"For a lawyer, you mean?"

"For a lawyer. For my freedom. For you."

"Is that a bribe, Yassar?"

"Yes, yes." He nodded vigorously, hoping they'd struck a bargain.

"Yes, you're trying to bribe me?"

"I don't want to go to prison. Please. This hurts no one. I am a good businessman. One little misfortune for you and me to forget, eh? Why don't you be a good businessman, too, and consider my money an honorarium?"

"And how much money would that be?"

"Five hundred dollar?" When he saw the look in G. A.'s eyes, he said, "No, a thousand dollar and you forget this. You agree? Now let me out of these. I am Christian. I know Jesus. I have converted three times. I have ten children. I have two wives. Does none of this affect your humanity?"

G. A. pulled a miniature tape recorder out of his pocket. "How much do you stand to collect from all this, Yassar?"

The man in the suit heaved a sigh and squatted on his haunches. "The house? Not very much. The contents? Another hundred. I have lost some gold and jewelry. I have lost—"

"Okay, okay. Let's say three-fifty. Sixty percent of that would be two-ten. I'll give you a discount here. Two hundred. You fucked up. Now you pay the piper."

"I don't understand. Who is the piper?"

"Me, Abdul. I'm the piper."

"My name is Yassar. Yassar Himmeld. I am a good man."

"There are plenty of good men in prison."

"But how to repair the premises? You leave me with less than half of my losses. You leave me with—"

"Sixty percent is about what it takes to keep you away from those tattooed biker boys up in Monroe. It's that or you shave your legs and dab on eyeliner. Your choice."

"How do I know this isn't a trap?"

G. A. popped a Motrin and chewed it, then held up the tape recorder, which was still running. "I don't need to trap you, Abdul. I've already done that. What I need is some of that extra green you got coming in from Aetna."

"Allah, help me," Yassar said, sagging against the porch support.

# 54. PARANOIA IN CHURCH

Finney was escorted to the third pew in St. Mark's Episcopal Cathedral on Capitol Hill, to the section reserved for speakers, family members, and dignitaries. Finney didn't feel as if he belonged in the pew, but by the time he realized where they were putting him, it was too late. He knew people were staring at him. He wanted to think it was only because the burns on his ears and the back of his neck were highlighted with white silvadine cream which stood out in a sea of black uniforms like some sort of misapplied clown makeup, but he knew it was more than that. He knew it and he hated it.

During the past two days he'd been out of the house only to visit his doctor. He continued to feel disoriented and at times dizzy, some of it from the medication, some from the delayed effects of heat stress and smoke inhalation, and from the chronic lack of sleep. He still hadn't sorted out the events of the fire in his own mind. Although he believed he and Gary had been set up, he wasn't certain. Even Diana hadn't believed him.

As did every other attending member of the Seattle Fire Department, Finney wore his black wool uniform, a ribbon of black tape across the coat badge. The church was filled with uniforms from departments all over the Northwest. Festooned in wreaths and black ribbon, Engine 26 stood outside waiting to carry Sadler's casket to the family plot in Bellingham.

Surrounding him in the first three pews were Sadler's mother, his two married sisters, their husbands, assorted nieces and nephews, some of Gary's old drinking companions, and a crop of current friends, mostly AA members and former girlfriends. Also in attendance were members from all the shifts at Station 26, as well as Charlie Reese and, at the opposite end of the pew, Captain G. A. Montgomery, who had been quoted extensively by the media over the past two days as saying their star witness had yet to give a statement. Finney was, of course, their star witness.

Finney found himself barely able to sit, unable to concentrate, and reluctant to listen to the eulogies. He caught a few words from the podium. Sadler had been an Eagle Scout. He was part of the Big Brothers program and had nurtured two young men to adulthood. He was an attentive uncle who took his nieces and nephews camping and fishing every summer, skiing every winter. He was an avid hunter as well as an amateur taxidermist. As the eulogies continued, sweat ran down Finney's neck and stung his burns like lemon juice on a fresh cut. He still couldn't figure out why Sadler was babying him during the fire, and that pained him almost as badly as the sweat on his burns. Sadler had saved his life, and Finney let him down.

With almost no conscious recollection of how he'd gotten there, he found himself outside the church among a forest of firefighters in dress uniforms. Engine 26 had left and so had the rest of the cortege.

"You okay, buddy?" his brother, Tony, asked.

"I guess."

"What you need to do, John, is you need to lay low for a while and let some of this blow over."

Diana Moore approached them. "Hello, Captain Finney."

Tony nodded and swung his dark eyes back onto his brother, as did Diana.

"I've been meaning to come over to see how you were doing," Diana said, to Finney.

"Don't bother. I'm fine."

"You been listening to the news reports about the fire?" Tony asked.

"No."

"G. A. Montgomery was on KOMO saying Bowman Pork was set with a time-delay device. The way G. A.'s hinting around about what they found in the building, it was done by somebody who knew how to light a fire. Maybe a pro."

"Or a firefighter?" Diana asked.

"That could be, too."

Finney listened to his brother rehash the details. The initial fire had been set in a small room off the loading dock, additional devices set to kick in later at various other points in the building. At least one of those devices must have gone off between the time Finney put Sadler in the doorway and when he went back inside. That was assuming he'd actually placed Sadler in the doorway and hadn't been hallucinating. He and Tony talked it flat, and then Tony said, "God, I feel bad about all this stuff."

"Yeah, well . . . it wasn't your fault."

After Tony left, Finney turned to Diana, whose hair was pulled into a knot at the back of her neck to facilitate the wearing of her dress uniform hat. The dull light from the sky made her face look radiant. He wished he wasn't so angry with her, but he was. "I know you don't believe me, but the fire was a trap," he said, dully.

"I'm sorry about what I said to your parents."

"Don't ever regret telling the truth."

"Just because the fire was set doesn't mean it was a trap."

"That civilian the night of the fire said there were victims inside when he knew there weren't. Then somebody locked a door behind us. They killed Gary. You don't believe me, do you?"

"Gary died. It happens to a firefighter every week somewhere in this country. Maybe every day."

"What about our victims?"

"I heard Parkhurst talking before the service, and he said the man who told him about the victims hung around for about five minutes and then disappeared. Said he was probably one of those freaks who get off on lying to the fire department."

"They torch a building in our district when I'm on shift. Get somebody to report trapped victims, so we're taking chances and going deeper than necessary. I practically handed Gary to those firefighters, and still he died inside the building. You've never believed any of this, have you?"

"I can't believe two firefighters would take Gary back inside."

"It was dark. Maybe they thought they had *me*."

"That's just a little paranoid, isn't it?"

Finney took a deep breath. A raindrop the size of a marble fell out of the sky and struck him in the forehead. Another fell on Diana's shoulder. Clumps of mourners on the street began to disperse. Moments later the air was electric with the smell of rain. Finney said, "You don't believe anything I've said, do you?"

Diana swung her wide-spaced gray eyes on him and brushed back a wisp of hair over her ear. A raindrop trickled down her cheek, or was it a tear? "It's not that black and white, John. Besides, it seems to me you're standing here imagining this is all about you, when Gary's the one who's dead."

# 55. THE OZARK

Five hours after Gary Sadler's funeral, Finney's father answered his doorbell in West Seattle and found his son on the porch with a hot pizza and a six-pack of beer. Stepping inside, Finney deposited the cardboard pizza box on the kitchen table, while his father popped the top on one of the beer bottles; Finney put the rest in the refrigerator. "Where's Mom?"

"She's got her ceramics class on Fridays. Take a seat. They got some great chopper shots of the fire. Interested?"

"Yeah."

A devoted film buff, his father had thousands of still pictures chronicling his family and career. At last count, he'd cataloged over six thousand videotapes, many of which lined the shelves of four large bookcases he'd built in the family room. He'd collected hundreds of feature films, plus any television documentary involving World War II or firefighting or any other topic that caught his eye. He had one row devoted to real-life car chases and accident footage. When he played them, it became obvious he had all the crashes memorized.

As he led Finney into the family room, his father said, "Missed you at the funeral."

"I didn't see you either."

"We were in back, old Ralph Marston and me. Marston was one of Gary's instructors in drill school. He actually tried to get him fired. Said he was cocky. Can you imagine?" This last said sarcastically. "It was funny. I saw Gary just the other day. Sure you don't want a slice of that pizza? It smells good."

Finney noticed his father had barely sipped the Heineken. "No, thanks."

"How'd you see Gary?"

"Oh, he dropped by. A lot of people are paying their last respects to the old bastard. It's kind of nice, really."

"Can we take a look at the tapes?"

"Sure."

Finney senior turned on the television and put the cartridge into the VCR, while Finney sat on the sofa, trying not to exacerbate the burns on his neck. His father dropped the remote in Finney's lap and sat heavily. They were both wounded warriors, though Finney's wounds would heal, most of them. "I thought this might give you a little perspective."

By the time news cameras reached the scene, firefighters were directing two-and-a-half-inch hose lines into the building from the parking lot. The interior was raging, but because they'd committed to an exterior attack, all they could do was wait for the flames to breach the walls; one of their primary missions would be to knock down floating embers before they ignited secondary fires up the hillside in the woods.

When Finney saw an injured firefighter being half dragged to the rear of a medic unit, it took a minute to realize that injured firefighter was him. He looked bigger than he thought he would. He also looked half-dead. It was a frightening piece of film.

What frightened him more than anything was his father's running monologue, which was basically a roll call of the faces they were seeing on the footage, his father calling out names with calm regularity as they appeared on the screen. Finney was unable to conjure up any names at all. He hoped this memory impairment was temporary but had been told there was a good chance, given the extent of his carbon monoxide absorption, that it wasn't. He didn't even remember much of what the doctors had told him, only that forty percent of severe cases such as his ended up with long-term memory problems.

They'd been watching the compiled news reports for almost thirty minutes when his father said, "I don't know where he gets off standing at the command post like that."

"Who?"

"Back it up. There he is. If I was B-One, I would have kicked him ass over teakettle."

Finney backed the tape up and saw a man standing five feet from Chief Smith, the picture blurred and fuzzy. It was Oscar Stillman. It took another long moment to bring up the name and remember where he knew him from.

"I didn't realize they were friends," Finney said.

"They aren't. Not that I ever heard."

"Oscar Stillman." Finney remembered Stillman's kindness on the fire ground Tuesday morning, how Stillman had been one of the few people who'd spoken to him. He remembered being rude to Oscar, too. That was his inclination, he'd learned, to be rude to people who were kind when hc was down. "What was Stillman doing at the fire? He's not on the call list for a multiple alarm. Now that I think about it, he was at Leary Way, too. I remember seeing him when we were changing bottles."

"I talked to Smith at the funeral. Oscar was the reason they switched from offensive to defensive. Oscar was the one who warned him about the LPG inside the Bowman Pork building. Of course, later on they found out he'd been mistaken. But what the hell. Better safe than sorry."

"There was no LPG inside?"

"There was one tank outside. The fire never got close."

"You still have those tapes from Leary Way?"

"I put 'em all together on one master."

Finney stood up. "Where is it?"

"You want it now?"

"If that's all right."

The Leary Way footage seemed endless, and was just as painful to watch as it had been last summer. His father, who always came to life when playing a videotape of a fire, gave a running commentary, noting hose lays that had gone awry, rigs parked too close to the building, and naming just about everyone who came across the screen. In some ways his father was like a Little League coach, the entire fire department his team. They watched for forty minutes before Finney backed up the tape and manipulated the remote to freeze a frame on the screen. It was another shot of Oscar Stillman standing at the command post next to the incident commander. "Look," Finney said. "He's talking to Chief Smith again."

"You said you saw him."

"I didn't know he was at the command post."

"If he hadn't been there, we probably would have lost you. He knew that building from his inspection program. He's the one told Smith which side of that fire wall you guys were on. Otherwise they would have sent everybody to the wrong side. They wouldn't have found you. I heard about it when you were still in the hospital last summer."

"Everybody searched the west side of the fire wall at Leary Way."

"That's what I mean. Who do you think told Smith you guys were on the west side?"

"Dad, we were on the east side."

"You sure?"

"I've been back. I've traced the whole thing. They were all searching on the wrong side. And nobody found me. I was on my way to the exit when I bumped into Reese and Kub. I've talked to everyone. They were the only team on that side."

"Don't that beat all? It goes to show sometimes a little information is worse than none at all."

"What it goes to show is that I've been in trouble at two fires, and for no discernible reason Oscar Stillman was at the IC post dispensing information that could, if acted on, make things worse for me at both of them."

"I don't think he meant any harm."

"You don't think it's odd he was at both fires?"

"Does seem strange."

They sat back and watched the rest of the footage on Leary Way. When G. A. Montgomery showed up on the tape, Finney said, "You worked with G. A. What was he like?"

"Biggest pussy I ever worked with. George Armstrong? God, he hated combat. He worked at Thirty-four's when I was Battalion Two, and every time I said I was coming down to give them a drill, he'd have a bloody nose when I got there. People used to call him Captain Kotex. Said he should keep one up his nostril in case his period started again. I haven't thought about that in years."

"You think he might be crooked?"

"No way. I knew his uncle. Good people."

"What about Oscar Stillman?"

"Oscar used to ride Attack Ten in the days when they were getting a lot of fires. That boy could eat smoke. I swear he'd still be in operations if he hadn't hurt his back. He tried to get out on a disability, but they called it phantom back pain. Instead of handing him a pension, they ended up sticking him down at the Fire Marshal's office. For a while there, he was real bitter."

Finney got up and stood at the window of the family room looking down over the backyard. As children, they were never allowed to leave so much as a toy in the yard, but when he was ten he'd asked his father for permission to build a tree house in the apple tree behind the garage, and his father, for some reason, said yes. Finney worked on it alone for weeks, and then one overcast Saturday afternoon while he hammered away, his father showed up and began helping. It had been uncharacteristic of him. His father worked with him all afternoon, and the memory of that day remained one of the brightest of Finney's childhood; he rarely visited home without checking to see if the faded boards of the tree house were still in place, always felt an inner warmth when he saw they were.

His father stood beside him at the window. "I ever tell you about the Ozark Hotel, John? The college basketball championships were on TV. I was on Ladder Four. We could see the column of black smoke from the station, and then we rolled up on it just as two jumpers hit the sidewalk right smack in front of us. Smoke and flame coming out of everywhere. Every window had a head in it. Me and Samuelson, we got the thirty-five, and we put it up to the first person we came to. The guy jumped for the ladder before we even got it upright, almost knocked it out of our hands. He missed the ladder, of course, fell at our feet. Brains exploding all over our boots."

Finney knew the details by heart, but he let his father ramble, knowing the telling of it was somehow soothing to his father, perhaps in the same way that telling the tale of Leary Way would be therapeutic to him some day.

"They had transom windows above all the doors to the rooms, so the fire went down the hallways and burned through these simple-ass windows and got into each of the rooms before the poor bastards knew what hit them. We put up every goddamn ladder we had and then moved them as fast as we could. I never worked so hard in my life."

"The Ozark drill," Finney said. It had been a staple of ladder company evolutions in Seattle for years, a race to put up every ladder from the truck as quickly as humanly possible and then to move them from window to window even faster.

"When we put up the fifty-five, some old man started down before we could get the tormentor poles out. His weight made the ladder start to creep along the side of the building. Then a woman came out and climbed right over him. We thought they were both goners, but that ladder slid down the side of the building, and by God, the two of them rode it down without a scratch. When it was all over, we lined up twenty-one bodies under tarps in the alley."

As his father escorted him to the door, Finney found himself crying. It was the damndest thing; the tears wouldn't stop. "John, you know if I was hard on you boys, it was because I loved you. You know that, don't you?" His father had tears in his eyes, too.

"Of course I do. I love you, too."

"John, all I want from you after I'm gone is a kind word. Can you do that for me?" It was an old family joke, something John's grandfather had said.

"Don't worry, Dad. You'll get plenty of kind words."

# 56. SIX WAYS FROM SUNDAY

The less imposing of the two plainclothesmen and the one who did most of the questioning, Rosemont, was one of those people who, for whatever reason, made a habit of pretending to be smarter than he was. They were almost polar opposites, because his partner pretended to be dumber than he was.

It was Thursday, the sixth of November, and early that morning while surfing the Internet, Finney had found a business news article that said, "Due to concern among building occupants, Cole Properties has agreed to increase its insurance coverage on the Columbia Tower in Seattle to an amount commensurate with industry standards for a building of its size, this to take effect as of November 2. Morganchild Insurance has—" Et cetera, et cetera. The article convinced Finney to see the cops.

The police would have his testimony, his suspicions, a videotape of the Bowman Pork fire with Oscar Stillman loitering near the incident commander, and not much else. He explained that there was a cabal of conspirators intimately connected to the fire service whose goal was another major arson. That he suspected D-day was tomorrow, November 7, primarily because Monahan had been so sneaky about getting it off, that other than Monahan, he wasn't sure who was in the group but suspected the individuals on the list Cordifis's wife had found among his effects. He didn't mention that his own name had been on that list. He still didn't know why it was there.

He knew this group had built a fire engine worth a couple of hundred thousand dollars, that they killed Gary Sadler, that they were probably responsible for Leary Way. What he hadn't known until this morning was the upcoming target; and now that the insurance coverage on the Columbia Tower had been raised, he thought he knew why the prefire book for the Columbia Tower had been in the copycat fire apparatus.

The second plainclothesman, Freeman, a big man with a flat nose and a prominent jaw that had a blue, stubbled look, took notes. He looked like an old-time cop, a strong contrast to Rosemont, who seemed almost prissy, a college professor type—eighteenth-century French poetry.

Rosemont had short, greasy hair that he parted meticulously down one side and small, manicured hands he waved in front of his face as he spoke. "Okay," he said. "You think there's going to be a fire tomorrow. Let's hear your reasoning again."

It had been three days since Gary Sadler's death, and at times he still felt as if his head were spinning. He had to think through his sentences painstakingly before he uttered them, because he had a tendency to jumble the order of the words. "I told you. The Columbia Tower was underinsured. Now it's fully insured."

"My house is fully insured," said Rosemont. "That doesn't mean I'm going to burn it down."

"Leary Way was some kind of practice run."

"I read in the paper that Leary Way thing was an accident. You can prove it wasn't?"

"Not so it would hold up in court."

"But you think Patterson Cole is trying to convert the Columbia Tower into cash?"

Finney nodded.

"He'd have to be awful desperate."

"He's getting divorced. And he's a skinflint. My guess is his wife is taking him to the cleaners and he doesn't have the ready cash to buy her off. He gets a large insurance settlement, he'll have the cash."

Freeman swiveled his dark eyes onto Finney and said, "Look, we're trying to keep this on a friendly basis, but when a firefighter comes in saying he knows there's going to be an arson at a specific place on a specific date, we get a little worried. Why don't you read back your notes, Stu?"

"The Columbia Tower. Oscar Stillman, Gerald Monahan, G. A. Montgomery, and Marion Balitnikoff. He any relation to the football player?"

"I don't know."

"God, he could hit. You ever see him play?"

"A few times." He'd been one of his father's favorites, his father, who always admired the toughest players on the field. Finney was not planning to mention his own surname had been on the list, or that he had a brother in the department, or a father who'd retired just weeks after Leary Way. He didn't mention Kub either. There had been a question mark after Kub's name.

"Why didn't you take this to your fire investigation unit?" Rosemont asked.

"Politics."

Rosemont gave Freeman a dubious look, not his first.

Since Tuesday morning he'd been unable to recall familiar phone numbers, routes of travel he'd used for years, all sorts of simple words, even the name of his cat. The phrase "it's on the tip of my tongue" applied hourly. He wondered if anything he'd said to these two made sense. Already he'd caught himself in a couple of embarrassing misapplications of language, though neither Rosemont nor Freeman bothered to correct him, practiced as they were at letting people hang themselves with their own words.

When a uniformed officer came to the door with a note, both men exited the room. The officer gave Finney a snaggletoothed smile and blocked the doorway, arms folded. A large woman, she looked as if she played rugby—with the guys.

After a few minutes of silence, Finney said, "Am I under arrest?"

"Not that I know of."

"Then I can leave?"

"I wish you wouldn't."

Finney had thought about relating this tale to the police for so long that now he was acutely aware that he had only one shot. And they weren't buying it. He wasn't sure he would have believed it himself. The more he explained, the more he realized he was spinning a classic tale of paranoid delusion.

Five minutes later, when Rosemont reentered the room, Charlie Reese stepped through the door behind him. It surprised Finney, until he realized Reese had been called in not only as the resident expert on fire operations in the city, but as an authority on Finney.

"Morning, John," Reese said, as amicably as if they were meeting for coffee. "I understand you've been entertaining these gentlemen. The Columbia Tower. Is that what we're talking about?"

"That's it," Rosemont said.

All eyes were on Reese now, who took his time with it, his voice silky smooth, his dark eyes unwavering.

"Gentlemen. One of our people had already brought up the possibility that something was going to happen at the Columbia Tower. I don't know why that particular building has become so popular with conspiracy theorists, but I can assure you we've checked it six ways from Sunday. There's no way we're going to let so much as a cigarette burn unattended in that place."

"You already checked it?" Finney asked. "Who told you about it?"

"I can only give that out on a need-to-know basis."

"Diana Moore?"

"I had Chief Murray check it for me. After he was finished, I sent in a second team, and they spent most of yesterday examining every nut and bolt. Then we had the building engineers go around behind and double-check one more time. Right now the Columbia Tower is probably the safest building in the state."

Rosemont, Freeman, and the uniformed officer who'd remained in the room watched Finney for a reaction; there was none. Finney didn't know what to say. He didn't know whether Reese was lying or he'd really checked the building. Reese strode to the door in a manner that signaled the others to follow and said, "Gentlemen."

"Wait a minute," Finney said. "Just because somebody inspected the building's life safety systems doesn't mean something isn't going to happen. You get one or two floors going in a building like that and it's a grounder, systems or not. Somebody could get in there . . . somebody could . . ."

Reese's voice grew smaller as they walked down the corridor. "Just like every other big city department, we have our resident two-twenties. This nutcase's father was a dear friend of mine, so it's particularly sad for me to tell you this, but if I could eject this poor bastard from our department, I would. Just like you guys, this is a civil service job, and we have to carry the deadwood. In case you didn't recognize him, this is the same guy who survived Leary Way last June. A few days ago he managed to get one of our best lieutenants killed at that pig plant fire. We're still trying to figure out how he did that. Also, and this isn't for public consumption, we're building a case against him for arson. Airtight. The trouble with—"

A door closed, insulating Finney from the remainder of the conversation. Now all Finney could hear was the sound of his own heartbeat in his ears. It didn't matter that the house he found prepped for arson had burned down the morning after he reported it, or that he'd discovered a replica of a city fire engine, or that somebody driving that engine had tried to kill him. It didn't matter that Sadler had been dragged back into the fire building and left to die. It didn't matter that these men, whoever they were—Oscar Stillman, Jerry Monahan, whoever—were going to do it again.

It didn't matter because nobody believed him.

"You all right?" asked the officer in the doorway.

"Pardon?"

"You look like you're having trouble breathing."

"I'm okay."

"Good. Because I think they want to talk to you again."

Moments later the three men paraded back into the room, and Rosemont put his foot on the seat of a straight-backed chair. "Why don't you run through this again?"

Finney got up. "I told you what I came here to tell you. Now I'm leaving."

Rosemont looked at Reese. "Want us to dig up some charge to hold him on until you boys are ready with your own charges?"

Charlie Reese stepped forward. "I don't think that'll be necessary, gentlemen. As you can see, he's not much of a threat."

Rosemont said, "If the Chief wants you out of here, I guess you're free to go."

A few moments later Reese approached Finney in the corridor. It occurred to Finney that if Reese was part of the conspiracy, it would make sense to keep Finney out of jail so he could absorb some or all of the blame for whatever was going to happen next.

"Sorry to burst your bubble, John, but I couldn't go on letting you make a fool of yourself."

"Who else inspected the Columbia Tower?"

"An engineer from the building and Lieutenant Stillman."

"Oscar? Oscar's part of it."

Reese turned and looked at him. "You're not kidding, are you? You really think this is going to happen. John, get a sound night's sleep. In the morning make an appointment with a shrink."

It wasn't until he looked down the hallway and saw the redheaded officer who'd taken his report after his tangle with the fake engine that something became clear: Rosemont and Freeman had been eavesdropping on him and Reese. Eyes locked on Finney, the redhead began whispering to the detectives. Finney could imagine what she was saying. "Yeah, we found him in his truck all mangled up one night, raving about being run down by a fire truck. Nutty as a pecan pie."

# 57. RIDING LIES LIKE A HOBBYHORSE

During the afternoon a carpet of fog rolled across the lake and began bunching up around the downtown skyscrapers.

At four o'clock Finney was in his kitchen on his hands and knees scrubbing and scouring. He found simpleminded tasks aided his convalescence from the CO poisoning. During the day a dozen messages had stacked up on his answering machine—from Diana, his father, Robert Kub, from news agencies wanting to interview him about Bowman Pork. He'd listened to each and replied to none, though he was tempted to pick up the phone when he heard Kub say, "John. Get your things in order. You can expect visitors this afternoon." Finney's houseboat was the second from the end on a narrow dock, not such a hot arrangement for moving pianos or dodging widows and a definite dead end when the police came calling.

He realized there was a good chance he would never be allowed to put on the uniform again. Losing the uniform wasn't the worst thing that could happen, but for some reason it felt as if it were. So much of his identity was wrapped up in being a firefighter. It left him with a satisfaction he couldn't imagine finding anywhere else.

He was almost finished with the kitchen. His checkbook was balanced, and his insurance and bank account information were neatly typed onto a single sheet of paper. He would ask Tony, who was allergic to cats, to keep an eye on Dimitri, and to put his personal effects in storage before renting out the houseboat.

At four o'clock a pensive group showed up on the dock: Charlie Reese, G. A. Montgomery, Oscar Stillman, as well as three uniformed Seattle police officers wearing black leather gloves and bulletproof vests.

G. A. Montgomery unfurled an arrest warrant, then stepped inside and bowed his head, a somber Stillman and Reese following. As if by prior arrangement, the SPD officers waited on the dock. Breathing through his gapped teeth with a whistling noise, Stillman gave him an avuncular look. With the moment upon them, G. A. seemed to have picked up a case of stage fright. In the tight quarters of the living room, G. A. seemed larger than life; his head looked as large as a bowling ball. Reese was the most chipper of the bunch.

"You're under arrest, John," G. A. said, almost apologetically from the back of the room. Without moving from the wall, he read Finney his rights from a printed card. He'd been crowing to one and all that he was going to put Finney away, and now his slow words and funereal tone were puzzling.

Chief Reese said, "Annie Sortland is finally alert enough that her doctors up at Harborview allowed G. A. to interview her. Says she saw you on Riverside Drive the morning of the fire. Right before somebody socked her upside the head."

"A captain, a chief, and a scoundrel," Finney said, looking around the group. "And you finally found your witness."

"I never put anyone away who wasn't guilty," G. A. said, reaching for the handcuffs on his belt.

Reese said, "Hold up a minute. John gave the police some interesting theories yesterday. Maybe he wants to share those with us."

"You want to say something, John," added Oscar Stillman, not unkindly, "you go right ahead."

Finney looked the trio over. "Yeah, I want to say something. I didn't set the fire. It offends me that any of you think I did. G. A. framed me. He knows it and I know it and I'm beginning to think you guys know it, too."

"Turn around and put your hands on the wall, asshole," G. A. said, stepping past Reese.

"No, no. Go back over there," Reese said. "You're beginning to think we know what?"

"This is my gig, Charlie," G. A. said, forcefully.

"No, I want to hear what he has to say." Reluctantly, G. A. moved back. "Let him talk. Maybe he'll say something else to incriminate himself." Reese turned to Finney, his brown eyes teary with gloating. "You thought you were hot shit, didn't you? Voted top of the class. And there I was at the ass end of things. It's turned around a little, eh?"

"Is that what this is all about? A drill school that happened eighteen years ago? Jesus, get a life."

"I have a life. Yours is the one going down the toilet. Leary Way is what started it for you, John. If that hadn't happened, you'd probably be all right. But then, with guys like you, something like that is bound to happen sooner or later."

"I've been back there. I cleared out the corridor where we met that night. I found the exact spot."

"Have you now? What an astronomical waste of time."

"Bill knew something was going to happen at Leary Way. One of you guys must have given it away somehow. I'm thinking you didn't realize just how much he suspected. The night of the fire Bill ran into Stillman and cursed him out. I heard him call Oscar a bastard, but I thought at the time it was in jest; now I know he was serious. I didn't hear what he said after that, but I think he was probably accusing Oscar of having something to do with that fire. A few minutes later when Bill got into trouble, Oscar steered the rescue teams to the wrong side of the building. And you, Charlie, you went in on the good side and made sure nobody found him from there."

"You actually think we went in to keep Bill from coming out?" Reese's face didn't often show emotion, but he was incredulous now.

"You wanted Bill to die the same way you want me in jail. To shut him up. To shut me up."

"This is bullshit!" G. A. said. "Let me cuff him."

"No, no, no," Reese countered. "I find this intriguing. Go on. Please. Weave your web. Let's hear more."

"I excavated that corridor where we met. My PASS device was maybe seventy-five feet straight down the corridor, twenty-eight paces. There was no way you couldn't have heard it."

"We never said we didn't hear it. We heard it. We just couldn't find it. Your directions took us in circles."

"You said before that I didn't give you any directions at all. And there weren't any circles. I can take you or anybody else there right now and show you there were only two directions you could have gone: the way I showed you or back down the corridor the way you came in. The only other possibility was a corridor to the left, and that had a locked gate closing it off. You either went out or you went in. You couldn't have gone around in circles."

One of those people who only pretended to listen while waiting for his own turn to talk, Charlie Reese found an opening now and began telling his story, a story that had been told so many times it came almost by rote.

"No. Here's what happened. You guys got lost, you and Cordifis. My personal theory is you panicked. You know how I know that? You never spoke on the radio. Bill did, but you never did. Later somebody said you were too amped to speak. I'd have to agree with that."

"I didn't speak because Bill had my portable. And we weren't lost. A wall fell on us."

Reese continued as if Finney hadn't spoken. "The search didn't sound like it was going well on the other side of the building. Nobody really had a clue where you guys were or how to get to you. It was such a huge complex, and there had been so many remodels. I'd listened to the captain's directions and thought I knew where to send a search crew, but they were all on the other side. The only person I could find was Bobby Kub. I couldn't send him in by himself, so we grabbed a couple of spare SCBAs and went in together. We searched a couple of rooms near the entrance-way, then went down that long corridor with the jogs in it. That's where we bumped into you. We could barely understand a word you said. We took you outside and—"

"You didn't take me anywhere. I went out by myself."

"Anyway, Kub and I continued on, but the fire was getting worse every second. We ended up crawling. We crawled along the right-hand wall. We hadn't gone far when the heat got so bad we had to put our noses on the floor. We went down the corridor like that, on our bellies, searched a couple of rooms near the end, then worked our way back. It was so hot. I can still remember the sound of my facepiece sliding along the linoleum."

"You have any trouble getting over the pipes?"

Reese stared blankly.

"In the corridor. You know. The pipes?"

Reese gave Finney a coy look. "You and I both know that floor was smooth as a baby's butt. There were no pipes."

"Is that a question or a statement?"

"If you found something on that floor when you were digging, it came down after we got out."

"They fell in the corridor as I was coming out. A couple hundred of them right behind me. I heard it. You heard it. I didn't know what made the noise until I went back. They would have been impossible to walk on and hard to crawl over, and they sure weren't smooth. You didn't go down that corridor at all, did you?"

Reese glanced at G. A. for help and then at Oscar Stillman. "I risked my life, is what I did. You don't believe me, check out the award on the wall behind my desk."

Finney's mind was racing down new pathways now, and he was

furious. The problem had never been his directions. The problem had been the rescue team. The problem had been two liars who'd taken medals for their lies. Bill had been within reach of two masked firefighters who'd refused, for whatever reason, to step off twenty-eight paces to find him. From the first he'd been ill-at-ease with Reese's version of events, but because Kub went along with it, because it had been their word against his, and because he'd been confused about so many other things, he'd tried to live with their version.

"You're a damned liar," Finney said. "I don't know what you were doing, but you weren't looking for Bill. You lied, and then you rode those lies into the chief's office."

The room grew quiet.

When G. A. stepped forward with the handcuffs, Finney said, "No need for those. Just let me get dressed. Can you do that for me? You know how drafty the King County jail is. Give me two minutes to get some longjohns? One favor. It's the last one you'll ever do me."

Reese and G. A. exchanged looks. Stillman said, "What if he's got a gun in the house?"

"I hope he does," G. A. said, touching the sidearm on the back of his belt.

"Two minutes," Reese said, looking at his wristwatch.

# 58. TEN MINUTES TICKING

## 1630 HOURS

Finney could hear voices behind him across the water, maybe two hundred feet off, several men shouting at once. He'd taken his oldest single kayak, knowing he would be forced to abandon it somewhere along the shoreline, had stepped out through the missing wall in his spare bedroom and paddled quietly into the fog on the lake, leaving behind confusion and outrage.

He knew G. A. would call the police boat stationed on Lake Union and that, if not for the fog, they would be on him in minutes. Still, G. A. couldn't know for certain he'd taken a water craft. There were three kayaks left in the spare bedroom, the new single, the double, and a half-completed kit on sawhorses. Who would guess he owned four kayaks? When a lull came in the shouting at the dock, he guessed they were conducting a search, possibly extending to the neighbors. Mrs. Prosize next door wouldn't be happy. The last people to raid her domicile had been Nazis in World War II Poland.

## 1805 HOURS

Accompanied by a tall, elegant-looking woman with narrow hips and long, pipe-stem legs, Robert Kub, dressed in slacks and an open-collar shirt under a sport jacket, was exiting his house when Finney's cab scraped its tires on the curb. Finney thrust a handful of bills at the cabbie and climbed the front steps of Kub's house.

Kub began to retreat back inside, but Finney ran up the steps, jammed his foot in the door, and shouldered it open. Walking across the room as Kub backed across it, he pushed Kub's chest repeatedly with both hands, forcing Kub up against the living room wall. The drapes were open, the television on. Kub always left his television on when he left the house as a deterrent to burglars. Finney reached over and killed the big-screen.

"What's going on?" Kub said. "You get my call? They're looking for you right now. What?"

"After everything you've done, you're still trying to be my friend?"

"I haven't done anything. Tell me one thing I've done."

"Leary Way."

"Where do you come off saying that? We almost got fried trying to get out of there."

"Yeah? Tell me about the pipes." When Kub gave him a blank look, Finney said, "You don't know any more about the pipes than Charlie did."

"You been talking to Charlie?"

"Enough to find out you're both liars."

"Okay. I'll bite. What pipes?"

"You guys never went down that corridor." Kub had no answer for that. "Where did you search?"

"Not in that corridor."

"I don't get it. Why lie about it?"

Clenching his jaws, Kub said, "I never lied." Kub glanced at the long-legged woman, but oddly, she didn't seem interested in the proceedings. She sat down in a leather armchair to wait. "I never took no award. I didn't want it."

"That's supposed to make me feel better?"

"God, I'm sorry." Kub dropped down into a squat, his back propped against the wall, his long fingers cradling his face. "You know how long it had been since I had a mask on?"

"Save the excuses for your mother. Just cut to the chase."

"Shit. I hadn't been in a fire in eight years. I almost couldn't even get the mask to work. We were just a couple of guys who hadn't fought fire in a while trying to do our best. We honestly thought we were going to find you both."

"Go on."

"We searched two rooms right near the entrance, but the smoke was so disorienting. Then before we knew what happened, we ran into you, and you were like some sort of . . . Your face shield was half-melted, and smoke was coming off your shoulders, and you looked like you'd just been dragged out of a steamer trunk somebody'd put in a furnace. Skin was coming off your ears. You could barely move, but you told us to go down the corridor you'd come up, that we'd hear your PASS device outside a hole in the wall. Twenty-eight steps, you said. Like we were going to go down there and end up looking like you. We were scared, but we were headed that way after you left, and then a gust of heat came down the corridor and forced us onto our knees. Reese was leading, and for the longest time he just knelt there in front of me. Finally I said, 'Aren't we going to do anything?' And he said, 'Calm down. Wait another minute.' We couldn't see shit, man. It was like somebody put sticks in our eyes. To make matters worse, we heard electrical wires popping. Every time we moved I kept thinking we were going to get electrocuted. Tell you the truth, I think we both figured if we waited long enough, Cordifis would come marching out of the smoke just like you did."

"I *told* you he was trapped."

"I know."

"How long did you wait?"

"I'm not sure."

"A minute? Two minutes?"

"Longer."

"Five?"

"Longer."

"Are you kidding? Ten minutes?"

"Maybe."

"But you were practically on top of him."

"I kept tapping Reese on the shoulder. He kept saying not yet. It wasn't like we sat down and said we'd wait *ten* minutes." Tears were running down Kub's face. He wiped them away with his opposite index fingers, moving them side to side like windshield wipers.

"What were you waiting for? As long as there's fuel and oxygen, a fire gets worse. You know that."

"We were calling him. We never stopped calling him."

"I'm sure that gave him some comfort as he burned to death."

"When it started coming down on us, we turned around and made a run for it. By then we could hear flame ripping down the corridor. Man, it sounded like a freight train. I've never been that scared. Next thing I know, I'm trying to cool off under a jiffy hose and Reese is in front of the cameras. I never heard what he said until the next day. I swear. Then what was I supposed to do? Call a news conference and say he was conning everybody? You know how I freeze up in front of a camera. After a while I thought, why not make it all a little more heroic than it was? What was it going to hurt?"

"Oh, yeah. You didn't hurt anybody."

"I didn't think about you until later. All I knew was I couldn't start a scandal, and nothing I said was going to bring Cordifis back. Then, after a few days, Reese told me if I contradicted him, it would blow any opportunity I might have as an insurance investigator for a private company. You know I been counting on that second income after retirement. The way that fire was running, we probably couldn't have got him out anyway. You know that."

"You've had a lot of time to work on your excuses, haven't you?"

Somewhere in the room a pager went off. As Kub went to get it, Finney became aware they'd been hearing sirens for some minutes. "I gotta go," Kub said wearily when he returned. "They got two multiples going on. Plus, there's something at the Columbia Tower."

# PART FOUR

# 59. THURSDAYS WITH SHEILA

Patterson Cole watched Norris remove the contracts from the safe and pack them into the briefcases, musing that there was something about Norris that made him look like a poof, something about the way he used his hands. He'd had this thought before, and deep down he supposed it didn't really matter whether Norris was a poof or not, but still, it bothered him. The bow ties bothered him. The manicured fingernails bothered him. Did he actually apply polish? Norris was using a cane today, had stubbed his toe walking to the pissoir in the middle of the night. Norris was always nursing some sort of ache. Just thinking about it made Patterson old. Maybe after this was all over, he'd send Norris to Sun Valley to oversee his Idaho holdings with Dithers. Maybe it was time Norris had a little change of scenery. Time he did, too, for that matter.

Norris Radford and Patterson Cole had taken a series of elevators to forty-two where they'd removed forty-seven thousand dollars in cash from the safe in the main office. Now they were on floor seventy-three in Patterson's private hideaway. Nobody ever came up here but Norris and, every other Thursday, a woman named Sheila from the service. It was a luxury apartment with a desk, computer, fax, and in the back room, a double shower, a Jacuzzi, and a bed about half the size of a tennis court. When he wasn't using the bed for his play time with Sheila, Patterson would sneak up after lunch to take a siesta, maybe twenty, thirty minutes of shut-eye. It was his guilty secret—well—one of them.

They'd planned this meticulously, and now all they had to do was empty the other safe and skedaddle. Everything else was taken care of. After tonight all of Patterson's troubles would be over. He would pay off the damn bitch, sign the divorce papers, and in time, they would rebuild this tower with more safeguards than the original.

Why couldn't they all be like Sheila? No fuss. No muss. He'd found her ad in the back of *The Stranger*: ALL THE COMFORT YOU WANT FROM A WOMAN, $175. NO EXTRA FEES. NO DISAPPOINTMENTS. She wore a little too much makeup, but her body was as advertised. And it didn't hurt that she was fifty years younger than he was. The one thing he was going to miss about this building was Thursdays with Sheila. He'd have to find another cozy spot.

Looking around the office, Patterson saw several personal effects he wanted to take with him. Sure, the firemen had told him to leave everything, but there was a montage of photos on the desk he needed, photos of his first wife, Ruth, their two children when they were toddlers, and shots of himself as a young lumberjack. They'd worked his ass off at Weyerhauser, but he found more and more he was looking back on those days as the happiest of his life. He picked up the montage and stuffed it under his coat.

"What do you want out of this safe?" Norris asked, looking up at him from across the room.

"The bonds. There's some jewelry in that black box. Any cash."

Patterson sat in the leather office chair and rolled it over to the window. Four floors lower than the famous women's rest room stalls with their panoramic view, it looked out over the same vista: the east portion of the city and, beyond that, Lake Washington, the growing city of Bellevue, and the bedroom community that was Mercer Island. The lake was fuzzy with fog, and most of the east side was already sketchy. He glanced at the clock on the wall. Six-fifteen. Plenty of time.

His eighty-fourth birthday would be coming around in March, and he knew he was slowing down. He'd thought about retirement, but then who would run things? He had two sons, in their sixties now, but they were both numbskulls. One, Hardy, hadn't spoken to him in four years, not since he married the bimbo.

The whoop-de-whoop mechanical screeching in the corridor outside the office started without any warning. The fire alarm.

"Go see if you can get that turned off," Patterson said. "Also, you get the lottery numbers today?"

"Yes, sir." Norris was heading for the phone, but he stopped, took a notebook out of his pocket, and began reading numbers off, while Patterson compared them to a pair of tickets in his arthritic fingers. No winners tonight. Norris made the phone call, spoke for a few seconds, then hung up.

Cole said, "I suppose they think a bunch of false alarms will put everybody off their guard, make it that much easier, eh?"

"I'm not entirely sure this is a false alarm, sir. Apparently there's smoke on one of the floors below us."

"Some idiot burned his popcorn in the microwave again?"

"Quite a lot of smoke."

Patterson turned away from the window. "What do you mean?"

"A *lot.*"

"You got everything out of the safe?"

"Just about."

"Get the rest. Let's get moving."

"Yes, sir. Shall I call the garage and have the car ready?"

"Absolutely."

Five minutes later Patterson Cole stood near the elevators. "Is that smoke I smell?"

"Sure seems like it."

"What the hell's wrong? Where's this elevator?"

"They don't work when the building's in alarm."

"I know that, goddamn it. But they work with that special key. The firemen have it. The security idiots downstairs have it. Why aren't they up here? Get somebody up here."

"Yes, sir." Norris Radford set the briefcases at his feet and took a cell phone from a pocket. "This is Radford. I'm on seventy-two with Patterson. You need to get somebody up here with an elevator. Now." He listened for a few seconds. "Uh, huh. So where are the engineers? Uh, huh. Okay. Call us when you're ready." He gave a phone number.

"What is it?" Patterson said, thumbing the elevator button again with a gnarled index finger.

"They can't make them work even with the key, and they don't know why. They've got a couple of people running up the stairs to see what's happening on twenty-six. That's where the alarm is."

"Shit, boy. You look like you need to hose out your trousers. This'll work itself out. Let's go up to the restaurant and get some grub while we're waiting."

"How are we going to get there?"

"We could walk," Cole said. "Or don't you think you can handle four flights." The old man was already headed for the stairway.

Hobbling along with his cane and the two briefcases, Norris passed the old man and opened the door for him.

"God! What the hell is that?" Cole said, as a blast of smoke came out the door. "Close it, for Christ's sake! Close it!"

"I thought it wasn't supposed to start until two A.M.," Norris said, his eyes watering. Cole wondered whether it was from the smoke or because Norris was such a damned pansy.

"The bastards started early," Cole said.

Norris glanced around helplessly at the empty floor, his brow beginning to bead up with perspiration. When the lights in the corridor went out, he said, "Now what do we do?"

"Give me that goddamned phone."

# 60. THE WEDDING PARTY

ecause of a shortage of rigs in the city, Diana and the other overtimers had been forced to walk the few blocks up the hill from 10's to the Tower. On the west side of the Columbia Tower, on Fourth Avenue, uniformed police officers in bulletproof vests and winter coats began taking charge of the street. When Diana looked up, she couldn't see anything but dark windows, and then, near the ten-story mark, just above the reach of the tallest aerial ladder, a halo of fog.

Inside at the security desk they found a bewildered county chief surrounded by three county firefighters and a couple of building security people. There were alarms on twenty of the seventy-six floors, floor sixteen being the lowest, the highest seventy-six, although the report by phone to the security desk was that the smoke on seventy-six was extremely light. The first real smoke was on sixteen.

Nobody'd been able to make the elevators work, so a team of county firefighters ran up the stairs to sixteen, where they reported via portable radio that the stairwell was full of thick, black smoke. They'd been forced to axe open the door to sixteen, which should have unlocked automatically when the building went into alarm.

They investigated sixteen, seventeen, and eighteen, and twelve minutes later reported a small room fire on what they believed was the north side of the building on eighteen. They radioed that they were going to hook up the two hundred feet of hose line a second team had lugged up to the standpipe in the stairwell and make an attack on the fire. The officer in charge was a county lieutenant, and he seemed to know his stuff. He said they thought the fire was being fed fresh air from an unknown source, possibly a broken window.

Diana hoped it was only a room fire on eighteen and that the smoke on the other floors had drifted up or been pumped down through ductwork. A room fire on eighteen was doable. More likely it was the malfunctioning ventilation system in the building, Diana thought. There was smoke on too many floors. The elevators were not running. Doors that should have been open were locked. Finney had predicted this.

Three minutes later, the upstairs team reported they were not receiving water from the stairwell standpipe. Outside, Diana had seen Engine

10 pumping into the building's connections, so there should have been water. The county chief dispatched a pair of firefighters to trace down the problem, then told the firefighters on eighteen they'd have to wait.

At the incident command post on four, the county chief, two of Seattle's newly arrived lieutenants, and a pair of firefighters from Station 10 who were familiar with the building began poring over the heavy, yellow, looseleaf binders that held the prefire plan for the building.

The lobby was filling rapidly with weepy civilians who'd straggled down one or another of the smoky stairwells and were stumbling around the open spaces on four, trying to figure out where to go next. Many had come down without car keys or purses or coats. All were coughing; one woman vomited. Several more mutual aid companies from outside the city showed up, most from jurisdictions where the tallest buildings were four or five stories. An alarm in a seventy-six-story building had to be daunting for them. Diana knew it was certainly daunting for her.

Diana remembered a fire they'd had at the Morrison Hotel. The Morrison was only five stories, but one of the elevators hadn't worked, so they'd been jamming men and equipment into the remaining tiny, slow-moving elevator. Most of their lines, pump cans, ladders, and fans had been hauled up four flights of stairs, and she still remembered how so many of the firefighters, after a couple of trips up and down those stairs wearing fifty pounds of protective equipment and carrying another twenty or thirty of firefighting gear, had knelt by open windows in the hallway, gasping for breath.

An Engine 10 lieutenant, Wilder from A-shift, quickly took the over-timers and the personnel from outside fire departments and began forming them into teams, passing out assignments as they came up. They established a medical area downstairs in the food court. A team of three firefighters was sent outside to set up a base area well away from the building, where the incoming apparatus would park. They announced the command post would be on floor four, which was actually at street level from the Fifth Avenue side of the building.

"What about all these other floors in alarm?" asked the county chief, who turned out to be from Bothell, a small city at the north end of Lake Washington. "When do we send somebody to investigate?"

Lieutenant Wilder said, "Use sixteen for staging. Send a backup team for the first crew, an RIT to back up both of them in case they get into trouble, and then have extra crews investigate the higher floors one by one. Bottom to top. We're going to have to send runners up with spare bottles so they can change right there in the stairs. It's all we can do."

"What good's a backup team without water?" asked the chief.

"We'll get water. We also have to pressurize those stairwells. The building engineer is on his way."

During the next few minutes they received reports over in-house phones—just before they inexplicably conked out—that there was smoke on floors eighteen through twenty, on twenty-six, sixty and sixty-one, seventy-six, as well as unconfirmed reports that smoke had been sighted drifting off the roof. "Probably coming out the vents," said one of the nearby county firemen, but even as Diana wondered how anyone could see smoke coming off the roof in this fog, she began to doubt the veracity of some of the information they were receiving.

By now forty or fifty civilians were wandering the lower floors, cleaning personnel and office workers who'd been putting in overtime. There were gawkers and a couple of homeless men who'd walked in off the street carrying bedrolls. Even as they organized the rest of the fire, the command post area began to deteriorate into bedlam.

Diana remembered reading about the First-Interstate Bank fire in Los Angeles, where the flames could be seen from eight miles away. She hated to compare this to the First-Interstate, because she had a gut feeling this was going to be worse. For starters, L.A. had poured four hundred firefighters into the effort. Seattle had two hundred on-duty firefighters, so even if they used the entire shift, they would need another two hundred to duplicate L.A.'s effort, as well as another fifty or so to give minimal coverage to the rest of the city.

So far, including the county chief, who was overwhelmed with the situation, Diana counted sixteen firefighters on the command floor, a few more upstairs, another handful outside. The building security people were tied up trying to explain to the firefighters how the fire suppression systems worked, even though none of the fire suppression systems seemed to have activated properly, none that is but the piercing whistle and loud honking from the alarms. A firefighter from 6's finally took the bull by the horns and broke the closest speakers off the wall with a pike pole. It was remarkable how much confusion the noise alone had caused.

A Seattle air rig arrived, and spare masks and bottles were brought in for the overtimers to use. The man running the *up* elevator would take people up and come down empty. The man in the *down* elevator would go up empty and come down full. Trouble was, the elevators weren't working.

Waiting for an assignment with the others, Diana drifted over to a console of television monitors in the security enclosure, where she was astonished to see one of the upper floors had dozens of people milling about in formal dress.

"What's this?" she asked a short, balding man of around thirty, who sat in front of the monitors reading a magazine called *Combat Readiness Quarterly.* The building security personnel all wore dark gray blazers, and she'd heard rumors they were ex-FBI men, though that was hard to believe. This guy seemed particularly unimpressed with their predicament.

"Some sort of wedding party," he replied, growing more interested when he looked up and saw Diana.

"Those people don't even look like they know the building's in alarm."

"Oh, they know all right." He sat up straight. "They're on emergency power up there right now."

"How many people are in the building, total?"

"Probably a couple hundred."

"What floor is that?"

"Seventy-five."

"So why don't we send someone up there to bring them down?"

"The elevators above forty aren't working. In fact, we've been having trouble with these down here. We're trying to figure it out now."

"What about the stairwells? I thought they were automatically pressurized with clean air when the building went into alarm? Why don't they come down the stairs?"

"Maybe they're supposed to be pressurized, but they're all smoky now. I don't know how that's supposed to work, but you could be right. Hey, is it hard to get in the fire department?"

"It's not hard at all," Diana lied. "I think you should sign up."

"Really?"

"Absolutely."

Diana knew that in L.A. the First-Interstate Bank fire had burned at temperatures close to two thousand degrees, that it had taken most of the night to extinguish. Yet there was one notable difference between that fire and this: Except for a few stranded office workers and about forty maintenance personnel, L.A.'s building had been vacant. The Columbia Tower was like a bee colony.

It was all too easy for smoke and heat to travel upward and sometimes downward in a high-rise building via plumbing and electrical chases, ventilation shafts, air-conditioning ducts, elevator wells, and tenant staircases. It was possible for a fire to be contained on a lower floor while people twenty or thirty stories higher were dying from smoke inhalation. It was even possible for this to happen with almost no smoke on the floors in between. And this was not a building where people could open windows for fresh air. Diana had seen a 250-pound man slam away at similar windows using a pick-head axe with absolutely no effect. None of the windows opened in the conventional sense, and the only ones that could be broken were those designated by small decals in the lower corner.

There were two ways of looking at this. The first as a tactical fire problem. The second as a trap. John had been right. Leary Way had been rigged. Bowman Pork had been rigged. And this building was rigged, too. They were standing on a big piece of cheese in a very tall mousetrap, cheese oozing up between their toes.

In L.A. they'd done their rescues with fire department helicopters and teams of specially trained paramedics who'd rappelled down the outside of the building from the roof. Seattle didn't have any helicopters, nor did they have rappelling paramedics. Even if they did, Diana knew the roof of this building was filled with antennae and microwave dishes and wouldn't accommodate helicopters on a good night, much less in the fog.

Floor four, which acted as the lobby from Fifth Avenue and accessed most of the elevators, was still accepting stragglers from the smoky stairwells. These latecomers had traveled farther and looked worse than the earlier escapees. Because the doors to the stairwells kept opening and closing, the area soon began to reek of smoke.

Moments later Chief Reese rushed in, flanked by two administration chiefs who hadn't seen combat in some time. This was going to be good.

Chief Reese began reorganizing in a surprisingly calm and methodical manner. After assigning division commanders, mostly lieutenants who would later be replaced with captains or chiefs, Reese ordered SPD to clear floor four of nonessential personnel and to have any civilian who'd been in the smoke taken downstairs to the medics.

Thirty-five minutes into it they managed to get water to floor eighteen. Thirty-five minutes was an unacceptable amount of time to leave a fire burning, and now reports from upstairs said it had spread to the entire wing. The original teams had been replaced by fresh troops, a move that had all but exhausted their meager resources. Diana was one of the few people left in staging, a factor she attributed to the county staging officer's reluctance to put a female at risk. She could wait. There was going to be plenty of fire to fight.

Now that she was witnessing it firsthand, the whole thing seemed so much easier to pull off than she'd imagined. A natural gas leak at Northwest Hospital, twenty-one firefighters and assorted hospital personnel tied up in the process of evacuating two wings. A multicar accident on the 520 floating bridge with persons trapped. Eighteen firefighters and five units sent to that one, the bridge gridlocked with thousands of cars backed up into town. Two additional engines locked up in traffic because of the backup from the accident on 520. A warehouse burning in Ballard. A ship fire, also in Ballard. Short of a once-in-a-lifetime natural calamity, it was improbable, if not impossible, for this many large incidents to occur coincidentally at once. On the other hand, it would be easy for an individual to break a gas line at the hospital. Easier still to drop some debris from a moving truck and cause an accident on either of the two floating bridges that spanned Lake Washington.

She was thinking about all this when she saw Finney enter the building in his bulky yellow bunking suit.

# 61. CARRIED AWAY BY THE CROCODILE

Engine 10 was parked at the base of the Columbia Tower on Fourth Avenue, the motor roaring as it powered the dual stage internal water pump, hose lines sucking water from a nearby hydrant. Finney walked over to the engine and ran his hand along the underside of the wheel well on the driver's side before going inside the building.

Once inside, he was directed up the frozen escalators to the command post on four where Chief Smith had been temporarily left in charge.

"John?" Diana came toward him in full bunkers, her coat unbuttoned, flashes of a Hawaii Ironman triathlon T-shirt underneath. "John? I should have believed you. I'm sorry."

"You would have been crazy to believe me."

"What are you going to do?"

"Try to get them to listen."

"They have to listen now."

"Don't bet on it."

Several homeless people who'd been asked to leave were protesting their ouster. On the other side of the room firefighters still awaiting assignments lugged equipment inside from Fifth Avenue, building a stockpile of compressed air cylinders, hoses, spare nozzles, chain saws, pike poles, forcible entry equipment, gas-powered fans.

Chief Smith was talking on a cell phone when Finney arrived. "Chief, whatever you think you know about a high-rise fire, put it out of your mind."

"I'll call you back," Smith said into the telephone. "You know something I don't, John?"

"I know if you fight this according to Hoyle, you're going to lose people."

Chief Smith grew more alert; he'd already lost two firefighters that year and didn't need to lose more. "Did you have anything to do with this?"

"Of course not. But I know this place is booby trapped. Whatever you try, it's going to backfire. Don't go by the numbers, and don't count on any of the building's systems kicking in. I wouldn't count on water from that engine outside either."

"What engine? What are you talking about?"

"The engine pumping into the standpipe is a phony. All it's doing is tying up the standpipe connection."

"What do you mean a phony?"

"It's not the real Engine Ten. It's a fake built just for tonight."

Staring resolutely at Finney, Chief Smith picked his white helmet up off the counter and held it under one arm. "Look around. Nobody has to tamper with any systems to make this bad! This is as bad as it gets. We've got what? Thirty firefighters? We need five hundred? Don't tell me to break the rules. And don't try to feed me any more of your harebrained conspiracy theories."

Several people had been clamoring for Smith's ear, and as he turned his attention to a police sergeant at his side, a large volume of ankle-deep water came gushing out the doorway of the nearest stairwell. Smith turned to Finney and said, "I guess that phony engine outside is pumping phony water, huh?" Several firefighters ran over to contain it, stacking rolled canvas tarps inside the landing to dike the flow. Even so, long fingers of water spread across the floor.

After a couple of minutes, Finney found Chief Reese speaking to Oscar Stillman in a cubbyhole on the other side of the elevators. Finney stopped just short of the corner and listened. "No, you will not call in a task force from Tacoma. Or from Bellevue. You will limit your losses, and you will fight a defensive fire."

"Damn it, Oscar. I'm the chief, not you. And I am not going to let all those people upstairs die. You think that's what I want as my legacy?"

"Screw your legacy. Get those guys out of the stairwells. Then get as many civilians out as you can. After that, pull back. What we're talking about here is saving firefighters' lives."

"I'm not going to pull twenty firefighters out so I can lose two hundred civilians."

"You want me to spill my guts about Leary Way?" Oscar asked, lowering his voice.

"You do what you have to. Our first directive is to save lives."

When Finney stepped around the corner, he looked at Reese. "God, I thought you were part of this. One day I saw you coming out of this building behind one of them."

"I come out of this building every day. My wife works here."

"I hope she's not here now."

"She's home."

"And you're being blackmailed."

Reese considered Finney for a moment. "Did you have anything to do with setting this?"

"Don't look at me. Who checked out the building and told you it was invulnerable? Who's telling you to pull out? Look, Charlie. Get somebody from the company that installed these systems and get them here fast."

"I suppose we're fakes, too?" Marion Balitnikoff stepped around the corner behind Finney, followed by Michael Lazenby in full battle gear. "And I suppose that rig we've got out in the street is a fake."

"They're part of it," Finney said. "And yes, that rig outside is a fake."

Reese said, "You're going to have to leave, John. You're in the way."


1932 HOURS

Everyone's attention was captured by four burly SPD officers wrestling with a firefighter in yellow bunkers. Diana's heart leaped into her throat when she recognized Finney. Working together, they wrestled him to the ground and snapped handcuffs onto his wrists, one officer's knee on his back, another putting his full weight on his neck. They dragged him through the foyer toward the doors on Fifth Avenue, past Reese and Smith, who both ignored the commotion, past the building security guards. It looked as if Finney were being carried away in the jaws of an animal, perhaps a great crocodile.

As they exited the building, Finney turned and looked back over his shoulder, and for just a second he caught her eye.

When she turned around to gauge the reaction of the other Seattle firefighters on the floor, most of the looks were shocked, but the faces of three men bore the definite aura of triumph: Balitnikoff, Lazenby, and Oscar Stillman.

Diana followed Finney and the police officers outside to Fifth Avenue, where one of the officers began speaking into the remote mike on his collar. Several engines were in the street, hose lines connecting one of them to a hydrant across the street, firefighters loading hose on their shoulders at the rear of that rig.

Keeping Finney in the center of their phalanx, the officers headed across the street.

It took a few moments for Diana to take in what happened next.

There was a noise high above. She didn't know what it was until she saw Finney turn and, using his chest and shoulder, bull two of the policemen back toward the doorway she was standing in. They had retreated six or eight steps when a loud impact occurred in the center of the street. Particles of something small and hard stung Diana's face. Water began spraying into the air in several directions, some of it onto her. A second impact in the street struck the roof of the engine and threw more particles at the building and at her. Then all was quiet except for curses and the water gushing into the street from severed hose lines.

The two police officers who'd been in front had turned and chased Finney, so that all five had missed the explosion by eight or nine feet. A window had fallen into the street. If Finney hadn't turned them around, they might all be dead. The officers were wet from the hoses, and even though they'd missed the center of the impact, two of them were bleeding.

"What the hell happened?" asked the officer closest to Diana. "I thought he was trying to escape."

"A window broke out upstairs," Diana said. "He was trying to get you out of harm's way. I think he saved your life."

"That was a window? Shit, it sounded like a cannon."

Another section of glass crashed to the street, this smaller than the first. Pushed by flame and heat and maybe by firefighters attempting to ventilate, falling sheet glass would probably continue to come down into the street like guillotine blades all night.

Diana knew those large sheets of windowpane wouldn't fall in a straight line. Like maple seeds, they fluttered this way and that, some landing a hundred yards or more from the base of the building. Some would land flat, others on edge. They would cut hose lines, destroy cars, kill people.

When Diana looked up, she saw a dull glow in the sky. "You think that's one floor or two floors burning?" she asked two firefighters who'd taken shelter beside her.

The shorter firefighter, Murphy, said, "Doesn't matter. If it's not two, it will be. They don't have water on it yet, so you know it's going to lap.

It's going to gut the whole building. I wish I could remember what temperature steel loses its integrity at."

"Two thousand degrees," Diana said.

"It won't be the heat," said the second firefighter. "The smoke'll kill those people upstairs long before the fire reaches them."

"They better start evacuating this whole downtown core area," said Murphy. "I think this is coming down."

"Where is he?" asked the tallest policeman, approaching the firefighters. "Have you seen our prisoner?"

There was nothing in the street now but three engines, severed hose lines, and spurts of water taller than a man.

Diana watched as the officers spread out on the sidewalk trying to locate their prisoner. One by one, the fire department drivers ran to their rigs and moved them out of range. Somebody yelled to the drivers that base was being set up two blocks away on Sixth Avenue between Cherry and Columbia. While the police officers warned her to stay out of the street, she crossed Fifth Avenue on foot.

She found him two blocks away staring at her from the shelter of a darkened doorway, his hands still cuffed behind his back. Their eyes met. He seemed surprisingly calm, as if waiting for a bus. Or for her. "Just a minute," she said, and walked to Ladder 9, opening compartment after compartment until she found their bolt cutters, then, sans cuffs, they walked back down the hill together. The police were gone. More hose lines were being laid to standpipe and sprinkler connections outside the tower, while other firefighters stood guard for falling objects; pumpers were set up to pump in tandem in order to build more pressure. They were going to have to raise the water an appreciable distance. No sooner had firefighters laid a line to a nearby sprinkler connection than a large wedge of glass fell and severed it, water gushing into the street like blood from an artery. Firefighters began raiding a construction site half a block away, carting plywood sheets to protect their hose lines. A group of civilians from a restaurant down the street helped.

Finney said, "They're pumping all that water onto an open floor somewhere. They're going to have to lay hose up the stairs as high as the fire."

"The fire's on eighteen," Diana said.

"You mean the first fire's on eighteen."

They could hear trucks and engines as, two blocks away, the base area began filling with new arrivals. Most of the newcomers had sped from earlier emergencies with empty water tanks, half-empty air bottles, and dirty or missing equipment. Most of the firefighters Finney and Diana saw coming down the street were already exhausted.

Carrying a ladder at waist height, a tarp laid out on the rungs, equipment stacked on the tarp, a quartet of firefighters trudged down the sidewalk. Their load was so heavy they could barely walk. Although Diana warned the officer that, in order to avoid falling glass, the ongoing procedure now was to enter the Columbia Tower via the tunnel in the building across the street, he ignored her and made a beeline across the carpet of broken glass on Fifth Avenue. When one of them dropped a portable radio unnoticed, Finney pocketed it.

Listening to the division reports on the radio, they heard the officer who was running the operation upstairs say, "Columbia Command from Division Sixteen. We have a report from our standpipe team. They're on fifty-one. They're okay for now, but they're trapped and out of air. They've encountered a lot of heat but no fire. No sign of any more survivors. None of the standpipe outlets they checked were open. The water's coming from above them. I'm not going to send anybody else up. Repeat. It's too dangerous to send anybody else up. The stairs are getting hotter every minute."

Finney looked up at the fog.

"What are you going to do?" Diana asked.

"What makes you think I'm going to do anything?"

"Whatever it is, I'm with you."

"Like hell."

"You're going to need help, and you know it."

# 62. IN THE MOVIES THEY ALWAYS SCREAM

The flashing red, blue, and yellow lights from nearby emergency vehicles reflected off the wet glass on Fifth Avenue, so that it resembled a street full of pirate treasure. The tread on the heavy tires crunched nuggets of broken glass. The street was beginning to stink of burning plastic, as smoke from the fire in the building mingled with fog and the heavy odor of diesel exhaust.

Finney pulled Ladder 9 to a stop, put the transmission into neutral, pushed the parking brake on the dash, and reached across to throw the rocker switch that would allow the transmission to power the aerial.

Without checking to see whether the cops barricading the street on the far corner had recognized him, he put his helmet on and walked around to the small control panel at the rear, where he put the hydraulic outriggers down on either side of the apparatus.

As a group of civilians watched from across the street, he climbed up onto the control tower on the turntable eight feet above the street, placed the toe of his boot on the dead-man control, flipped the switch to raise the RPM on the engine to fast idle, and pulled the black-knobbed elevation lever. The aerial raised out of the bed. He swung it around, extending the sections toward the Columbia Tower. A few moments later, fully extended, the tip grazed a window on what he calculated to be the seventh floor above the street. He wasn't doing this to bring people down. People trapped on the upper floors in the building had no hope of rescue from outside the building.

Diana ferried equipment to the base of the turntable, while Finney slipped his arms through the straps of one of the MSA backpacks rigged with a one-hour bottle.

As he was cinching up the shoulder straps, Jerry Monahan came out unexpectedly from behind a gaggle of spectators on the corner of Fifth and Columbia. Monahan was wearing all his gear, including a mask in standby position. He was carrying a large plastic suitcase that contained his high-rise civilian escape invention, Elevator-in-a-Can.

"I don't know what you're trying to do, John," Monahan said, breathing heavily, "but you're not going up there."

"Get away from me, Jerry. I'm pissed."

"I don't want anybody else hurt, most of all you. My God, I . . ." Monahan's words were heartfelt. "What are you going to do by yourself?"

"He's not by himself," Diana said, approaching the turntable with two bags of six-hundred-foot ropes they'd appropriated from Station 14's inventory minutes earlier, right after they stole Ladder 9.

"John, don't make me do something we'll both regret."

"It would take a conscience to feel regret."

"No, I feel awful about what's happened. That's why I'm going to save those people up there. I've got this invention. There's a few bugs left in it, but I think—" Without warning Finney knocked the older man to the ground. Monahan landed on his hip, his air cylinder striking the pavement with a loud, metallic thunk.

"Okay, okay," Monahan said, raising a hand as a gesture of supplication. His helmet was upside down beside him, his knuckles cut and bleeding from the glass on the street. "I deserved that. Just remember. You can't change anything."

As Finney walked to the rear of the apparatus, screwing the low-pressure hose from his facepiece onto the regulator on his belt, another firefighter approached unexpectedly. Robert Kub had on full bunkers, an hour bottle in an MSA backpack, and a pick-head axe. He was already sweating. "You guys need help," Kub said.

"You've helped enough," said Finney.

"Give me a chance. I want to do this with you. Whatever it is you're doing."

Finney brushed past without a word.

"Okay," Kub shouted to his back. "But I've been inside. Reese is running this like it's any other fire. The building engineer keeps telling them it will only be a few minutes until he gets water to the sprinklers, so they're all basically in a holding pattern until that happens. Every fifteen minutes he takes a break to stand in front of a television camera and yak. They're not going to get water to the sprinklers, are they?"

Finney turned and looked at Kub. "No."

"Let me help. I have to prove myself."

Finney had already calculated that if they each carried a spare bottle and paced themselves, he and Diana might just be able to climb seventy-odd stories before running out of air. That they would drain most or all of both air bottles on the way up was a given. A third person to help pack equipment up might make the difference.

278

"Take me with you. You need me, and I need to do this."

Finney looked into Kub's eyes for a few moments. Kub was right. They needed help. He extended his hand; they shook. "Go get another hour bottle."

Kub said, "They sent a team to rescue three or four people on fifty-one, but they never got past twenty because of the heat. Two of 'em got burned and are headed for the medics. What happens if you can't get up?"

"We'll get up."

While he waited for Kub to ready his equipment and begin his ascent, Finney turned to Diana. "If we don't get out of this, I love you."

Gray eyes twinkling, she said, "And if we do get out of it, you don't?"

He laughed. "I know we haven't known each other that long. And my life has been in such turmoil. But I do love you." When she didn't reply, he continued, "So? What do you think?"

"I don't know. I guess I need more information."

He took her in his arms, an awkward maneuver, considering they were both wearing close to sixty pounds of equipment, MSAs on their backs, facepieces slung around their necks, portable radios in their chest pockets, axes in scabbards at their waists, full bunking trousers with multiple layers of heat and vapor barriers, rubber boots, and Nomex coats. Her lips made him want to whisk her away and watch the fire on TV over the bar in some cozy Italian restaurant in Belltown. When they separated, two or three spectators across the street whistled and applauded. "Is that the sort of information you were looking for?"

She smiled, and he knew that if she didn't love him now, she would. Then, as he looked into Diana's eyes, Finney said, "Look, if things get too rough, I want you to turn back."

"Sure, you, too."

"I mean it."

"Yeah? What else? You going to open the doors for me? Carry my handbag? Listen to yourself. Ordinarily, you're stronger than me. I'll grant you that. But you've had a lot of shocks to your system. You're not anywhere near a hundred percent, and you're going to need all the help you can get."

Finney put his helmet back on and looked up at Robert Kub, who had secured his spare bottle and a rope bag and was making his way up the rubber-coated rungs of the aerial. Shards of glass were embedded in the soles of his rubber boots. His progress seemed painfully slow until

Finney remembered how much weight he was carrying: fifty-odd pounds of personal protective equipment, a spare bottle, a rope bag with six hundred feet of rope in it. They all knew this could be their last fire. If they succeeded, they would be terminated. If they failed, they would be dead.

Before they could follow Kub, two chairs and a flaming desk fell to the sidewalk, crashing to the pavement forty feet away in sequence like lopsided meteors. When it landed, the desk sounded like a gun going off.

Moments later a large yellow package struck the pavement with the sound of a tree breaking in half, bouncing as high as the roof of Ladder 9 before dropping back onto the ground. A yellow helmet bounced off the base of the building and spun in the street like a broken top. A firefighter had tumbled into the street.

Diana, who'd been facing the other direction, realized what had happened, and said, "Oh, God. No."

The face was unrecognizable, but the name across the tail of his jacket said "Spritzer."

"Barney," Finney said. "Works on Engine Nine. He's got kids."

"I just saw him at the funeral," Diana said. "He's the nicest guy in the world."

Kub, who'd stopped halfway up the ladder, glanced down and said, "The street's going to be full of our friends if we don't get moving."

Before he'd proceeded five more rungs, another body hit the street, a woman in a skirt that had blown up over her waist on the descent, her mouth and nostrils ringed with soot and blood. She didn't bounce. She just broke and lay splayed out ten feet from Spritzer. They looked like a pair of discarded rag dolls. It was odd, Finney thought, that neither had made a sound during the plunge. In the movies they always screamed.

# 63. THE OLD MAN TRIES ONE MORE TIME

For almost a full minute, Diana watched Robert Kub pounding on the plate-glass window with his service axe, the pick head bouncing off with no discernible result. They all knew the designated breakout windows in a high-rise had white dots in one corner, but nobody had ever bothered to tell them how to locate them from the outside, especially when the windows were tinted.

After a while Diana heard the sound of glass breaking and looked up to see parts of a window dropping to the sidewalk. She could hear the two men talking through the intercom at the tip of the aerial.

"Damn," Kub said, gasping. "If I'd known it was going to be this much work, I wouldn't have volunteered."

"You never did like work," Finney joked.

"Look who's talking. I'll be dragging your sorry ass up those stairs."

"I'll clip a carabiner to your backpack to make it easier for you to give me a tow."

The next voice Diana heard was so close it startled her. "Listen to me." Jerry Monahan was on the turntable behind her, one of his eyes beginning to swell shut from Finney's fist.

"There's no stopping this," Monahan said. "Bail out now, while you can."

Tinny and laced with the sounds of rubber boots on broken glass, Finney's voice came across on the speaker. "Diana. Come on up."

They'd left a spare hour bottle, the Halligan/flathead axe combination, and a bag of webbing for her to carry, the tools banded together with a strip of rubber. It was going to be tough enough without battling Monahan. As she reached for the spare bottle, Jerry Monahan took her in a bear hug from behind, from which she quickly managed to extricate both arms, though he kept hold of her torso.

"Let me go."

"No can do, Miss Moore. I've done some boneheaded things in my life, but one of them is not going to be letting you get yourself killed."

Diana freed the flathead axe from the tool package and dropped the Halligan. "Let me go."

There was an intimacy to the assault that Diana couldn't escape, this old man breathing into her ear like a lover, smelling of cloves and hair oil and perspiration and the blood on his face. "Listen to me. Finney doesn't have anything to prove. Finney didn't have anything to do with that woman in the burn ward."

"The police think he did."

"Paul was at Riverside Drive that morning. After Finney left, Paul set the fire. That old woman just happened to get in the way."

"Lazenby?"

"Yes. When he realized that old woman could ID him, he hit her over the head and dragged her upstairs; tied her up with some twine."

"What about Gary Sadler?"

"They set that other fire to get rid of John and Gary both. Gary was on to me. They hauled Gary back into the building. It was hard for me when I found out. I mean, I worked with both those guys. None of this has been easy. But we can change that. We can do something good here. We can use my invention to get those people out."

"Let go."

"I know it doesn't make any difference in the real scheme of things, but I can't let you guys die the way Gary did."

With the flat head leading, Diana swung the axe between her legs. A short, crisp blow. Monahan dropped onto his side, then rolled off the apparatus and fell eight feet to the ground. She'd broken his leg.

# 64. HERDING CATS

Using a grease pen, Oscar Stillman scrawled a floor plan for the building on the wall next to the stairwell. Chief Reese had appointed him information officer in charge of briefing the stairwell teams. The teams would, directly after speaking to him, climb to floor sixteen, take a short breather, and from there go to the fire on eighteen.

Years from now when people asked Oscar what part he'd played in the Columbia Tower debacle, he would tell them he'd been at the hub of the conflagration, had been head information officer. With time, Reese would, of course, develop into a pitiful and despised figure, especially since he'd personally vouched to the police that Finney's allegations about the building were spurious. It tickled Oscar to think of Reese trying to explain himself, particularly after Oscar and the others denied Reese had asked him to inspect the Columbia Tower's fire suppression systems. There was supposed to have been a written report, but Oscar hadn't turned it in.

Information officer. He liked that. It was a lofty-sounding moniker and would lend credence to the details he would parcel out in the years to come.

So far, most of the groups Oscar briefed were comprised of mutual aid companies from outside the city, young men eager to die in a building they knew little about and had no stake in. Oscar had to admire their gung-ho attitudes and youthful faces, even as he mentally ridiculed their commitment to this folly.

The Columbia Tower had been built with pressurized stairwells to keep the smoke at bay, phones for firefighters on every floor and in the elevators, water tanks on floors twenty-five, thirty-seven, and fifty-eight, as well as a five-thousand-gallon tank on floor seventy-seven, which should have supplied the initial water for the sprinklers. There were fire pumps on level A and floors thirty-six and thirty-eight. On paper the system worked great.

Because of the elaborate preparations Oscar and his partners had made, few of those systems were operable. What they'd left intact were blinking lights and shrieking alarms, anything that might amplify the chaos. The phones didn't work. They'd scuttled several key sections of sprinklers and standpipes, so that no matter how much water was pumped into the system it would never pressurize. There was little danger in leaving the fire pumps and water tanks intact—any water from them was destined to bleed down the interior stairwells through a series of strategically broken pipes. A torrent in the stairs would not only make work difficult, but would, after some hours, cause ungodly problems in the basement.

As another group approached with hose lines on their shoulders, Oscar collared the officer and tried to gather everybody together. It took a full minute. Firefighters. Unless they saw flame, it was like herding cats.

"Okay," Oscar said, surveying the eight firefighters and two officers. It tickled him the way the officers made their men stand with hose loads on their shoulders while he spoke, even though in an hour none of them would have the strength to lift a dirty sock. If they'd been his men, he would have been filling their gullets with Gatorade and making them rest before the ordeal.

Oscar pointed to the diagram on the wall. "You'll find that most floors in this building will have this approximate layout. The elevators are in the center. They're not working now, but we have a specialist looking into it. The two main stairwells are fairly close to each other. You are about to enter stairwell A, which we have designated as the firefighting stairwell. When you get inside, you'll notice lines have been laid. That's because there's a problem with the standpipes. The building engineers tell us they're going to get that licked in the next half hour or so."

Oscar pulled open the stairway door to reveal a dark and noisy stairwell with eight inches of fast-running water blurring the steps, enough to knock a careless man off his feet. A cloud of smoke drifted out as he closed the door. Water might have escaped, too, but somebody'd diked the inside of the doorway with rolled-up canvas tarps. The whole thing was turning into a delightful clutter. The worse it became, the harder it was for Oscar to stifle his laughter. He'd even heard a story about a dead firefighter in the street. These county guys were so panicked they were inventing their own urban legends on the spot.

"We've had smoke problems down here, but you'll have more higher up. Use your masks. And think about whether your five-minute warning bells are going to give you enough time to find a fresh bottle. The second stairway is not to be used for firefighting. If and when we get it pressurized properly, B will be reserved for bringing down victims. We start fighting fire from both stairways, they'll both be contaminated with smoke. Understood?"

The first officer, a heavyset man with a florid face and webs of burst blood vessels across his bulbous nose, took off his helmet and said, "I heard stairwell B was shitty already."

"It is. We're working on it."

"Why not put up our own fans? We can clear a stairwell."

"That's been tried. It made it hotter. It also fed the fire on eighteen. Okay. Now, there's a restaurant on seventy-six. The Tower Club. There was a wedding banquet going on below that. We think there's around two hundred people up there, including staff."

"No sprinklers anywhere?" asked a firefighter.

"All we know is they're not working on the lower fire floors."

"What do you mean lower fire floors?" asked the first officer. "We were told there was one fire. On eighteen."

"Figuring out which floors are involved and which are not is going to be one of your assignments. We have TV cameras, but there's so much smoke they're not telling us much." Oscar might have told him about the fire on fifty-six, which had been raging for some time, but he thought that was better coming as a surprise; besides, he didn't officially know about it yet.

"How long are these bottles going to last?" asked the officer. "Going up stairs."

"What you've got here is a seventy-eight-story building—seventy-six actual tenant floors. When they run the Columbia Challenge each spring, even the fittest athlete firefighters running these stairs in full bunkers need a change of bottles before the top. One firefighter who's run it said he used two bottles and ended up unscrewing his low-pressure hose so he wouldn't suffocate when he ran the second one dry. Remember, you move slower, you use less air. I'm no physiologist. I couldn't give you the numbers.

"Okay. Listen, it's going to lap on you. It's going to break out the windows and work its way outside the building to the floor above. There are plumbing and electrical chases cut through the floors, so it's traveling up in that manner, too. Remember the three firefighters in Philadelphia? They ran out of air, called for help, and gave the wrong floor number? By the time they found them, they were dead. Keep an eye on those gauges. Know which floor you're on. This isn't a pissy little house fire, where you can bail out a window. You bail out of one of these windows, you better sprout wings.

"Now, one important fact we do know is that none of these doors have unlocked the way they're supposed to unlock when the building's in fire mode. If it hasn't already been broken into, you'll have to break into every floor you enter."

"What about master keys?" somebody asked.

"We got some keys, but for some reason they don't work. This also means any civilians coming down are in serious trouble unless they can hold their breath for seventy-odd stories; they won't be able to rest up on a clean floor. Hasta la vista, amigos."

After the group left, Oscar began to wonder why he felt so smug. A typical house fire drew temperatures around twelve hundred degrees. This would be a lot hotter. Cold-drawn steel, such as that used in the elevator cables in this building, failed at eight hundred degrees. The building was constructed around a steel core, and the heat would eventually deform that at around two thousand degrees. More than one of these boys probably weren't coming back. Still, he felt smug.

Oscar couldn't even imagine the commissions they were going to convene trying to explain tonight. Not that he had to worry about it. When this was finished, there would be no evidence and no witnesses. The others would be long gone and he would be in Costa Rica reading about it four days late in the *Wall Street Journal*.

The question was, did he feel anything over the fact that he had planned and was in the process of murdering some two hundred souls, including one Patterson Cole, who'd paid for the whole thing? It was hard to tell. Oscar's primary concern right now was whether they would actually get the money. A million five in his pocket would go a long way toward assuaging his guilt. There was so much testosterone and adrenaline in the air, Oscar didn't really know how he felt. Besides, there was no stopping it now. They'd done it, and they would have to live with it.

# 65. GETTING DOWN TO BUSINESS

Stillman had just sent another group upstairs, this with two women firefighters in it, their round faces reminding him for some reason of a pair of semi-pro women softball players he'd once met in a bar in Portland. He turned back to the wall just as G. A. Montgomery stepped out of the confusion, G. A.'s face dripping with perspiration, his nose and cheeks red.

"Everything moving along according to plan?" G. A. asked.

Oscar glanced around to see if anybody had noticed them. "Yeah, yeah, yeah. I understand we've been getting cell phone calls from upstairs, from Patterson. You got the cash?"

"Jerry started it early. Stupid bastard."

"I wondered what happened. I got your call that everything was starting, and I just went ahead and did what I was supposed to. I guess the others did their share 'cause the city's in a tizzy. But what about the money? You got it?"

"You know I do."

"Where?"

"Don't get your nose out of joint. It's close. Right now I need to know how things are going."

"There's three firefighters trapped in the mid-fifties. Everybody else is below the lower fire. On sixteen, seventeen, and eighteen."

"And they're sending people to get above it?"

"They tried. The stairwell's too hot. You get up around twenty, it's hotter than a hooker on payday. It gets worse as you go up. A lot worse."

"What about elevators?"

"With the exception of one we left for ourselves, they're all disabled."

"How many more hours do you estimate this will take?"

"Not long. Our highest fire has been burning over an hour with no water on it. Hell, by now every floor between fifty-four and the roof has to be full of smoke."

"Nobody's going to believe this is an accident," G. A. said. "The papers will be full of speculation. It will go on for years."

"All the same, it couldn't have gone better." Oscar tried to smile, feeling his lips and cheeks stiff with the trying. G. A. always had been a worrier, ever since the night he'd recruited Oscar into this little group. G. A. had received the initial offer from Patterson Cole's man, Norris Radford. Together they'd approached Jerry Monahan. Monahan had in turn suggested Marion Balitnikoff, and Balitnikoff brought in the Lazenbys. He couldn't remember how Tony Finney got into it. One or more of them might have backed out, except that Norris Radford had been FedExing Oscar bundles of cash so that they'd been paid nearly $50,000 each for their practice runs, $10,000 a week to prepare for tonight. And that didn't take into account the cost of the engine they'd had built to ensure they were the first firefighters responding to the Columbia Tower. Good thing, because tonight the real Engine 10 was in Ballard fighting a ship fire.

"Know where everybody is?" G. A. asked.

"I think so."

"Good. Round them up. I need to see the whole team. Now."

# 66. IT'S TOO DAMN HOT

On floor fifteen Finney took stock of their situation. They were one floor below staging. They'd climbed seven stories on the aerial and then scurried up the remaining floors at a pace he knew they couldn't maintain. Kub, who could move like lightning for a hundred meters on the flat, was having trouble keeping up. Finney wondered whether any of them could make it another sixty stories. His thighs were trembling from the load. Diana looked ashen.

He wanted to stop and strip off some of the nonessential equipment, maybe remove the liners from his bunkers, wear only the light Nomex shell without the vapor barriers that kept in all the body heat, but if they did that and got caught by fire, they'd be as bad off as the civilians. They certainly couldn't jettison the spare bottles. And if they didn't take the rope bags and hardware, they might as well not make the trip.

It would get easier by seventeen pounds, he knew, after they emptied their first bottles and off-loaded the empties.

Floor fifteen was clear enough that all three had taken off their face-pieces and were gulping building air. When Kub sat against the wall, Finney noticed the nose cone of his facepiece was half full of sweat, the fluorescent lights glaring off the tiny moving puddle like a mirror. Kub had unsnapped his coat, and his T-shirt was sopping. Diana took her coat off and then her T-shirt, dropping the shirt, which slapped the floor like a wet dishcloth. She was left with a damp sports bra and bunking pants.

Diana scouted out a watercooler and began tossing down water from a small paper cup. "If we don't drink," she said, "we're going to get dehydrated, and that's going to cause us to start making bad decisions."

"Hell," Kub said, struggling to his feet. "We already made one bad decision. We're here, aren't we?"

Diana's smile was weak.

Finney said, "This next is going to be the tricky part. We not only have to get past stairwell division, but we have to get past the fire."

"It's already way hot," Diana said, pulling her facepiece back on and opening the valve on her regulator.

As he began breathing bottled air again, Finney laughed at their audacity. The three of them didn't stand a chance of bluffing their way past stairwell command, much less plunging into what would probably be the worst heat they'd ever encountered. The higher they went, the hotter it would get.

Moving with a load again was not a pleasant experience. After only one floor Finney's thighs began burning and his shoulders ached where the air-pack straps pulled. The insides of his bunking coat and pants were still wet and clammy from their first climb. Soon that clamminess would feel like a sauna. It didn't help that the air coming through Finney's regulator didn't come fast enough. Nor did it help that he secretly believed this whole wrong-headed idea would get Diana and Robert Kub killed. Just what he didn't need. More dead partners.

They climbed past sixteen and encountered smoke so thick they had to keep one hand on the guardrail to maintain equilibrium. They slogged through running water that came down the steps like a mountain stream. Finney assumed the water was pouring out the door on the fire floor, that the panicked firefighters on that floor were using too much water, but sometimes pranksters opened one of the stairwell valves, and these could remain open for weeks, or until somebody charged the system and water began spilling out the way it was tonight.

Finney led the way, though the others followed so closely that when he slowed they bumped into him. On eighteen they ran into five firefighters kneeling under the heat. Just inside the door to that floor another crew worked a hose line.

A short man in an orange captain's helmet rose from a crouch and approached. "Okay, I want you three on this backup line, while these others rotate inside. Give me your passports."

"This isn't the firefighting stairwell," Finney said. "I thought everyone was in A."

"We're using both now. Give me your passport."

"They told us to go higher," Finney lied.

"Forget that. Nobody's going higher. And give me those spare bottles."

"We're supposed to take the bottles with us."

"We tried that. It's too hot. Who the hell are you guys?"

Finney didn't hear the rest—he was moving.

They were already hot, but as soon as he reached the turnback on the stairs, he could feel severe heat beginning to crawl inside his bunkers. Because he was first in line and higher than the others, it would hit him first. He hoped that would give him some measure of control, that he could turn back before Diana and Kub were burned too badly.

They passed nineteen, and by now the stairwell was so smoky their flashlights were useless. Last week's burns on his ears and neck began to feel raw and sore. He welcomed the pain; it was sharp and precise and took his mind off what they were walking into.

By the time they reached twenty-three, it was hotter than anything Finney had ever known.

Waiting for the others, who had slipped back, he dropped to one knee.

He sensed rather than felt Diana making her way up the last half-flight, but Kub stopped below on the turnaround landing and said, "I'm on fire! Goddamn, I'm on fire. Damn, my neck. Goddamn!"

Finney could hear him splashing water from the floor onto himself. He grabbed handfuls of water himself and splashed it around his own facepiece.

"It's too hot," Diana said, dropping her load in the water on the floor at Finney's feet. "It's way too hot."

Finney stood, and when he did, the sweat inside his bunkers scalded him in a half-dozen places.

He found the wall and felt along it until he had the door. "We'll go in and cool off."

Not only was the door locked, but it was hot to the touch, which usually meant there was fire on the other side. In this situation Finney couldn't be sure. It was a metal door, and convection from the stairwell might be responsible. As he thought about it, the dispatchers announced on the radio that Columbia Command had been on scene sixty minutes, plenty long enough to warm the door from the outside.

"Give me the Halligan," Finney said.

A pry bar about three feet long with a simple straight claw on one end and a set of short, right-angle levers on the other, the Halligan was designed so that, in combination with a flathead axe or a sledge, the right-angle levers could be pounded into the crack in a door, which then made it relatively easy for someone on the long end to lever the door open.

Finney inserted the end of the Halligan, then reached out until he found Diana. "Hold this," he said. "Keep your hands back."

Working blind in the smoke, he struck several blows with the back of the flathead axe until the Halligan was securely in the crack in the door. Metal screeched as Diana pried the door open. A tongue of flame shot out. Together, they shouldered the door closed.

In the brief light from the flames, Finney caught a glimpse of Diana and Kub both. Neither looked happy about the situation. Kub was kneeling in the running water. "What do you want to do? We can go up and try another floor. We can go down and quit."

"How many floors have fire on them?" Kub asked. "What floor is this?"

"Twenty-three," said Diana, who'd been counting as painstakingly as Finney.

"It couldn't have spread that far," Kub said. "The next couple have to be free."

"So we're going up?" Finney asked. No answer. "If you're nodding, I can't see you."

They both mumbled yes.

At the turnback midway between twenty-three and twenty-four Finney was again burned inside his bunkers. It was not possible, he realized, to endure this kind of heat without burns, no matter what he wore. He tried to stop on twenty-four to open the door, but Kub nudged him in the smoke and said, "One more. This might not be any good."

Finney didn't think *anybody* could climb one more set of stairs. But if Kub could, he could. They forced themselves to twenty-five and pried the door, pulling it open against the rushing water on the stairwell landing. There was something else, too, something on the floor.

Except for a small, nasty cloud that followed them in from the stairs, there wasn't much smoke on this floor. The fluorescent lights were on. Kub closed the door behind them. They dropped their gear and tried to cool off. After he'd thought about it awhile, Finney went back and opened the door, curious as to what the obstruction in the stairwell had been.

It was a woman in her fifties dressed in jeans, deck shoes, and a gray uniform shirt with the name "Alma" stitched across the breast pocket. Finney dragged her inside.

Diana took her mask off and knelt beside the woman, feeling for a carotid pulse. She looked up at Finney and Kub and shook her head.

Hoping to find safer passage, they checked stairwell A, but found it as hot as the one they'd come up.

"What are we going to do?" Diana asked.

"Let's check the elevators," Finney said.

"Even if they work, we'd be crazy to use them," Kub said.

"We wouldn't be crazy to use the shaft."

# 67. ROGUE PENNY

All three took off their MSAs and dropped the cylinders and backpacks onto the floor near the elevators. They took off their helmets and hoods and opened their coats. Diana's hair was plastered to her head with sweat, her bare shoulders sleek and tawny. Though his torso was lean and muscular, Kub's face looked haggard and drawn.

Finney opened the hardware bag and began rigging carabiners on a sling that he draped over his shoulder, clipping a small loop of webbing onto each carabiner. "See if you can scrounge up a coat hanger, anything we can use for an elevator key."

He took out a pulley and extra webbing of various lengths. He got out a pair of thin, leather gloves he kept in his inside coat pocket for rope rescues, stepped into a waist harness, and cinched up the leg and waist straps. He put a carabiner through the ring on the front of his belt, tied a figure eight in the end of a six-hundred-foot rope, and clipped himself in.

"Let's see if this'll work." Diana went to the elevator and inserted a long elevator key into the small hole on the upper right side of the door.

"Where'd you find that?" Finney asked.

"In the box." She nodded at a small, red box on the wall next to his head.

Elevators had two sets of doors, the inside door was attached to the elevator car and traveled up and down the shaft with the car. It was generally finished on the inside, innards exposed when viewed from the outside. In addition, each landing had its own door that was finished on the tenant side.

From inside the car, the doors could be opened with hand pressure. From the landings, the outer door required a special key consisting of a piece of steel tubing, the end of which flopped down on a hinge. The key was inserted into a pencil-size hole in the door, placed just far enough inside for the shorter portion to flop parallel with the door, so that when twisted the end fell across a latch mechanism and released the door lock.

Working together, it took Diana and Finney thirty seconds to open the door.

It was perfect. The shaft was four cars wide and there was a ladder on the wall.

Out of a perverse whimsy, Finney found a rogue penny in the thigh pocket of his bunking pants and tossed it into the shaft. For a second he thought he'd lost the coin, but then he heard it ping far below.

"I'll string up a lead line. One of you can follow, and then we'll haul up the equipment. Then the last one can come up."

"Sure you're strong enough?" Diana asked. "Those stairs were no picnic, and you've had a rough week."

More like a rough year, he thought, and no, he wasn't sure. But there were two reasons why he needed to go himself. The first was that Kub wasn't a truckman and didn't know how to rig ropes. The second was that (and he hoped this wasn't only male vanity) even in a weakened state his upper body strength was greater than Diana's. "I'll manage."

"What if fire breaks through the elevator doors on one of the lower floors?" Kub asked.

"Then you two go back down and be safe."

"John," Diana said. "We're on twenty-four. You're not planning to climb all the way to seventy-six? That's got to be over five hundred feet."

"If I remember the prefire for this building, these elevators only go to forty. We'll regroup there."

Finney couldn't shake the feeling that he was asleep and he would awaken in a hospital bed. Or a box. After all, it had happened before—the hospital bed. The box was yet to come. Far in the future he hoped. Though it could easily be tonight. For some time now he had the feeling he was going to die, and as he readied himself to step into the elevator shaft, the feeling intensified.

"You okay, John?" Diana touched his face with a bare hand.

"Double-check my rigging. I'm going to put a carabiner on every floor. You two belay me. Find an anchor point down here, and we'll feed the rope through a couple of prusiks. That way if I fall, I won't go far."

"Already done."

Kub found a portable television in one of the offices and brought it out to the elevator lobby, set it on the floor, and plugged it in with an extension cord he'd bootlegged. He was soon watching television pictures shot in the street a block from the building, and then from the lobby, where Reese was chatting with a reporter. Reese felt confident that the fire teams would extricate everybody from the building. No, he could give no time line.

"Sure is weird to watch this on TV," Kub said.

By jamming a desk into a nearby doorway and throwing webbing around it, Diana had managed to set up an anchor that was both close to the shaft and stable. She had rigged up the anchor with the webbing, a carabiner and two cords tied onto the main rope with prusiks. They clipped the two loops onto the carabiner and then looped the prusiks onto the rope. The prusiks created enough friction to easily hold the rope and Finney's weight should he fall, yet when the person controlling the prusiks gripped them, the rope passed through, allowing him to climb.

When Finney stepped into the shaft, Kub was in the doorway monitoring his progress. Diana would be forty feet away on the floor, her gloved hands tending the prusiks, Finney's rope sliding through as she allowed it. Should anything happen to her, the prusiks would hold him.

Finney was tethered to the end of a six-hundred-foot rope, most of which, after being fed through the prusiks, would remain in the bag near Diana's boots. He had nineteen floors to climb in his bunkers. As he stepped into the shaft and reached with his left arm for the steel ladder on the wall, he felt a frisson of fear.

He began climbing, reached the next floor and stopped to wrap a short loop of webbing around a ladder rung, clipped a carabiner to that, and slipped the rope through the carabiner.

His pulse was pounding, first in his ears, then his temples. Normally he wasn't afraid of heights, but he was so shaky from the climb and from the heat he didn't trust himself. It helped that he could not see either up or down. In fact, with his flashlight bobbing from the clip on his coat, what he saw mostly was wall.

After four stories, he began resting briefly at each floor.

Midway through the trip, his hands began trembling. When he rested at each floor, he looped his elbows through the ladder and worked his fingers to pump blood into them. He was dehydrated. He knew it, and there was nothing he could do about it now. All he could do was climb one floor at a time.

It seemed like it took a week to reach forty. When he got there, he attached a carabiner high over his head and clipped his rope through it.

His arms were shakier than ever. As he stepped from the dark ladder to the elevator door ledge, he found the latch, and released the door.

Forty was almost entirely free of smoke.

The lights were on. The lights didn't surprise him.

What surprised him were the two men pointing guns at him.

# 68. CORPSES THAT BITE

F inney must have seemed like a leprechaun coming out of a hole.

"Who the hell are you?" said the one with the portable radio.

"Just the sonofabitch who's going to get you out of this," Finney replied, calling down the shaft for slack on the rope, then stepping out of the shaft.

A small portable television was set up on a desk in the lobby area, tuned to the same channel Kub had been watching downstairs. Faces heavy with incredulity, the two men stared at Finney.

They were with building security. They'd been trapped since the beginning, had used phones and their radios, but nobody had been able to give them a prognostication of their outcome or even any advice. In the beginning they thought about making a run down the stairs, but they'd hesitated and now the stairs were too hot.

The two men looked at one another. The one with the radio said, "Buddy, if you were a woman, I'd propose. What do you want us to do?"

"First, don't propose. Second, help me find a place to tie off this rope. There are two more coming up."

"We been watchin' the news," said the second man, who had a thick southern drawl. *Fire* sounded like *fur*. "You know there's fire below us. There's fire down around eighteen or twenty, and there's another fire above us on fifty-four or -five. It was just on the TV." He pronounced it *teeee-ve*. "I don't get it. Fire below and above. How does it skip so many floors?"

Veins on the side of his face bulging like beetles, the man with the radio said, "It goes up the toilet holes." He looked at Finney. "Right?"

Finney said, "Not in this case. These were set."

It took Finney a minute to work the kinks out of his arms and back and neck. He turned his coat inside out to let it dry and set up an anchor for the rope. Kub would come up using the second of their three waist harnesses, sliding a couple of simple prusik knots along the rope as he went, the prusik clipped to his harness with carabiners. If anything happened, the mechanism of the prusik would hold him.

While Kub was climbing, Finney found some bottled water and explored.

Not surprisingly, both stairwell doors were hot to the touch. When he put on his gloves and opened the door to B, a balloon of black smoke rolled in on him, so hot he wondered if he'd burned his scalp. Without his bunking coat and helmet it had been a foolish thing to do.

The design of the trap was clear in Finney's mind. Disable the sprinkler and standpipe system. Immobilize the elevators. Turn both stairwells into chimneys. Cripple escape, hamper firefighting, stand next to the IC, and give tainted advice. The fog had been an unexpected bonus.

After Kub reached forty, they rigged a hauling system for the equipment and hoisted all of it. Diana climbed the sixteen stories on the end of the rope, stopping at each carabiner and collecting it and the webbing Finney had used to fasten it to the rung.

When she stepped onto the floor, the security man without the accent said, "You're a woman!"

"No shit," said Diana. Finney could see she was getting tired and irritable.

"No, I meant . . ."

"She knows what you meant," Finney said.

"No, I just meant a woman firefighter. You know, that's great. A woman doing a man's job. That's just great."

"It's not a man's job," Diana said.

"That's what I meant."

Drinking bottled water Finney had scavenged from an office, Robert Kub came back through the lobby after reconnoitering. "The stairs are clearing."

"They can't be," said Finney. "I just checked."

"I think we can make it."

When they went back together and looked, he knew Kub was right. In bunkers and breathing from an MSA, the stairs might just be bearable. Still, the higher they went the hotter it would get.

They donned their masks, pulled on their facepieces, tugged the rubber cheek straps tight, and loaded all the equipment bags and spare bottles onto their shoulders.

"What about us?" asked the security guard with the southern drawl.

"We'll be back," Finney said.

"Promise?"

"Thirty-four floors," Kub said. "It's going to be a bitching climb."

"You've got my word. Just keep the door closed. Closed but not locked. Somebody else might need to get in here."

As they began the journey, Finney wondered why the air was suddenly clearing. Had the building engineers pressurized the stairs, or had somebody closed a door on a fire floor below? Or was somebody down there using gas-powered fans? The stairs weren't clear of smoke, they were simply cooler than they had been—he couldn't feel any breeze that indicated they were being ventilated. Unless the gases in the stairs had been vented at the top, the higher they went, the hotter it would get.

Six floors up, they stumbled over a pair of dead men. Kub took off his gloves and checked for life. "Ouch," he said.

"What happened?" Finney asked. "He bite you?"

"His watch was hot."

"Don't touch the steel railing with your bare hand either."

They were on fifty-seven before the warning bell on Kub's air tank began ringing. After traveling another two flights, Finney's went off, too. Hoping to squeeze them dry, they ran the bottles another couple of floors; then, as they were changing, Diana's bell went off.

After the bottle change they climbed steadily to sixty-five without stopping. Though they were each seventeen pounds lighter, they'd inhaled plenty of smoke, had climbed fifty-eight stories, and were near the breaking point—Finney was going to be surprised if they made it. His limbs inside his bunking suit felt as if they'd been dipped in hot oil, his thighs wet and slippery, his arms sliding around inside the coat. His neck was cramping. He had a tick in one cheek, and his eyes stung from the salt.

Near seventy-four, Kub's warning bell began ringing again.

The door to seventy-four was locked. Of course.

Before Finney could bang on it, the door opened and a small Asian woman in a simple black dress and too much mascara gave him a wide-eyed look and waved for him to enter. "Yes?" she said, as if afraid he wanted to sell her magazines.

Seventy-four was well-lit and relatively cool inside. Working their way out of their backpacks, helmets, and coats, the three were quickly besieged by a crowd, the men in suits or tuxedos, the women in dresses appropriate for a wedding party. Still breathing heavily, Kub slumped to the floor and onto his back. Finney and Diana followed suit. Finney felt as if he might not ever sit up again. The ceiling began spinning. He couldn't catch his breath. His underwear was soaked, one ear stopped up with a constant flow of perspiration. The tick in his cheek felt like a small bird trying to hatch out of an egg. After a few moments, he felt as if he were glued to the floor. Diana lay next to him, Kub somewhere above his head.

"I'm beat," Kub said.

"Me, too," said Finney.

Diana sighed deeply.

For a while everybody clamored at once. When it calmed, one of the building security men leaned over Finney. He had wiry hair that had probably been red in his younger years but was mostly gray now, a lined face, and compelling brown eyes that wouldn't let Finney look away. Long hairs grew out of his ears and nostrils. "What's going on, partner?"

"How about you give me an update first?" Finney asked, his throat raw from smoke. He sounded like Tallulah Bankhead, cigarette larynx.

"Sure. According to the TV there's a couple of fires down low. They got control of one and then went higher and found another. There's a third one burning somewhere around fifty-five or sixty. The last half hour or so our air has been getting smokier."

"You have a plan?" It was Patterson Cole peering over the security man's shoulder. Cole was the last person Finney expected to see here.

"I have a plan," Finney said, sitting up on his elbows. Cole looked like an actor, a look-alike playing the part of an old man. But it was Cole all right, his sidekick in the bow tie hovering beside him.

Finney explained that they'd brought ropes and three climbing harnesses and had been planning to lower people down the side of the building to the roof on sixty. Now they had decided they would try the elevator shafts instead. It would take time, but it could be done. They could lower people using a pulley and the brake rack they'd brought along. He and Diana could rig it in five minutes. The air in the elevator shafts was still breathable. It was probably better than the air outside the building.

Several minutes later, the three of them reluctantly climbed to their feet, groaning as they stretched damaged muscles and felt chafed skin where their loads had dug in and where they'd been burned. Finney's wounds from the Bowman Pork fire were oozing.

With the assistance of the security people, they opened the elevator doors and set up a rope and anchor system. One of the guards had rock-climbing experience and volunteered to go first. Knowing he was fresher than they were, Finney agreed. With the help of his two friends on forty, he would set up a receiving system. Finney, Kub, and Moore would send people down in the three harnesses they'd brought up, recycling the harnesses back by rope. It wasn't going to be particularly elegant, but once the system was running, they could refine it on the fly. There were, by head count, 189 people to lower, plus the two on forty. There might also be firefighters trapped somewhere, but if so, Finney hadn't heard about them.

Finney used his portable radio to advise Columbia Command where they were and what they were doing. When he received no reply, he sent the transmission again. After a few moments he heard Reese asking the dispatcher, "Is there somebody on our channel? We're getting some odd radio traffic. Who's on channel one?"

Finney keyed his mike and said, "This is John Finney. We have a crew of three on floor seventy-four with ropes and harnesses. We're going to send people down the elevator shaft to forty."

"Do not be sending people down without ropes. Repeat. Do not be sending people down without ropes."

"We have ropes."

"Clear the channel," Reese said. "We've got fire traffic here. Repeat. Clear the channel." After their conversation, Reese called Division Sixteen and asked whether anybody had gone up the stairs. Division Sixteen, who may or may not have been the same captain they'd chanced upon earlier, replied, "Negative. It's too hot in the stairwells for anybody to get past our level. Repeat. The stairwells are not usable at this time."

They would be receiving no help from below.

# 69. THE BALLROOM DANCER

Almost immediately upon the arrival of the firefighters, the people on the floor separated into cliques, the family of the young bride in one corner, the family of the groom in another. Most of the staff and hired help congregated in the kitchen area in back by the freight elevator.

Off in a corner, the top of Patterson Cole's head was visible over a couple of shorter security men he'd kept by his side.

His sidekick, a small, stumpy man with a soft neck that overflowed his collar, broke away from the group and towed the older man across the room, shadowing Finney.

They'd set up the rigging. Diana was managing the lowering operation, and Kub was getting people into harnesses, each teaching their job to others. Finney was examining the system, checking knots and trying to figure out if there was anything they'd missed. He'd given his speech; he didn't know whether this was going to work or not, didn't know if these people would make it all the way down to forty or not, didn't know how tenable forty would be by now if they did. Should the security man they were lowering run into trouble, they would haul him back up.

"Sir? Sir?" It was Cole's yes-man. His suit had been tailored to make his pear-shaped body look leaner. He had pale, wet skin and tiny silver eyes that were delicate and set too close together.

"What is it?"

"Norris Radford. My name's Norris Radford. This is my boss, Patterson Cole. We need to talk. In private."

"Right here is fine," Finney said.

Nervously looking around, Radford said, "Some fool saw *The Towering Inferno* last week. They drew numbers in the movie to determine what order to go in, so we drew numbers. Mine is going to put me at the tail end of this Chinese dragon. Mr. Cole's is even higher than mine. There's no way we're going to make it before the fire reaches here."

"Things should move along pretty quickly," Finney said.

"I don't see how. The television people are saying it's climbing at the rate of thirty minutes a floor. It's on sixty now, and it'll take twenty minutes to lower each of us . . . you can do the math."

"First off, I doubt the fire is climbing at thirty minutes a floor.

Second off, the first few people we lower will take longer than the rest, but nobody is going to take twenty minutes."

"Whatever it takes, it won't be fast enough."

"Sure it will." Finney made a point of sounding more certain than he was, if not for Radford, then for those bystanders listening in.

Finney knew this was like trying to swim a horse across a swift river. You might make it. You might not. Whatever you did, you didn't stop in midstream to calculate the prospects. Once you launched out, you kept moving and you didn't think about anything except the opposite shore. Besides, trapped or not, these two were part of the machine that had initiated this. He'd just that minute recognized Radford as the little bastard at Bowman Pork who'd told them there was a family in the warehouse. He wanted to beat the tar out of him, but there were too many witnesses and not enough time.

"You weren't listening to the mathematics," Radford said. "We're not going to make it."

"If you're not, I'm not, because I'm not leaving until everyone's down."

"But you people have those oxygen tanks."

"Compressed air. And they're almost empty. If the rest of these people are willing to go with their numbers, you should be, too."

"They don't have a choice. We do."

"Oh?"

Radford looked at his boss, who, until now, had been letting Radford do all the talking. Cole took a deep breath, scratched an ear with an arthritic finger, and said, "You take us down on the elevator. You'll have to keep it on the QT. Otherwise we could cause a stampede."

"Even if we could call a car to this floor, I wouldn't get in an elevator under these conditions."

"Why? It's dangerous? What's more dangerous than burning to death?"

"Mr. Cole, I think you started this fire. Or had it started." He turned to Radford. "And you were at Bowman Pork. You're the one who set us up. They gave you numbers? Keep the numbers. If it was up to me, I'd throw you both out the window."

When Finney began to walk away, Radford tried to grip Finney's bare shoulder, still slick with perspiration. Then he stepped ahead of Finney and danced backward, carefully wiping Finney's sweat off his hand with an embroidered handkerchief. Finney had a feeling from his intricate foot movements that he was a fair ballroom dancer.

"Let's make a trade. I'll give you information, and you give us lower numbers. My eyes are already bloodshot. Can you see this?" Using his thumb, he pulled on his right eyelid.

Finney addressed his next statement to Patterson Cole, who was following them. "No trades. You killed my partner."

Cole said, "How do you figure I killed your partner?"

"You had somebody set the fire at Leary Way. Bowman Pork, too."

"You've lost two partners?" the old man asked.

"That's right. And you're responsible directly or indirectly for both."

"I'll pay them. The family. Whatever you think they need. I'll write his wife a check right now. Both wives. I'll write you a check. Thirty thousand each sound okay? No, that's a little on the cheap side. A hundred? You're looking at a man who still saves used tin foil in a drawer. Let me think. A widow. Lost her husband. Your friend. A million?"

"The price isn't for the widow. The price is for your life, isn't it?" Finney and the old man stared at each other. Finney didn't think Cole and Radford were going to die up here, but he didn't mind if they both believed they were. A little bit of hell was just what they needed. "Tell you what," Finney said. "You go out to the cemetery and you dig up Bill and then you dig up Gary and you breathe life back into them. You do that and I'll get you out of here before these others. A couple of walking, talking corpses would put you right at the head of the line. You like to play God. Go ahead. Bring 'em back."

Finney turned and walked away.

# 70. LIAR, LIAR, PANTS ON FIRE

Oscar Stillman was upset with G. A.—he'd wasted a lot of time separating his men from the frenzy and getting them down to the meeting room. Supposedly, G. A. was to have distributed the communications equipment, which would have made it a whole lot simpler, but he confessed to Oscar that he hadn't had time to stop by Kmart, as if this were a grocery item he'd forgotten to bring home for the wife and she could divorce him if she didn't like it.

Had Oscar been in charge of communications, they would have been purchased out of town a month ago with cash, and long since passed along to the troops.

Now they had only their fire department radios, which they didn't dare use lest their exchanges were immortalized on the master tape down at the alarm office.

They held their meeting three floors below the command post and directly opposite the entrance to Fourth Avenue in a small back room adjoining a closed taco stand.

Oscar had found Marion Balitnikoff and the Lazenbys in the standby area on four playing dumb. He'd seen Tony Finney walking up the frozen escalators carrying his bunkers and boots in a large red canvas tote bag.

There was a great deal of tension in the room, even more than these men had shared after Leary Way.

G. A. tended to get flustered at every little snafu, and tonight they were compiling a litany of snafus and he was beside himself. Monahan had set the fire nearly seven hours early. They had no walkie-talkies. Reese, after months of granting their every request, was not listening to them. And worst of all, John Finney and company were somewhere loose inside the building. The only lucky break was that Monahan was injured and wouldn't be able to deploy that silly contraption of his.

"Are we all here?" Stillman asked. "There should be six of us."

"All except Jerry," Paul Lazenby said. "Can you believe it? She hit him with an axe."

"Bitch," Balitnikoff said.

"Listen up," said Oscar. "I want you to bear with me. I know everything hasn't been going exactly as we thought it would, but I don't see any reason why this building is not going down."

"You don't consider that wedding party up there a problem?" Michael Lazenby grumbled.

"Not our affair," Oscar said.

"How do you figure?"

"Those people just ran into some misfortune."

Michael, who'd been edging forward, said, "Anybody who put a little thought into it might say we're about to murder two hundred people."

"Don't say that," Oscar warned. "Don't ever say that."

"You shouldn't have called the meeting," Balitnikoff said. "Just gives people a chance to bitch."

"Called you here because there's been a modification of plans. G. A. and I have decided we need to go upstairs and make sure"—he turned to Tony and gave him a questioning look—"that John doesn't make it back down."

"What's my brother got to do with anything?"

"He's at the top of the building," Oscar said. "Him and two others. Don't ask me how."

"I don't get it," Paul Lazenby said. "Those stairs . . . I was in 'em. It's one thing to have some smoke hanging around, but those stairs'd roast a lobster."

G. A. said, "They must have used an elevator."

"Elevators aren't working," Stillman said. "The elevators are fucked, and only me and G. A. know how to unfuck them. I guarantee they didn't use an elevator. In a few minutes we'll turn one on for you guys, but they're not going to work for anybody else."

"We're going up, I'd just as soon do it in an elevator," Michael said. "Standing in those stairs is like sticking a road flare up your ass."

"That a new sex game you boys are playing?" Balitnikoff asked.

"The point is," continued Oscar Stillman, pacing, "he has to be stopped. Anybody have any problem with that?" All eyes in the room turned to Captain Finney.

Biding his time, Tony looked around the group. Until now he had done everything asked of him. He'd made no secret of the fact that he needed the money as badly as any of them, that there were loan sharks who wanted to break his toes with a sledgehammer. He turned to Paul

Lazenby and then to Balitnikoff. "Down on Marginal Way. That fire in the pig factory? That was a setup, wasn't it?"

"Liar, liar, pants on fire," said Paul Lazenby, laughing.

"Shit happens," said Balitnikoff with a shrug.

"Bad luck," said Oscar.

"We tried to arrest him so he wouldn't be part of this," G. A. said. "Didn't we, Oscar?" Oscar nodded. "Be safe in a cell right now if he hadn't run."

"He's trying to do his job. That's all he ever wanted."

"What he's trying to do," Stillman said, "is put us away for life. Think about it."

G. A. folded his arms across his chest. "Don't kid yourself. There won't be any life sentences. Not with these corpses piling up. Think more along the lines of the gallows or some ten-dollar-an-hour prison medic putting a needle in your arm. Your choice."

Oscar saw Balitnikoff fingering the pistol in his bunking coat pocket, a hammerless five-shot .38 designed to be carried in a purse. Balitnikoff would never shoot Paul or Michael, his own crew members, but Oscar had a feeling he'd do Tony in a heartbeat. Balitnikoff had never been pleased with Captain Finney's inclusion in their club, had never been a fan of the Finney clan, father or sons.

All eyes were on Tony, who said, not too convincingly, "I got no problem with this."

Good, Oscar thought. Once they turned on each other, nobody would feel safe. All they had to do was get through one night. In a month Oscar would head for Central America, where he would live like a king with the most beautiful women on earth. Paul and Michael had their eye on a condo in Cancún, where they figured they could party for the rest of their lives. Tony would pay off his gambling debts, and after that, even though he thought he was going to Tahiti, he would fritter away the rest of his share, probably at an Indian casino. Tony was the weak link they all knew would eventually end up in prison—that is, unless he was eliminated by G. A. or Balitnikoff after this was over.

"I don't want any more mistakes tonight," Oscar Stillman said.

"Don't be jumping down our throats." Paul Lazenby's voice grew louder. "It was your pal Jerry who started early. We had a schedule."

"I'm not jumping down your throats. I just want everyone to be particularly conscientious from here on out. And Tony. I know this isn't going to be easy, but it's him or us. It's not like we have a choice."

"I know."

"I don't understand why we have to go up," said Michael Lazenby, stepping to the door of the small room. "Everybody above eighteen is as good as finished anyway. Right?"

"Maybe," Stillman said.

"It's bullshit," Michael said. "We set this up to happen at two in the morning. Then all of a sudden we have twenty minutes to do our shit. If everybody had done what they were supposed to do when they were supposed to do it, there wouldn't be anybody upstairs and we wouldn't be having this conversation."

"If ifs and buts were nuts and candy, this would be Christmas," said Oscar. "Don't go all Boy Scout on us. You guys are going up, and you're going to make sure Finney and his friends don't come down. If he's found dead in the building, G. A. can make a pretty good case he started the fire, just like he started Riverside Drive. Riverside Drive didn't give him the glory he wanted, so he tried this. But the minute he sashays down here and starts talking to reporters, we'll have a whole 'nother kettle of fish."

Michael Lazenby unsnapped his bunking coat and said, "It was supposed to be a couple of janitors. Maybe one or two security guys. We're talking two hundred people."

"Get over it," G. A. said, his voice flat. "None of us are happy, but we're stuck with it." G. A. took out a handkerchief and wiped the sweat off his chin. His face appeared to be sliding off one damp layer at a time. "Tomorrow morning before breakfast we'll be counting out shares."

"So who's going up?" Michael Lazenby asked.

G. A. said, "I think it should be Engine Ten. You guys work as a team anyway. It'll look more natural."

"I'm coming," Tony Finney said.

"Sure. The four of you. Oscar and I will handle things down here until you get back."

"I still don't like this," Michael said.

"Quit your bellyaching," said Balitnikoff. "We ride up on the goddamned elevator. They turn their backs, the rest is history."

"We don't even know where they are," Michael said. "I think this whole thing stinks."

"It stunk from the beginning," said Stillman. "That's why we're being paid so exorbitantly. Exactly because it stinks to high heaven."

G. A. said, "And no guns. They find a firefighter with a bullet in him, the investigation will run into the next millennium."

"Only as a last resort," Balitnikoff said.

"Not at all," said G. A. Then, as the others filed out the door, Stillman felt G. A.'s touch on his shoulder. "Got a minute?"

"Sure." Oscar was finger-combing his hair, staring at his warped reflection in the chrome on the refrigerator near the door. He wondered what a balding, aging gringo looked like to a seventeen-year-old señorita in Costa Rica. Probably not too bad.

The others were out of earshot before he realized G. A. had slipped something around his neck, at the same time closing the door with his foot and pushing his shoulder into the middle of Oscar's back so that Oscar bumped up into the corner behind the door. It wasn't G. A.'s habit to wrestle for fun. Balitnikoff, sure. Or those damn brothers. But G. A. preserved the personal space around himself with a fierce self-regard.

Oscar turned as far as G. A. would allow and saw a look in G. A.'s eyes that told him he wasn't playing. Hell, he was strangling him. It was his necktie around Oscar's neck. "I'm okay," Oscar said. "I don't—"

The tie was being tightened from behind, tightened and pulled and tightened some more. Had G. A. gone mad? The idea was to go upstairs and get rid of Finney, not each other. Oscar wanted to speak, to reason this out, but his windpipe was closed off, his face squashed against the wall so hard his dental plate was twisting out of place. He tried to reach for the knot at the back of his neck, but G. A. was a large man, surprisingly strong, and he held him like a lion holding a young wildebeest.

He began to see stars, and it was then that he remembered what he'd learned in his emergency medical training. Once the carotid artery was blocked, unconsciousness occurred in as little as fifteen seconds. Sometimes only seven or eight seconds. Sometimes . . . the last thing Oscar heard was a gurgling in the bottom of his own throat.

# 71. THIS IS YOUR BRAIN ON FIRE

Norris was making a second call to his mother when one of the waiters who'd been loitering near the freight elevator burst into the men's room and whispered loudly to his friends who were passing around a joint. Intrigued by their words, Norris slogged through a haze of marijuana smoke and followed them out of the john.

It seemed a pair of waitresses had noticed that for no particular reason and without any fanfare the freight elevator had returned to seventy-four, empty. So far twelve waiters, one supervisor, eight waitresses, and three chefs knew about it, and word was spreading. Everybody knew the responsible thing would be to alert the firefighters in the other room, but nobody budged. Most had picked high numbers in the lottery.

Since the building alarms had gone off, the staff had been more or less relegated to the back room like servants, and then just before the numbers were drawn, one of the wedding party, an older man with silver sideburns, had suggested the help not be included in the drawing. Although they eventually had been included, it was hard to ignore the underlying group arrogance and assumed superiority that led to his suggestion. Everybody in the back room had taken umbrage.

The freight elevator was behind several tall wheeled carts, in an area that smelled of baked halibut and smoke from the fire that was climbing toward them from below.

While the waitresses and kitchen staff debated whether or not to use it, Norris knew instinctively what needed to be done and, in one of the few truly decisive moments of his life, he returned to the main room and retrieved Patterson Cole and both briefcases. They brushed past the group of debaters to the rear of the car. Norris proceeded to unbuckle his belt and loop it around the waist-level metal bumper in case anybody tried to remove him forcibly. They might get Cole out, but he was strapped in.

The stampede that took place next may have been provoked by the belt business or by the recognition of Patterson Cole. By now everyone on the floor knew Cole owned the building and that he'd been working his way around the room trying to purchase a lower lottery number than the one he'd drawn.

For just a second, the area outside the freight elevator was silent.

Then, like an implosion, people filled the car—waiters, chefs, waitresses. Several women shrieked as their feet were stepped on, and one chef began to look faint as his toque was knocked off and he was flattened up against a wall. As the car filled to capacity, the stronger men and some of the women in the forward part of the car began pushing latecomers back out. A shoving match ensued. Fists were doubled up, blows exchanged, and then a woman stopped the melee by saying, "The firemen! They'll stop us if we don't leave now."

A contract was entered into wherein the car would transport the first load down to the street and then quickly be sent back for the others. Norris did some rough calculations. Say they were taking twenty-five down at a time—that would be seven, no, eight trips.

When the doors closed, Norris found it difficult to breathe. Men cursed. A woman giggled. Somebody passed gas. It would be intolerable if he didn't realize the alternative was waiting to be burned to death.

Norris found himself scrunched sideways, the wall on one side, a lanky waitress pressed up against the other. He began to smell body odor and bad breath. He was glad he had thought to fill his cheek with Tic-Tacs in the bathroom. He didn't complain. They would soon be safe, while those left behind had nothing to look forward to but headaches from the smoke and whatever came after that.

Somebody pushed a button and the car began a rapid descent. For a few moments Norris felt as if he were floating on sheer relief. In minutes they would be cooling off in the fog in the street.

Somebody jokingly said, "I wonder what the weight limit on this baby is?"

A man with a rich baritone voice said, "About four hundred pounds."

Muffled laughter broke out. They were headed toward freedom, and a feeling of conjoined euphoria was sweeping over them.

Norris's ears started to pop, but he stifled the yawn, wanting to savor the sensation of escape, of descent. They'd only been moving ten or twelve seconds when the elevator began to lose speed. One didn't descend seventy-five floors in a few seconds. Everybody knew it was too soon. Norris had worried about a lot of things, about the sheet metal in the walls collapsing, about the elevator crashing into the basement, about not getting unbuckled before they sent it back up, but it hadn't even crossed his mind that they might end up on the wrong floor. This was terrible. Now the firefighters would not be able to find them. Now they'd never get their spot in line back.

When the car came to a halt, one woman who didn't understand the implications of their abbreviated trip said, "Oh, goody, we'll be home in time to watch *The X-Files*."

The doors opened, and a wave of heat engulfed them.

Then came the crushing weight against the rear of the car, the screams, more heat. And more. Norris would have sworn he heard bones breaking. For many long seconds he couldn't breathe or move or even think.

He tried to squat, but there were too many people crushed up against him, and besides that, he was buckled to the rail. Suspended in place by the crush, the woman next to him lost consciousness. The pressure against Norris at the rear of the car became greater.

Norris realized with a start that he smelled burning hair. For a few moments as the hot smoke rolled in and enveloped them, he had a flashback to his childhood. Once, while baking peanut butter cookies with his grandmother in Iowa, he'd stood too close to the oven, so that a blast of heat struck him in the face when the oven door opened, frizzing his eyebrows and causing him to cry out. He'd been seven, and his grandmother had spanked him for getting too close. He never forgot that searing heat. Even as an adult it defined hell for him.

"Close the doors," Norris whimpered. "Please close the doors."

He had no idea how long he remained upright, or how much heat he endured, or what the temperatures were, but after a time, maybe ten seconds, maybe a minute, the pressure began to moderate. Not a lot, but enough. The deafening screeches began to wither away, and Norris sensed a space under two women next to him. He tried to move but found himself hanging by his own belt on the railing. Burning his hands on the metal, he unbuckled himself and dove under the women. It wasn't until then that he discovered the lower he got the cooler it was. He began burrowing.

# 72. NEVER TAKE AN ELEVATOR IN A FIRE

The building security man—the rock climber they'd dropped down the elevator shaft on a line—had been given several tasks, one of which was to check out floor sixty as he passed it. He radioed back with just a trace of a Bronx accent that there were still a few small fires on that floor and that everything was black and stinking. Nothing was intact. He didn't see any people or bodies. Many of the outside windows were missing. Then he radioed that he could feel a slipstream of air coming at him from outside on that floor. Most of the heat seemed to be residual, not dynamic, if those were the right terms, he said, and he believed the floor was now habitable. What did they want him to do?

"Stay there," Finney said, on the radio. "Set up to start receiving people." The fire wouldn't revisit sixty; the fuel load had already been consumed. People might get burned if they touched hot metal or tried to walk barefoot over the smoldering carpets, but they weren't going to die there. Also, there was a roof on sixty, and it would be airy.

Even as Finney was speaking, three firefighters who'd been trapped on the lower floors showed up on sixty and offered to help. They would set up a receiving station that would, after the first wave descended, be staffed with rotating personnel self-selected from among the rescued.

The first three civilians were outfitted in waist harnesses, secured to the main line at intervals, then sent down the ladder in the shaft. They soon had three more people headed down in harnesses, rope handlers selected from the security details. Kub was the rescue group leader.

As he scouted seventy-four again, Finney confronted a dozen agitated workers in the space near the freight elevator. A perspiring man in a waiter's outfit stepped forward and said, "They didn't make it. We heard screaming in the shaft." Others, nodding their heads and shivering, seconded his words.

"They didn't make what?" Finney asked. "Don't tell me somebody used the elevator?"

"A lot of somebodies," said the waiter.

"How long ago?"

"Two minutes, maybe three. We heard the machinery stop, and there was all this screaming."

"Like a bunch of cats in a box," somebody volunteered. Several people gave the speaker dirty looks.

Finney keyed his portable radio and asked Columbia Command whether anybody had arrived in the freight elevator. Reese and company had been studiously ignoring his transmissions all night, so he wasn't surprised when he received no answer now.

"We heard screaming," said the waiter. "I know we heard screaming."

"But it stopped," said one of the waitresses, a ribbon of hope in her voice.

"It took a while," said a guest from the wedding party.

"They must have stopped on a fire floor," Diana said, glancing over her shoulder at Finney as she pried the doors open and peered down the shaft. "I see them. Our guys are on sixty. The elevator must be between us and them."

Some of the men and most of the women were crying. All of these people had fought to be on that first trip. One man kept repeating that his fiancé was in the elevator. "She's not dead," he sobbed. "She's not."

"We'll go down and check it out," Diana said, looking at Finney.

Finney gave her a grim look. They both knew the most dangerous thing you could do in a fire was ride an elevator. Once the doors opened on a fire floor, the electric eye wouldn't allow them to close again.

While the others followed, Finney and Diana walked back to where they'd left their bunking coats and MSA backpacks. Just before they pulled on their facepieces and stepped into stairwell B, Kub caught Finney's eye and gave him a thumbs-up.

Inside of thirty seconds the temperature in the stairwell siphoned off most of Finney's remaining strength, fingers of heat stealing up under his suit to tickle his arms and legs. His burns throbbed. Already his legs were shaky.

"Too hot?" he asked, half-hoping Diana would say yes.

"No."

Finney led. "You think any of them are alive?"

"No. But we need to check."

Standing in the elevator shaft, they'd both inhaled the distinctive odor of burned clothing, singed hair, roasted flesh.

Physically, the descent was easier than the ascent, partly because they weren't doing as much work, carrying no equipment except the Halligan and flathead axe, because they were descending instead of ascending, but mostly because the heat decreased with each floor.

After descending ten flights, they used the Halligan to force a door on sixty-five and found heavy smoke down to their waists. They used the Halligan again to force the doors to the freight elevator and found smoke pouring out of the shaft. They heard talk coming from above, but nothing from the blackness below. Finney knew the car was maybe three floors down from here, certainly no farther.

There had been no heat in the shaft they were using for the rescue operation, nor had there been much heat in this shaft when Diana had looked at it upstairs, yet now there was a great deal of heat and black smoke. The smoke stunk as bad as any Finney had ever tasted.

Back in the stairs, they heard voices in the stairwell, masked firefighters. It was hard to tell how far away they were, or whether they were above or below. Whether they were approaching or retreating.

Finney said, "Reese must have sent a team up."

"God, I hope so."

On sixty-three they pried the door and found heavy black smoke rolling at them like a series of huge black balls. They closed the door.

"Ten minutes ago this wouldn't have caused any screaming," Finney said. "This is all new. They've got to be on the next one down. Sixty-two. Or sixty-one."

The door to sixty-two was hot enough that they decided there was fire behind it.

On sixty-one, most of the fire had already passed through, blasting out the windows, gutting offices, leaving a desk melted into a lump on the carpeted floor, flame limply dancing off it. As they walked onto the floor, melting black plastic from overhead pipes oozed onto their helmets and shoulders until they began to look like leopards.

"Look," Diana said, "why don't you go intercept the group in the stairs? We don't dare miss them. I'll go look for the elevator. We'll meet back here. Any problems, we'll call each other on the tactical channel."

"I can't leave you."

"We don't have enough air to do everything together."

"You're right. Okay." They switched their radios to channel seven, and he went back to the stairs. It was never a good idea to separate in a fire building, but they were depleting their bottles rapidly and lives were at stake.

Finney thought he heard the distinctive clank of spare air bottles knocking together below. This group might be ten floors below, or fifteen. If they had instructions to do a search, they could vanish onto a floor at any moment.

He inspected the gauge on his waist-belt. A fully charged bottle had 4,500 pounds of compressed air; he had 1,400, probably not even enough to get back to the wedding party.

Carrying the Halligan/flathead axe combination in one hand, he descended slowly, stopping from time to time to quiet his breathing and to listen. He counted the landings, sixty, fifty-nine, fifty-eight, and continued to hear sounds of movement and conversation below. The group climbed at what seemed like an excruciatingly slow pace.

Wanting to be refreshed and able to make sense when they reached him, Finney paused on fifty-one and turned on his flashlight. It occurred to him that his thoughts were growing fuzzier by the minute. He knew he was in the incipient stages of heat exhaustion, because his mind was beginning to wander. Logical connections from one idea to another didn't seem to matter anymore. He went for long periods without thinking at all. Soon the hallucinations would begin.

Judging by the sounds of their MSAs, there were either three or four firefighters.

One was a floor ahead of the others, and as he approached fifty-one, Finney met him and peered into his facepiece. He wore an orange captain's helmet. The face, what he could see of it, was familiar, but it took some seconds to place it. "Tony? What are you doing here?"

"Where are the others?"

"Upstairs. Boy, am I glad to see you."

Finney wanted to ask if Reese had sent them or if they'd come on their own, but he was too tired.

Tony said, "Come on, let's go." Even as he spoke, the next man in line arrived. With his brother tugging on his arm, Finney shone his light on the next man: Marion Balitnikoff. He was carrying a pistol.

A third firefighter came up the steps below Balitnikoff, and as he arrived, Balitnikoff said something over his shoulder. He was still talking as Finney shoved Balitnikoff, sending both firefighters sprawling backward.

Finney turned and ran.

Tony yelled, "No, wait."

A gunshot echoed in the stairwell.

Another.

# 73. TI-I-I-IME IS ON MY SI-IDE—SING IT

Finney rounded the corner and sprinted up the half-flight, then swung himself around the next turnaround on the banister and raced up another. A second shot rang out, and he felt a dull thud against the air bottle on his back. The sounds of hurried movement behind him grew louder.

Exhausted as he was, Finney never would have guessed he could move this rapidly. He knew the adrenaline propelling his speed wouldn't last long. He'd been near the end of his rope when he met them. He counted the floors carefully to make sure he didn't accidentally lead them to Diana.

The sounds of their boots, the steel of Balitnikoff's pistol on the railing, the heavy breathing, all these sounds in a stairwell that had been tomblike minutes earlier, combined to spook Finney.

Though he was gaining a couple of steps each floor, his thighs were rapidly losing strength and felt hollow and trembly. It wouldn't be long before his legs gave out entirely.

He'd met them on fifty-one. And he'd gone two floors, three . . . He was on fifty-four and gaining. They had to be almost an entire floor behind now.

By fifty-six he found himself using the railing, working his arm and shoulder muscles as much as possible, trying to distribute the workload among various muscle groups, lest one fail before the others. He wanted to drop the axe and Halligan, but that would only give them encouragement. He felt as if his lungs were on fire.

Each floor seemed to take forever, and each time he reached the top of a half-flight, he expected to be shot.

For a few moments he considered stopping and setting up an ambush, but the masks were loud, and his sounded like a megaphone. If he stopped, they would easily home in on his breathing and shoot him in the smoke.

On fifty-nine, he began to slow involuntarily. He'd reached some sort of maximum overdrive, and no matter what was behind, he couldn't maintain the tempo. On sixty he slowed even more. They were now one full flight behind.

319

He bypassed sixty-one; Diana was not on the landing.

He bypassed sixty-two and went through the door he'd jimmied earlier on sixty-three. Most of the doors were locked, but he and Diana had pried this one.

His five-minute warning bell hadn't begun ringing yet, but once it did, he'd be the belled cat.

He'd gone thirty feet beyond the door on sixty-three before he realized that the fire had progressed significantly since he and Diana were there; the smoke that had been boiling around on the ceiling had become flame, an orange cloud sweeping across the upper portion of the lobby area from the direction Finney figured was the Fifth Avenue side of the building. Keeping low, he crawled toward it.

Most of the doors were locked, each office another buffer to the fire.

Rolling onto his side, he kicked open the door on a nearby suite of offices, scrambled through the doorway on his belly, and closed it. It was cooler in here. There was smoke, lots of it, but as yet no fire. He still couldn't understand what Tony was doing with Balitnikoff. Behind, in the lobby, he heard voices. Surely his brother wasn't going to let these bastards kill him. He listened as they moved around in the heat, speaking to each other in low tones.

He was in a reception area. Dense black smoke had banked up on the ceiling to a depth of five or six feet. A calendar on the wall had rolled into twelve separate tongues. The windows were black with smoke tar. Kneeling, he waited with the axe—his plan to peg the first one who came through the door and try for a gun.

Time was on his side, he thought. "Ti-i-i-ime is on my side," he sang softly to himself. "Ti-i-i-"

After a few moments, his warning bell began clanking, and he realized he was an idiot. Time wasn't on his side; it was on theirs. They had the air. All they had to do was wait outside the door until his was used up.

# 74. A SHORT PRAYER FOR THE FALLEN

Leaving her heavy firefighting gloves on, Diana waded into the mass of bodies. About half the party had spilled out of the elevator; the other half was a spaghetti snarl of bent limbs, scorched skin, and melted clothing. Trying not to step on any bodies, she searched for signs of life. As much as she wanted to avoid it, the melted mattress of humanity was too closely packed together for her to move without her boots crushing something. They were all dead. Everybody she saw.

Less than fifteen minutes ago she'd been upstairs talking to these same people. Against the wall was the short waitress who'd been chewing bubble gum. In the center sitting up, one side of his face burned black, was the heavyset chef.

In front of the elevator, she'd encountered the bodies of two males who'd made a run for the stairs. One almost gained the stairwell entrance but had apparently been cut off by flame and more or less barbecued in place. Judging by how much more progress he'd made than the others, his force of will must have been tremendous. She had to admire that. The second male was sprawled on his face forty feet from the elevator, one shoe still smoking, the sock melted onto his leg. All the other bodies were either in the elevator or within a dozen feet of it.

Diana said a short prayer, pleading with God to let her find someone alive. Anyone. Just one.

It was a large elevator, the walls half-metal, half-wood, scarred and dented from years of careless baggage handlers. Even though she knew it wasn't the case, the scratches and indentations presented themselves as the work of a large animal trying to claw its way out in every direction but the door. The effect was disconcerting. Most of the clothing on the top of the pile had been melted or singed off. People didn't realize how flammable modern synthetics were. Among the corpses, Diana recognized another waitress, a petite brunette with glasses who had expressed the intention of applying to become a firefighter. At the time Diana wondered how she could be strong enough, but she'd dispensed encouragement anyway and, in fact, had her phone number on a scrap of paper in her bunking coat pocket.

Working her way through the bodies, Diana spoke through her tears, "Anybody here? Anybody?"

After examining every corpse in the car, Diana found several near the bottom who might have escaped the worst of the heat but who had expired of smoke inhalation, nostrils and mouths ringed with soot, eyes staring, lungs wheezing when she moved their bodies.

There were two layers on top of him, which was the only reason he'd survived, that and the fact that his lips were pressed against a hole the size of a rivet-head on the floor of the car through which he had been able to suck clean air. A portion of his jacket collar had melted, and there were burns on the back of his head and on one leg, but other than that, little of the real force of the heat seemed to have bruised him.

He sobbed and fought when she tried to pull him away from the hole in the floor.

"Come with me," she said. "There's air out here."

"Give me some from your bottle," he said, without looking up.

"That won't work. You come out or you die here. Your choice."

He was wobbly and made a squeamish show of not touching the others with any part of himself or his clothing, even though it wasn't possible to move without doing so. As he moved, he reached down and tried to pick up a briefcase off the floor.

"Come on," Diana said, tugging his coat sleeve. "This isn't an airline. We don't stop for luggage."

The briefcase blew apart, turds of blackened cash fluttering across the bodies. He stooped, picked up a single intact bill, stuffed it into his pocket and said, "Christ. That's a shame. All that money."

"Isn't it, though?" she mocked, as she escorted him to the stairwell.

"Don't look at me. It sure wasn't my idea to take the elevator. I told them not to."

"I'm sure you did."

She marched him down the smoky stairs.

Sixty was cooler, a burnt-out hulk of a floor, the steel girders of the building showing through like a bra strap through a torn dress, everything else filigreed with tendrils of smoke as if somebody had just that second snuffed out a million candles. There was fresh air from broken-out windows on this floor. She could hear the rope-handling team deep inside the floor. Her victim would recuperate here and join the others coming down the elevator shaft on ropes.

Diana went back to the stairs to look for Finney.

# 75. STANDING IN THE BACK ROW AT YOUR OWN EXECUTION

Too late, Finney reached around and muffled the bell on his backpack with his gloved fist. If he'd had a gun, he would have shot through the lower quarter panel of the door, for surely they were crouching under the heat and flame just outside the door.

But he didn't have a gun, and his only option was to run. Scuttling through the reception area and down a long corridor, he kicked in the last door on the right and crawled in. Too late, it occurred to him that by going right he'd taken just one more turn into a dead end. His only compensation was a paucity of smoke in this office, little enough so he could stand up and cross the room on his feet. When he swept the flashlight beam behind him, he noticed his boots had left black marks on the carpeting like a dance pattern on the floor of a school gym.

The smoke on the ceiling was three feet thick, curling in on itself, a collection of gases waiting for ignition. When these rooms took off, they would go in a burst. Even crouched low on the rug in his bunking clothes, the heat in such an enclosed space would broil him alive.

Then, unaccountably, the sounds in the outer office grew weaker. When he heard his pursuers moving to the far end of the corridor, it became clear that their job wasn't to kill him.

Their job was to keep him pinned down. To make certain he didn't leave.

In not too many minutes the fire would kill him, and his demise would look like that of any other luckless firefighter who'd become separated from his companions.

Knowing he had a few moments to think, Finney went around the desk and sat in a plush office swivel chair. It was awkward with the bottle still on his back. His flashlight played across a silver-framed photo on the desk, a man, a woman, and three little girls with ribbons in their hair. He tried to think the problem through, but for the first time tonight he found himself beginning to panic. He'd been moving quickly earlier, fighting for his life, but he hadn't been panicked. Not till now.

He knew if he treated this as a logistical problem rather than the last five minutes of his life, he'd have a better chance, but how could he not think about these as the last minutes of his life when that's exactly what they were? In minutes the fire would gallop through this dead end he'd fashioned for himself.

He did his best to slow his breathing. To conserve what little air remained in his bottle.

He tried to contact the dispatcher via radio. No answer. He attempted to raise Diana, but there was no reply on the tactical channel either. The telephone on the desk was dead.

At the same moment his air bottle gave out, a *whoosh* outside the office door signified flames had flared up in the corridor. Already, long fingers of orange crept over the top of the partition separating this room from the next. Lazily, flame crept across the ceiling toward him. He ripped off his facepiece so he could breathe. Surprisingly, the air wasn't too bad in here.

Should he make a dash for the stairs, the inferno outside the door would eat him alive, and even if he made it, he'd be burned horribly when he faced down the three men with guns.

He couldn't help reminiscing over all the stories he'd heard about firefighters who'd ended their lives trapped in small rooms such as this.

He was as good as dead. They knew it. He knew it.

There were two large windows in the room, several metal file cabinets against the far wall, and a coat tree. Finney ran his light over the windows. On the nearer of the two down in a corner he found the two-inch white dot signaling a breakout window. He could break it out and jump. Or ...

There might be a chance.

Several years ago somebody'd thought to put a small bag on the side of truckmen's masks, fifty feet of nylon climber's webbing stuffed inside, ostensibly to be used as a lead-in line, but the line was strong enough to be used as a lifeline. Because he'd appropriated this mask from Ladder 9, he had the bag with the fifty feet of webbing.

Yarding out the material, he put a loop around his waist under the MSA backpack. He doubled-up the webbing and grasped it in front of himself. Then he looked around the room for an anchor point, something to tie the other end to. He overturned one of the heavy file cabinets and dragged it toward the windows, then opened a locked drawer with the axe. He hit the cabinet with the pick on the Halligan and made a hole in the side, then tied the webbing through the hole and out the drawer.

He shattered the window with the Halligan and hurriedly cleaned out the remaining shards of glass on the sill.

As the fresh air from the window rushed into the room, the ceiling ignited with a soft, puffing sound like an old man sucking on a pipe. Flame began banking down the other side of the room, cloaking the door in a reddish-orange sheet. In another thirty seconds it would creep across the carpet and make a complete vertical sweep of the room.

Using half-hitches, Finney affixed both tools to the end of the nylon webbing and dropped them out the window. He tugged his thin, goat-skin climbing gloves on, then draped a leg over the sill.

He pulled tension on the line and worked his way over the sill, feeling the file cabinet begin sliding as his weight pulled the nylon webbing taut. His stomach started doing flip-flops. In the fog he could only see eight or ten stories, but he knew he was six hundred feet above the street.

At least it was cool out here.

Tools clanking against the building like a junkman's chimes, he lowered himself so that only his head was above the sill, walking on his knees down the side of the building. Above, the room boiled with fire. One gloved hand kept the webbing together at his waist, the friction of the webbing wrapped around his butt slowing him down. He slowly let the webbing slide through his glove and began working himself down the face of the building. The file cabinet shifted again.

He lowered himself a few more feet. He was so dizzy he didn't even know if he'd tied the webbing properly. Even if he had, it wouldn't take much heat to melt nylon.

He dropped a few feet, a few more. All the white-dot windows in a high-rise would be in line above each other. He had to go down just far enough, because if he went too far he would not be able to climb back up on the half-inch nylon webbing.

When his rubber boots made contact with the next window, he saw through the glass that the room behind the window was fully involved.

He dropped down to the next floor and crab-walked to the center of the broken windowpane, held the webbing tight, and kicked at the remaining triangular-shaped plates of glass until they fell out. A hot stench exhaled into his face from inside the building. Below, swinging to and fro, his tools clanked against the building. Blades of flame shot out over his head into the grayness.

He kicked the remaining glass out of the sill, then found himself dangling, half-in and half-out. If he were to drop now, he'd slide down along the face of the building for hundreds of feet. Attempting to get some momentum, he pushed off the sill and swung out as far as he dared. Any second the webbing would melt through. He pushed out again, and on the second backswing, he managed to hook one leg inside the window, then pulled himself toward the building and slowly lowered himself.

As he settled his weight on the sill, a burning loop of nylon slapped his shoulder from above. He'd avoided a free fall into the fog by seconds.

He hauled his tools up, then rolled onto the blackened floor.

Near the window a current of foggy air allowed him to breathe almost as freely as if he were downstairs in the street. Wisps of dark smoke snaked up from various objects in the room. Even though he wanted to stay and revel in the fact that he hadn't plummeted sixty stories or been burned to death, he knew if he loitered here for any length of time, he'd become too lethargic to do what he had to.

This was the floor where he'd last seen Diana.

Carrying the axe and Halligan over his shoulder, he made his way to the freight elevator and found it filled with bodies like junked manikins at a going-out-of-business sale. There were lighter spots on the blackened clothing of some of the victims that indicated they'd been moved after death. Diana had come and gone.

He walked toward Stairwell B on legs that felt wooden. In the stairwell, from above, he could hear the Darth Vader sounds of three masks as the men wearing them waited for him to burn to death. It was like standing in the back row at his own execution. In a moment, he'd be in the front row.

# 76. FREE FALL

Finney caught the first man completely off guard, grabbed the bottle on his back and jerked him down hard. The man flew past him in the smoke. There was a series of thuds and muffled yelps before he came to rest out of sight in the smoke on the next half-landing.

With barely a pause, Finney turned back and swung the flathead axe at ankle level, blade leading.

A man screamed into his facepiece and collapsed on top of Finney, who quickly lifted the heavy body off his shoulders, flipping it down the stairs to join the first man. He knew by their voices neither was his brother.

"What's going on? Can't you morons keep your balance in the smoke?" barked Lieutenant Balitnikoff.

Finney raised the axe over his head and swung downward. But the blade bounced off the concrete with a jolt that went through the axe handle and into his arms like an electric current. He must have misjudged the distance.

An instant after the axe hit the concrete, something small and metallic clattered to the floor. It took Finney a second to realize he'd missed Balitnikoff but had nicked the gun out of his hand.

"Hey, who is that?"

"The ghost of Christmas past, big boy."

"Who?"

"Next time you kill a man, do it face-to-face." Finney's voice was hoarse.

When Balitnikoff ran up the stairs, Finney tried to give chase, stumbling to his knees just as a gunshot rang out from below. A bullet ricocheted against the wall next to his face, and chips of concrete spattered his cheek. He groped around on the floor, picked up the Halligan, then raced up to sixty-four, where the door was just closing on its pneumatic closer. At least one of the men behind had a gun, and though he believed Balitnikoff had lost his, he couldn't be certain.

When he stepped through the door onto sixty-four, he could see the rooms were absorbing heat and poisons from the fire below through the ductwork and pipe chases. This would be the next floor to explode into flame. Even so, he could see here more clearly than on the stairs.

Marion Balitnikoff stood facing him, an open Buck knife with a four-inch blade in his left hand. No gun in sight. He weighed in at two-fifty, was quicker than a cat in a dog fight, and had a keen little smile on his face that he reserved for situations such as this. It occurred to Finney that he'd never been in a fight as an adult. By all reports, including his own, Balitnikoff had been in dozens of brawls over the years.

Finney stepped forward with the Halligan bar raised over his head. Balitnikoff feinted, then forced Finney back, then feinted again. Even with all that equipment on, the knife blade moved with surprising swiftness.

Careful not to place himself in a position where Balitnikoff would step inside his swings and gut him, Finney swung the heavy bar. He missed, He swung and missed again, the bar whirring in the air. Balit-nikoff flicked the blade at him and cut a banana-shaped wedge out of the Nomex shell on his shoulder.

As they fought, Finney began to think about all those sleepless nights he'd endured. He thought about Annie Sortland and her burns and rictus teeth, about Gary Sadler saving his life and then dying in the smoke. He thought about the dead waiters and waitresses in the freight elevator. He thought about Spritzer, the firefighter who'd fallen into the street out-side, and the woman who'd fallen beside him. About the corpses they'd found in the stairwell. He thought about Bill Cordifis, and as he thought about these things a rage welled up in him.

Stepping forward, he swung right-to-left and then left-to-right, us-ing his arms as if the heavy bar were a kayak paddle. He swung again and again.

Stunned by the rapidity of the assault and the fact that Finney was swinging from both directions, Balitnikoff began edging backward. In the middle of his assault, Finney recognized Balitnikoff's strategy for what it was, an old Muhammad Ali ploy—the rope-a-dope: let the other guy punch himself out. It would work only as long as he could evade Finney's blows or absorb the punishment, and only if Finney actually wore himself out.

Working like a farmer with a scythe, he forced Balitnikoff back a step at a time until the bottle on his back butted up against the wall with a melodic clank. Then, before he could get his bearings, Finney stepped in and hit him in the left shoulder, the right hip, left shoulder, right shoulder. Finney fought as if possessed. With all the equipment Balitnikoff was wearing, no single blow was going to bring him down.

He hit Balitnikoff across the side of the helmet, knocking it half-off and cracking the lens on the MSA facepiece. When he connected with Balitnikoff's forearm, the knife flew off and skidded across the floor.

Weaponless, Balitnikoff bulled forward and grabbed Finney around the shoulders. Face-to-face now, they danced a cumbersome dance. Clean air blew out the sides of Balitnikoff's dislodged facepiece. Arm-weary, Finney struggled in Balitnikoff's powerful grasp, managing only to twist around so that they were facing the same direction, his back to Balitnikoff's chest, the larger man's arms encircling him from behind. It was a mistake, because in a matter of seconds Balitnikoff maneuvered the crook of one arm around Finney's throat and began choking him.

Like a pair of mating monsters, they staggered backward out of the room and crashed through a hollow-core door into one of the tenant areas. Finney, seeing stars and streaks of light in front of his eyes, knew he was beginning to black out.

He pushed the larger man off balance, forcing him backward. When he heard Balitnikoff's composite air tank clank against a window, the sound of the cylinder on the pane solid and heavy, for a split second he thought the glass would break and they would catapult into the street, but these windows didn't break that easily. The ones without the white dots didn't break at all.

Finney had only seconds. He pushed with every ounce of strength, but all he accomplished was to run Balitnikoff along the surface of the glass from one side to the other. He still had the Halligan in his hands. He swung hard between his own legs, thinking to hit a leg. Instead, the sound of shattering glass startled him, small plates falling onto the floor, others disappearing silently outside.

Balitnikoff whispered, "Oh, shit!" His grip loosened.

Their combined weight had been pushing hard against the glass when the Halligan cracked it. Balitnikoff had his heels firmly up against the window base and was now holding onto Finney in order to maintain his balance. He might have stepped forward, but the heels of Finney's boots were against the toes of Balitnikoff's, locking his feet in place.

Now Finney swung the Halligan hard over his head and down, digging the pick into the surface of a nearby desk as they teetered for a moment, and then Balitnikoff began sliding backward, his feet inside the broken window, his body and rump out. As much as he tried to right himself by pulling on Finney, he continued to drop. His grip had slipped, so that now he was grasping the tail of Finney's coat and his backpack. Finney couldn't tell if he was trying to climb back in or take Finney with him.

Finney held tightly onto the Halligan, which he'd buried in the desk.

Balitnikoff, Finney, and the desk all began to slide toward the open window. Only Balitnikoff's ankles and wrists were inside now.

"Help me," Balitnikoff said, his words brushed smooth by the hissing from his displaced facepiece. "Help!" There wasn't anything Finney could do but hold onto the steel bar with all his might.

When the tugging stopped, he turned his head in time to glimpse the soles of Balitnikoff's boots as they rolled backward out of the building, the only sound the whispering of his facepiece as his body merged with the mist.

Finney peered over the lip of the open window in time to hear the body land in the street below. The composite air cylinder exploded.


Diana's MSA cylinder had only six hundred pounds of air left, barely enough to get her back to sixty. She was finding that the lower she went in the building, the longer it had been since the fire had touched a floor, the more tenable that floor was. Sixty was dicey. Fifty-nine iffy. But fifty-eight was definitely inhabitable despite sparking wires in the ceiling.

She'd failed to contact Finney by radio and believed he was probably with the rescue team and in the process of getting a full air bottle. She certainly couldn't squander any more of her air waiting for him.

Fifty-seven had so many missing windows she was able to conserve air by turning off her waist regulator. Midway through her exploration of the floor, she spotted a man dragging a large canvas package out of one of the elevators.

He wore a bunking coat and helmet with civilian trousers, along with a mask in stand-by position. It was G. A. Montgomery. When he looked up, she saw nothing but his smile.

"The elevators are working?" she asked.

"Just this one. I have to get this out, though."

Helping him slide the heavy canvas-clad lump out of the elevator, she said, "Looks like a department tarp."

"Am I ever glad to see you. We've been looking all over for you guys. Have you seen what the fire's done to these floors? This is incredible."

"I didn't think the elevators were working," Diana said. "If they are, we have a lot of people upstairs who need help."

"I don't know how dependable it is. I only just found it."

"And you came up without full bunkers? Bring anybody with you?"

G. A. looked around. "They were here a minute ago."

Waving her flashlight along the burned carpets so they could both step safely through the debris, Diana surveyed the floor. She noticed the doors on a second elevator were propped open, a gaping black hole showing—the elevator car was not on this floor. Before she could turn around to address G. A., a loop, possibly a section of curtain cord, dropped around her neck from behind. "Hey," she said, as the cord tightened. "Hey. Cut it out." She grabbed the cord and managed to get a glove under it before it tightened fully.

G. A. pulled the cord taut and then placed one of his feet between hers, jerking on her neck and tripping her like a cowboy roping a calf. Without realizing how it happened, she was on the floor on her hip. Oh, God, she thought. He's one of them. He began dragging her across the floor by the cord. It took her a few moments to realize he was dragging her toward the elevator shaft.

"What the hell are you doing?" she gasped. "Are you crazy?"

Her free hand grasped frantically at the floor, but there were no handholds. She grabbed at the wall and caught a feeble purchase on the corner molding next to the elevator doors. They were at the shaft opening now, and she could hear the sounds of their movements echoing in the elevator well. She was on her back, digging in with her boots, anything to slow her momentum.

Pinpricks of white light had been rotating behind her eyes, but now they began to turn to large black circles. She could feel the deep, open space under her head and neck. Of necessity, he had loosened the cord and was pushing instead of pulling. One of her shoulders was now beyond the lip of the opening. Another few seconds and she would be falling.

Finney walked down to the next landing and felt around on the floor for the pistol Balitnikoff had dropped. He hadn't encountered either of the Lazenbys since he threw them down the stairs and had no idea where they were now. As he swept his gloved hands around on the floor for the gun, he touched a pair of boots and realized there was a man standing in front of him. He rose to find the dim outline of his brother, Tony, a battle lantern in one hand, the missing pistol in the other. He was still wearing a facepiece and breathing bottled air. "What are you doing with these guys, Tony?"

"Get out of here, John. Leave the building. Go away and don't come back."

"I can't leave. There are people in trouble."

"Get out or—"

"Or what? You going to shoot your own brother?"

"John . . ."

"Give me the gun, Tony."

"I can't."

"Shoot me or give me the gun. I'm not giving you any other choices."

"Damn you, John."

"I've been damned for a while. You want to see what it's like, pull that trigger."

Tony raised the pistol to his brother's face and held it. After a moment, his arm began shaking. Then his shoulders slumped and the gun skittered down the stairs. "Ah, shit! The whole thing just ran away with us."

"Where are the others?"

"Mike has a dislocated shoulder. You broke Paul's leg. I don't know where Marion went. There's no one else up here."

Diana was almost to the juncture where her own body weight would carry her into the shaft. She'd kicked him two times in the face and blood was gushing out his nose, but it didn't seem to faze him. He continued to push and shove like a man putting garbage down a chute.

Then she heard a familiar voice say, "You sonofabitch!" Immediately the pressure against her hips ceased. She heard scuffling as she balanced on the brink of the shaft, uncertain whether she was going in or not. After some moments of flailing, she managed to touch the wall inside the shaft where she found a metal flange that gave her enough purchase to slowly stop her teetering and lever herself out. She propped her back against the wall, stripped the cord off her neck, and tried to move air into her lungs. Her throat was swollen, her face itchy with what felt like needle pricks.

G. A. was making almost no headway against the intruder, even though, legs pumping, he was shoving with all his strength and weight.

Finney wasn't wearing a bottle, his sooty face and shoulder dappled with blood from G. A.'s nose.

Finney walked G. A. backward, the two performing a strange, lethal dance, until they were standing next to the exposed elevator shaft. As Diana watched, G. A. pulled a small automatic pistol out of his pocket. She tried to shout a warning, but couldn't get any sound out of her swollen throat before G. A. fired a single round into the center of Finney's coat.

It didn't seem to affect him. At the sound of the shot, Finney gripped G. A. by the lapels and whirled him out from the wall, spinning him around the room in a circle, like a man playing with a child, until the centrifugal force brought G. A. back around and slammed him into the raised edge of the floor of the elevator. Striking his rib cage and arm with a dull cracking sound, G. A.'s legs collapsed and he slipped, his legs disappearing into the shaft.

As gravity slowly inhaled G. A., Finney stood over him, his soot-streaked face dispassionate. Without meeting Finney's eyes, G. A. slipped to the lip of the hole. Diana wanted to tell him to let go of the pistol—if he let go he might be able to hold on—but she still couldn't get any words out.

"Why?" Finney asked. "Why did you guys do this?"

"You'd never understand," G. A. gasped.

"Try me."

"Why bother? You're a loser."

Locking eyes with Finney, G. A. slowly raised the gun for one last shot, a shot he was certain he could manage, just as he'd always been certain about everything else in his life. Finney didn't bother to move out of the line of the pistol. He'd taken a bullet to his gut and didn't feel like moving. Besides, he had it two to one against G. A. getting off the shot.

He was right. Instead of pulling the trigger, G. A. slipped into the hole. On the way down they could hear him screaming, "Aw, shit!"

When he hit bottom, the ugly thump came back simultaneously with a hollow-sounding gunshot, as if his finger had reflexively jerked the trigger.

"Am I ever glad to see you," whispered Diana, hoarsely.

"You okay?"

"I think so."

"He was trying to throw you down the shaft."

"It was the damndest thing."

The door from stairwell B opened, and four men wearing MSAs and full bunkers entered in a whirl of smoke, their helmet shields identifying them as crew members from Ladder 7. They carried spare bottles and rope bags. The door opened again, and four more firefighters appeared.

"You the ones set up the rope system?" the officer asked.

"We are," Diana whispered.

"Is it working?"

"So far."

"Can you show us what you've done?" asked the officer.

"Maybe she can," said Finney, backing against the wall where he slowly lowered himself to the floor. "I have to take myself out of service here."

When they opened his coat, his T-shirt was soaked with blood from his navel down. The bullet had gone in at an angle, had zipped around the outside of his rib cage so that, using their fingertips, they located it just under the skin near his spine.

"What the hell happened?" asked the officer.

"It's a long story."

"Where did you guys come from?" Diana asked.

"Reese got this great idea of using ropes in the elevator shafts. The stairs cleared a little bit, so we came up to try it."

# 77. A PAIR OF FEET UNDER A BLANKET

As they reclined in lounge chairs on the deck atop Finney's houseboat, the late autumn sun glinted off Lake Union; boat traffic paraded across the surface of the lake like colored geegaws in a shooting gallery.

Diana doing the lion's share of the work, they'd kayaked all morning in the double sea kayak, up the Montlake Cut to Lake Washington, past the razzle-dazzle homes and condos on Lake Washington Boulevard, and then along the lee side of the new floating bridge. They'd tied up at the sailing club at Leschi and lunched, then paddled back to Lake Union.

Their leisurely day was to have been capped off with a medal ceremony at the Seattle Center, a commemoration of heroes at the Columbia Tower that Finney had, at the last minute, decided to boycott for reasons he could not explain.

Diana and Finney were sitting in deck chairs so they could absorb the sunshine and watch the sailboats while they listened to the football game at nearby Husky Stadium on a portable radio, the announcers occasionally drowned out by the drone of a seaplane dropping down onto the water. In order to keep them warm, Diana had tucked her stocking feet into a provocative nook under the blanket in Finney's lap.

They were both still on disability leave, and she had spent the last week at his place, returning home only to pick up fresh clothes, check messages, and water her mother's houseplants. "What's the score?" he asked.

"You just asked. Twenty-seven ten. Sure you don't want to go to that ceremony?"

"When I think about medals, all I can see is that plaque over Reese's desk."

"If you're not going, I'm not going."

"That's silly. Go ahead."

"Not this time."

After a minute or two, Diana said, "Rumor has it, when you get back from disability, Smith is going to make you a lieutenant." Smith had been appointed interim chief of the department following Charles Reese's abrupt resignation.

"That would be nice."

"Is that all? Nice."

"Yeah."

Once Reese had staffed the upper floors of the Columbia Tower with truckmen, it had been a relatively simple, though time-consuming, process to evacuate the last of the wedding party out of the tower. Since Oscar Stillman was no longer available to manipulate the air pressurization system, the stairs had become passable first for firefighters and later for civilians.

The morning after the fire nineteen firefighters were sent to the hospital suffering burns or smoke inhalation. Finney was treated for burns, cuts, a gunshot wound, smoke inhalation, and a chipped tooth he'd incurred during his scuffle with Balitnikoff.

For twenty hours the fire raged, and after it was tapped, the Columbia Tower had a distinct tilt to it. One local newspaper columnist proposed that it be left that way and transformed into a tourist attraction.

During the fire Jerry Monahan gave a rambling confession to the medics who were treating his broken leg. He wanted to come clean in time for somebody to stop Balitnikoff, Tony, and the Lazenbys from killing Finney and his friends. Monahan didn't seem to mind murdering two hundred strangers, but losing three people he knew bothered him no end, especially after having suffered guiltily through Gary Sadler's emotional funeral a few days earlier. He'd admitted the Lazenby brothers had been inside the Bowman Pork fire giving bad directions to Sadler and Finney, that they'd taken an unconscious Sadler back into the building after Finney had carried him out.

Tony Finney turned state's evidence, admitting he'd been desperate for money after a succession of gambling losses. Tony had always coveted the good life, and just to make sure he never got a piece of it, he'd gambled away most of his paychecks. As had the others, he'd done it for the money, tax-free and ankle-deep, as well as the promise, initially, that nobody would get hurt. After their first major fire resulted in Bill Cordifis's death, they all realized they might well be prosecuted for murder—that was when denial, rationalization, and justification set in.

Gil Finney reluctantly told his son John that Sadler had visited him with theories about Monahan, and that he had breached Sadler's confidence by telling Tony, who in turn must have told the others. Thus, the booby trap in Bowman Pork—intended to kill both Finney and Sadler.

For a few hours after they picked his body up off the street, Marion

Balitnikoff was hailed by television news reporters outside the building as the second heroic firefighter who'd fallen to his death battling the Columbia Tower fire. It was the only glory he was to squeeze out of this.

Wrapped in a canvas tarp, Oscar Stillman's body was found upstairs on fifty-eight. The most popular theory for why G. A. Montgomery had transported him up there was that he'd been planning to pitch him down the elevator shaft so it would look like an accident.

Paul Lazenby was found on sixty with a badly broken ankle. Michael Lazenby was picked up two days after the fire in L.A., waiting to board a Mexican Airlines flight to Mazatlán. Currently they were both in the King County jail, charged with the murder of Gary Sadler, the attempted murder of John Finney, and conspiracy to commit arson.

The day after the Columbia Tower fire was tapped, Charlie Reese gave a series of media interviews in which he attempted to fob off blame for the catastrophe on shady building contractors. Four days after the fire he resigned, saying he was going back to college to pursue a degree in social work, that he wanted to work with wayward teenage girls.

Later that week, Robert Kub came out with a public statement laying out what had really happened at Leary Way when he and Reese went inside to search. When reporters tried to contact Reese for his rebuttal, he'd already left town.

All in all, the Columbia Tower was the worst fire tragedy in Seattle history, the runner-up a 1943 plane crash in which a B-29 missed the runway at Boeing Field, crashed into the Frye Packing Plant, and killed thirty-two people.

In addition to Barney Spritzer, Stillman, Balitnikoff, and G. A. Montgomery, twenty-eight civilians, including building owner Patterson Cole, died, most in the elevator fiasco. Only one man survived the freight elevator, Norris Radford. His was a curious case, because a week later he managed to disappear from a hospital in Bethesda, Maryland, near his mother's home, and hadn't been heard from since. Patterson Cole's right-hand man was now being sought by the FBI.

Annie Sortland died in the burn ward a week after mistakenly naming Finney as her attacker.

Although dozens of people were treated for burns, heat exhaustion, smoke inhalation, and cuts from falling glass, the rest of the wedding group upstairs made it out safely. Two were already slated to publish books on their experience.

Though it was known that money had been funneled from Patterson Cole to finance the group of renegade firefighters, Cole was dead and his assistant missing, so nobody yet had the full story. Monahan and Tony Finney both maintained that the go-between for the money was G. A., and that he had, by his own account, dealt only with Norris Radford. Cole, desperate for cash to pay off his wife in their divorce settlement, knew he couldn't sell off enough assets at fair market value in time, so he'd decided to get the cash in his own way.

When all was said and done, the fire department found an abandoned engine in the street in front of the Columbia Tower, an exact duplicate of Engine 10.

A day and a half after the fire, one of the building engineers, a man named Adolph Piacentini, drove his car across the Canadian border at Blaine, Washington, and, a few miles later, parked under some trees just off Highway One outside New Westminster, where he blew his brains out with a .357 revolver he'd smuggled illegally into the province. As was the case with some suicides, it had taken him two shots. He left no note, but his adult daughter said he had medical debts and had been especially troubled the past few weeks. Always safety conscious, he'd inserted ear plugs prior to the shooting.

"You expecting somebody?" Diana asked, turning her head casually toward the dock.

"What?"

"Those people coming down the gangway. Some woman. Your father. Looks like Smith, and I bet that other guy's the senator who's giving out the medals tonight." Finney was already scrambling down the ladder to the lower deck. He'd called in with the excuse that he wasn't well enough to attend the ceremony.

There were four of them: the personnel director for the city, a woman named Roetke; acting Seattle fire chief Smith; ex–battalion chief Gil Finney; and Senator Jon Stevenson, who was to present the awards at the Seattle Center in two hours. After they'd shaken hands all around— Finney remaining on the couch under a blanket—the senator said, "It's a shame you're not well enough to attend the ceremonies."

"I pleaded with the doctors," Finney lied.

"And you must be Diana Moore, the other firefighter I've heard so much about."

"Yes, sir."

A well-dressed, silver-tongued man in his sixties, the senator had spent most of his career in the state legislature before going to Washington, D.C. Neither Finney nor Diana bothered to correct his misimpressions of the Columbia Tower fire, of which there were many.

When they were ready to leave, Finney's father approached the couch. "Both my sons are heroes. You went up and got those people. And Tony came forward and confessed. That probably took more guts than what you did."

Once again, even though he was headed for prison, Tony had come out ahead in his father's mind. It didn't matter. People were screwed up. Finney smiled and said, "I love you, Dad." His father nodded and stepped to the back of the room.

After everyone left, Finney and Diana went out onto the lower deck of the houseboat. The sun had sunk over the hill behind them, and a great shadow was quickly sweeping across the choppy waters. On the far shore, cars on the freeway sent the occasional sliver of reflected sunlight across the water.

After a while, Diana touched Finney on the cheek with the back of her hand. "Something bothering you?"

"A lot of things."

"Me, too. But the farther we travel away from it, the smaller it gets."

"Some philosopher say that?"

"Yeah. Me." When he sat down, she straddled his lap, facing him. They kissed. After a few moments she said, "You coming back to the department?"

"I don't know what else I'm good for."

She looked into his eyes and kissed him again. "I can think of a couple of things you'd be good for right now."

"Oh, yeah? You going to show me?"

Kissing the tip of his nose, she said, "I think I just might."